Incident at Akabal

Incident at
AKABAL

Joanne Omang

*To Marty + Susan —
friends, authorial role
models and wonderful hosts —
All the best —
Joanne*

HOUGHTON MIFFLIN COMPANY

Boston New York London 1992

For information about permission to reproduce selections
from this book, write to Permissions, Houghton Mifflin
Company, 215 Park Avenue South, New York, New York 10003.

Library of Congress Cataloging-in-Publication Data
Omang, Joanne.
Incident at Akabal / Joanne Omang.
p.   cm.
ISBN 0-395-58840-5
I. Title.
PS3565.M33I53   1992
813'.54—dc20   91-18230
CIP

Printed in the United States of America

Book design by Robert Overholtzer

AGM 10 9 8 7 6 5 4 3 2 1

Quotations from the *Popul Vuh* are used by permission.
Saravia, Albertina: *Popul Vuh*, illustrated with drawings
from the Mayan Codices. Published by Editorial Piedra
Santa, Guatemala, 1991.

This novel was inspired by the dazzling people of
Central America and by fellow journalist Marlise Simons,
from whom I stole the idea. My agent and friend Kathy
Robbins kept me going, and editor Henry Ferris kept me
honest. I am also grateful to those in Washington,
Mexico, Nicaragua, Guatemala, El Salvador, and
Honduras who provided crucial help but would probably
prefer not to be named here. They know who they are.

For David, sine qua non

PART I

One

HE WAITED alone in the darkness, cramped a little in his crouch, but nothing he couldn't handle. It was all going very well this time and the night would soon be completely black. Nahual had been right to insist he wait until the moon set. Nahual thought of everything, Miguel reminded himself. He shifted his weight against the fence.

It was chilly, the way it gets in the mountains, even here where the days can be so hot the dogs weep, and Miguel shivered a little. The white shirt was too thin, maybe too easily seen through the weeds if the soldiers were to look right at him, but that would mean they were checking the fence instead of staring down the road. No, he was sure they wouldn't be checking the fence; they weren't that smart. They really were asking for it here, had been for a long time.

The fence was a joke, just chain link, not even barbed wire on top, though it was the only barrier between the barracks compound and the road. Not that the road was any danger. Like the fence, the road was halfhearted, a gesture to somebody's idea of a road, full of potholes, melting away to rubble even when it was new, meandering through the cornfields to

Santa Rosa not with any sense of purpose, but because some fat general got tired of muddying his boots. No vision, they had no dreams, those people, that was their fundamental problem, not from the day they first got here four hundred years ago, nothing but take what's there and get out, the rest a nuisance. The barracks was from the same philosophy, a tired thing plopped down here when the rebels first were organizing, not with any strategic point, no, but because some official somewhere decided a provincial capital needed a garrison; it was only proper. Nahual had often told Miguel the whole place was a sloppy insult to the revolution, a disgrace to any serious army. It was time for this mission, more than time.

Miguel fingered the watch he treasured, a huge old tarnished thing his father left him that hung loose on his wrist as a belt on a pole. He waited, checking the black plastic tape that held it together. It was secure. Five minutes. Slowly, so as to move no faster than the nodding weeds, he tilted his head to see the top of the guard tower, blacker against the black, stars showing through the regular gaps in its flat roof. The tower was the worst part of this place, an arrogant thing of gun slits and massive walls, built to dominate, to overwhelm the road, looming up over it like some crumbling castle turret in a Bible epic. It was deliberately awesome, and the villagers were cowed by it. But like anything contrived to impress, it was vulnerable at least to parody. Clearly, Nahual had said, the tower was some colonel's dream of what a fort should be, a colonel raised in white suits on a cotton plantation on the southern coast, reading fairy tales, seeing too many movies, joining the army on a commission his father bought him because he was too stupid or too corrupt to take over the family business.

Nahual said one could learn a lot from movies, even the badly dubbed relics that made it this far into the hills, if one paid attention. He had studied that barracks and pointed out what Miguel had stared at for years and never seen: the colonel's vision had no walls. Beside the dark bulk of the tower, the chain-link fence wandered out like an afterthought, propped up by rust, an illusion of a barrier along the road, and the fools had put the rows of bunkhouses just across a dirt path inside the fence, almost up against it. A hundred yards of sleeping men were strung practically along the highway, so close their snores were like a taunt. If he had wanted to, even Miguel with his stringy arms could have thrown a grenade into any one of the buildings. But that would have been risky: he might miss. This way, Nahual had told him, he would not miss.

It wasn't a serious army either. Nahual always insisted on that. The garrison was like the barracks, like the road, thrown together out of material scrounged in haste from the dregs of the country, drunks and parasites conscripted into a false front of an army. Nahual called the soldiers vegetables baked in Yankee camouflage dressing, garnished with M16s and turned loose in the mountains as a snack for the fighters waiting there. Other times he said they were a patchwork blanket stitched up for an unexpected baby, the temporary emergency, and had fallen to rags as the emergency grew, kicking and biting, into revolution. Miguel kept that in mind, smiling to himself, as he hunched in the dark, waiting.

Odd to be part of a temporary emergency that had existed since before he could remember. But the revolution would be permanent, an endless transformation of time and history, the final triumph of the last over the first, just as the Bible said. A soldier coughed inside the tower, and Miguel's hand twitched. As he shifted his feet the grass rustled and insects sang in irritation at his rubber sandals, his dried-sweat smell, urging him to hurry and to leave. Yes, he would hurry; only a few minutes more and he would be gone. The barracks would then be its own temporary emergency; a nice joke, that one. It would be over quickly, part of the past, like the time before the country's temporary emergency, so far back now that even the soldiers must be embarrassed to use the words, but they still called the rebels subversive delinquents, a bunch of bandits, just as they had during the first pacification campaigns. The world knew the truth, but the generals hung on to those words as though they were the dreaming beans, charms that would somehow make the upending of the world into a matchstick, a thing small enough to handle.

That attitude had helped the revolution a lot, according to Nahual, who knew everything. How had he put it? Miguel repeated the lesson like a catechism, finding warm reassurance in the words. "They want to believe very badly that we will go away, that we are tiny and irrelevant, and so they can only take tiny little measures against us. But a little wall will not hold back the sea. In this way they will defeat themselves."

The barracks, typical of slapped-together shacks, had survived hurricanes and earthquakes and fires and the usual disasters of fourteen years, without real repair or reinforcement. It had been sustained by the force of people's image of it, the feared and terrible fortress. Nahual had laughed at the incompetent reality, saying the army should have put up cement walls, gun emplacements all along the perimeter, with regular patrols, and now they talk of it, but no, at that time, they had underestimated everything, the costs, the time, the strength of the people's feeling, the horror they were just beginning to get into, and no sign of an end to it yet. Temporary emergency, Nahual practically spat in contempt, and rubbed his hands as if to wash off dirt. Then he shrugged, explaining to Miguel that the military toads were desperate all over the country and it kept their spirits up to lie. In this way also they will defeat themselves, he said.

Miguel repeated it to himself again, certain that the soldiers in the tower were dutiful, doing what was expected, but only what was expected, so that what listless attention they could muster at that hour would be directed at the potholed road.

He pictured them, smaller and younger even than he was, guns propped against the cement sill, sighing for the end of their watch, shifting uncomfortably on the wooden chairs. They had heard the van coming a long way off, the tape deck blasting the latest cheerful salsa, and it had distracted them completely, just as it was supposed to. Oh, his comrades had played it perfectly, rattling past the barracks just as the moon went down, singing and shouting cheerful obscenities like a bunch of drunken villagers going home from the soccer game. The guards no doubt had grinned as the van hit the speed bumps too hard, jouncing oaths and yelps from the passengers, careening a little but not too much, just enough to remind the watchtower soldiers of their own nights out, before the army took them: simple nights of beer and rum, escape from the cornfields and the rows of beans, and they dreamed for a moment, as the van went by, that they were going along, home to the dark warm shacks piled with sleeping women and children, to stumble fully dressed onto the mats by the dark red fire, to the rough blankets, to sleep a long time. It had been easy then, the soldiers lightly dreaming, for Miguel to slip up against the fence, to duck behind the tall weeds at the back and wait. The soldiers kept this part of the road fairly clear, but not clear enough to save them now.

Only a minute left. He thought he should move back a bit, but he wanted instead to be closer, although that was impossible, to make sure again that everything was all right in that other, lethal plastic that waited beyond the fence, layered in the bottom of the Coca-Cola box. A good joke, that one too, Nahual's idea of course, to execute the fascist oppressors with the Yankee poison they brought so carelessly into their barracks. They couldn't see that it would destroy them, he had said, had destroyed them already, the way all of these useless Yankee toys were destroying the country, dulling the minds of the people, putting everybody to sleep. Nahual had told Miguel it was too bad the soldiers would never know that this box of Coca-Cola had put them to sleep forever. But they would know in the capital, and in Washington and in Moscow and in the hills and the slums and the cornfields where people labored to survive, sweating and gaunt and never a drink of water all day to keep them going, much less a Coca-Cola. Yes, they would know and they would marvel at it, the clever bravery of it, the truth it spoke, and even those who fought against it would see that it was true. Miguel's breath came faster. Oh God, let this message be heard, let my heart in that plastic sing to the people, you are not alone, we are one against the crushing weight that sucks the meat from your bones, and I promise you that burden shall be lifted. He pushed the watch stem.

The blast shattered the dark in blinding white, smashing heat like an earth tremor against his body. He was too close, he was lifted off his feet, flying backward with fiery boards and chunks of metal, screaming joy and triumph and revolution. He floated out over the road, the world gone white in front of him, all sound obliterated in ultimate sound, the world annihilated that it be reborn. Finally his feet touched, running backward on the gravel, but he did not fall. It was all perfect, perfect. He stared a moment at the conflagration, the wall of flame, stood there too long, until dark figures were running behind, shadows, shouting and waving arms, faces staring at him through the smoke. Then he turned and plunged across the road, into the black, stinging arms of the cornfield, running low and fast.

So that was how it started. Actually it had started years before, of course, but for the villagers of Akabal it started that night. Even Lieutenant Gomez dates it from then, and he was the last one likely to feel the way he does now. The blast hurled him from his bunk, making a roar so deafening he half dreamed it was a volcano. He came to, sitting on the cement floor in his underwear, screams and shouting all around in the smoke and dust, staring at the jagged boards and rubble beside him, piled on his legs like hot sand at the beach. The roar solidified at his back into heat, a wall of fire, and he scrambled away, over the shattered timbers and the stinging metal, stumbling over a glistening outstretched arm, noticing the irrelevant detail, the way one does at these moments, that the man's dark undershirt rounded beautifully over his shoulder. He dragged the limp form along across the ravaged room, finally reaching air, the courtyard, and the night outside. Men ran shouting in every direction, their faces orange in the fire's light, waving and pointing, hunching over other men stretched on the ground. Gomez stared and dropped the man's arm to turn back to the burning building, engulfed now in flames, licking through the roof, towering orange fingers flickering and reaching white and gold, dazzling against the black sky.

"Gomez! Gomez! Is that you? For Christ's sake, Gomez!" He turned and gaped toward the high-pitched voice, Captain Lorenzo coming at him across the courtyard, his briefs colored gold by the fire, but Gomez couldn't figure that out at first. Lorenzo had a small white dog clutched under one beefy arm. The captain knelt quickly beside the man at Gomez's feet. "Dead," he said, and stood up. "You needn't have bothered."

Gomez looked down at the body and up again at his commanding officer. "Dead," he repeated. "How many? What happened?"

Captain Lorenzo patted the shivering dog fiercely as he spoke. "One man, we think. The guard saw him just outside the fence. He was laughing. Can you believe it?" Gomez blinked. A dead man, laughing? Only one dead? But he could see other bodies . . . "He was right there, a fucking Indian, maybe twenty, skinny, a white shirt. Laughing! But we'll get him, don't worry. You all right?"

Gomez surveyed himself. Now he understood: Lorenzo had forgotten the dead and was already talking about catching the terrorist. One man ... Gomez ran a hand through his thinning hair and leaned over just enough to see his toes below the T-shirt stretched taut over his belly. All seemed normal, although he felt as if he had made a long trip in a jouncing truck — everything was quivering slightly. "Yessir, I'm all right."

"Well, get your men together and go after him. This one's all yours. Go on."

Gomez blinked. "Yessir. How many men, sir?" His voice sounded practiced, calm in his own ears, and his heartbeat eased.

"As many as you need. Get going! Get that bastard, whatever you have to do. Sonofabitch!"

"Yes, sir! Right away, sir." Gomez drew himself into a salute. The captain returned it and walked away.

Lieutenant Prospero Jesús Gomez took charge. Men came up to blurt damage reports, fear and anguish pouring from their faces. Teenagers, hardly more than children; what were they doing here? He nodded: only his barracks had been hit. Two dead for sure, a couple more not likely to live, at least six injured, five men not located yet. A major hit. How had they done it? Was it aimed at him, his Special Forces unit? The arrogance of it was infuriating, and he felt a familiar chill below his breastbone, the preparation. He put a reassuring hand on the messengers' shoulders, feeling thin bones under a veneer of army muscle, the hungry blood of generations coursing now with army beef and beans. Their sons would be stronger yet, taller, healthier, happy in a free country — if any of them lived to reproduce. He grabbed a private running by.

"You, go find Sergeant Joyabal, Unit Three. Bring him

here, quick." The soldier gave him a walleyed look and ran off. Chaos still roared all around but Gomez hardly noticed. He had done this so many times, too many times as the country spiraled into violence and counterviolence, the cycles accelerating until each side's responses were automatic. He was too good at it. He watched himself: the noise was background harmony to the gears meshing in his mind as he eased out of his shock. Like one of the new computers in the capital, he recalled lists of supplies, named men, counted hours and distances, remembered intelligence reports. He waited for the right information to surface, selected by an instinct for the relevant honed over many mountain chases, many miles of retribution.

Several of his "ears" in the district had been evasive lately, shaking their heads, mumbling about something cooking somewhere that they couldn't pin down. One man named Tijax; he had been more specific. Benedicto Tijax, that was the name. Where was he from? Gomez mulled it over, not pushing it, letting it come, keeping half aware of it as he grouped and calmed his men, a hand on an arm here, a pat on the back there, locking gazes and giving directions, checking for guns, ammunition, water. Somebody brought him some clothes, boots, a heavy semi-automatic rifle, the latest from the Israeli catalogue. He dressed there in the open courtyard, soldiers around him like servants, handing him a shirt, pants, a belt. He would need this respect later, when he remembered the rest of it, when he began to think about what would follow. He drew in their trust like food hoarded against a hungry future.

Two

IN AKABAL the morning began like any other, although for Gregorio it was just an extension of the day before, because he had been up more or less all night, like Miguel. It seemed right, later, that Gregorio was one of the civil patrol on duty that night, watching and waiting for subversives to attack the village.

Of course Gregorio wasn't going to shoot anybody — he would be the last to fire on a bird — but he did look good with that rusting gun, big and muscular with farm work, and he could stand smartly to attention without seeming as ridiculous as most of the villagers did. Also he could read and write, and he would sometimes add a comment to the overnight reports that made them look authentic: "dog barked, nothing found," or "bad storm." One time he wrote, "clouds like quetzals," but the mayor erased it and made him promise not to do that again. The army has no imagination, the mayor told him, unless it is the wrong kind. Some corporal would surely decide that was a subversive remark, evoking the national bird of freedom in a civil patrol report.

Still, Gregorio was always agreeable, and since it was up to

Don Cristóbal as mayor to make out the nightly duty list, he put Gregorio on it any time army patrols were nearby, in case they came to check on Akabal. Gregorio didn't mind; he wasn't interested in why or when he was chosen. The patrol was officially voluntary, the army had said, but every man in the village had joined after the mayor pointed out that only communist subversives would refuse, as the army had also said. So Gregorio probably didn't notice that Don Cristóbal wasn't exactly fair about rotating the names. If he did notice, he never said anything.

There were seven of them on duty that night, a normal number, and they shouldered those ridiculous old rifles the government had sent up a few years earlier as proof the people were trusted — as though Indians were too stupid to see the irony in that — and made the regular rounds according to the army order. Every patrol had to plod all around the tiny little square of dirt in front of the church, barely thirty paces to a side, as though it were some magnificent plaza that could not be seen completely in a glance, like the one in the capital, where there were trees and flowers and tiles in patterns, where bands played on Sundays and children frolicked in the fountain! No, Akabal's dusty parking lot was carefully paced out every hour, just as every last one of its eight or nine rutted alleyways had to be marched like a boulevard, its grave passageways between the leaning houses where the patrol had to walk single file, almost able to hear the sleeping people breathing through their open doors. But those open doors had to be checked, lovers ousted from their trysts and sent home because of the danger that communist subversives might sneak in and take everybody hostage, so the army says.

The patrol thus would wind up every hour or so at that drafty lookout shack on the next hill to put their X's on the report Don Cristóbal wrote out for them in advance: 12 midnight; all quiet. One A.M.; all quiet. They could see up and down the valley from there, when the moon was high, and even on black nights like this one, it was easy to make out Akabal's scrubby mountains dark against a sky full of stars, the nearer hills rounded and blurred with trees, the higher mountains sharp and jagged beyond. But they knew every rock and ravine like their own corn patches, and they knew any sensible subversive would be asleep by a fire somewhere, and they couldn't see any fires. So they marked all their X's at once and tried to sleep too, like any men who have a living to make the next day. The soldiers never could understand this.

Yes, the civil patrols were a farce in Akabal, as they were everywhere, but worse than that. From the moment Captain Lorenzo announced them three years ago, standing in the back of his jeep in front of the church, the villagers could see they would be required to shoot at shadows that might be sons or brothers. And the shadows would have to shoot too, to defend themselves. Yet such is the habit of subjection and hypocrisy in this country that the crowd nodded and praised this idea of the new president's, hoping, even as they stood there in the hot sun, to ignore the whole thing if they could. The highland Indians have never confused change with progress, not since the Spanish came.

But the army insisted, demanding to inspect the reports, and so on this too Akabal went through the motions. When the mayor drew up that daily list of walking targets, he thought about the others, the thousands of ragged farmers trudging dutifully around the numberless villages of this poor country, pretending to be warriors with their antique rifles, and he laughed to keep from cursing. The dogs and the children chasing around are at more risk from tripping over those guns than are any subversives, and if the boys do come in from the hills, the first ones they kill are the civil patrol, of course, the collaborators with the army. As if the farmers had any choice! They did their job and the mayor did his, grinding his pen into the paper at the waste of it all.

But it was an accident Gregorio was on patrol that night, nothing Don Cristóbal did on purpose. The army hadn't been through in months, nor the rebels either, and he didn't expect anybody. Akabal sat on its hilltop in peace, and the civil patrols were fairly perfunctory matters. It was chilly, the stars staring down unblinking as searchlights. Gregorio got cold and went to the church to try to sleep a little there, out of the wind. But he had a lot on his mind and the benches were hard, just boards on blocks, so he sat half awake and aimed his rifle at a candle guttering on the altar.

"Boom," he said to himself. "Boom." He waited, holding his breath, but nothing happened. He raised the barrel to the toes of the white body floating in its dirty glass cage, to the purple cloth painted over the loins, to the bloodstained chest, to the eyes staring into the gloom. "Boom. Boom. Boom." He pictured the eyes swiveling to pin him there against the wall, the hand coming down from its nail to point at him in accusation, a voice thundering out . . .

Nothing. He exhaled. No response. The statue hung inert, mute, suffering, doomed, as passive as a chicken, as resigned as Akabal itself. The guns of the rebels, the guns of the army, the gun of some half-awake farmer, what did it matter? The town was as doomed as Christ.

The notion became a picture in his mind, as so much did. Perhaps he could draw the village hanging on a cross, but a modern cross; better, the village hanging on the tips of the bayonets of crossed submachine guns. But such guns had no bayonets; they slaughtered from a long way off. No matter, the jutting sights and the open triangle of the metal stocks would do for hooks. He frowned. The church would sag forward in the head's place, its three arches like a crown of thorns, the plaza drooping below like the bleeding chest, with houses

strung out like arms along each side. The crosses of the cemetery would trail down to be the loincloth, white and bloody . . .
a town martyred. A good picture. No, too obvious — in fact,
almost hackneyed. And it would be dangerous as well. He
could never show it to anybody. And martyred for what?
There would have to be redemption in some way, for comple-
tion's sake, or it was pointless. But that was the point, the
pointlessness. Was there anything that everyone in Akabal
would die for? He smiled to himself. Argument was the town's
chief entertainment when no outsiders were around. He
thought of women waving their arms, men shaking their
heads, youngsters fighting — no one in Akabal agreed with
anybody else about anything. There wasn't even anything they
had all considered. But if they were asked? Gregorio thought
for several minutes. The shrugs, the constant dismissive hand
gestures, so hard to capture on paper — they were the uni-
versal last word here, and they all said the same thing: you
know the rules, do what you want, just leave me out of it. Could
a town be martyred for the right to be left alone? Would an
army rally for that? In Akabal it would. He would be the first
to sign up.

But of course there would be no rally. The town had survived out of luck, nothing else, inert on Akabal's ridge, and
it would go when its luck ran out, as so many villages had
already. Like that statue. He could have blown its pious face
off, or made a crater of the loincloth, very realistic. But then
he had not pulled the trigger, had he? In fact he had never
intended to pull it. Of course: God knew he was a coward, that
he was bluffing and would never shoot in a church. Gregorio
sighed and smiled at himself, a dumb farmer trying to out-
smart God.

But what if he hadn't been bluffing? What if he had really
shot? Would the statue have moved then? He frowned, trying
to put himself in the mind of a man who would shoot in

church at the body of Christ. Even after everything that had happened to his family, even after what had happened to his sister, Cecilia, he still would have to be someone else altogether, a not-Gregorio, to shoot at Christ. He could have done it, but he could not have done it. Gregorio sighed again and gave it up. The priest was right: the church was too complicated for the likes of him.

He hooked his fingers together before him and stretched, feeling the shirt taut across his back. He thanked God the night was nearly over. What a charade. Only once in the last six months had the patrol challenged anybody, calling out nervously from the hilltop shack, and then it was only Benedicto Tijax, the town labor organizer, coming back drunk from some whorehouse in Santa Rosa. The dogs hadn't even barked. The guerrillas didn't need to sneak in by night; they came in the daytime, parading openly up the long hill past the cemetery into the plaza. The black emptiness of the night made your eyes hurt from trying to see something in it, but Gregorio, if he wasn't too sleepy, saw it flat, a screen for his drawings, uncluttered with the rest of life. It tantalized like an unopened gift, and he would have loved the patrol nights for their black potential except for the lack of sleep, which made him achy and groggy and irritable and the sun too bright for two days afterward. The crops suffered too. Last year, fighting in the hills had kept everyone out of the fields for weeks at a stretch and the corn withered, unwatered. Even now no one had any money; the war had emptied the markets. The wispy stalks in his own small plot called to him all night, wailing for water, stifled by weeds. He rubbed his eyes. His mother had been working late at the baking cooperative, and when he went by with the patrol she had given him such a tired smile he had to look away.

He was wasting time even now. He should be sleeping, he should be out walking up and down, he should think how to

tell his parents about Cecilia. He rubbed his eyes, his calloused hands rough on his face. He should pray for help, he
should talk to somebody. He should be pulling weeds, he
should spend more time helping his mother, he should be a
better person. He blew a long breath. Once, to apologize to
her for everything, he had done just the wrong thing: made a
drawing of her working at the oven, the shack around it filled
with shadowy forms bending in the smoke, the pathos wrenching as a Goya. She had looked at it without expression and
handed it back.

"A pity we can't eat this," she said. She was right, he thought,
and tore it up. The doodlings were ridiculous, squanderings
of time, arrogant and self-indulgent. But the images kept
crowding into his head, demanding to be put on paper or
whatever was handy. The slightest thing would set them off, a
parrot looping over the church in a flash of green, a baby goat
tossing its head, the moonlight catching a faraway river. Then
a chain of pictures billowed in his mind until they took up all
room, and he would stand with his eyes glazed, transfixed by
the private panorama. At last he would draw quickly, sketch-
ing Tecun Uman soaring over the final battlefield, his long
quetzal feathers a snake across the sky, or an infant grasping a
machete, eyes crazed and innocent. He was unable himself to
say how these associations occurred.

He put all the villagers into his pictures, sometimes in
realistic poses, more often in the fantastic scenes he invented
from nothing. He seemed to capture something deeper than
just their faces, something that showed an attitude, but he did
that unconsciously, because it puzzled him when people were
not always pleased.

Gregorio said later he could see everyone in the village
in the church statues of the saints that night, sometimes two
or three in one plaster face. Poor crumbling things, most of
the paint long gone and the edges of the robes ragged and

chipped and black from generations of rough stroking fingers. The little chapel was nothing like the pictures in the books Father Edmundo had brought to show Gregorio, carefully turning the big pages for him, after he saw some of Gregorio's drawings. The heavy books showed lacy cathedrals in fruited gardens, white-faced saints in flowing robes, blue eyes fluttering skyward, gold-edged parks full of unicorns and dragons, blond and chubby angels like no babies Gregorio had ever seen around Akabal. That glowing god of palm trees and olives lived a long way from scruffy Akabal on its bony ridge and surely had never heard of the place. Gregorio's real gods were much more accessible; they lived right here in the fields and the rocks and had since long before the Spanish came. His mother could talk to them, bargain with them for a good crop or a healthy child, a new shirt or a trip to work at the plantations on the coast without illness or flat tires. She gave them chickens or fruit or a promise, and if they didn't perform, she took the offering back and gave it to some other god, one who might be more agreeable. Other people would just knock the failures down, gone and good riddance. But this Jesus was already dead, like the saints, and if the answer was no, there was nothing for a poor mountain Indian but acceptance. A hard business, all part of the mystery one was supposed to love. Gregorio kept trying to figure it out. But not at the Mass. No, he wanted to take on God on his own terms and wound up in church at odd times, like that night.

It wasn't as dark in the little nave as Gregorio had expected. The single candle fluttering on the table that doubled as an altar had spattered wax all over the plastic cover, blotching the purple and yellow squares with white. But it cast an amazing amount of light. He stared at Saint Helena in her niche, patron of the province, protector of the cross, and for an instant she stared back. Her eyes were familiar. Yes, they were

Irene's eyes, direct and honest, patient, waiting for him, unhurried and unafraid. Sweet Irene, Miguel's sister, as solid as Miguel was scrawny, built like their late father, Lucas, sober as the mountain under Akabal. She was big enough for a big man like Gregorio, not one of those tiny ones that might break underneath. He had been courting her for ten years, more or less, and at twenty was finally old enough to marry her. She was sixteen and finally old enough too, if only her mother Flora would admit it. But crazy Flora would not, at least not for Gregorio. The de Córdobas were too poor, too loud for her, always in trouble . . . Saint Helena's eyes flickered, and the face for an instant changed to Cecilia's, mobile and mischievous, always laughing at her younger brother and his skinny friend. The ache rose in Gregorio's chest and he stood up, the boards creaking in protest.

The dim chapel suddenly seemed too warm, crowded with faces, and he gave up on sleeping any more. He decided to go back to the lookout shack. He stretched, pushing the dark away. It was almost dawn anyway, time to wake the others for the end of their duty. He leaned to pick up his gun just as Father Edmundo came stomping from the shed into the halflight of the church.

He lurched like an angry mule, flapping the laces on his ancient running shoes. He banged back the door to the shed where the cot was kept for his visits, once a month in normal times, less often if the fighting nearby was bad or if some other village on the circuit took more time than usual for funerals or confessions. Gregorio winced at the sudden noise. He felt heavy and tired and sat down again, hunching over. "G'morning, Father. How are you?"

Edmundo jumped. "Uh! My God, you startled me! Gregorio? Is that you?" The priest peered into the darkness, his thin hair a halo in the flicker of the candle. Under one arm he had a load of new candles. With the other hand he struggled to zip up his shiny baseball jacket. "Well, since you ask, I had a rough night, thank you." Letting go of the jacket, he waved in annoyance. "I dreamed I was in my cassock and it was on fire, little blue flames licking up all around at the edges." He gestured toward the puckered ankles of his blue jeans. "Isn't that something? But I wasn't afraid, I was just kind of curious, looking at it, you know, until all of a sudden it sort of billowed up higher, and then it reached my . . ." His hand fluttered at his hips. "And then I woke up, and I had to get to the outhouse immediately."

Gregorio laughed, but the priest scowled. "Just a little flu, a touch of the flu, that's all. Nothing serious." He smoothed his jacket front and strode across the front of the nave, three steps, turning down the center aisle to the bench where Gregorio sat, elbows on his knees. "Is that a gun? Why do you honor me with your annual visit so early? I was expecting Miguel."

How like a Ladino, Gregorio thought, to be embarrassed over such a trifle as gut trouble. No Indian would even notice normal human frailties like diarrhea and pimples and smelly feet, and the Spanish would be above such things. It was the pretensions of the Ladinos to out-Spanish the oligarchs that made them so unhappy, always dissatisfied with the half of themselves that was Indian. Edmundo would be God's perfect servant if it killed him. Gregorio sat up and stretched.

"I confess, Father. I've been sleeping, right here." Not strictly true, but close enough. He picked up the rifle and sighted listlessly along the barrel toward the altar. "It's my night for civil patrol. I was looking for Miguel too. You haven't seen him?"

"No, no. He's supposed to be here at sunup and it's nearly that now." Edmundo stepped toward the back of the building, leaning to set a fallen board back on its cement block. "Better not let the mayor catch you goofing off." He walked on to the big arched door and pulled it open with his free hand, letting in a gust of chilly air and a pinkish burst of light.

"It's all right," Gregorio said. "The rest of the patrol is up in the lookout. I don't know how they can sleep in such cold. Your benches are hard but it's warm in here at least."

"Well, it needs airing. Smells like a chicken coop." The priest took a deep breath but did not look up. If he had, he might have seen the rising sun glinting off Lieutenant Gomez's field glasses, although it is not clear even now whether the soldiers were hiding at that point or wished to be seen. In any case, Edmundo saw nothing but the dusty plaza, the usual dogs and chickens and the shacks that ringed the square, clinging gray and shadowed to the fading night. His breath puffed before him. "Ah, this really is the best possible time of day, the very nicest light, the very sweetest air, the best, don't you think?" His eyes were closed. "Anything can happen on a day like this."

Gregorio shivered. He hoped he wasn't catching cold. He smoothed his thin cotton shirt and gave an envious glance at the blue and white baseball jacket and the American jeans, the obvious trophies of some priestly day off at the black market in the capital. Someday, Gregorio thought, he would go there, but not for a while yet, until he had saved a little more money. He was afraid he wouldn't know how to behave in such a place, full of noise and cars, foreign women and people in suits. His father had gone there, Cecilia had gone there, and what had it got them? Only trouble for everybody.

The priest turned and genuflected before the bleeding Christ in his glass cabinet, then marched back down the aisle to the wooden table below the statue. He dumped the candles onto the spattered plastic and peered at his god, the image fuzzed through the murk of decades of dust and candle smoke. He shook his head and muttered something, bending over.

He had a rip in the right rear pocket. Instantly Gregorio saw a drawing: the priest standing tall in his running shoes, raising high the Host to reveal his T-shirt, which said in English JESUS SAVES, and his knees showing knobby through tears in his jeans, while the penitent before him wore the shawl and robe of Bible pictures. Or perhaps one hole was patched; that would be better. Edmundo never wore anything frayed or damaged. He was fastidious, obviously from a manicured life in a moneyed family, well educated, showing the way to the heathen. A drawing like that would baffle him completely.

Gregorio touched his own ragged collar, the missing buttons, and reached for his tattered straw hat. He was starting to feel better.

"Well, busy day today, Gregorio." The priest blew on his hands to warm them. "More than the usual thirty women at Mass. We'll need all these new candles. Will I see you at the procession this afternoon, hmm?"

Gregorio thought of the special ceremony, the solemn parade that would shuffle through the town to honor the name day of the patron saint of San Clemente de Akabal. Edmundo loved these medieval rituals, fussing over the draping on the caïque that bore the statue, the number of flutes and drums, the niceties of which of those bearing the litter should stand foremost and which behind. He was scrupulous that the regularity of his parishioners' devotion and not their social rank would determine the order, with the result that the mayor often marched near the rear, herding the children, and Gregorio was behind even him. But Gregorio had not marched at all since his sister was taken away six months before. Edmundo's question irritated him.

"Which procession?"

The priest snorted and snatched up one of the altar's old beer bottles crowned with candle stubs, tugging at the multicolored wax blob. It came loose with a pop, and he jammed a long white taper into the opening. "I suppose Maximon will stay on the far side of the square, at least," he said. It was more a warning than a question, and Gregorio ducked his head to hide a smile. "It's a sad thing, a sad thing," the priest muttered, "that there should be a parade today of all days for that — that idol. I don't understand how these things get scheduled." He snapped another candle from its bottle.

"Just an accident, surely," Gregorio said. Maximon sat enshrined in his open-air throne on the other side of Akabal, as far from the church as Edmundo's irritation had been able to push him. The cheerful statue is a sort of secular god, a modern caulk for Christianity's cracks of age and distance, although Edmundo didn't see it that way. If a prayer is a little too worldly for John the Baptist, a little too earthy for the Virgin Mary, or if the saints prove deaf to a just petition, Maximon will hear it and smile in understanding from under his flat black hat. He looks like a jumble of leftover authority figures, with the toothy grin of the old Mayan death gods, the menace of Herod and Judas in his rigid posture, and the black suit and tie of rich landowners and government bureaucrats. Gregorio often sketched him above a pile of the peasants' offerings of cigarettes and aguardiente as a god of modern last resort, a giver of new trucks and money for prostitutes, of sequined shoes and virile lovers. A half-burned cigarette hung from his leering lips.

Gregorio leaned forward, wide awake at last. "Have you ever heard the story of how Maximon got his suit?" he asked, his smile innocent. He wished he had a cigarette to dangle dangerously like Maximon's.

"No, and I've always wondered," Edmundo said. He turned around in real interest. Invariably the hard-drinking rake appears in a white shirt and a suit fixed forever in the 1920s, whether he is a little statuette sold in kiosks or a life-sized altarpiece. He wears a four-in-hand tie — or is it a Windsor? — rather than a bow tie or a Spanish-style string knot, which

Edmundo thinks would be more appropriate. "You know, I asked Don Cristóbal about it as your final authority around here and all he said was, 'It is the custom, Father,' that's all. I never did find out."

"Well, I'll tell you. He wears that suit because it is the custom, Father." Gregorio grinned broadly. Edmundo grunted in annoyance and turned back to his candles.

It was the answer to much about Akabal that the priest never seemed to understand. He had railed for years about the village habits, calling them pagan: men on the left of the church, women on the right; the women's blouses that had to be of lightweight pastels and laces here, but of heavy red and black woven cotton in Chilango, just over the mountain to the south, a different pattern for every district. He harangued them about the traditional drinking on weekends, on holidays, at night. He got impatient when the elders tried to explain the villagers' obligations, the ritual festivals, their respect for those who save and work to provide liquor and fireworks for the entire town, sometimes even a band, their celebrating as a way to push back the nights that are so often punctuated by gunfire in the hills a long way off. Edmundo said it was wrong for a poor man to spend himself back to poverty for such occasions, and complained that Don Cristóbal as mayor and storekeeper should not allow them to buy so much. But Don Cristóbal was Ladino too, and felt no remorse. He knew he gave good weight, as the saying goes, for their meager money. After so long among them he understood what Edmundo did not, that complete generosity was the whole idea, that it was the gift's totality that made it worthy of respect. In a way he was a vehicle for their honor, a storehouse for it: the mayor's wealth was proof the customs are defended in Akabal, even in the depths of hell.

This made no sense to Edmundo, and he would raise his eyebrows and his shoulders when the mayor told him the customs were very old, as old as the villagers' Mayan ancestors.

The trouble with Maximon, the priest said, was that he wasn't so old. It was as though the door to a forgotten tomb had been pushed aside and some ominous new life form had crawled out, oozing evil.

Gregorio was relentless. "You know something else I've always wondered about? Who was it who hid Maximon under the sand pile that time?"

The priest's hands paused an instant, then resumed replacing the candles. "How should I know?" he muttered.

Gregorio smiled, satisfied. This was a sharp needle indeed, because the little statue and all the cigarettes and liquor bottles had disappeared from the thatch-roofed shrine one night several months before, and of course Edmundo was immediately the chief suspect, even though he was a priest. Don Cristóbal had convened the village elders to consider the situation. The seven of them decided everything of importance in Akabal, and their debates were public, according to custom, so that everybody knew what went into the decision. After a lot of talk, in which they considered blaming even the subversives to avoid confronting the priest, they had agreed that the best way to let Edmundo know he was suspected would be to ask him for advice. That was Don Honorio's idea, the wily old baker always so subtle he seemed to be simple. So the elders had stood in a row outside the church door, their hats off, and Don Honorio had spoken to him. "Father, the Maximon has disappeared and we respectfully ask your advice in seeking its return."

"Gone? Gone? But who would do such a thing? Who?" Edmundo waved his arms, a bit too much. "Perhaps Maximon himself decided to leave you. Perhaps his mission is complete here. Have you thought of that? Hmm?"

Don Honorio ignored the sarcasm. "We can think of no one who might know what to do better than yourself, Father."

Edmundo raised his chin. He was not easily intimidated.

"Well, I suggest you take it as a sign and leave well enough alone. I'm sure Akabal is better off without Maximon anyway."

"Will you come and bless our search, Father?"

Edmundo's face reddened. After a moment he had made a swift, small cross over them, mumbling, and swept back into the chapel. A week later Maximon and his offerings were found in the sand pile of a house being built nearby, and he was restored to his open-air throne. Don Genero, the sweet old fool, actually suggested the elders go formally to thank Father Edmundo for his blessing, and he didn't understand why the mayor laughed. Genero had never had a mischievous thought in his life.

Gregorio smiled to himself, remembering. He waited now, watching Edmundo with the candles, and started humming "Onward Christian Soldiers." He had learned it from the Pentecostal amplifiers booming onto the streets in Santa Rosa, delighted, knowing Edmundo detested the Pentecostals, the upstarts who were taking so many of the Indians away from the Catholics with their emotional chanting and shouting about a personal savior. Like a mighty army . . .

"Are you going to talk about Maximon again today, then?"

"As a matter of fact, yes," Edmundo said, turning. "It's odd, you know, but for the feast of San Clemente the ordained reading just happens to fit right in with idol worship. It's about the writing on the wall, all about false gods." He held a beer bottle forgotten, his face alight, as though he were about to take a swig. "And then the other reading is from Luke, just perfect. It says loyal Christians may be arrested and tortured and betrayed, even by their families — and you know everyone here will listen to that — but belief in the one true God will save them. That's all perfect, don't you think, really aimed right at the Maximon business."

"It is?" Gregorio's biblical education was spotty at best.

"Well, if you get arrested around here, maybe it's divine punishment for believing in Maximon, see?" He saw Gregorio's eyes widen and went on in haste. "Well, not directly, of course, certainly not your father or your sister, or anybody else in particular, but in a symbolic sense, really. Arrested in the sense of — of led astray, carried off, by any kind of false idols — money, or Maximon, or a new car, things like that." He bit his lips. "Distractions," he added, waving the bottle. "I mean, poverty itself is a distraction; so are children, or politics, getting involved in politics. We have to keep focused on God and what God wants of us, see? That's the problem with Maximon."

Gregorio didn't see. He shook his head. "It's hard enough figuring out what I want myself —"

"Yes! Exactly! That's Maximon exactly! It's backward! That's why he's so dangerous! We must focus instead on what God wants from us!" The priest smiled broadly. "You've got it. That's wonderful." He lifted the beer bottle in salute. "Inner change is first, and then it changes the world, not the other way around. That's right. Many people don't understand that."

Gregorio sighed and gave up for the third time that morning. "Well, perhaps." He paused. "You have so much energy so early in the day, Father. You're too much." Edmundo grinned and turned back to his candles. "You came here yesterday from Tekan? How many places now in your circuit?"

Edmundo glanced over his shoulder but Gregorio kept his face sincere. "Well, it's hard to say. I think it's down to sixty, maybe fifty-five. A sad thing." Gregorio nodded. There had been eighty when the priest, fresh out of seminary, first jounced up the hill in his jeep four years ago, but four years of fighting had weeded out the rest: little clumps of humanity in three or ten huts between the trees, larger collections of twenty or so in clearings, villages like this one of thirty or more real houses, erased from sites that had been old when the conquistadores marched by. Even generous towns of yards and fences, some with a paved street or two, even some of those had been burned, crushed, abandoned, the people swept out and blown away by the gales of revolt and repression, the *xocomil* wind of the rebellious mountains.

Yet every month Edmundo drove dogged through the rubble, spending a day here, two days in Zacapa, going back to the big stucco church where he lived in Santa Rosa, out to Kanil by jeep, and by donkey on to Chucuyub; eight o'clock Mass, six o'clock Mass, baptisms, funerals, a dozen candles each. A morning of weddings up in Tibal and an afternoon of confessions down in Kerat, and to Tekan when he could fit it in. Where the saints have trod . . . Sometimes he had to stay someplace longer than expected because the fighting blocked the roads, or because his jeep broke down, and then he would write out new lessons for the catechists to use until his next visit. The last time, Gregorio gave Edmundo a sketch of that jeep, detailed to the last dent, flying empty like a boxy bird over a rocky landscape.

Edmundo had laughed. "That's what I need, all right. But why is there no driver?"

Gregorio considered the answers he could give. It's carrying the Holy Spirit. It's the church defying earthly difficulty. It's you, Father; draw your own conclusions. "I didn't think it needed one," he said.

The priest narrowed his eyes and shrugged, tossing the drawing on his cot. "Well, many thanks. So, then. Are you drawing full time now, or what?"

"I wish I could. No, the usual — the corn patch, the bakery. We survive."

"Yes, good. The Lord helps those who help themselves. And your father is all right?" Gregorio nodded. "Any word about your sister — Cecilia, isn't it?"

"Yes, Cecilia. No, nothing. We put in another petition last week."

"Well, keep at it. Knock and the door shall be opened. I'll bring you some more paper next time." He had forgotten to take the drawing with him, and of course this time he had forgotten to bring the paper. But Gregorio was not disappointed. He had not expected the priest to remember such trivia.

Gregorio contemplated the priest's narrow shoulders as he labored over the candles. How many candles in how many beer bottles, crooked and straight, long and short, lit by matches and black-market Bics to shimmer in the shining eyes of how many exhausted farmers over the past four years? The priest spent too much time on the candles. One big central light would be easier, more modern. Gregorio envisioned an ornate chandelier of gold and crystal, intricate like the cathedral giants in Edmundo's books, but festooned instead with beer bottles, candelabra of the poor. How could such a thing be hung from the flimsy rafters here? It would take up half the room. It would clash with the pink and yellow plastic fringes tacked to each beam, maybe set them afire. Perhaps the bottles could glow with little light bulbs. But would the generator make enough power for so many? Clearly not. The pathetic machine slept in the shed, reeking of gasoline. Only with Arturo's coaxing would it mutter reluctantly into life, and then it roared, noisy as a tank, to chug out power for Edmundo's microphone and two weak light bulbs on their long cords, one by the cot so that Edmundo could read at night and the other glowing in the eyes of God on his cross. The town needed more power than that.

Edmundo's gut rumbled so hard Gregorio heard it five meters away, and he laughed aloud. The priest backed away from the altar, dusting his hands. "Well, that's done. Now where is Miguel Angel? He was supposed to be here by now. I didn't see him last night either."

"He'll be here if he said he would," Gregorio mumbled. He stood again and picked up his rifle and his straw hat.

The priest turned around and his eyes widened. "Look there! The blessed chickens are back." Gregorio followed Edmundo's gaze to some scrawny black birds scratching in bits of grass and corn on the cement floor. "This place is such a mess." He wheeled and marched into the shed. He emerged with a broom. "Gregorio, here. Make yourself useful. Get those chickens out of here." He tossed the broom at Gregorio and, fumbling with his belt buckle, hurried back into the shed toward the outhouse.

Gregorio dropped his hat to catch the broom. Slinging the rifle across his shoulder, he advanced on the chickens, who lowered their heads and screeched at him. "G'wan, shoo, get outa here." Gregorio swept madly, herding the flutter of birds through the square of pink light at the big open door, bursting into the plaza in a cloud of dust and feathers.

A peach-colored flash drew his eye to the ridge glowing pink across the gully road from Akabal's hill. A short rifle barrel. Another. A line of heads misshapen by slouch hats, moving. Soldiers, no question. With a gasp he wheeled back into the church and ran up the aisle, vaulting the front bench toward the shed. He flung open the door and grabbed the rope hanging in the corner and hauled on it with all his might. *Bonk, ca-lonk!* The cracked old bell awoke in its arch high above the gate, sounding the news again and again and again, as it had for centuries: Wake up! Come here! Come find out! Something is happening in Akabal!

Three

LIEUTENANT PROSPERO JESÚS GOMEZ had been lying propped on his elbows on the ridge overlooking Akabal for at least two hours. At first he had just been able to make out the cemetery through his field glasses. The crypts so early were only smudges on the opposite hillside; the church above was three smooth arches in the black fringe of treeline behind, the sky growing gray in the distance. This was Gomez's favorite hour, the morning infinite with possibility, a time when practical men could open their hearts to hope that rare surprise and fresh experience awaited them in the new day. Gomez had savored the minutes as long as possible, turning the church silhouette to a playful snake rolling gold-edged over the hills, the pinkening sky to fields of orange sheep, himself at ease in a hammock, lord of the lush plantation below. He gave a long sigh and lowered the binoculars to examine the village taking on reality against all his will, his gaze as careful as if Akabal were a woman dressing in the gathering light.

The Akabal he saw was a contemptible place, he thought, a dirt creature barely risen from the mire, dull and hopeless, exhausting even to look at. The huts were brown; the roofs of straw or tin or tile were brown with age or dirt or rust, the plaza before them a dusty lighter brown. The cornfields, the starving dogs nosing about, the sleeping Indians with brains of carrots, all were a drab, eternal brown, so deep they sucked in light. The little church had been whitewashed once, but the sandblasts of the dry months and torrents of the wet ones had tanned and streaked its adobe face to brown noncolor, the color of sleep, a passive wash of indifference even to looming death.

That was what he felt himself to be, peering across the gully into the plaza that had to be holding his quarry, an angel of death and retribution for the fire and blood of last night, the terror of the past fifteen years. For Julio his brother, dead in the blast at Cotzal three years ago, walking by the guard post when the bomb went off, just bouncing the soccer ball Gomez had given him, for Julio there could never be retribution enough. This place wouldn't be worth even mentioning on any list of payment for that debt.

But because of the blast, Lieutenant Gomez and twenty of his best Kaibil Special Forces unit had tracked the terrorist here, starting fast through the cornfields east of the military base. It was an easy trail at first, even at night, with the high-powered Israeli flashlights showing the bent stalks as clearly as though a truck had gone through. The subversive had swung north toward the meager lights of Santa Rosa, skirting east again in the shadows of the Esso station and the baseball park to circle up toward the new highway that came out of the market quarter like an arrow aimed along the eastern valley. There the pursuers had halted in indecision, flashlights probing the gullies to the north, into the market warren, looking for signs. Gomez had stood on the gravel where the road began and considered what the terrorist might have done there.

The lieutenant hated that road, still oily black in the crev-
ices, its nubby surface scarcely grayed in two years of traffic. It
had been the first gift of the gringos to General Torres after
his coup two years before, the latest in the kind of antiguer-
rilla thinking that made Gomez spit: move the troops in quan-
tity into rebel territory, overwhelm them with numbers, build
roads to boost the economy and open up the land. But a road
like this couldn't quell a revolution, and a revolution was what
they had here, although nobody used the word. This was a
highway transplanted from Nebraska. Its two lanes of asphalt
had oozed from the huge Yankee machines like black slime
behind yellow snails, coating sixty kilometers of cratered ruts
to chain Santa Rosa with half a dozen villages in the eastern
valley, as though that would be enough. Large pale gringos
tended the herd of Caterpillars, toting rolls of maps, yelling
at the drivers in atrocious Spanish, drinking all the beer for
miles around, and passing out candy bars and chewing gum
to the children as though they were invading Europe. The
villages so honored were no bigger or smaller than a dozen
others that did not happen to lie along the straight line the
gringos liked so much. The road ended abruptly at the west-
ern edge of each cluster of houses, replaced by mudholes and
meandering goat paths sweating with sewage, cobbled streets
barely wide enough for a truckful of soldiers to inch past
children and babies squeezed up against the walls. Then the
sleek highway resumed again on the eastern edges of the
towns as though nothing had interrupted its blind conversation with itself.

Between the towns, the road seemed embarrassed by its
emptiness, almost shy, calling out for traffic to the watching
patches of corn and beans as though crops were coming in, as
though the power lines hummed and the bridges in the mountains weren't bombed out, as though there were tourists. It
sang doggedly of money, promising smooth, dreamy passage

to market or to the southern coffee and cotton plantations for extra work, even in the rainy season, but it couldn't produce more buses or trucks to give body to that promise. The few buses that hadn't been burned by the guerrillas or confiscated by the army rattled along like backfiring hills of people, sheep and peasants piled on top and hanging from the sides. Private cars stayed safely in Santa Rosa; taxi drivers tried to sell their ancient heaps in order to eat, but there were no buyers. Yet this was the road that would bring order and democracy into the surly heart of this treacherous province. Or so General Torres had said.

In fact the last time Gomez had seen the former president was when he came to Santa Rosa with the U.S. ambassador to open that road, giving the first major speech of his presidency to a vast crowd of soldiers and a silent sea of farmers trucked to the plaza for the occasion. "This highway represents a neeEEEEEEK . . . a new era," the general had shouted, backing away from his shrieking loudspeaker. Gomez could catch only a few phrases after that: ". . . peace and economic devel . . . brotherhood . . . all the people. The bloodbath is over! This symbol of . . . binds the people of our fatherland . . . great friend the United States." Everyone clapped. The new president shook hands with the ambassador and the other sweating dignitaries on the top steps of the church, and Gomez and his troops paraded in the hot sun.

To Gomez the road was worse than a lie to the farmers. They had been lied to for so long that the truth would only have confused them. The road's real evil was for the army, for whom it had become a sweet zone of safety that seduced away from vigilance. It was a well-lit street through this dark and threatening slum of a province, and the troops barreled through without seeing when they should have been scouring the place clean, inch by corrupted inch. The corridor of false security made the surrounding hills seem full of subversives, inaccessible, looming over the soldiers, who sat coddled in their trucks. Nothing but rocky suggestions of tracks led north and south from the highway into the hills, habits of passage that only four-wheel-drive jeeps and men on foot could hope to follow, men willing to risk ambush and blood. Those were the only men who would be able to quell a revolution, men as ready to die as the rebels were. Too many patrols had found it easier to reconnoiter the highway and declare the zone safe and free of subversives. That was why the country was in the state it was in. But soldiers were only soldiers, and Gomez knew some of his troops hoped he would decide now that the subversive had taken the road, impossible to track him there.

He had allowed himself to sound impatient. "Well, which way?" He and Joyabal and the tracker Emidio Tijax, the silent one, bent to study the loose gravel at the point where the blacktop emerged from the town, looking for the slight dampness of just-turned stones, the newly broken weeds, scuff marks that would tell the path. If the terrorist had gone into the market labyrinth, he would be easy to find, or someone would be easy to find, someone who looked enough like a terrorist to be arrested, and the hunt would be over that way too.

The market was a huddle of tin roofs over black pathways, low adobe huts, and cardboard shacks divided by gauzy cloth and flimsy sticks, breathing silent life and a murmur of rats. Gomez considered the hundreds of peasants who lay awake inside these hovels, waiting, hardly daring to breathe, listening to the soldiers' whispers and the crunch of their boots, flinching as the flashlights shot across the walls. He smiled to himself and imagined their hands in the darkness, making a quick sign of the cross, creeping toward the pistol, gripping the machete.

The criminal might be in any one of those pigsties. Gomez considered a full-scale raid, dragging them all out, taking everyone in the district in for questioning. He imagined frightened children reading his mind, cowering on the mats, men and women willing the boots to turn away, bracing for the hammering on the door.

"Here, Lieutenant." Sergeant Joyabal's low call was wide with satisfaction. He pointed to where Emidio crouched over two skid marks, faint ridges shadowed like mountains in the flashlight beam, running down the low shoulder of the road on the north side toward the ravines. Gomez bent to touch their slight dampness, his right knee crackling. He stood and nodded. Joyabal nodded back and gave a low whistle. "All right, move out," he said. His voice was barely louder than a conversation.

Gomez switched on his radio. "We're going into the hills after him, north and east. Bring a unit up toward Zacapa on the highway and I'll be in touch."

The men and their flashlights flowed around him off the road, into the brush and rocky wasteland that stretched a hundred trackless miles to the north, rising in tortured ridges and gullies to the high northern mountains, where the rains and the mist never dried, where the ancient ruined cities slept under vines, and monkeys and quetzals still screeched, invisible in the jungle canopies. The terrorist had fled to a rebel camp somewhere in the gutted land of the high plateau, or to one of the stubborn villages scattered through here, hopeless places that clung to their barren rocks like barnacles, forever old and crumbling. Gomez would have to be very careful, very good at tracking to pick the right way.

But of course he didn't have to pick the right way, or really put himself through any of this. All of these villages were collaborating, feeding the subversives or hiding them, farmers by day and terrorists by night. Almost thirty years now since the communists had been ousted from the government, bombed out of the capital with Yankee money, driven over the borders and into the mountains that should have absorbed them without a trace. Instead they had festered here, in this province especially, living on God knows what and spreading their poison ideas, erupting fifteen years ago in the cities like boils all over a man's body. He could just pick any town and name anybody and be done with it, and he'd probably be right. He had a list of names ready, suspicious people and troublemakers, and no one would question him about it. At least no one would have until recently, and even now it probably wouldn't matter. But he had a trail here, and troops that were trained to follow it, so they might as well see where it went.

Was it only fifteen years? Half his life. It seemed much longer. Gomez scanned his troops loping along, following Joyabal and Emidio with their eyes on the ground, flashlight beams darting this way and that, bold probes into the hostile wastes. Gomez marveled at the outrage that seemed to well up naturally in Sergeant Joyabal and some of the others. They appeared actually to be enjoying themselves in this frosty air, stumbling through the ridges. The recruits were young and eager to learn what to think: calls to patriotism and the fatherland gave them wings. But Gomez had a belly now, and a bad knee, and Melinda, kids, debts, responsibilities. He saw her in the window of the narrow apartment in the military section near the capital, strand of dark hair over one eye as she stood at the sink, suddenly seeing him and smiling through the peeling kitchen window that looked through banana palms to the suburban bus stop. The kitchen — was it blue? Yellow? The bedroom sheets were white, he knew that. Nothing out here was white, nothing pure or clean or even safe. He could hardly remember when a dirt road was just a road and not a possible minefield, or when sandbags and machine guns were something in the movies, not part of the doors to every building.

The troops stumbled and shuffled along over the rough

ground. These ravaged hills hadn't changed since the 1520s, when Pedro de Alvarado had come through on his bloody way south. Gomez pictured the Spanish demigod on a capering white horse, armor gleaming as he rode along this very ridge perhaps, tossing his famous blond hair. Hundreds of foot soldiers plodded along behind, nobody glancing at the scruffy villages that marred the countryside. Their hunt was for gold, not for men; much easier and more predictable than Gomez's job tonight. This chase could go any which way. Melinda was always after him to quit, and maybe she was right. Maybe it was time for him to get off these death runs, move on to a desk job before he got hurt again. His knee ached permanently now, deep inside, harboring a grudge from too many long nights like this one.

In fact the track wasn't very hard for Gomez to follow. The terrorist had been overconfident. The soldiers exclaimed in satisfaction as they learned his character, seeing how he had zigzagged through the night at first, stopping often, probably to listen, repeatedly packing the dry earth with many turns and shiftings, making them search up and down the stoniest stretches for the sign of his direction. But soon his tracks were tearing straight through the dry yawns of gullies, following the goat paths that led only to Akabal or Tekan, his distinctive sandal prints clear as billboards. Now when he thought he had escaped, now they would catch him.

Miguel had tried for a while to be a thicker darkness in the night, standing long among dark rocks no more immobile than he while he watched and listened, focusing a little to the side of his central vision as Nahual had taught. Comforted each time by silence, he decided early that the troops would stay on the main road as they usually did. The only danger might be a small unit camped in the hills above Akabal, part of General Torres's reluctant net spread at the Yankees' insistence to catch guerrilla fish. But they would be easy to spot, advertising their presence with leaping campfires, as happy as he to avoid disturbance. Miguel ran on easily to Akabal, slowing at the top of the last ridge before the village. He lay down on the rock to peer over the rim.

Not a sign of life. The crown of huts and houses that ringed the hilltop opposite was so cradled on its sloping cornfields as to be part of the nurturing earth, hardly visible from the dirt road below the ridge even during the day. He could not see them but he could sense each familiar building there, exuding soft warm calls of sanctuary and hot coffee, a welcoming murmur of friends and family snug in piles of blankets, fuzzy with sleep. Miguel got up and worked his way down the incline to the rutted track between the hills, where he paused and listened. Only the stream trickled eternally below the road. He looked up the path that led to Akabal and worried briefly about the dogs dozing in the plaza. If they barked, if the civil patrol challenged him . . . but his luck would stay good that night; Nahual had thought of everything. He started at a lope up the wide path, past the last bit of corn, past the cemetery with its tottering wooden crosses and boxy crypts that held the dead aloft, away from the ravaged earth. The low mounds reeked of turned clay and bitter marigolds strewn and growing there, left over from the picnics and the drinking of the Day of the Dead three weeks past. Not for him yet, that quiet place.

Suddenly he heard gravel move on the path ahead and caught his breath. He waited, his heart racing. In the starlight he made out two of the town's spavined mutts, ears forward, sniffing the air. But he knew them both, and did not move. They relaxed and sidled toward him, whining a welcome home to the plaza at the top of the hill.

Now Gomez, lying on the same ridge overlooking Akabal, possibly on the very spot where Miguel had lain, turned to check his resources. The soldiers of Kaibil Unit Three were scattered below and behind him on the ridge, lying with guns forward like a fallen fence. They pretended to be ready to move, but one or two had their heads down, probably asleep. He was briefly sympathetic. He was as tired as they were from the long run of maybe fifteen, twenty kilometers, fifteen years more tired, actually. He scanned the smudged faces under their slouch hats, camouflage print shadowed into the rocks. It was appropriate that soldiers spent so much time face down in the dirt they had sworn to defend. These were just children, most of them Indians like the villagers, following orders as they had for four hundred years, trained redundantly to be passive and obedient. Twenty of them, and another forty waiting for his signal on the highway ten kilometers south over the mountains. Akabal center, if you could call it that, had maybe a hundred people, with another hundred out a kilometer in every direction who came in to market here. A pathetic market that would be, he thought: a few piles of peppers and corn, bags of flour and sugar, cornmeal and white lime for their endless tortillas. But most of them would be communist sympathizers in this area, even the women and the children. They wouldn't have many guns, maybe twenty or twenty-five, and that many only if the subversives had come in during the past few days. There was probably a camp nearby, although Benedicto Tijax had said nothing about it last week, and he had been paid. A dozen guns max.

Gomez decided he could probably level the place with just the men behind him. It would hardly be missed; it was a wonder it had survived this long. Towns like this spawned murderers. To be born here was to be sprinkled with the blood of chickens by some witch doctor, to drink muddy water, and if you were lucky to die before you were six months old. To survive was to be hungry for life, to carry firewood or cow dung as soon as you could walk, to breathe smoke all day from the open cookfire in the hut, watching your father drink the corn money, watching your mother waste away among tumbles of children, all of them sick and small. The children drank too, first at the festivals and then every weekend, falling in their own vomit before they were old enough to go to school, only there was no school. It was incredible; why didn't they leave? How could they be fully human, living in such filth? They never washed. He remembered the blocks and blocks of soap stacked in translucent candles at his father's little store in Cotzal, in the civilized central part of the country. Two cents each, one would last a week of scrubbing clothes. Nobody was too poor to afford that, not even the Indians, but all he had ever seen them buy was sugar and aguardiente. But they were trainable: his unit was proof they could learn to wash and wear boots and shoot. In fact they were almost too trainable when they wanted to be. He thought of that northern village, what was its name, where soldiers entering empty huts had triggered snares that hung them upside down from the rafters, or fell through mats into hidden pits and were skewered like pigs on the spikes below. Anyone could see the communists had brought that trick straight from Vietnam, and yet the leftist agitators claimed the rebellion was purely domestic. Akabal would do that sort of thing. It was that kind of place, a pile of traitors, collaborators. The word clattered in his mind like rocks falling off a truck.

He raised his binoculars and noticed that the church door was open, although he hadn't seen anyone. He wondered whether there were binoculars staring back at him, cross hairs of rifle sights over his forehead from all the dark corners.

He heard a noise behind him, and Sergeant Joyabal joined him on the ridgetop. The wiry subaltern was a confusion of allergies, and his nose ran constantly. "So, Faucet Face, what do you make of it?" Gomez almost smiled. Their relationship

was new yet, only a year or so together in this unit, and the
sergeant's ambition struck Gomez as quaint.

Joyabal wiped his nose. "A little too quiet, I think."

"They're Indians. They're always quiet." Gomez imagined
his quarry, Miguel Angel Kanak, a sharp-edged name like so
many of them, the one underlined at the top of the list of
troublemakers Benedicto Tijax had given him months before.
He had forgotten Tijax, forgotten Akabal until the track led
here; now the memory of that list scrolled behind his eyes like
a dusty tape dredged up from some long-forgotten mental
vault. He could see it all: some runt in a crumpled cowboy hat,
throwing himself through one of those doors across the ravine
an hour ago, two hours, lying exhausted on the dirt floor, but
too nervous and scared to sleep. Or no, he was elated, proud of
his murders; he slept the instant peace of the damned. He
would be awake now, refreshed, ready to get up, sitting on the
straw mat he might have for a bed, perhaps eating breakfast —
a tortilla and beans? Coffee? Bragging about the bombing to
his woman wrapped in her stinking striped blankets as she
served him. Gomez clenched his teeth. Kanak. Tijax. It was
time to find out more about the connections.

"Any of the men know anything about this place?" He kept
his voice careless.

"Yessir. Emidio is from here, or from this area, Private
Tijax, sir."

"Right. Get him up here." Joyabal wriggled backward down
the ridge, and Gomez turned sideways to watch him, dislodging pebbles that bounced down the ridge toward the road.
Gomez had noticed the tracker's name when he got caught in
one of the regular draft roundups of the locals, eight, nine
months ago, and wondered briefly then if he and the infor-
mant Benedicto Tijax were related. But he had said nothing.
The Indians were all intermarried, cousins of cousins with
the same names who had never met. There were dozens of

Tijaxes in this province; it wasn't likely these two knew each other, and the lieutenant had decided to wait and see. Still, if they were related it would complicate matters, and he considered the two men.

Benedicto Tijax, just a few years younger than Gomez, was ambitious, shifty; you wouldn't trust him with a centavo, and therefore he was a useful spy. Emidio was five or six years younger than Benedicto, about twenty, still a kid, silent and tireless, a faceless cipher who happened to understand trail marks, a soldier invisible in the ranks of other soldiers and therefore also useful. If they were connected, well, that might be useful too. Now all of it was ready to Gomez's hands, as though he had never forgotten.

The sergeant returned, crawling beside Emidio Tijax, who gave an awkward salute. He looked a little like Benedicto, Gomez noticed: the hooded eyes, the broad Indian nose, high cheekbones, and wide, slack mouth, but then most Indians looked like that. Enormous teeth. Did they used to eat their human sacrifices? "Well, Emidio. You're from here?"

"Yessir." The voice was low, flat, without either respect or offense. A mud turtle would have such a voice.

"What do you know about this pig wallow of a village that I don't know already?" Gomez lay propped on one elbow.

"Ordinary village, sir. Nothing unusual." Tijax stopped. Gomez waited. He could wait as long as they could. Emidio's Spanish was ramshackle. The lieutenant could not remember which of the twenty or so Indian languages Akabal used. The old Mayan had subdivided so many times in the mountains that the Indians in his unit often could not even understand one another. "Just Indians, sir," Tijax said at last.

"You know this guy Kanak, Miguel Angel Kanak?"

Tijax shrugged, expressionless. "Sure. Nothing special. A good shooter. Farmer." He stopped again, his jaw ajar, eyelids heavy. "Family poor, like all here."

"He's a troublemaker, a subversive?"

Tijax shrugged again and looked away, his gaze unfocused. "Any other roads out the back?" Tijax shook his head. Gomez knew that was true. Only footpaths led down the steep hill to the wilted cornfields behind and below, and to the stream for water, and his gringo maps showed all of them.

Gomez looked at the tracker. No point in asking him about Benedicto Tijax. Better for Gomez to suspect a link and act carefully, much better than to bring it up and risk creating a connection where there might be none. He waved dismissal and turned back toward the ravine. He picked up his field glasses and peered through them at the village, now a pink and orange topping to the brown pile below.

The crosses of the cemetery leaned brilliant among the pastel crypts, and Gomez frowned into the cold metal circles. Any display of irritation was unprofessional, but his soldiers watching him would expect it. This Tijax grunted and the other one babbled, and neither one said anything. The silence of these people rivaled plant life. He had seen Indians stand an hour in a rainstorm waiting to be asked what they wanted; he had seen them discover their dead, remove and bury them with barely a flicker of their lizard eyes. Nothing seemed to move them. Strange how so many had turned into terrorists, but they had, especially around here.

In his ten years of fighting subversion in this province he had always been able to tell when he was in friendly territory, and this wasn't it. Sunrise now and nobody in sight. The little plaza ought to be alive with busy farmers, women feeding the chickens, youngsters carrying water and wood. They must have been up late, probably waiting for this Kanak to come back from his mission, Kanak or whoever it was.

At that moment Gregorio erupted from the church door in a dusty cloud of chickens. Through his binoculars Gomez saw the burly fellow turn and gape upward, saw astonishment on the dark face, watched as he tore back into the church, heard the old bell ring out across the ravine. Damn fools, sounding an alarm as though the army was their enemy, not the only thing standing between them and communism, he thought. Why didn't the guy's face light up with welcome, why didn't he wave in pleasure, in friendship? Gomez got to his feet and raised his arm, hearing the scramble of his men behind him. He waved them up to the top of the ridge. "All right, let's go! Let's get this over with."

Four

HEARING THAT BELL was a great relief to Don Cristóbal Clemente. The mayor had been crouching nearly an hour by the window that looks out over the road from the back of his store, trying to think clearly, ever since he first got up, stretching, and glanced outside. Along the ridge, dark against the whitening sky, he had seen the unmistakable barrels of guns, the crumpled hats of at least a dozen soldiers, probably more behind. His heart had crashed into his throat and his knees buckled, and he clung to the window ledge for support. Never before had they come to Akabal in such numbers. His first thought had been the logical one, that the end had come, that this could only be a massacre squad, sent to wipe out the village for harboring the cancer of subversion. Akabal, serene and quiet on its mountaintop, his healing refuge, source of nourishment for so many, this harmless place would be burned to the ground, a blackened bit of rubble.

In his terror he tried to hold that awful scene in his mind, examining each charred stick in horror, so as not to think about what would happen before that, as it had in San Martín, in Cuarto Pueblo, in Agua Escondido, in Chacúl, in Tucuallpa:

first to all the women, Irene Kanak and Ana de Córdoba and beautiful Caterina, raped and raped by the troops who would not resist the thrill of coming as each woman writhed, screaming in death, her throat slit; to the howling children, spores of rebellious infection, skewered on their fathers' own machetes; to the men, forced to watch as a lesson of their impotence; then powerless as the soldiers stripped them, laughing at their nakedness and suddenly vicious, seizing the strongest and youngest, hacking off penises, balls, the future . . . his groin would shrivel as he watched; his turn would come quickly, too quickly, the unthinkable agony, and then the blackness, his head cut off to stop the screaming. He would be among the most unlucky; he panted as he thought about it: one of those left to the last, to be questioned, gasping, as the others died before his eyes, then the knives upon him, so that only the animals remained to watch, until they were killed too in cruel kindness so that they wouldn't starve. Then Akabal would be burned, its stucco cracking and the tin roofs melting all around the heaps of bodies.

No, it was impossible, not here, not now; those massacres had ended in the past year or so, two governments back, before Morales, even before Torres, or so the radio had told them again and again. Times of change, times of progress, the Yankee human rights commissions had come as far as Santa Rosa and everyone had heard the speeches. But why else would so many soldiers come here? Maybe there had been another coup d'état in the capital last night, a policy reversal? But Akabal would never be first on any new government's revenge list. The mayor could think of nothing that had ever brought this many soldiers to an insignificant place except a massacre, and he could not think of that.

Perhaps someone was to be arrested, as the radio endlessly told them was now the policy for suspected guerrillas. But the group that had arrested Cecilia de Córdoba was only five, jouncing up the path in a jeep, a good jeep, because only a good jeep could survive the ten kilometers from Santa Rosa over the boulders and craters of that so-called road. And the garrison there didn't have enough jeeps for this many men. Anyway, the whole town would have heard them coming a long way off. No, he could not escape it: so many men must have come over the hills. Maybe then they were one of the Torres terror units camped somewhere nearby, chasing guerrillas through the gullies. But why were they waiting up there? They weren't even hiding; they couldn't be planning to attack. It was silly to keep thinking about it. How their guns flashed in the sun! Probably they had the town surrounded — but why? His thoughts flew in these circles a thousand times in minutes, faster and faster, and when the bell rang it was a jolt, derailing his panic so that he nearly fell over. It meant the priest had seen the soldiers too, was calling everyone to the square; he must know something about it. The mayor got up quickly as he could on his old legs and grabbed his long-sleeved white shirt off the chair, putting it on to look as official as possible while he went through the store into the plaza. But his belt was too tight and he struggled vainly to stuff the flapping shirttail into his pants behind as he went out.

The big church door was open but he couldn't see anybody inside. No one was in the plaza yet either, but a few people started coming as he hurried toward the road: two women wrapped in stripes emerging from the shed just above the cemetery, another couple out of the corner where the Coca-Cola sign is, Gregorio's father, Andreas, coming around the houses behind the mayor's green store, hobbling along on his crutch. That bell crashed like a stuck record, *bonk-bonk-bonk*. Cristóbal waved at everybody, trying to get them all into the plaza as fast as possible, a united front, nothing to hide, they had done nothing wrong. The soldiers were standing up by then, looking down across the ravine, but at least they weren't pointing those guns. Cristóbal raised his arms and yelled.

"Halloo-oo! Good morning!" No response. He waved

again. "We are at your orders!" Maybe they were just on routine patrol. Maybe they only wanted breakfast. He recalled those thoughts later as frantic, a fool's dash toward hope in denial of all experience, but such is human nature, a blind life force driving toward the tiniest excuse from death. Behind the mayor the town gathered together, men and women stumbling into the bloody light from every hut on the hilltop, pooling their uncertain strengths to waver as one before the flashing guns.

In the morning light the women's pastel blouses glowed different shades of pink, the lace elbow cuffs and collars frothy above the long wrapped skirts. Cristóbal motioned to the men to take their hats off as a sign of respect, and as they moved, the tattered straw swooped arcs and shadows in the dusty light.

"Halloo! Chief! What's going on?" Cristóbal yelled again, cupping his hands. "Good morning! I'm in charge here. How may we serve you?"

Gomez yelled back. "Hello! Bring out the chief of the civil patrol! We're coming over."

They rolled forward, spilling over the ridgetop like a mud slide down into the ravine toward the road. Ten, fifteen, twenty . . . Cristóbal kept inhaling as they appeared, until he thought he would faint. So many! So early! Why? Why? People behind him were murmuring, starting to whimper, and he turned on them. "Shut up! Quiet! We're all right now. Just be careful. We don't know anything. Let me talk." His mind raced but nothing came out.

The mayor recognized Gomez, the Special Forces chief. The lieutenant had been to Akabal before, once when his jeep broke down, once again on some reconnaissance operation, maybe once or twice more. Cristóbal had seen him in Santa Rosa a few times, and they had spoken pleasantly enough. He was older than the usual lieutenant, not noisy like some of them, and had gained some weight since the last time they met. With him in charge this couldn't be a terror unit, not a massacre squad, but a special detail for something. What? Cristóbal was sweating already in the cool morning air, trying to make some kind of plan, trying to appear calm for the sake of the others, failing at all of it. He had helped them survive so far by being one step ahead of whatever they wanted, first the soldiers and then the rebels, then the soldiers again, being agreeable to everybody, but this time he didn't know what to offer. He straightened his collar and they all stood there together, waiting for the soldiers to come up the path by the cemetery.

Perhaps so many armed men gave off a faint scent, of leather or sweat or gunmetal, or perhaps their presence changed the way the morning sounds murmured on the rock. Perhaps their breathing or their body heat changed the breeze or the shimmer of light over the ridge. Somehow, below awareness, the villagers of Akabal had been slightly tense before the bell rang, finding little things indoors that needed doing, fiddling with the fire, the day's tools, nursing the baby a little longer than usual. Miguel had slept fitfully after his hard run home, adrenaline jolting him awake at every crack of the glowing embers by his mat. Each time he lay taut and listening, deafened by his heartbeat, but each time there was nothing to hear. He had escaped; Nahual would be proud of him, call him the protector demon of Akabal. "Well, Helado," he would say, using Miguel's battle name, "Old Hurakan has nothing on you!" Miguel warmed and turned over under his thin and scratchy covers, imagining Nahual slapping him on the back. He would reply something witty, something modest, but not too modest, acknowledging that it had been a dangerous job meriting respect. Nahual would put his arm around Miguel's shoulders and grin and talk and laugh so that the others would know Miguel had done very well. He was a warrior now; no one could doubt it. Comforted at last, he had slept late, dozing until his mother, Flora, prodded him, reminding him of his promise to help the priest with morning Mass. Fogged with sleep, he had grumbled and stumbled into the narrow lane just as the bell rang. He turned the corner toward the plaza as the soldiers poured over the ridge face.

His knees went numb at the sight and he tripped. He staggered toward the church, keeping the low shacks between himself and the plaza. He thought, as Cristóbal had tried not to think, that it must be a massacre squad. How ironic that they should come today of all days! It couldn't have anything to do with him. Soldiers from the barracks were incompetent; they couldn't have tracked him over the hills. They could not have known where he was going. If they had tracked him, they wouldn't be waiting on the ridge; he'd be dead already. What else could this be? It had to be something else. It was almost funny except that it might be something horrible. Maybe it was a routine patrol, or someone coming in to make a speech. No, too early. More likely they were here by accident, maybe a terror unit mobilized by radio because of the blast to make an example of someplace, and they just happened to be near Akabal. So many! It had to be a massacre. He panted like a trapped jack rabbit and leaned for support on a nearby wall.

Every instinct screamed at Miguel to run. No one had seen him. He could hide somewhere, below the bluff near the stream, in the corn behind the hill, until they had gone away. Yes, that was it; he would survive and bear witness to the killings, carry the word of it to outrage the world. He looked around wildly and saw people moving along every rutted passageway toward the square. He would have to shoulder past them, go in the opposite direction, to get out. Why was the stupid bell ringing anyway? Were they all goats to walk so passively to their own slaughter? Were they all crazy?

He realized then that he had panicked, thinking only of

himself. What of his family, Irene, Gregorio, Caterina, what of them? What would happen to Caterina? The bell stopped its clonking and he peered carefully around the corner. The plaza was filling up, everyone looking toward the soldiers. Nobody glanced at him. He could slip behind the crowd, into the church, hide in the church shed, and see what happened. He could always escape the back way, down the bluff to the stream, if anything happened. Perhaps he might save others. He would know better than the rest what to do; the whole village might survive this if he kept calm.

He forced himself to remember his battle name: he was Helado, Ice Cream, the Cool One, whose open smile blinded enemy eyes. His breathing slowed and he straightened up. He turned the corner and pushed into the crowd at the door of the church, entering the gloomy nave as Father Edmundo emerged from the shed, zipping his jeans.

"For God's sake, what's going on? Miguel? What happened —" He broke off, looking past Miguel at the anxious faces peering in from the square.

"The soldiers. You didn't ring the bell?"

"No, it must have been Gregorio. Where is he? You — what? Soldiers? At this hour?" Eyes narrowing, the priest hurried past Miguel into the crowd, which parted to let him onto the three narrow steps. He looked quickly at the soldiers, by now spreading over the road at the bottom of the ravine, and came down quickly into the people, who pressed around him, murmuring urgent questions. He put his hands up to ward them off. Miguel halted in the shadow of the big wooden door, where he could see and hear but could not easily be seen himself.

Gomez led his soldiers across the road below the ridge, sending three men to stand guard fifty meters back toward Tekan and three more to the civil patrol shack on the next hill. Four more trotted up the streambed that led behind the town; God knew what kind of swamp that was. The rest followed the lieutenant up the path past the cemetery and into the square to face the villagers where they stood huddled together.

It was clear they were all terrified but were trying stupidly to hide it. Children clung to the adults' thick legs and peeked at him as if at some bottled obscenity in a village fair. Everyone was wearing the most vacant possible look, a pathetic attempt to appear open-minded. He felt a mixture of disgust and despair. The lieutenant recognized Don Cristóbal immediately, the only Ladino in the village. The old goat was wearing a pasty smile, bowing and working hard to be obsequious. "Good morning, Cristóbal," Gomez said, scratching his stomach deliberately. Someone had to stay relaxed around here. Neither man offered to shake hands. "Where is the head of the civil patrol?"

The mayor bowed again. "A very good morning to you, Lieutenant Gomez. I have the honor to hold that position. How may I serve you?"

Gomez gave him a tired look. "You, my old friend? Aren't you busy enough being mayor and catechist and robbing these people in your store? Isn't that enough for you without the civil patrol too?"

Cristobal laughed, a little too loudly. Behind him the villagers who spoke Spanish were murmuring behind their hands, translating for the others. "I never refuse an opportunity to serve my country, Lieutenant," he said. "We are so few and poor here that those of us who have good fortune — you understand, God wills us to contribute our fair share. It is my blessing to be head of the civil patrol." Gomez appeared not to be listening. His eyes flickered over the faces behind the mayor, probing vainly for connection in those dark walls. Cristóbal kept going without missing a beat, strewing verbal flowers as fast as he could. "You know that the patrol is a special honor here, for every man in San Clemente de Akabal is a member. Here we are all true patriots, all of us, and all of us are at your service this fine morning, the name day of our patron saint — and my own name day too, I am happy to say. We are at your command. You are most welcome here." Still Gomez did not respond. "Perhaps you have come to join us in our festival? You will have a fine day, a procession, a special market. Very fine vegetables from all over Santa Rosa. We are very proud of our festival —"

"We're looking for a terrorist here," the lieutenant interrupted, the word hissing into the crisp morning air. "A subversive named, ah — Kanak, Miguel Angel Kanak. You know him?" The crowd behind whispered a staccato echo: Kanak, Kanak, Kanak . . .

In that moment's pause before Gomez said the name, Cristóbal saw his disgust with the whole business: to the soldier the villagers were faceless annoyances, pestiferous dogs he as a man of honor had to clear away. Extermination was surely possible, but animals were not a cancer, not the plague; alternatives existed. Through that slim crack Akabal might escape, like a rat. He tried to appear confused and ran a hand through his hair. "Kanak? A terrorist? What do you mean?"

"Kanak, yes, a terrorist. Bring him out."

The mayor looked around vaguely. "Miguel . . . I haven't seen him today. I don't know if he's here or not." He turned to the faces behind and spoke in the village tongue. He was careful; some of Gomez's troops would understand. "None of you have seen Miguel Angel, have you?" Heads shook obediently. "No, I didn't think so." He turned back to Gomez, who had his hands on his hips and was nearly laughing. "Are you sure you want him?" he was almost begging. "He's a good man, never been in any trouble —"

"Yes, we want him! Quit wasting my time!"

The mayor reached quickly for the nearest boy, a swaybacked

seven-year-old with a withered left arm, one of Caterina's children. "Diego, go to Miguel Angel's house and if he's there, tell him to come here. Yes, it's okay. Go on." The child's eyes rounded and he gazed up at his mother, luminous in her red cotton blouse, but she stared impassively at Gomez. The boy ran off. Maybe the warning would allow Miguel time to escape.

Gomez was almost amused by this pathetic pretense of cooperation. He relaxed a bit and scanned the plaza, recognizing Father Edmundo and a few others. Finally he spotted Benedicto Tijax standing back by the church wall, his arms folded, a little apart from the rest. Tijax looked sober, his pressed pants and leather shoes the only ones in the plaza, smoke curling from his cigarette. He lifted it to his lips and his eyes locked with Gomez's, narrowing in the smoke. He nodded slightly, little more than an exhalation, and Gomez was unaccountably irritated.

Tijax hadn't always been so sure of himself. Gomez remembered the furtive, unshaven face, the sour breath, the nervous hands fastening and unfastening the two remaining buttons of the fetid shirt the day the soldiers dragged him in for questioning about the car bombing two years ago that had killed a colonel outside Cachabel. As a labor gang organizer, Tijax had access to trucks, machinery, and money and was a logical suspect. But he had talked nonstop, eager to please, full of nervous laughter, and Gomez had recognized him immediately as an opportunist, not innocent but certainly no subversive. Well, in these secretive mountains one took informants where one could find them, and Gomez swallowed his distaste to agree with Tijax's broad hint that for a few dólares each month the fatherland would receive a great deal of useful information. Ever since, he had provided more gossip than Gomez wanted.

They met from time to time in one of the cafés of Santa

Rosa, and Tijax drank two, three, five glasses of aguardiente, wriggling in his chair, chain smoking, grasping Gomez's elbow, his whispers punctuated by bursts of high-pitched laughter. The traveling priest, he confided the last time they met, had stayed overnight twice at the home of a widow in Tekan. The weaver Irene Kanak was getting free sugar from Cristóbal's store in Akabal. Men gathered there to talk politics every morning; he was watching this suspicious activity. Gomez had yawned and signaled for the bill.

Tijax had seized the lieutenant's forearm. "But listen, this is important. That Kanak is up to something. He's gone too much. His sister Irene, the one who makes that new cloth? He brings it in to sell and they're making real money, but he's doing something else with it. I know it," he said as Gomez stood up. "There's never any sign of it in Akabal. But I'll find out what it is, I promise you. Don't worry."

Gomez hadn't worried; he recalled that the tip that led to the arrest of the communist Cecilia de Córdoba had come not from Tijax but from the capital. Even in this useless backwater, even with so little to hear, one's ear could sometimes be deaf. He turned around and scanned his troops for Emidio Tijax, but the tracker was not in sight. Must have gone to the other hill lookout post, or up the stream. Gomez was annoyed with himself; another sign he was slipping. He should have brought the local man into the village, had him identify this Kanak, watched him for signs. He scowled and turned back to the mayor. "Were you on duty last night?"

"No, ah, but we all —" Cristóbal turned again to the villagers. "Who was on duty last night? All of you, step forward!"

The craning crowd of sixty or so appeared to quiver, the murmur increased, and heads swiveled to make little circles of faces around seven men. The patrol group shuffled forward and fell into a ragged line, shouldering those guns and coming to a pathetic semblance of attention. Gomez surveyed them and shook his head. He walked slowly from one end of the line to the other, stopping to examine each face.

To him they all looked like Tijaxes: leather skin, high cheekbones, the close-set eyes dark and blank, almost sleepy. None of them approached Gomez's two meters in height, not to mention his girth, and they all had the sloping shoulders and slight bowlegs of a hungry childhood. The younger ones clutched high-brimmed straw cowboy hats in various stages of shredding, and most stood in plastic sandals. All wore faded cotton shirts over beltless trousers of green, blue, or black, worn in spots to shiny brown. He stopped before one middle-aged man, who stood swaying in a Grateful Dead T-shirt, apparently drunk.

"You, what's your name?"

"Arturo." The village mechanic was surly, the stupid belligerence of illness in his stance, his eyes red and mean, his belly straining over his belt like dough overflowing a bowl. His rotting gut was the one thing he could not fix with his bits of metal and wire, and he radiated resentment like a broken motor. Gomez stared at him until he looked away.

"You?"

"Genero, sir." The old carpenter bowed twice from the waist and smiled broadly, showing off his three teeth. Gomez smiled faintly and nodded. He glanced at the next, a thin old relic who swallowed thickly as his gaze slid away.

"Joselino, excellency." Gomez heard no hint of sarcasm in the high-pitched voice, only the fear of a creature elusive by nature.

Gomez walked on down the line. For the first time, he considered a new option. What if he took all seven of them in for interrogation — and the mayor too, and Kanak as well, of course, if he was stupid enough to turn up — just to see how it would work? It would call the bluff of those posturing colonels. He could announce a formal inquiry, make the episode a test case for the — what was it? — the dawning era of investigation and judicial procedure; that was the phrase, the standard speech of the new president, General Morales. Gomez had been surprised to hear such rhetoric from Morales. He was a military hero, a helicopter pilot known for leading strafing runs on enemy positions, no pansy. He had helped in the cleanup sweeps through here two, three years ago; he ought to know you couldn't put Indians in a courtroom. They didn't know what a courtroom was. Bringing in half this village would show the colonels in their thin city boots that the real world was different: Indians wouldn't know how to testify, or they'd start one of their chants, create a street disturbance, and the ruckus would bring the newspaper people and maybe even the TV cameras. That would fix the colonels.

Gomez smiled to himself. Yes, my colonel. No, my colonel. Of course, sir, how difficult, so sorry. But then he reconsidered. Even if the thing didn't get completely out of hand, making the point would be risky; he would be blamed for anything that went wrong. And if nothing went wrong and they all disappeared forever under the garrison, Lorenzo would be furious at the paperwork and the tedious hassle of dealing with so many people, after he had told Gomez to take care of the business himself. The general's written order for arrests and trials was beside the point: Lorenzo trusted him on this.

He stopped in front of the tallest, strongest man in line. "Your name?"

The youth straightened up just slightly from his slouch. "Gregorio de Córdoba." That was foolish; there had been no need to give his full name, and he was looking the lieutenant in the eye, an additional provocation.

"Why aren't you in the army?"

"I was exempted."

"Exempted! Why? By whom?"

"Your Captain Lorenzo. Family problems."

Gomez stared at him. That de Córdoba family again. Gregorio's father, Andreas, had been a notorious radical around here, organizing farmers and agitating, and his sister Cecilia the same, but the old man had been wrung out and crippled and crushed, and the girl was still in prison, as far as anyone knew. Gomez thought it a strange oversight that Gregorio had not been arrested as well. He made a mental note to ask Benedicto about this one, grunted, and moved on. He passed the thin, gnarled form of Honorio Luxit, who said he was a baker and looked it, with his powerful hands, and Diego Saraf, white and also stooped, the oldest man in the village. Gomez barely looked at either of them.

Gomez gave a brief glance and almost smiled at the last in line, Daniel Malik, the baker's grandson; he was only fourteen and looked about nine, not much taller than the kid with the withered arm. That reminded him. Gomez looked around, and sure enough, the boy had come back. Gomez raised his eyebrows in a question and the kid shook his head, raising his narrow shoulders in a parody of a shrug. The lieutenant grimaced, not sure himself if it was a laugh or a scowl.

"Why did none of you sound the alarm when this Kanak arrived last night?" Gomez asked gently, his tone almost conversational. He saw no flicker of response. "Didn't you hear anything? Were you all asleep?" All seven stood mute, Genero and Arturo with jaws ajar. The two oldest men were barefoot, their toes as horned and curled as dusty lizards in the dirt.

Gomez decided the villagers had not yet realized how serious their situation was. He thought of the soldiers blown to bits last night, the rounded arm on the private he had pulled from the barracks, the others' brains and entrails bubbling in the fire, the screams of the wounded men, medics pumping painkiller into them, tying off their bloody stumps of hands. If Kanak had escaped him, every soul in Akabal was responsible and the village would pay, pay for last night and for Julio,

for fifteen years of all that, the dead generation, the gutted
land, the ruined country, the national shame, and the world a
mess; they would all pay the highest price he could exact from
them, and that a puny nothing, their useless lives, but perhaps even Indians might benefit from a chance to regret their
choices. Perhaps one or two would be allowed to live in order
to spread a warning to the rest of the province. He raised his
voice.

"We trailed a murderer here last night, a killer of women
and babies, a stinking worm without a heart, without a soul,
without the tiniest piece of humanity." Gomez paused to let
the translation catch up, a whisper of clicks and sibilants and
ringings like water over faraway stones. "We are the defenders
of your homes, and of your families, against the subversion
that would make slaves of us all. We have come to you expecting justice for these crimes, knowing that patriots would
never, never allow such a criminal to enter here unchallenged.
But what have we found? Incompetence!" He spat the word.
"Collaboration! Conspiracy!" The murmur rose before him in
clicking gusts.

Gomez shifted to a near-whisper. "Can it be possible, is it
believable, that this entire village, all of you people, sons of
Tecun Uman, daughters of the quetzal, all of you, everyone
here before me, all of you are — traitors?" He paused again
and his voice rose. "Betrayers of the nation? Subversive criminals?" He clasped his hands behind his back and leaned forward slightly. "Well?" he bellowed. "What can you tell me?"

The murmur subsided slowly. Miguel, watching from the
church door, held his breath. Cristóbal opened his mouth just
as Gregorio looked up from his slouch and raised his hand.

"With your permission, sir — we know nothing about this.
It was a quiet night. The dogs never barked, no one came."
Cristóbal translated hastily for Gomez. The lieutenant stared
at Gregorio as if he were a statue come to life. The mayor

babbled on as Gregorio continued, his hands shaking only a little. "We are patriots here, sir, not traitors. Please, could you tell us what happened? We only want to be of service."

It was an amazing speech. Gomez was clearly impressed. Heads nodded across the square and Gomez looked thoughtful. He had not expected a challenge and his knee throbbed. He wanted to sit down. "Sergeant," he said, and Joyabal stepped forward. "Sergeant, the patriots of Akabal want to know what happened. I think they deserve this honor. Go ahead, tell them."

Five

MARTÍN JOYABAL, thin and shorter than Gomez, could see only the first few rows of villagers, so he craned his neck and scowled over his nose like a vulture scanning the capital garbage dump. Every eye was on him, but all were dark, opaque as marbles in a wall of blank faces, the hair matted, dusty as the feet, leathery hands loose and hanging. Passivity itself stood before him. In the first morning breeze, the women's striped skirts stirred a little, and the children stood behind them gaping, one bare foot upon the other, brown toes tiny as flowers. The sergeant blew his nose through his fingers and tried to cover his surprise at being asked to speak.

"All of you are familiar with the military post in Santa Rosa," he began. "Some of you have served your country there; the rest have sons or brothers or husbands, loved ones in the armed forces here or somewhere else." He rose up and down on his toes as though daring them to snicker at such banality. He cleared his throat, the effort of deciding what to say visible in every muscle. Clearly Gomez did not expect him to reveal what had actually happened. Not even the soldiers behind Joyabal had been told the full extent of the damage, detailed to the lieutenant and the sergeant on the two-way radio: that one man had half blown away their invulnerable barracks, killing three sleeping soldiers and injuring ten. It was humiliating news, a report the high command would immediately stamp secret so as not to encourage the guerrillas, so as not to give the American military attaché another chance to sigh and talk about improving intelligence capacity. Of course the guerrillas would claim ten times that many dead, but the only proper response to such lies was silence.

"For many years we have fought the subversive communists together. You know their tactics. They lived among you, but they were the first to be tricked by the lying propaganda of the Russians and the Cubans, the international conspiracy. They were the ones who listened to the communist priests and their so-called liberation theology, or rather they listened to communists who slander the sacred church by calling themselves priests. Yes, these lying scum promised everything — a magic end to hunger, an end to poverty. They said all you had to do was believe in the foreign invasion and betray your government, betray your fatherland, and your misery would disappear. Well, the communists lied! Those who listened were tricked! They were duped!" He spiked the air in punctuation. "The outside influences lied to them, and they lied to you! They came here and tried to make fools of us all!"

This was safe boilerplate from speeches everyone present had heard a dozen times, speeches Gomez and Lorenzo and even Joyabal had made all over the district. But the phrases warmed the sergeant's heart, like familiar food in a foreign country. His dark eyes shone as he searched the faces for signs of sympathy and support.

Cristóbal tried to look receptive. In his lack of cynicism, the sergeant was almost interesting, and the mayor wondered whether the soldier knew that Marxism was more than a swear

word, whether he had any notion of the true danger of communism — that it awoke a surge of futile hope for a better
life. Did the sergeant hope for anything beyond a good fuck
and the lieutenant's smile? The mayor thought not.

Imitating Gomez, the sergeant lowered his voice. "They
promised you land, didn't they? They promised protection
from criminals, and schools and water and clinics, and toma-
toes the size of footballs, and rain every Tuesday!" He paused
again, hoping for smiles or nods. He was disappointed. "And
some of you believed them. Some of you thought they would
give you land. Some of you went with them, and helped them,
and you know very well who I mean." The sweep of his arm
included them all. "But the truth is that you were betrayed,
weren't you? They lied to you, didn't they? The subversives
have no land to give. They have no schools for you. They have
no water, no doctors, no nothing, nothing but the slavery of
communism! They promise you freedom, but they offer only
slavery!"

The sergeant glared at the crowd. No one appeared to have
changed expression in the slightest. A few heads tilted the
other way. Arturo in his Grateful Dead T-shirt swayed alarm-
ingly, and Gregorio still held his straw hat motionless. Even
the children's mouths remained agape.

"The subversion has failed!" Joyabal fairly shrieked, raising
his arms in triumph. "The brave resistance of the armed
forces has revealed this trickery for what it is! The subversives
are responsible for all your suffering, lying to you with false
promises, dragging your sons into combat with the army of
your fatherland!" He stopped, his arms in the air, and waited
for the applause he had often heard at this point, the cheers
he had occasionally supplied himself. But in this place it
appeared he might as well have spoken in Chinese. The villagers stood mute and motionless as corncobs in the breezy
plaza.

After a moment the sergeant's face turned red and he dropped his arms abruptly. He leaned forward and hissed. "Now here we have subversion at its worst! To cover up this failure, to divert attention from their lies, the subversives have turned to obscenity, to horrible violence." He held up a finger. "Not ordinary violence, not honorable combat between men on the field of battle. Oh, no. The subversives are not honorable!" He paused, breathing heavily. "You know this. Think about it!" He was reaching them now. "They have forced you off the buses and burned them so you have to walk. They have burned the trucks that carry your crops. They have cut down your power lines, bombed the bridges! They shoot the leaders of the civil patrol, your friends and neighbors!" This was all true, the villagers knew it was true. "The subversives take your money, your papers. They are nothing more than bandits, delinquents, common criminals!"

He leaned back and looked down his nose, preparing himself. "No, they are not patriots, not real men, but cowards, robbers, miserable pansies who attack only when the defenders of the nation are resting from their labors! Do such worms deserve to be called men? Of course not!" Inspiration took him. "Now listen well, all of you. Last night, not only did the subversive delinquents attack sleeping soldiers at your barracks in Santa Rosa, not only did they set off a cowardly explosion that harmed your patriotic sons and brothers! No, not just that! Last night the ringleader among them, a truly evil coward, this Kanak, last night he took a hostage in Santa Rosa, a young innocent girl, a beautiful young mother. This cowardly subversive violated her, assaulted her repeatedly, without shame, without honor, without any human feeling, and he forced her little son to watch while he did it. Yes!"

Miguel, still in the shadow of the church doorway, felt his gut heave. A rush of fury joined the fear that was choking him. He stifled a shout, "Lies! Lies!" as it rose in his throat, and his fingers turned white around the doorjamb. Gregorio looked, frowning, at his rubber sandals, turning his hat in his hands. Gomez, watching his protégé, smiled faintly.

"Then"—Joyabal dropped his voice to a whisper—"the communist traitor used his knife on the little boy, the poor defenseless angel of god . . ." The sergeant moved his hands in front of his groin, shook his head, and looked aside, as if unable to continue. "And then he stabbed them both. Again and again he stabbed them, an innocent mother and her innocent child. He left them dead . . . and he fled from Santa Rosa."

Miguel bit down hard on his knuckle as the murmur of translation rose and fell. Cristóbal frowned. This had clearly happened, sometime, somewhere, and Joyabal had obviously seen it, touched the blood, felt his heart pound in horrified excitement that he now made plain to them.

Joyabal's voice shifted higher. "He fled from the scene of this terrible crime, from these dead patriots and innocents, and he came here, to Akabal!" He waited until the murmur of translation died away. "And here we have tracked him. There is no doubt. This killer is among you right now. He is a common criminal! Not only a terrorist, a traitor, but a murderer!" The sergeant stood panting, exultant, arms and legs spread wide in triumph. "And so you see why we are here in Akabal. We have come as the servants of the people, your faithful army, to bring justice, to deal justly with that killer Kanak, and with those who have helped him, with all those who are responsible for these unforgivable things. We are here to defend the national dignity! We will save Akabal and save the country from subversion! We will guard the nation's honor! We are here"— he paused—"to guarantee the freedom of the people!"

Martín Joyabal was sweating. He clenched and unclenched his fists and glared at the villagers. He focused on the mayor, who almost nodded.

Cristóbal tried to communicate understanding back to the

indignant face. Joyabal had earned that much. He was not corrupt like some, not jaded like Cristóbal himself or exhausted like Gomez. No, he was telling his own truth, a political truth in that hundreds, thousands of women and children had died like that, and if this particular person Kanak had not killed anyone last night, he might have done it earlier, or someone like him had, or would in the future, or by his mere existence he might have caused someone else to do it, perhaps even a soldier — who had acted of course only to save the country from the poison of subversion. And so all the death on all sides was all Kanak's fault, and it would happen again and again until they were all stopped. In this way Joyabal had taken upon himself the responsibility of bringing all the criminals to justice; to himself he was a hero and his face shone with righteous fury.

Cristóbal felt sorry for the boy, a naïve passionate tool that jaded men wield to change the earth. Then he felt sorry for himself, to scorn passion. Old, he was getting old . . . but he indulged that self-pity only briefly, for Joyabal had revealed much the mayor could use. The speech was almost encouraging. Ah, he was lucky to be able, even for a moment, to listen with a truly open mind, as though he might really hear something convincing, for only then could he heft the honest weight in facts of any argument. And the sergeant was right in part: many bloody things had happened as he described. But they had not happened by Miguel's hand. The boy was simple, shy, quiet — he would be capable as any of throwing bombs, shooting rifles, of dealing death at a distance. That was easy for most here, like shooting a rat, but hands-on murder required something else. To touch the victim risked giving it life, humanity, presence before the slaughter; to kill then, especially to kill slowly, was a pure ecstasy of power, and power was not a common feeling here.

No, Miguel was too simple to see beyond ordinary horror.

He would not sense, much less seek, the consuming pleasure of godlike capacity that such a murderer would feel. The sergeant in his sincere effort to reach the villagers had picked the wrong target, the wrong crime, and had savored the description a little too much. Perhaps he had seen such a murder, perhaps he had committed it himself, perhaps a friend had. If he had blamed it on Cristóbal it would have been believable; the mayor knew himself capable of such a thing, somewhere far away inside, and was grateful never to have seen a victim's eyes.

And so Cristóbal knew what Joyabal could not know, that the soldiers had nothing real against Miguel. Irrelevant as that might be, it meant they had probably chosen Miguel's name at random, perhaps even come to Akabal by whim or accident, and by whim or accident might be turned away.

Gomez nodded approval at his subaltern, at the passion the lieutenant would never have been able to simulate. He surveyed the crowd again, his broad face openly looking for signs of support and cooperation, or at least acceptance. Again he was disappointed. He saw only anxiety, bottomless pits of faces into which all the wisdom of the planet could vanish without trace.

Gomez drew a deep shuddering breath and shook his head. Was he going to have to go through with it once again? His orders were like mist, hiding and permitting everything at once: Get the bastard, whatever you have to do! It was clear Kanak was not going to materialize on his own. Three years ago Gomez would already have wiped the earth clean of these ciphers and been on his way back to Santa Rosa, thinking about dinner. But the new governments, the new orders, the new rhetoric . . . he flushed in sudden anger. What right did the politicians have to change the rules in the middle of the game? For centuries justice had been swift and sure; the peasants knew not to cross the army, and in return they were protected. Agitators were easily spotted and shot, and the lesson kept things peaceful. The generals were wrong to blame the current flood of subversion on the 1981 sweeps, to listen to the international crybaby groups that wailed human rights, human rights whenever a cow died. War wasn't pretty, war was not a bunch of speeches or a classroom lecture, and this was war, that's what it was, and he cursed the generals for mincing around the word. The sweeps had been bloody, but they had been successful, as such things had always been: a pile of dead communists made a sobering impression on the peasants, the only kind of warning they understood.

The problem was that the sweeps had stopped when they should have gotten tougher, just when the subversives were on the ropes. Stop and go, stop and go — the army had been called off at the worst possible moment. The generals had no convictions; they were hopeless, forever conniving against each other in their cliques instead of paying attention to the field, backstabbing and countermanding orders issued the week before. It was impossible to keep track of who was in and who was out, and little people like Gomez were trapped in the middle.

Why couldn't life be more like soccer, he wondered recklessly, where rules formed a permanent, structured universe that rewarded those smart enough to explore every limit, while those who could not or would not crack the code were punished? Options should be those of strategy within the laws of the game, not choices about the game itself. One didn't simply decide to pick up the ball and run and get away with it; the generals couldn't say a general cleanup was all right one day and forbidden the next.

Of course there were moments in every game when you could run with the ball. He had always been good at soccer despite his bulk and his clumsiness, filling it with practice and his thorough understanding, and in the same way he had

been a model army recruit, spotted early as a natural en-
forcer. He took quickly to counterinsurgency training, ab-
sorbing the lessons in hunting and tracking, guerrilla warfare
and field survival; they were a kind of deadly gloss on soccer, a
version where the army wrote the rules and the winners imposed their own penalties.

Here in Akabal there were options, there had to be, for
someone as thorough as Gomez. He decided he was in no
hurry. He would study the situation a bit more.

"Well, that is how it is," he said into the silence. "We are here
to bring justice. Now you must do your part. Now it is up to
you." He paused.

The air seemed to stop moving. Cristóbal was barely
breathing, and Gregorio's jaw muscles worked. The women's
skirts rustled in the silence.

"We call upon you to do justice in this case. We have been
worried about Akabal. I am not certain, I am not confident,
that Akabal is truly a town of patriots. It is possible that all of
you here, all of you," Gomez said, separating each word, "all
of you are subversive traitors." A murmur of translation followed, then of protest. Heads shook.

"No, sir. It is not true." Cristóbal was astonished to hear his
own voice.

Gomez shot him a glance. "Well, then, you must prove it.
You must demonstrate that you are not traitors, all of you." He
raised his index finger. "We know that at least one of you here,
this Miguel Angel Kanak, is a murderer, a subversive, a communist, a terrorist murderer of innocent women and children.
Look among you! Where is this worm?" He watched. Not an
eye flickered. Dust blew toward the cemetery, and white puff-
balls scudded across the deep blue sky.

"Where is he? Some of you know, perhaps all of you. Where
is he?"

Silence. In the church Miguel held his breath.

"Perhaps you all helped him, eh?" More murmurs of denial. "He came here. He is here now. This murderer is here in Akabal." Gomez let his eyes sweep the plaza and continued in a low voice.

"I advise all of you, as a friend. Do not make any mistakes here. Think carefully. We know how to deal with terrorists. We know what to do with anyone who collaborates with terrorists, with villages that collaborate." He stopped to let them remember the stories, some of them true, some vivid rumors concocted as labor-saving devices late at night over many drinks and much bitter laughter: of Amachel, where children were hurled head first against the river rocks — Joselino had reported the bits of scab and hair; of Macalbaj, where fifty-four men were beheaded; of the sixty shot in Cochob, the one hundred in Mangal, the two hundred whose throats were slit in Zacuallpa, the hundreds killed in Lempa, the five hundred vanished from Pajarito, the thousands in refugee camps across the borders, the thousands upon thousands more in this province alone who lived in terror in the mountains, their squalid villages ransacked, burned, and abandoned. The names, the faces, the blood fused together in a towering mindwall of horror through which no reasoned thought could pass, and that was the idea. Touch those thoughts on their edges, jagged and bloody like a shattered window, and turn away quickly to anything, anything else.

"We expect you will deal with this terrorist in the correct manner. We will leave it to you." Gomez stopped again and looked at each of them, one by one. When his eyes reached Cristóbal's, he held the gaze only a moment, no longer than the others; he refused connection and moved on, and the mayor's heart sank.

"The people of Akabal must administer justice here. You know what I mean. You know who the guilty one is. You know what justice must be done. You must act yourselves, to defend your families from communist subversion, to defend your nation. It is the responsibility of every one of you." He paused and raised his voice. "If you do not act, well, then . . ." The silence hung like fog in the sunny plaza.

"You have until dawn tomorrow. We will watch. Do not try to leave, do not think we will hesitate a moment. We give you until dawn. We will see then whether Akabal is a town of patriots . . . or a town of traitors."

The lieutenant seemed to have grown an inch. He stood silent, unmoving a few moments, then turned to look hard at the mayor. Don Cristóbal Clemente swallowed and managed a croak. "Yes, sir. We understand. Dawn tomorrow. Thank you, sir."

Gomez turned to his soldiers. "Let's go," he said.

PART II

Six

OBSCENITIES rushed against the mayor's teeth as the villagers stood breathing the dust of the soldiers' boots. Cristóbal could dismiss a flood of oaths in others as pathetic, the screech of impotence against outrage, and he pitied the weakness and self-disgust of people who could only swear. But Gomez's mocking laugh had shattered the delusion that he had kept these people safe, and bitterness flooded his gut. The vilest words he knew surged up like vomit, enraging him the more for their futility. So silently, under his breath, he called down on those slouch hats the hopeless venom of a jilted lover. He wished them the humiliation of every agony, every violent dismemberment and bloody slaughter ever known; he swore until he was savoring his wrath, building murderous energy to face its source. Gregorio took his arm, and he realized he was shaking.

"Don Cristóbal. Listen. We need you now." The mayor unclenched his fists; his fingernails had dug half moons in his palms. He rubbed the stiffened fingers on his pants and tried to smile at this beefy youth, at the circle of anxious faces behind him. They were right. There was work to be done. But what could he do?

Like the sergeant, he breathed deeply and stuck out his chin. "All right! You have heard the lieutenant! We must act now and decide. We must decide what to do." The faces relaxed and nodded, turning away to reassure others that the mayor had not gone mad just yet. He looked beyond them. A few villagers stood talking behind their hands, staring down the road after the soldiers, and others moved out of the plaza in twos and threes, shaking their heads. A cluster of people had formed around Father Edmundo back near the church, tugging at his sleeves, and the group with the mayor began to talk.

"What do they mean about Miguel, Don Cristóbal?"

"They're lying, aren't they? Where is Miguel?"

"What happened? Someone has denounced him!"

"No one has done anything here, have they? Miguel is no subversive!" The voices grew louder.

"Who is this woman he talked about? Is she from here?"

"Will they come back? What did he mean, sunrise tomorrow?"

The questions rose and fell over the plaza like raucous birds. He put out his hands to calm them. "Now be quiet. We have to think carefully about this. We have to be very careful . . ." But he was drowned out.

"What the hell are we supposed to do?" Arturo the mechanic boomed over the clamor, waving his heavy fist. His words were slurred. "Who's the woman who died? She a relative of his?"

"The patrol should say if they were awake . . ."

"We better do what they say . . ."

"No! Those days are over! They're just bluffing . . ."

The voices clattered on. No one waited for answers, expecting none: the chance to express a fear before it was upon them was luxury enough. Gregorio stood silent in the tumult and looked at Don Cristóbal, waiting for him to say something.

But the mayor had nothing yet to say even to himself. He busied his hands in calming movements, patting arms and urging quiet on everyone, and Gregorio shook his head and backed out of the crowd.

Cristóbal was just as glad to see him go. Gregorio's trust stung like a needle through the clouds of air the old politician routinely manufactured for the others, and what the mayor needed at that moment was not more reality but less, in order to think.

He was certain of this much: Lieutenant Gomez was not bluffing. For most of his fifty-eight years Cristóbal had watched the armed forces play stern parent to the country's infantile politicians, and they took that job seriously. Gomez had not come to Akabal to make an idle threat, especially to a mayor. He had followed orders, whatever they were. The astonishing difference, the fact Cristóbal had still not managed to absorb, was that these orders had brought the district's Special Forces chief and so many soldiers to Akabal for something other than instant, mindless slaughter.

Akabal and countless villages like it had forever been irrelevant, daubs of life scattered through the wastes, invisible as ghosts to the politicians and the commanders in the capital. Rural lives were nuisances to them, buzzing flies to be swatted away or ignored to live or die as nature willed. And like flies that die in their millions and endure forever, marginality had preserved these ancient people more than it had hurt them.

That was why Cristóbal had come here in the first place, after all, fleeing too much involvement, looking for a place to rest, an eddy in what seemed to him then a torrent of political energy roaring through the country. In those days, when he was in his twenties and caught up in it all, that river was vast to him, flooding all his understanding. But obviously it was much smaller then than it was now, when history came lapping even at the walls of Akabal. The mayor still could scarcely believe it. He thought how it would amaze the old Spanish priests to hear that such places as this were even named, those priests who kept the first records, listing the few places and people who mattered here for three, nearly four centuries after the conquest: the viceroys, the generals, the army hangers-on. Those people had come to plunder but had stayed to run the mines, the plantations, the railroads, to put down the occasional Indian rebellion. Even by the time he was a boy growing up in the capital, working in his father's print shop, the people who mattered were still the ministers and generals who sent in announcements to be engraved on fine vellum, who ordered election posters in screaming six-inch block letters he helped to set by hand.

Oh, they were a tight little group, interlocked families known by their names on the banks and the stores and the warehouses, and government was a grave formal waltz among them all. Their intrigues had all the creative predictability of the Indian festival dance that re-enacts the Spanish conquest, an art form of self-destruction. Their houses, when he went to deliver the parcels, were dark halls behind the servants who answered the doors, hung with portraits of grandfathers, men on horses, the armies of independence. Those men had been full of self-congratulation and generous speeches, had had idealized notions of civilian rule, absorbed from France and the Yankee colonies already roaring along to the north. They didn't notice their civilians weren't a yeasty gringo mix of misplaced Puritans and outcasts and gentleman farmers, but were like themselves, homesick Spanish nobles who tried to re-create their lost lives here, enclaves of starched gentility in a sea of Indian dust. They had owned the land, they thought, first by grant of popes and kings, and then because they had bled for it, and their eviction of Indians here for millennia was as weary and unthinking as a farmer's removal of a tree stump.

No, there was never any open land in this country, nowhere for the displaced natives to go, and when the immigrants continued to come, there was no land to spare to absorb their energies either, none to make new people try new ways, no work except the old work in the landowners' farms or factories or armies. For malcontents there was no room at all, no place to thrash out new systems or for any outlandish notions to sprout uncrushed by imported tradition, religion, values. So the Indians were crowded out. They withdrew to the mountains and finally, when they were followed there, they withdrew into themselves, hoarding only the memories of the old ways, learning the guise of dull incomprehension that made the aliens throw up their hands and stomp away, exasperated.

But the newcomers would come back, and back and back again, beating their single god into the Indian animism, dressing the spirits in saints' clothing, forcing Spanish names and rites on towns and people who died like flies, defenseless and impervious, silent, invisible at last.

And in the cities, where the markets boomed with forced labor, when the civilians became too incompetent or venal for the Yankees or the international banks to bail out any longer, the army that still saw itself as moral would step in to salvage the national honor. Every few years the troops would march on the capital and purge the presidential palace of that year's rubbish, as the conquerors had swept down from the mountains on their magic horses. Half the country's politicians would flee the country crying massacre, and the other half would emerge from hiding singing hosanna. The Yankees, who loomed forever over the land, would waffle for a week or two, wringing their hands and urging democratic reform, and when the sandbags were finally stored away, they would resume military aid.

Things would be calm a while as the uniforms swept off the cobwebs, orating about order and discipline and counting what was left in the treasury. With no battles to fight, the colonels would relax a bit and court the landowners' daughters and move into the big houses, accumulating medals, letting out the seams as their bellies swelled with peace and afternoon siestas. In time, often a very little while, they would grow mellow and lax with success. They would at first be deaf when the national grumbling started up again, the waltz resuming, the businessmen complaining about the rising cost of labor. The commanders would fume at dimwits in neckties who questioned their orders, exclaim about fumbling bureaucrats who couldn't get anything done without another meeting, about thieving businessmen who grudged them their bribes. Used to command, the soldiers would tire of argument, and bodies would appear in the streets, bodies of rabble-rousers, labor organizers, loudmouth writers. The young politicians would start pushing for their turn, and soon the satisfaction and the cheering that were the true fruit of victory were only memories, replaced by sour calculations, negotiations, the daily losses of governing.

Finally, in the old days, the soldiers would yield grandly and with thin regret. They would announce elections, handpicking the official candidate, putting down the protest riots, making the ballots come out right. Then in clouds of bunting they would hand over the presidency to a civilian once again and march back to the barracks, washing their hands of the stink and mess of politics.

It had become a routine as predictable as a gavotte. Storing the sashes and plaques and photographs and memories of their days as cabinet ministers and presidents and diplomats, the military men would sit in their officers' clubs and judge the politicians like so many horses at a third-rate track. They expected every crop to be the same and were rarely disappointed: charlatans who bloomed and then decayed in the shower of cash from landowning families and the United Fruit

Company, who lost their bearings in the gaudy bedrooms of the businessmen's wives. Soon, the soldiers knew, the sleek politicians would become arrogant, thinking their power was their own, and they would start to haggle with the soldiers about their portion of the take. Worse, a young legislator or a union leader or some other demagogue would emerge and begin spouting socialism, power to the people. The riots would start, disorder would hurt the nation's image, the national dignity would once again be threatened.

Yes, it was inevitable in those days that judgment would come, that there would be another bloody coup. That was the way life was. So the military men, cool in their barracks, studied management and government and history and economic theory along with Clausewitz, waiting for the day that always came again. The army was used to wielding the power of life and death; killing, after all, is the military problem-solving method.

So Cristóbal wasted no energy doubting Gomez's sincerity. But still he could not make sense of what the soldiers wanted. To search every house, drag everyone into the square, torture a child until someone pointed out Miguel, that would have been understandable, standard procedure in the old days. This speechmaking, this appeal to some warped sense of justice, this leaving it to them — it was almost worse, a way of enfolding the villagers in the horror of whatever the soldiers were going to do. It was a ludicrous bridging of the chasm between the rulers and the ruled, a monstrous perversion of the democratic notion that they were all fundamentally the same.

Cristóbal cursed again. He had deluded himself into thinking he could keep Akabal forever on the sidelines, sitting out the dance. He was too much the Ladino, too used to being forever in the middle. He mourned the hybrids, his people, bastards in the early days, spawn of Indians most inundated by the Spanish flood, halfbreeds created first by rape and later by indifference. They belonged to neither of the two histories and grew up loyal to nothing, adapting, like all hybrids, to their found conditions, becoming the army, the shopkeepers, the urban workers, his people, Edmundo's: unpoor, unrich, unsentimental. Where the land was fruitful, they were overseers, farm managers, wooing landowners' daughters in secret and buying parcels where they could. In the cities, they filled niches that both Indians and Spaniards shunned, hauling trash, cutting hair, building walls, printing leaflets. His grandparents borrowed a future where they could and stole it where they had to, in the capital that spread over the valley like mold over bread.

He grew up in one of thousands of identical shacks within sight of the cathedral spires, on a street three meters wide that was more a run for rats and sewage than for people. As children, he and his brothers and sisters were steeped in talk about business, endless complaint about prices, haughty customers, bureaucrats, hatred for the secret police and their protection racket, which took a thick wad of the father's cash every month, contempt for the interchangeable generals and presidents who waved at them from the lacy palace balcony. Oh, the Ladinos lived in political chatter, unimpressed by tradition and unfettered by the niceties of antique Spanish law: he threw rotten oranges at fat businessmen and soldiers and Indian market women alike. But he went to school, by day with the Jesuits and by night at home, where his parents read him the tracts they printed in lieu of books they were too poor to buy.

In those days, almost forty years ago now, a revolt surged around his people's dinner tables, in the candlelit shacks of Ladinos tired of living like mussels on the wastes of the ruling families. Arrogant to the point of blindness, the dissolute governors disdained to see that his father was fed up with

paying bribes, that factory workers had listened to labor organizers bringing dreams from Detroit, that university and high
school students were choking on the jingoistic newspaper
tales of the far-off Second World War, that young army officers and bureaucrats were nauseated by the corruption above
them.

The Ladino rising came just after the Normandy invasion,
when the Yankees were so preoccupied with Europe they
barely noticed. The new majority swept away the old system
overnight, generals and ruling families alike, unhindered and
astonished at what they had done. And Cristóbal Clemente
was part of it, although now it made him sigh in exhaustion
even to think about it. He was nineteen, excited by the illegal
handbills and posters he helped print by night, ravished by
the rhetoric of liberation and freedom, drunk on sleepless
dreams of change and justice. He learned the intoxication of
feeling part of the engine of history, to know in his gut he was
right about everything, had been right forever, and would
now be recognized for it by all the world. He was dazzled by
how easy it had been, to join the crowd shouting for freedom, to overrun the palace with the help of rebel troops. He
climbed the statue of the Liberator in the plaza with dozens of
others, and he himself draped the rebel flag on its cold shoulders: Bolívar had thought that to govern such a people was
impossible, but they would help him learn to plow the sea!

And later, though he had no office, no title, he made
speeches from the steps of churches and printed up posters
supporting the changes. He laughed with delight as the new
leaders received ambassadors with grand gestures and fed
them Indian corn tortillas. He rejoiced that the constitution
was repealed, the secret police dissolved, the generals all
ousted and replaced with young lieutenants. At last, in his
passion, his sweet naïveté, he ran for congress. Yes, this old
wreck actually had stood in a suit and tie on platforms once,

making outrageous speeches, and in a fluke of history he was actually elected.

It was a secret he had hidden from Akabal, that he had once been part of the national government. It was the best, perhaps the only decent government the country had ever had, he thought, but it was still a government and in that way it was a failure, as they all had been. He had another name then, as irrelevant to him now as that person had always been to others, and at the time he was blinded by the light in his own eyes, so he became a rock in the government section of the legislature. He helped write a new labor code that legalized trade unions; he pushed the newspaper reform law that made the papers worth reading, full of argument, problems, proposals, criticism, energy. That was probably a mistake, he decided later, one of hundreds, for every day brought another demonstration, more demands, bitter refusals, triumph, anger, joy, all of it furious. He lived on coffee and talk, too busy and often too tired even to make love; he forgot what it was to sleep more than four hours a night.

It was too much. The reformers were like teenagers partying until the parents come home. Soon the world war was over and the gringos looked around themselves, conquerors returning to their abandoned plows. And right here in their yard, they discovered in horror, their neglect had allowed a terrible bud to sprout, the scourge already spreading in Europe, the dangerous weed of communism. There were communists in this little country's government, they announced, as if just the pointing finger would cause the plant to wilt.

Well, communists there were, and Cristóbal supposed he was one, as the word had lost all meaning in being thrown at anyone interested in change. But he had joined no party, read no theory, and he worked with fascists and democrats and socialists and oligarchs, all labels that once perhaps meant something too. They were sons of the rich and daughters of generals and workers and peasants and teachers. Mostly they argued, over health care and wage scales, over history itself, over land reform and peasant rights, whatever that meant. In their reckless faith in words, they told United Fruit to give up some of its unused land, and that was their final error.

The coup that followed was different from the old kind. The same faces and the same families returned to the presidential balcony, but they had a new self-righteousness, a crusading aura to their purge. Torture and show trials, of course, but this time they seemed more like inquisitions than retribution. This was something new, a liberation from a communist dictatorship, to be the first of many, a practice run for Eastern Europe, and then — well, who could say? So the Yankees, calling the national tune as usual, restarted the waltz as though the decade of revolution had been only a brief intermission. But there was a new undertone to the music, something like a hymn.

When the coup came, announced by planes bombing the presidential palace, Cristóbal had been lucky, out of the capital making speeches. He was, in fact, in Santa Rosa, then as now a truculent place, slow to move in any direction, and he was there exhorting the school directors to order the new government's new textbooks. The day thundered with rain, and the principal and his toady board sat lumpish in their folding chairs along the peeling green stucco, examining their fingernails as he babbled on, boring even himself. When the young teacher came running in, they all looked at him in hope of entertainment. "A coup, another coup! They've bombed the presidential palace and the generals have won!" Water ran from the messenger's clothes in a puddle on the floor, which Cristóbal remembered was tiled a dark, cool green. They all turned to stare at Cristóbal, the young deputy, already a solitary remnant of an extinct species, and he overturned his chair as he stood up.

"Well, gentlemen, I thank you for your attention. I don't think you'll need those books now. Good day." And Cristóbal walked out into the storm, down the street before anyone could move to stop him, taking off his tie and his soaked suit jacket and throwing them in an alley puddle, walking fast, away from anyone he might know. He went into hiding that very afternoon, getting his hair cut and starting the mustache he wore ever after, buying a pair of glasses and renting a room over a little general store where he could watch the street. He stayed there nearly two weeks without going past the door, listening to the news, sick with horror and loss and finally with something like pneumonia that sent him into a delirium.

It was a kind of death he suffered, a loss of time to heat and unleashed fancy, where he ran through all the speeches he had given and embroidered them into the ears of the astonished storekeeper, who washed his face and held water to his lips. If not for that old man and his silence, Cristóbal often reflected, he might have died there in that little room, mourning the loss of a mere government!

But he didn't die, at least not physically. Perhaps he purged himself of illness and of words, with the words of all that had driven him before, for when he recovered, with the storekeeper's help and over many days, he was a broken man. He was not yet thirty, but he thought he was through with life. He could not face such failure as he had seen, as he had caused; in his youthful arrogance he magnified his responsibility for the many deaths that had followed the liberation, as the generals called it, and he wallowed in his suffering. Even now he could not think often about it, but now he was angrier at his former self than he was then: so many friends dead or in prison or in hiding because they were naïve about the way the world works. He was stupid to care so much, and he cut that tangled netting all away. He let his parents think he was dead, for he was. He evaded the few old friends from the ousted government who tried to find him, ignored reports of comrades in the hills, in other countries plotting the next coup. He wasn't important enough for the generals to seek him out. He was no longer naïve; he ceased to care in order to live.

Gradually, as he regained his health, he made himself useful to the storekeeper in return for cigarettes and meals and a little conversation. He took the name Clemente in homage to his survival; he swept and cleaned and helped out behind the counter, and after a few weeks, months perhaps, he met Elena.

She had come from Akabal to market, into the little store to buy simple things, a young widow of plain thoughts and no ambition, a generous body and a quiet heart. Eventually she took him to Akabal to meet her family, and he saw that the village was identical with her, fundamental and poor, without pretense. In those days it was a happy place — not the kind of happy where children romp in sunlit fields and couples stroll idly through the moonlight, for those are icons of a culture that aspires to leisure. No, Akabal was a place where all the parts had working functions and people fit eternal spaces, knowing forever what to do. It was so many light years from the capital that news of the revolution had scarcely arrived here before it was over. None of the changes had made it this far; no schools, no electricity or running water or any sign that life was more than a featureless tunnel carrying generation after generation from birth to death. In Akabal the seasons ruled, the sky rolled blue and white forever over mud and dust, the cemetery was close and the cornfields thin. Nobody asked Elena why someone like Cristóbal would want to marry her and move to this dogged mountaintop; to the Indians it had always been everything there was, and they understood instinctively that Akabal was the small cleared ground he needed on the edge between life and death. He opened his store there the next year.

For seven years he lived in simple happiness. If he always rushed through the details later in the telling, it was only because that too was over, washed away by the growing river that lets no man sleep in peace. He and Elena had two daughters, beautiful children of warm smooth skin and thick black hair, and he supposed he loved them as a father does. They were not yet in school when the flu epidemics of the 1960s seeped through the hills the way the fighting later would, and they died coughing and gasping in the arms of his dying Elena as he watched without so much as a headache.

After that he just existed, buying and selling and living out of habit and inertia. He learned indifference at a deeper level than he had thought he harbored, and he took comfort in the patronage of the people of Akabal. He was useful to them: they needed his store, his help in reading and writing their letters. He told them where to find things in Santa Rosa, how to get around the capital, where to go on a Sunday. He could talk to the military patrols that sometimes climbed the hill into Akabal, and he was big enough to stop the fights that sometimes erupted after a late fiesta. He was no danger to their wives or daughters, a widower in permanent detachment, and they told him their stories and brought him their hurts. He gathered the people around him, willing them to come, and because he had no ambition, they in their simplicity made him catechist and counselor and, eventually, as his hair turned white, mayor. He grew fat on their acceptance.

So it was that he watched the brutalizing of his country as though at a movie, embedded and protected in his castle on the rocks as the rebel officers were hunted down in the hills, seeing little mentions in the corners of the flimsy newspapers that this former comrade had turned bandit and been captured, that one had murdered a landowner, another had been hunted down and killed by the police. Yet still the peasants told him of gatherings in the mountains where groups of four and five talked politics, where priests blessed the stolen rifles. The ousted soldiers and the stifled revolution festered in this desiccated province with no help from him, its crushed ideas crawling through the valleys inch by inch for twenty years. He saw the army growing, reaching, stamping on the past to keep it out of the future, and he wanted nothing to do with the gaunt apostles of revolt: their calls for justice were delusions and they were fools endangering everyone they knew. He had warned Akabal to stay away, led the village into the middle ground, hidden it in the lapses of attention that cracked the rebel front, the army buildup, the walls of violence rising on all sides. It was treacherous ground, but he was nimble and, he told himself, a clever old goat. Well, he had stumbled this time, tripped by his own pride.

"They have no right! No right to give such an order!" It was Gregorio's father, the old crippled firebrand Andreas de Córdoba who startled the mayor from his reverie, waving his crutch over the heads of the others in the plaza. "We are citizens! They have promised us justice! It is an outrage!"

"You are right, Andreas!" Cristóbal shouted back. "That is true — but irrelevant!" The crowd quieted and he felt control returning. "Remember the military mind! It gives and takes orders, that is all. What we must do is figure out a way to slide around the order."

He was rewarded with nods and a few smiles. They knew this strategy very well. It had allowed Akabal to sidestep demands from both the army and the rebels many times, filling out the forms with gibberish, forgetting guerrilla messages, losing parts. Under Cristóbal's tutelage they had all become good at misunderstanding translations and standing in open-mouthed inertia. In the old days, before the river rose, life here had been the same no matter who was running the government; civilian or soldier, they robbed and beat the Indians just as hard. Like their mother mountains the Indians had been stone to all the soaking changes, practicing so long their stolid pretense of indifference that many finally forgot its reasons. No, Cristóbal's strategy was a very old one, and it had worked a long time, right up until this very morning.

"We must not waste more time today," he called. "Let us talk together. Here, let's go . . ." With herding movements and many low assurances he edged the men who stood near him slowly back from the road to the side of the plaza across from the church, toward his little store. The plaza was gradually emptying, although a knot of people stood near the church and small groups were talking here and there. "We must decide what damage is absolutely unavoidable . . ."

Seven

GREGORIO'S first thought after leaving Cristóbal was to find Miguel. The mayor was too passive; he assumed the lieutenant knew what he was talking about, but Gregorio wasn't sure Miguel was even in the village. He hadn't turned up at the church to help Father Edmundo that morning, and the night before, Gregorio hadn't seen him anywhere. He had hoped as he made the patrol rounds to see Miguel's bony form propped against the mud brick wall of the Kanaks' little house. It would have been a nice excuse to stop a moment and talk, to greet Irene, who would surely have come to the door to see him, and to let the patrol go on a few yards ahead with their boring murmur of football teams and endless complaint. He might have been able to hold Irene's hand a moment, if her mother Flora wasn't watching, and maybe he could have told them both the bad news about Cecilia, gotten their help in telling his parents. But Miguel hadn't been home, and as the group trudged past the house, around the edge of the hilltop by the fallow hectare that served as a soccer field that year, Gregorio saw that the Kanaks' door was closed.

Miguel had not been at Caterina's later that night, either,

when Gregorio had knocked in passing, although he could hear a man laughing behind her thin wooden walls. Caterina had been flushed when she came to the door, amused at Gregorio's embarrassment, and he had left quickly. He didn't care who was with her, but Miguel would want to know, and Gregorio preferred not to be able to tell him, though he knew Miguel wouldn't do anything about it. Miguel's involvement with the town's *chiman*, his subjugation to her magic arts and electric yellow eyes — Gregorio shook his head. The affair was several years old already and had nothing to do with Miguel's commitment to marry Cecilia one day, but it made Gregorio uneasy. Miguel didn't talk much about Caterina — about anything, actually — but when he did speak of her, it was with a curious mix of jealousy and passive resignation, as though he had no control over what awful things might happen and no interest in trying to gain any. It was like watching a thunderstorm, Gregorio thought, or an earthquake. He still shivered at the thought of anyone being daring enough to touch Caterina. Miguel seemed to walk through that wall of fire as though it weren't there. It was, for Gregorio, just more evidence of Miguel's capacity to do something surprising, another sample of the constant discovery of unexpected corners in a person that keeps a friendship alive just as it nourishes love.

He knew he and Miguel were unlikely friends, but they had been inseparable since childhood, brothers from brotherless families of women and impenetrable men. Together they had defined the margins of their generation in Akabal, the restless edges of those born in the eye of a hurricane, trying to grow as their fathers had to ordinary manhood while surrounded by war.

Half their lives ago, when each was ten and the crushed rebellion was just starting to revive and fester in the hills, they had decided to marry each other's sisters. It would be a

further intertwining of their roots in what was old and real
and solid, another bulwark against the roiling days everyone
sensed were coming. They swore a blood oath at what they
fancied was their secret place in the stream below the town,
where sunlight dappled the rocks.

"I am pledged to Irene Kanak forever and ever," Gregorio
announced with a wave of his machete. He touched his thumb
to the blade and showed Miguel the welling red.

Miguel swallowed and teetered on the rock. "And I am
pledged to Cecilia de Córdoba, forever and ever." He was pale,
but on his second try he too drew blood. They raised their
arms high and pressed their thumbs together.

"We will be friends forever, no matter what our families say."

Miguel nodded. "Forever!"

The movie that inspired this event had faded to black at
that point amid soaring choirs of triumph, so the boys suffered an awkward moment. No choirs sang. Finally Gregorio
shouted, "Death to the invaders!" although it was not entirely
clear whom he meant, and leaped off the rock. Miguel burst
out laughing so hard he nearly fell, but together they charged
pell-mell up the bluff.

Gregorio had led Miguel through their youth, always the
first to kick the soccer ball, to learn the alphabet, to birth the
pigs. The smaller boy would gape at him, standing wide to
watch, and Gregorio would laugh and shake his head, returning to show Miguel briefly how to do whatever it was, seeming
to be patient. But Gregorio's attention flitted like the cobalt
butterflies, and soon Miguel would look up from the mystery
of dribbling, or the letter M, and hear Gregorio calling him to
some new excitement.

It was Gregorio who ordered that their mutual marriage
pact be kept a secret from the girls involved. That made it
more important, and besides, Irene was only six then, not
worth talking to, and Cecilia was two years older than they,

nearly twelve, and would laugh at them. She was always laughing. In fact, Gregorio's earliest memory was of shoving Cecilia off their father's lap to hear a story, and being shocked when she shoved him back and laughed at his astonishment. Andreas de Córdoba, of course, forever rational, made room for both of them, reading Bible verses. Later, he ignored his wife's objections that no mere girl needed to know how to read, and he set the youngsters against each other writing Bible summaries, poems, rhymes for saints' days and holidays, notes for birthdays. Cecilia wrote easily, but Gregorio never could describe the birds of the visions that roused such turmoil in his mind.

One day he drew a picture when he was touched past words, a lamb writhing on the end of a rope, its desperate plunges for freedom and prescient terror of the waiting oven much more wrenching on the cardboard than they were in the yard, where no one but Gregorio had noticed. His parents' exclamations at the power of the drawing equaled those for Cecilia's poetry, and they set the lamb free. They ate beans and rice for dinner that night — "Gregorio's lamb," Andreas called it, laughing — and it became a family joke. "We're having Gregorio's lamb again tonight." None of his drawings since had had as tangible an effect on his life, but Gregorio had found his tools, and the pleasure the act of creating pictures gave him was godlike, addictive, irresistible, constant. He hardly noticed there was no market for what he made.

"Miguel!" Gregorio called now, shouldering his rifle, heading for the church, looking here and there among the murmuring groups of people scattered around the plaza. The bare dirt was still cool under the whitening sun, but the sky was already an azure dome. It would be hot later, during the market, during the procession. How ridiculous a story from that slimy sergeant! Miguel a terrorist, of all people. Someone must have denounced him, someone with a personal grudge.

That was common enough: whisper communist, and the soldiers would come anywhere, like dogs called for feeding.

Six months it was since the soldiers had come for Cecilia, kicking in the de Córdobas' door one rainy night, shouting at them to get up, get up. Flashlights blinded them, rough hands hauled them to their feet. Two held guns on him and his mother and father while another two raised their gun butts and hit Cecilia, in the face, in the belly. She doubled over, crying out, and then they dragged her away, screaming, by her long black hair. Beautiful Cecilia, her fine nose spurting blood, her almond eyes contorted in pain, screaming for help.

The fog had swirled like demons' breath around the jeep as the men forced her in, shoving her down to the floor behind the front seat. Three of the soldiers climbed into the rear seat, kicking and grunting, and propped their feet on Cecilia's back. Gregorio could still hear the thudding of their rifle butts on her body as the jeep roared away. One soldier had looked back at them; he was just a boy, an Indian, and his eyes had been as wide and confused as Gregorio's own.

He thought about the soldiers this morning, picturing them gaping, drooling in a line behind the runt sergeant who brayed, bug-eyed, from the frame, all teeth and flapping tongue, his finger pointing like a girl's. Gomez hulked beside him like a bulldog in a hat, a faint smile denting his jowls, his sagging eyes sinister, his belly popping the shirt buttons.

The image crumbled and faded as Gregorio saw his mother in the group by the priest, near the church. He looked away. It was too early to face her with this week's news about Cecilia; too much had happened this morning already. He spotted a patch of deep red near the church door: it must be Caterina's blood-colored blouse, short-sleeved, heavy cotton, the only one in Akabal, so he pushed through the group surrounding her.

Caterina's back was to him, solid and heavy, her long black

braid swinging across it as her hands chopped the air. She was shouting at a slight, white-shirted figure no taller than she was, wearing a straw cowboy hat. It was Miguel.

"You idiot! You're a dead man unless you get out of here, don't you see? Oh! Why are you —"

"I don't know why they said me," Miguel replied, his big grin unsteady. He had both his delicate hands up, fending her off and reaching for her at the same time. "No, I can't leave, what are you talking about? You heard what he —"

"He lied! You ass! You think they would wait a second if they really —"

"I'm not going anywhere! I'm just trying to —"

"Gregorio!" Caterina, seeing him, grabbed his arm. "Listen to this maniac! Help me talk some sense into him. We have to get him out of here right now, don't you agree?" Her eyes flashed golden, the strange amber stigmata of those born to the witch's art, and they burned in worry. Only Caterina with her fortunetelling beans, her magic powers, her bastard children, only this electric woman cared as much as he did for this obstinate farmer, this slope-shouldered peasant in his tattered shirt. Gregorio supposed she loved Miguel, but she loved all the men in Akabal in the same way — amused by their hopeless wanting, their need for her generous affections.

Her touch burned his arm, and Gregorio covered Caterina's hand with his own to cool the heat and register silent agreement. She waved the other. "Miguel is a child. He refuses to understand! This is real trouble, not some — some story!"

Gregorio looked at his friend. The smile that had made Miguel's mother name him Miguel Angel, the smile that dazzled women and quieted enemies, that smile looked pasted on. Miguel glanced up at him, then at Caterina's anxious face, and back to Gregorio. He took a deep breath and shrugged.

"It's obvious I have enemies. I've been denounced, that's all, that's what this is all about, no? I swear to you it is all a lie, a fucking lie." He looked hard at the taller man. "I'm no subversive. You know that."

"Of course. It's crazy."

"Of course! You, a subversive! Hah!" Caterina's sharp laugh was harsh, like the omen bird that cries in the trees by the stream, fearing what it mocks. "Hah! My little Miguel, angel of the corn . . ."

She stepped away from Gregorio, and the others moved back a bit, away from her energy, giving her room. She put one hard, calloused hand on Miguel's cheek, but his eyes remained searching Gregorio's face. She raced on. "No one has been as careful as Miguel to stay out of politics, no one, isn't that true? This is all a terrible mistake, a lie . . ."

Gregorio was startled by Miguel's gaze. In it he saw fear and uncertainty; he had expected that, but there was also something cold, something measuring. He seemed to be waiting for a verdict. Gregorio opened his mouth to repeat his assurance, but others were crowding around now, calling Miguel's name, asking questions, offering support, jostling to touch his arm.

Little Diego with the withered arm pushed through the group and beamed up at Caterina. "I knew he was in the church, didn't I, Mama, but I didn't tell!" She put an arm around him.

Miguel smiled, the gentlest man alive, and ruffled the boy's dusty hair. "Many thanks, Diego. You did very well." He gazed at Caterina over her son's head. He hoped no one would notice that his knees trembled under his baggy trousers. How much fear could he show at such a moment? It felt volcanic, hot in the pit just above his collarbone, a bubbling terror that he had been discovered, named, condemned to die. Knowing what the army did to revolutionaries was enough to justify screaming hysteria, but that was for women and old people, not for warriors, and certainly not for an innocent man. He focused on Caterina. Her soft gaze at her son was a cooling stream of calm, like atol, milk of the corn, banking her fire. Loose strands of her black hair stood away from her head as though the wind blew through it, and when she looked back at Miguel her caring reached for him like sparks. He could drown in those burning eyes.

Suddenly Miguel wanted Caterina very much, wanted to burrow between her heavy breasts, hide his shaky center between the pillars of her legs, and disappear inside her just to rest a little while. He grabbed her hand and looked around in distraction. Where could they go? But his gaze fell instead on the birdlike figure of the priest, his blue jacket bright in the sunlight as he pushed through the noisy crowd.

"There you are, Miguel Angel!" Edmundo grasped Miguel by the shoulders and peered at him, his thin hair a wild corona. "What is this all about? What does it mean?" The villagers' chatter died away as they craned to listen.

"Father, I have no idea." Miguel's voice was low, humble, calm, ice cream for his dry and fearful throat. Nahual would be proud. "But what will happen now, Father? What should I do?"

"Well, we must all discuss this, decide what the choices are —" He stopped as the villagers clamored in suggestion.

"We can't turn him over!"

"No, he must hide in the cornfields."

"Let him stay in the church, Father."

"No, he must leave. They'll burn the whole village."

"They'll burn it anyway, and kill us all —"

"We have to send for the governor."

"Are you crazy? We have to fight them ourselves."

"Yes, there weren't that many —"

"No, we all have to leave, all of us together —"

The priest held up his hands. "Quiet! Quiet! Eh, listen now . . . we will talk more of this at Mass today. I expect all of you to come." The group fell silent at this reminder: ancient comforts, ancient obligations. Many feet shuffled. "Then there is the procession this afternoon. We will ask San Clemente, patron of Akabal, for his help on his name day." He raised his arms and everyone nodded. "Then tonight the elders will meet, no? To decide? Isn't that the custom?" Heads nodded again. "In the meantime let us all pray for Miguel and for Akabal, for San Clemente de Akabal." The priest clasped his hands and paused, dramatic in spite of himself.

"Now you should all go home. Let us make this day one of honor for ourselves and for Miguel and for everyone, by doing what we must at such a time." The priest lowered his voice. "Try not to be afraid. We must all think clearly and be very careful before we do anything." They nodded once more, then crossed themselves and backed away to open a path to the church for him. Thrusting his hands in the pockets of his blue jeans, his head down, Edmundo strode past them and went inside.

Caterina's whisper was fierce. "I still think we have time to get you out of here, if we move right now."

"Don't talk nonsense. The soldiers are watching the fields already. And if I did get away, they'd come and kill the rest of you for helping me."

"They'll probably do that anyway." Heads turned toward the crisp voice. Benedicto Tijax gave Caterina a jaunty grin over the heads of the others, who shook their heads and smiled as they always did at the dusty incongruity of his pressed yellow shirt, his creased pants, and brown leather shoes. As the labor organizer for several south coast plantations, he was a source of jobs and the owner of a truck, meriting respect, and they moved back to let him into the group. "Why do you waste time with that little subversive?" he said lightly to Caterina. "Come with me and let's make the most of our last day on earth."

Her worried face relaxed into a smile. "Ah, you monkey. You must charm the lieutenant for us, get him confused with your devil's talk so we can get Miguel out of here. What do you say?" She let go of Miguel's hand and shaded her eyes from the sun.

"No, your charms are the only ones that work in this place, my heart, you know that. You must tell us all how to do it." He came to her side and took her hand, and Miguel tensed. Benedicto ignored him and murmured to Caterina. "Come along, really. I have to tell you something."

"No, I can't. Come on, we're busy," she said, but still she smiled and did not reclaim her hand. "This is an emergency. Don't you think we have to decide what to do? It's all a mistake, so we have to get Miguel out of here somehow, isn't that right? We've all agreed —"

"No, that's not right. You think we have a choice here?" Benedicto's smile disappeared. "Weren't you out there? Didn't you hear what the lieutenant said? It's him they want; it doesn't matter what he did or what he didn't do. The army demands him, the army takes him. It's that simple. What makes you think anything else is possible?" Gregorio looked away; Benedicto had grown impervious to sentiment, surprised by pity, hardened by his landowning employers against all that was nonproductive. "It's always been that way, hasn't it? We are dust to them. Isn't it true, Miguel?" Benedicto turned to Miguel as if noticing him for the first time.

Miguel stared. "You can say that to an innocent man?"

Benedicto spread his hands. "Innocent? What does that mean? You think they care who's innocent? And even if they did, who around here isn't guilty of something?" He turned to the little group, suddenly a preacher. "Didn't we all listen with great respect when the subversives first came in from the hills? Did any of you shout 'Long live the government!' at that moment?" He looked at the circle of faces. No one spoke. Benedicto spat. "Yes, I remember very well those times when I was a kid, those boys all skinny and scared, coming in and standing on this spot right here, telling us all about the people's rights and the oppression of the landowners. That was what, ten, eleven years ago, the first time? Just before the earthquake. Only those speeches were the real earthquake, weren't they? And some of us even got excited about it, didn't we?" Miguel's face was a mask. Gregorio, watching Benedicto's dapper figure turn and gesture, wondered at the surge of confusion he felt.

Suddenly Gregorio was ten years old again, trying to disengage his hand from his mother's firm grip as they stood amid the scarlet peppers and the white piles of lime on market day, watching the wiry young men climbing up out of the cornfields, walking up the hill into the plaza from all directions, an invasion from another world. They wore rows of bullets slung over their bony chests and carried rifles and pistols at the ready. Relaxing into smiles, they had patted him on the head and grinned at his mother, who glowered in distrust and clasped him into her billowing skirts. He watched the young men, gaunt and more ragged than the villagers, as they reached hungrily for bananas and candies from the market piles, stuffing them down as though they hadn't eaten in days.

"Come and listen!" the thin one had called from the church steps where Miguel now stood. "We want only to talk to you!" When no one moved, the smiles narrowed and the rifles rose. One youth went into the church and the old bell soon clanked out the summons, bringing the old women from their hovels and nearby farmers in from the corn. Slowly, reluctantly, prodded by the gun barrels, everyone had herded together in front of the church as the bell called above.

The youth raised his hand and the ringing stopped. "I am called Nahual, the spirit that lives in us all, and I am the jaguar that fights for freedom," he said loudly. His voice cracked; he was only a teenager himself. He smiled at them, then bent to a nearby woman and gently took a baby from her arms. Gregorio's mother inhaled sharply. The youth tickled the infant and held it up to the crowd. "This is a child of corn," he cried. "You are the people of the corn, an ancient people of pain and suffering, and we are your brothers!" He rocked the baby and it smiled up at him. "You are the mountains, and we come to the mountains of our ancestors, as our ancestors did, in search of freedom and justice!"

Nahual gave the baby back to its mother. "You are the sons and daughters of kings, and you are many, many more than the corrupt thieves who rule this country! Yet you live here like slaves, without land, without property! You have no schools for your children! You have no clinic when you are sick! You have no roads, you have no electricity. Why is this?"

He paused, awaiting an answer. He put his hands on his hips and nodded at them. No one stirred. To Gregorio, peering around and through the crowd, Nahual seemed relaxed, cheerful, like a younger version of his father when Gregorio was being a dutiful student. Even the question echoed his father's talk, and he realized with excitement that he knew what was coming: a lecture about peasants' rights to the land, the evil of the landlords. "Mama!" he whispered. "He's like Papa!" She pinched his ear and shushed him hard.

"You know the reason. You do not own the land! You have no land, and what you grow with your sweat and your blood you cannot sell, because of the landlords. Yes, you know that! Your coffee and your corn, they go to the landlords, to the rich, and then to the Yankees, who live far away and pay nothing for it!" The crowd seemed to shift from one foot to the other, and a few heads nodded in assent. Gregorio's mother tightened her grip on his shoulders. In her tension was the same fear she showed whenever his father talked like this, when he made the boy write stories about the beauty of the fields. "Write about the land," he would say, "how fertile it is, how we have loved it and worked it since the days of Tecun Uman." He started one night to take Gregorio to a meeting of a budding peasants' union, but Ana de Córdoba forbade it in horror, holding her son tightly just as she did now, every muscle in her body rejecting what she heard.

"Well, that is all history now," Nahual called. "We are here to tell you the good news, that things are changing! All over this country, from the capital to Santa Rosa and even here in Akabal, the people are rising up to say we have had enough!" He raised his fist. "Enough of the landlords! Enough of slavery! You people deserve to own the land you live on! You deserve justice and freedom from this slavery. And we are here to tell you that the people will have what they deserve!"

He raised both arms in the air, and the other rebels scattered through the crowd raised their fists too, and cheered. "Long live the revolution! Long live the revolution!" The villagers looked at them with mouths open. Gregorio looked up at his mother, at the fear and hatred in her face, and knew suddenly, with the certainty of childhood, that the words were worthless air. They had to be; she was so sure, her face so hard. He looked around for his father, to see if he understood also, but could not find him in the crowd.

Nahual rose on his toes with excitement. "Everywhere the fire is growing! The people's revolution is burning strong! We are in the plantations in the south, the oil zones in the north, on the highways, in the towns where the tourists come, and in the capital, where the politicians and their corrupt army know they are safe no longer! Every day we have successful operations. We have thousands and thousands in the Guerrilla Army of the Poor, all of them people like you! Ordinary people, farmers, mothers, children, students, workers! All fighting for freedom! We are everywhere! We are strong, and we are going to win!" More cheers. "We will overthrow this corrupt government of the rich very soon! And then we will install a government of the people!"

The rebels cheered again, and this time some of the villagers raised their fists too and shouted with them. "We promise you this: we will end the repression. We guarantee you life and peace. We will free you from the rich oppressors! We will end all discrimination against Indians by the Ladinos!" Gregorio looked around the plaza and saw nodding heads. "We will create a new society, where all patriotic sectors of the nation, all the popular movements, all the democratic groups, everybody will be represented in the government! We will guarantee you freedom to write and say whatever you want! You can practice any religion! And we will end the forced time in the army!"

At this some villagers actually clapped. Ana's grip on Gregorio's shoulders was like steel, and he squirmed. "In the new society, women will have more rights! You will have the same rights as men — to vote, to work, to get equal pay!" Gregorio felt his mother's sharp grunt of contempt and disbelief. "And old people too! You will be honored for your wisdom and for your achievements!" Nahual paused. Sweat poured from his forehead and he wiped it with a grimy cloth.

"Now listen a little more. We know the soldiers will come here. We know they will threaten you and ask if you have seen us. They will question you and demand food, and eat it without paying. Yes, you know this is true. But listen now — if you are with us, we will protect you from the soldiers! Yes, we promise, we will protect you against them!" He lifted his hand in an oath and nodded solemnly as the other rebels raised their rifles and shouted, "Long live the revolution!" At this the villagers eyed one another, and did not clap.

"There is one thing more." Nahual shook a finger at them. "You must not collaborate. You must refuse to help the soldiers; you cannot become part of the repression." He put his hands on his hips. "We must all stand united against them! We must enforce this unity together! The officials who run the repression must face revolutionary justice, and those who collaborate with them. We will be harsh in judging traitors to the revolution, and you must help us." He looked around the square again, and there was silence. "But we know it is difficult. You are in a good position here. We are flexible with those we know are with us. So listen to me! You have nothing to lose! You have only the chains of slavery now! You are the future! You are the revolution, and we are your army. Together, together we will rise up, we will overthrow this slavery, and we will guarantee the freedom of the people! The people, united!"

"The people, united!" the other youths shouted back.

"Will never be defeated!" Nahual shook both fists.

"The people! United! Will never be defeated!" The rebels took up the chant and urged the villagers to join in. Many did.

Gregorio's mother shrank away from the nearest of these as the rhythmic shout rose in the square. Pulling Gregorio along, she edged toward the shadowed passageway that led to their house, shushing him. He was glad to escape, happy to see her fear and anger melt into relief as she shut the door behind her. She knelt before him and grasped his shoulders.

"Gregorio, listen to me. You must not pay any attention to those people. Do you understand?" She spoke urgently, staring deep into his eyes. "They lie to us. What they say is wrong, dangerous for us. We could all be killed, just for listening. Do you hear me? Please, look at me." Her voice softened. "Your father doesn't understand this. He's got these same notions from somewhere, talking about peasants' unions, trying to organize the farmers. It's crazy, crazy!" She released him and stood up, rubbing her hands. "But he won't listen, he keeps going on about it, and now he's got Cecilia doing it too. Oh, I wish this hadn't happened here, not now, not ever. Listen,

Gregorio — listen to me. Now. Promise me you won't pay any attention to what you heard today, none of it. It's all lies, no matter what your father says! Promise!"

"I promise, Mama. Don't worry." She wept, and hugged him long and hard.

But he had not worried then about Cecilia. He was proud to be his mother's good boy, favored for once over his sister. Guilty pleasure had made him fierce with love for his mother, hugging her in return, triumphant for a while over Cecilia and her bicycle. That bicycle, another memory tangled up with the subversives, the guerrillas, the war — he hadn't yet sorted it all out. At that time, ten years ago, he had still been smarting from the pink and gold bicycle Andreas brought back one day from Santa Rosa, a gift to the girl from an uncle, he said. Cecilia wouldn't let Gregorio touch it, the only bicycle in the village. She learned to ride it in the plaza by herself, falling again and again. He and Miguel roared in envious laughter as she careened down the hill, her long braid flying, vanishing over the rise toward the highway.

He had studied the machine with longing and drew over-lapping portraits of it on a piece of newspaper covered with whitewash. He detailed each wire and sprocket, a perfect vision of a bicycle, then drew half over it a bicycle shedding pieces like a molting bird. That yielded to pieces disintegrat-ing in all directions and finally to a pile of bolts, the seat forlorn over the dead handlebars. His mother had laughed and teased him for being jealous, but she marveled at the picture and Gregorio scored a small, secret win.

Cecilia had used the bike at first to go from door to door announcing their father's meetings, asking for signatures on petitions to the Agrarian Transformation Institute, protest-ing against the Torazo brothers. Men with surveying equip-ment had appeared in the cornfields, telling the villagers the land and any oil under it belonged to the landowner Bar-tolomeo Torazo of Tekan, and Andreas was indignant. The surveyors flashed pieces of paper covered with print and laughed when the peasants couldn't read them. But Andreas could read. They are fake, he said, waving his arms at the doubtful faces. "We have to get a lawyer to help us in the capital. Otherwise we are still slaves here. We have to stand together . . ." But the others shifted from foot to foot and looked around to see who was listening.

Andreas had walked miles through the province, taking Cecilia when Gregorio cried and refused to go, calling meetings, telling the tenant farmers they had to defend the land they had worked for generations. Cecilia half rode, half walked her bicycle with him, but the tires surrendered quickly to the rocky paths, and soon the machine rusted in silence behind the de Córdobas' house, slowly becoming Gregorio's portrait. His father grew more energetic. A few people came to the meetings, and Andreas gathered a centavo here, another there, money to hire a lawyer from Santa Rosa. The lawyer was friendly, a Ladino, and he said he would speak for the peasants in the capital. He took the money and went there, coming back a week later in a new suit, with leather shoes. He brought papers he said proved Torazo owned all the land in the area, and then he went to Tekan and began working for the Torazo family.

Andreas only got angrier. He took all of his wife Ana's money from the baking cooperative and hired another lawyer, an honest man. But in their honor he and the rest of them were simple, and they did a stupid, stupid thing: they made a public statement. They announced in every church in the region that the union had been formed and everybody should join it. Of course Torazo had him arrested right away, making up some story about embezzlement. The soldiers came and took him away just as they did Cecilia four years later.

For four months Gregorio and Ana and Cecilia had waited, standing for hours in the sterile anterooms of lounging officials, standing in line at the gate of the barracks to see the captain, bowing their heads in silence when they were told to come back the next day, and the next, and the next after that. One hot afternoon Ana had wept in despair as the big iron gate closed in her face, and the soldiers had laughed at her through the chain-link fence: "Cry some more! The earth is dry here!"

"We'll let the girl in if we can keep her."

"Let's hear you shout again!"

Their petition for help, painfully spelled out by Cecilia and corrected by a sleepy priest, grew gray and tattered by passage through many careless hands. It collected signatures, stamps, bits of ribbon and wax, and finally a big blue scrawl: Lorenzo, captain of the garrison, had signed it himself.

The following week Andreas was released. With no warning, no explanation, no papers, no hat, he returned to Akabal in the back of Father Edmundo's jeep, a broken man. His right leg was mangled, his face gray in new furrows. He told his family the police had slapped him, then beaten him, first with fists and then with rifle butts. They made him sit for days on a hard stool because he was defiant, refusing to confess to plots he had not made. At first he was willing to sit in his own urine and excrement rather than give in to them, he said, but they beat him awake when he slumped in exhaustion, they forced his shit into his mouth, they poured his vomit on his head, and finally, when he cried in sick humiliation, awaiting his death, they had smashed his right leg in three places with three blows of a hammer over three successive days.

All this he told Ana and his white-faced children. The truth, the part he could not say, Gregorio saw in his eyes. He had tried at first to overcome the pain in his guts, reciting to himself his name, his status, laying bricks of memory for what he knew would have to be a citadel around the core of his sanity when the pain from his leg pushed through his shock: Andreas de Córdoba, husband, father, farmer, human being . . . But the pain had grown, little tingles at first from his knee, needles of crystal so sharp they were almost interesting; then tiny starbursts, and slowly, like a fire spreading, his leg's screaming presence filled his mind, then the room. The pain became a hulking weight that crushed air from his lungs, narrowed his universe, collapsed the circle of his knowledge to a world no wider than his own skin. Gregorio understood that this was the intended outcome, the total eclipse by agony of all his father's delinquent ideas, notions expelled from a brain crammed so to bursting with pain that it had no space left for thought.

Later he remembered wisps of tubes, hypodermics, people coming and going, images in ripples that washed him briefly on the shore of consciousness and swept him out again to nothingness. In the end, wildly grateful at pain's easing, he had told the soldiers anything, making up names and jobs and plots beyond their questions, signing documents and confessions until he became tiresome. They had sent him home a babbling shell, an example to others of the price to be paid for spreading subversive notions. As he left, Andreas said, he had thanked them for his crutch.

"And the peasants' union?" Cecilia had asked him. Ana gasped in horror at the question, and Gregorio shoved his sister in the ribs, but Andreas shook his head.

"Yes, the union, subversive, illegal. I understand all that now. We must forget about it, don't think of it. It doesn't matter. Rejoice we are together and alive, alive . . ." Gregorio hugged his father's bony chest in fierce agreement.

But Cecilia would not cooperate.

She kept asking questions. Andreas resisted. He didn't want to talk. He waved away all mention of the Agrarian Institute, the land, of all the things that once consumed him. Ana moved about the house like a ghost, working longer hours than ever at the cooperative, never sleeping, shushing her daughter. Gregorio helped, kneading the dough, beating the soldiers' faces in with every blow. When the two of them returned late from the baking hut, Cecilia would be there by Andreas's side, asking questions.

"Stay out of all that," he whispered one night, waving her away. "It isn't worth it, don't you see?"

"Leave him alone, Cecilia! Haven't we had enough trouble?" Gregorio was too tired even to draw.

"I'm only telling the news, Gregorio. He wants to know what happened while he was gone. Don't you, Daddy?" The Torazos' men had taken over the land parcels of the old baker, Honorio Luxit, and Diego Saraf, the most honored elder, she told him, the best of the scrubby land in the region, and plowed the corn under. The council of elders met in the church to decide what to do, but after two days of talk they had no plan. They came out of the church with their shoulders bent, ten years older in those two days, Cecilia said, and had walked home with their eyes on the dusty ground.

Gregorio listened in horror. His sister's words were tentacles reaching out to drag them all to prison. "You're crazy! What are you doing? You're trying to get it started all over again!" He had rushed at her, stopping only at the sight of his father's anxious face, the gnarled fingers closing and twisting the threadbare cloth of that half-empty pants leg.

Cecilia's gaze was level. "It's started again whether I do anything about it or not. You think not talking about it will make it all go away?"

"It doesn't concern us! He's finished with that! Let it alone!"

"Doesn't concern us? They take our neighbors' land and nearly kill our father, and you say it doesn't concern us? What are you talking about? You think you can stay out of life? You want to find neutral ground in this place, somewhere you can just draw your silly birds? You're the one who's crazy." She waved a hand at him. "You want to hide in a corner somewhere, but don't you see? You're a — a bit of dust to those people anyway; all of us are. That's the problem, not the solution. We don't exist for them. We're just stupid Indians, worse than animals. We don't have any rights at all, no land, no life, no nothing. Look at him, a brave man. They nearly killed him because he told the truth." She smiled at her father and crouched by his mat, taking his hand. "But he still understands. He's just tired. He'll be all right, he'll recover, we'll get it done right this time, won't we, Daddy?"

"Oh, for Christ's sake, leave him alone! You'll kill us all with this kind of talk."

Her eyes narrowed. "I didn't think you were so empty as that, my brother."

Gregorio recoiled as though she had struck him. The old man's eyes clouded in distress and he raised a quavering hand. Gregorio whirled and stomped out of the house, nearly colliding with Ana, squatting on her heels just outside the doorway, rocking back and forth, her hands to her face.

After that, Gregorio watched in silence as Cecilia's energy lit the hut. She talked constantly about the peasants' union, brought villagers to see Andreas, read him drafts of petitions. She asked his advice on phrasing, on officials to talk to, and slowly, reluctantly, he began to answer. He corrected her grammar, he suggested other names, and when he waved away a question, she didn't push him. His leg healed; he leaned on Cecilia and Gregorio and hobbled around the room. He learned to use the crutch and he listened again to the radio in Cristóbal's shop. Gradually he offered his daughter tentative advice, and gradually he recovered the vocabulary of outrage that had been beaten out of him. She sat with him, polishing her boots and talking strategy, night after night.

Gregorio felt as though a choking fog had flooded the house. He warned until he bored himself that the soldiers would return at any moment. He dreamed at night of drowning, of falling into holes or off high cliffs. He screamed in terror and woke in a sweat-drenched jolt just as his body hit the ground. His pictures grew contorted and ugly, quetzals tearing at their breasts or being devoured by vultures, females brooding over dead nestlings. He drew the faces of their neighbors, but they wore cynical sneers or frightened backward glances. He grew haggard from lack of sleep, and exhaustion took over. He began to nod off in the corner as his father and his sister talked late into the night.

Cecilia took up where her father had left off. She was more circumspect, timing her organizing meetings with market trips to Santa Rosa. She became the village scribe, offering to help her neighbors get their endless birth and death and marriage certificates through the listless bureaucracy, charging a few cents and saving them the trip and the bribe they would otherwise pay the officials she could charm and bully into doing their jobs. In the Santa Rosa market, she talked with women in the teeming stalls, writing down their suggestions. She drafted proposed contracts and with Andreas's help composed petitions to landowners and the Agrarian Transformation Institute. She wrote letters to possible allies in the trade unions and awaited the responses they sent to "C.C." at a made-up market stall number. She spent every evening writing by candlelight, copying proposals, correcting drafts.

Gregorio watched in fear and irritation. "Why don't you get married like a normal woman? Miguel is ready."

"Miguel? That simpleton? He's worse than you!" Cecilia laughed. She had dismissed Akabal's male population long ago as hopelessly dull, and never really distinguished Miguel from the other useless boys around her little brother. "He should join the army. They're stupid and incompetent too — he'd fit right in."

"You've got to stop talking like that. You don't know who's going to take you seriously."

"Or maybe he should join the rebels, be another ant crawling through the hills, shooting up buses for entertainment."

She waved her hand in dismissal. Gregorio's heart ached to remember how often he saw that gesture: the church was a useless bore that blinded people to reality, the bakers' cooperative was a pathetic waste of time, the civil patrols were party nights for children. Such needles festered in her neighbors' flesh, and in the nervous climate of the time it was inevitable that someone, somewhere in the jealous market, somewhere in the suspicious city hallways, somebody would denounce her as a communist. Six months ago that had been enough to bring the soldiers by night.

But this time, this morning, the soldiers had come in sunlight, casually, without anxiety, many more than had come for Cecilia. They wanted her then, they wanted Miguel now, they were stronger, there were more of them, they wanted everyone in Akabal eventually, just as the bony young men had wanted everyone. The soldiers had called to them today just as the guerrillas had called before.

"Lies!" Benedicto was saying now. "All those kids told us was a lie! But we just stood there and listened. And when the soldiers came a few weeks later, did we confess? Did anybody tell them the subversives had been here? Pah! Of course not." He waved aside the thought. "So you see, we're all traitors here, just from that one moment. And how many times have they been here since then? Ten? Twenty? We've been traitors again and again, every time! For ten years we've been traitors! We're lucky we've escaped this long!" He laughed sharply, and Gregorio winced. "All the rest of this, the story about some bombing, some woman, that's all a formality, it's not even necessary."

Benedicto grinned at Miguel, who had clenched his fists, and he raised his hand as if to slap the smaller man on the shoulder. Then he appeared to think better of it. He waved instead.

"They want Miguel this time. That's too bad. A real pity. Next time they'll want somebody else. Just bad luck, nothing we can do." He glared around at them. "It's not right, you say.

It's wrong, it's unjust! Well, so it is. So what? That's the situation. At least let's not talk about innocence, for God's sake."

He stood for a moment, as though waiting for rebuttal. Abruptly he reached for Caterina. "Come on," he said, his voice low and rough. "I've got something to —"

"No! She stays here!" Miguel startled himself. He reached for Caterina's other hand. She looked at him and then at Benedicto and opened her mouth, but Benedicto let go of her and raised his hand to Miguel in mocking salute.

"All right, all right. As you wish, chosen one." Benedicto gave a low bow. When he stood again, he and Miguel stared hard at each other. Benedicto raised his chin and looked away, nodded at Caterina, and turned to leave, pretending to laugh. But his hands trembled and Gregorio saw hard fury in his eyes.

They all stared after Benedicto a moment, uncertain what had happened. Gregorio put a hand on Miguel's arm, and started. It was like grasping an iron rail.

"Ah, forget him," Gregorio said, surprised at the ease in his voice. "Let's go somewhere and talk about this. Does your mother know? What about Irene?"

"I'm not sure. I left them in the house. Unless someone went to tell them, I don't think so." Miguel blew a long breath and tipped his hat back. The others, distracted by Benedicto's departure, began moving off too, talking again, and Gregorio watched them go. "Forgive me, Caterina," Miguel said. "It's just . . . I didn't want you to leave just then."

She smiled at him, her gold-rimmed tooth flashing in the sun. "It's all right. You go on. Obviously you're not going to listen to me, so the hell with you. I'll talk to some more people and try to find out what happened. Maybe we can save you in spite of yourself." She reached to touch his cheek; he took her hand and kissed it.

"Many thanks," he murmured. She smiled again and left them.

Eight

DON CRISTÓBAL CLEMENTE's tiny shop, solid and reassuring on its concrete blocks, was glorious to him that morning in its bright green paint, its new tile roof. It was a kind of sturdy answer to the stained pale wreck of a church directly across the square, providing for earthly needs on this side of the hilltop just as the church offered spiritual provender on the other. He decided he would put up the pink and yellow plastic banners he kept rolled behind the laxatives that no one ever bought, partly to honor San Clemente on his name day, Cristóbal's assumed name day too, and partly to give the finger to this crisis. "We must look here at what the Yankees call the bottom line, no?" Smiles and murmurs of assent surprised him, relaxing the worried faces of these people who were his friends, his constituents, his customers, and even, he thought, his subjects. But that was foolish. He reminded himself he would sell a lot of beer that day, for fear is very thirsty. He thought crazily, just for a moment, that he was lucky the soldiers had come on a festival day when he was well stocked.

"I think it is all a mistake, just a misunderstanding," old Genero moaned as Cristóbal pushed open the door. His whine begged for absolution. As nominal head of last night's patrol, he would be the first one punished if punishing was done. "The dogs never barked. I only slept a little. I swear nobody came in —"

"Nobody's accusing you of anything, Don Genero," Cristóbal said.

Arturo's face reddened. The irascible mechanic was reliably as much a sentinel against indifference as he was against rust, and now his meaty fist banged the wooden inner wall. "The whole story is made up, a lie! Nothing like that ever happened!"

Half a dozen of these older men crowded in behind the mayor, jamming the little space, drawn together in a meeting that was partly conscious, partly unaware, knowing but not thinking yet of the formal gathering of the village elders they would have to hold later, with all the people watching, sometime before dawn. All talking at once, they pushed up to the wooden counter that ran across one end of the shop as Cristóbal ducked behind it. "Well, there's no reason he'd make up such a story and come all the way out here to tell us about it," argued Joselino, his foxlike face as sharp as his voice. No fixed job, no fixed opinions, the market's wiliest dealmaker was always quick to see other sides, even to invent them if necessary. "I think the first thing to do is find out where Miguel was —"

"Right." Arturo gave him a pained look. " 'Pardon me, esteemed sir, is it possible you happened to castrate a young boy and murder his mother last night?' Why don't you write out his confession while you're at it?"

Cristóbal put two bottles of soda on the counter between them. "Oh, come on, shut up for once," he said. He opened more soda for everybody, then turned to the radio behind the counter and flicked it on.

". . . the beer that satisfies!" An announcer's voice crackled off the walls. Teletype noise surged in the background.

"Now! In Sann-ta Rosa, a strong explosion! From Good Life Tonic, the news of the hour!" A trumpet bleated two tinny notes.

"Quiet! Quiet!" They leaned toward the brown plastic box.

"A very, ver-ry strong explosion woke all-l-l Santa Rosa in the earr-ly hours of the morning!" the announcer cried in Spanish. Cristóbal frowned; the others caught the name of the town and their eyes widened. The mayor motioned them to keep quiet. "The blast occurred in-side the military garrison of the national army, but according to re-liable army sources, it caused — only minor damage!" Cristóbal translated as fast as he could. The trumpet blew again. "An official spokesman said . . . that one person! Suffered superficial wounds . . . and that the event was — an ac-cident." The trumpet heralded another commercial.

The mayor translated the rest. When he finished, they leaned back and blew a long breath, looking at the radio as though it were a toad. "So something did happen at the barracks after all. That much is true. That's very interesting." Everybody nodded. The real astonishment was that the news meant something to them. In remote Akabal, for the first time in memory, they felt they were linked to an event important enough to be mentioned on nationwide radio, to be heard by people waking up in the capital. Suddenly their little village was connected to the world; a giant's eye was upon them on their tiny bit of rock.

None of them considered for a second whether the news report might be accurate or complete, or whether the radio might tell more later. Experience told them the story would either remain unexplained all day, or that it would change beyond recognition. They would learn nothing for certain. The capital's twelve-page newspapers would not get to Santa Rosa until tonight, but nothing about this would be in them until tomorrow's editions, and then only the official statement. Still, Akabal was connected to an event that would be mentioned, and that was momentous. "Remind me tomorrow to send somebody to Santa Rosa to get the newspapers," Cristóbal said.

"If any of us are still alive," Arturo said into his soda bottle. The newspapers. Cristóbal read them like the *chiman* Caterina studying the angle of sunlight on the dreaming beans, noticing the magic of absences and allusions, guessing at invisible forces shaping the words. Even here, even after all this time.

"So what do you know about this lieutenant, Don Cristóbal? Is he a friend of yours?" The mayor did a quick check of his audience. He could never be sure who the local ears were at any moment. They changed too often. But truculent Arturo, the old radical Andreas, Genero in his simple faith — even slippery Joselino, who lived by his wits — none of them were ears. He leaned back, folding his hands across his bulk, and thought out loud.

"Well, let's put him in context. Under that soldier's hat is a storekeeper like me. Yes, not as smart perhaps, but a storekeeper." He waved a deprecating hand. "Think of him for a moment not as Lieutenant Gomez but as Prospero Jesús Gomez, who drinks and sweats as you do, Arturo, only not as much. Maybe such a man can be reasoned with, eh?"

"Not if he's like Arturo," Andreas said.

"He came here the first time I think about two years ago. His jeep broke down a couple of kilometers away — he came in for a beer and some shade. He had his poor private sweating out there under the hood, but he sat here and talked to me" — the mayor smiled — "about monopoly capitalism."

"About what?" Genero squinted.

"Storekeeping. He called me a monopoly capitalist like his father, he said. His father ran a shop in Cotzal, a little bigger than this one, and he worked there after school, and so did his sister, so you know they weren't rich. He said he sold the same things as here — liquor, salt, flour, rice, candy, and so on, and more soap than we sell. He wanted to keep me in my place, you see, so he was full of little insults. 'Have you ever painted this hovel?' 'Do you carry your own water?' But I just listened, and pretty soon he told me his father used to pay protection money to the Cotzal police, and did I have to pay anybody here." Cristóbal swigged his soda. "I thought at first he was telling me I was going to have to pay him, but I wasn't sure, so I made a joke of it; I told him I paid myself protection as the only policeman in town. He said I was lucky. He said his father had to bow and scrape to the rich folks of Cotzal, who always shortchanged him and never paid their bills, and so he yelled at the peasants and the Indians to make up for it. I said I never yell at any of you, that you all yell at me instead. He kept saying I was lucky. I have to admit he surprised me, he never came back to the protection business, and after a while some other people came in here, and he left."

"He was just being friendly?" Arturo said in disbelief.

Joselino spat on the floor. "Nah, he was checking the place out. I bet he counted all the houses and looked around for hiding places. Didn't pay for the beer either, did he?"

"I don't remember," Cristóbal lied, and then frowned at himself. Gomez had not paid. Why had he not wanted to tell the others that? Was he trying to defend the bastard?

Andreas looked thoughtful. "Do you think he's someone we can argue with then?" Andreas argued with his son, argued with his wife, argued with landowners and farmers, and had even argued with his torturers. Andreas would argue with an avalanche.

"Well, depends on his orders, doesn't it? You know, I always say it's easier to militarize a civilian than civilize the military. We may be able to reason with the man Prospero Jesús, but with Lieutenant Gomez?" He shrugged. "This lieutenant loves his military uniform. You saw how his shirt was buttoned right up; even his belt was shiny. It gives him comfort, that uniform. I think he will follow orders. But what are they?"

"Why is that so hard?" Genero spread his hands. "The days of the bloodbath are over. General Morales said so, you know that. This Gomez is just bluffing. Now we have real investigations, honest trials — they won't just shoot somebody anymore."

"Right!" Arturo snorted. "Now they expect us to do the shooting. And even if we do, what's to keep them from killing us all afterward? He said already we're all traitors if Miguel is here."

Cristóbal raised his hands. "Let's think about that a minute."

Last year's coup, he reminded them, was by the younger colonels, field veterans, the names they had first seen three years ago in newspaper accounts of General Barcos's bloody sweeps. The colonels had seemed to like Barcos's massacres, judging from their triumphant rhetoric, but then they overthrew him and proclaimed an end to the slaughter. That was intriguing, although it looked at first like a standard power play, but then right away they put in General Torres, a religious man who prayed over the radio for the rebels' surrender. Torres insisted that the bloodbath was over, as Genero recalled, but that was a laugh, because the Torres terror units moved into the provinces in smaller units than Barcos had ever dared, and the civil patrol farces started up. Torres promised at the same time that new schools and clinics would halt the rebellion by — how had he put it? — winning the peasants' hearts and minds, that he would dry up the sea the rebel fish swam in. That was clearly the Yankees talking, getting Torres to try the approach they thought they hadn't had a chance to test properly in Vietnam.

Still, it was interesting, and when the older colonels got rid of Torres four months ago and put in this buzzbomb helicopter jockey Morales, the human rights speeches got louder than ever. Cristóbal said they had all been scared by the collapse of the Argentine generals after the Malvinas humiliation. The speeches were about international citizenship and freedom of expression, but that was rationalization after the fact. Don Cristóbal decided it all meant that the sweeps hadn't worked. The colonels never minded killing Indians as long as they thought they were cutting out the cancer of subversion, as they so charmingly put it, and they didn't care what any international worrywarts said about it, not that anybody said very much about a few Indians. But if the bloodletting stopped working, if three rebels sprouted where one fell, if the cancer fed and grew on peasants' blood and widows' wails, then the practical military would try something else.

"But what? And have they really changed tactics yet? Or is it all just talk until they fight it out among themselves? I don't see how we can know in time to do much about it today," Cristóbal concluded. "I think we have to take Gomez at his word —"

"Right! He'll take Miguel back and they'll give him a fair trial, and they'll let him go." Genero nodded vigorously, and stopped at the pitying looks from the others. "They promised! We don't have to do anything!"

Cristóbal reflected that this wizened carpenter, in his frayed hat and bare feet, was in every way a rock, impermeable, unchanging, the kind upon which any government built its palaces. Genero would hope forever for a brighter day, clinging to words the way he had clung to the church through forty years of disappointment. Genero had raised his scarred and blackened hands in hosannas to the saints when Torres announced he would arm the villages. He had got drunk on his first taste of trust and responsibility, savoring vinegar and calling it wine, the day the soldiers delivered those six rusting relics of the Second World War to the mayor of Akabal, saluting in mock seriousness, their faces barely straight.

On his duty days, Genero strutted about the town with the

ancient weapon cocked and ready, and he wore a fearsome scowl of righteousness when Cristóbal read them the presidential speech proclaiming the civil patrols: "The difference between the left and the right is like the difference between God and Satan. No one can stand in the middle. No one can have a little faith in the one as well as a little faith in the other." Cristóbal had repeated these lines twice in amazement, and Genero often recited them like catechism as though they made sense. And when General Morales overthrew Torres, Genero had nodded at the new speech, the new proclamation of another end to the bloodbath. He lit firecrackers to celebrate Morales's promise that the army would be only a caretaker to hold things together until the civilians organized for new elections. He found it reassuring that he had heard that promise many times before.

Cristóbal envied Genero's faith. What resilience one could have if he were not a cynic! So he made sure every night's civil patrol included at least one like Genero, someone in whom the president's choice resounded as fierce and simple duty to the fatherland, a shining city somewhere out there next to God, or perhaps the same as God, someone with total devotion to the only abstract concept he contained. The nationwide majority of Generos was either the nation's heaviest curse or its primary blessing. Cristóbal had not yet decided. As he had told Edmundo, "God's larger plans for humanity may include these humble wretches, but it is easier for them to grasp their importance in a great effort when they have a gun on their shoulders."

He had baser motives, he reminded himself. Men like Genero provided a model of dedication that reassured the army things were under control here, a conclusion absolutely necessary to Akabal's survival. Yet Akabal's Generos were so clearly inept that Cristóbal could laugh them off to the guerrilla commanders, whose suspicions of collaboration needed equally constant reassurance. If unknown challengers appeared at night, Genero's innocent valor was a spur to the rest of the patrol to fire, if only into the air. The shadows could be sons, brothers, friends. Failure to hit could be explained, but failure to fire was betrayal, one way or the other.

"Enough of this pig piss." Arturo waved his thick arm, dismissing Genero and demanding a beer. He tossed the soda bottle into a corner bucket. His T-shirt with the logo was grimy beyond color, and he moved in a thick, sour odor of decay and restless heat. His syphilis had put a wild edge around his eyes and given his words luminescence, for even Cristóbal believed dying men spoke only truth. "The army's going to take revenge here for that bombing no matter what we do," he said, thumping the bottle on the counter. It was like a verdict.

They fell silent. Andreas cleared his throat. "Why are you all so sure Miguel is guilty?" Propped against the wall, his good leg braced in front of him, he poked Genero with his crutch. "Eh? You believe that fat soldier? What do you know about it?"

"What does it matter, old one?" Benedicto's nasal drawl made them turn as he came into the store. "The soldiers say he's guilty and that's that. He's guilty. No use arguing. They have the guns; we don't. They decide what's right and wrong. If we don't produce Miguel, we die. It's that simple. We might die anyway; it depends on the lieutenant's digestion. I don't see what you're all babbling about." He pushed to the counter and slapped down a coin for a beer, somehow the triumphant youth silencing old men. He smiled as though he had said something cheerful.

"It's your mind that's simple," Andreas growled. "The army doesn't know Miguel. Gomez can't know for sure who did the bombing; he just got the name from somewhere, maybe out of a hat. Maybe the one who did it is not even from here. We're supposed to take the blame for that?"

Benedicto laughed. "You just don't get it, do you? You know, I lent the guerrillas a truck once, when they asked me politely with a gun to my head. They even told me where to find it later, and by God it was there, although the battery was gone and the tires were flat. And you, Joselino — you let some of them sleep in the church once, didn't you?"

"In the shed, in the shed! And you know it was raining and they said they would kill me. They were too many for me . . ."

"And Cristóbal, you gave them medicine from the store, no?"

"Not only medicine but sodas and beer and vegetables . . ." Cristóbal had even felt a stirring of the old light in his gut as he uttered the ritual phrases of welcome, but he would never admit that to Benedicto. He was careful even then, that first time, to speak to the rebels just as he had to the soldiers. "Good day, how may we serve you, we are at your command." Hungry and ragged, Nahual's boys had almost emptied the shelves, but they paid for about half of it and nodded and smiled as they left. Was Miguel there that day? Cristóbal could not remember. But the town had talked of little else for weeks, until the soldiers returned. Then they were dumb as corn-stalks. Cristóbal had welcomed the soldiers again in their turn with sodas and flattery, showing the town the two faces of survival. Ah, it was a delicate, dangerous path, contrary to Christian hearts. Jesus would have spat Cristóbal out of his mouth. But today's zealots were tomorrow's corpses, and Cristóbal planned to die of old age, pleading ignorance of politics on his deathbed and wishing everyone a good day.

"Sure you fed them. We all did, and why not?" Benedicto said between swallows. "Miguel too, somehow. So what's the difference? Only thing is to get him out there, or decide who to shoot instead." He grinned again. "Any volunteers?"

They regarded him with distaste, and fell silent. "Perhaps Miguel cannot be found," Cristóbal said at last. "Perhaps we shall try our best, search every house, hold interrogations, and find nothing, no one, no evidence. Maybe we'll invite the good lieutenant to conduct his own investigation here. We have nothing to hide, hm?"

"Pah! Miguel was right out there in the plaza a minute ago, holding court." Benedicto drained his beer. "You should arrest him, Cristóbal, tie him up to make sure he doesn't get away, and call the soldiers back. How about that?"

The others looked at him, at their feet, around the shop. Andreas shook his head and shouldered himself onto his crutch. He hobbled into the plaza, bright now with sunshine. The sky was the joyful deep mountain blue of another rainless day. Benedicto laughed and followed, stopping to stretch in the doorway. Cristóbal, leaning on the wall, suddenly felt it tremble.

It meant only one thing. "Earthquake!" He vaulted the counter, colliding with Joselino and the others as they scrambled to the door. They all spilled headlong into the square.

A rumble grew toward them faster than thought, rain driving across the rocky hills at impossible speed, arriving dry as shuddering dread underfoot, a taut band about to snap. Skeletal dogs crouched, whining in the dust, and instinctively the people crouched too, eyes huge and staring, fingers and toes digging in for the ride.

Cristóbal, his mind floating over his fear, saw that the horror of earthquakes was unlike fear of flying, of snakes, of gunfire, or any of the thousand things that petrify on first encounter. This fear did not subside with repetition, even with the dozens of tremors that rattled these mountains every year. On the contrary. He remembered his first tremor as intriguing, exciting — his mother swooped him into the street. What would happen next? The second tremor made him more nervous, and the third sent him running headlong to safety with his elders, grabbing his treasured soccer ball. After that, grim panic turned loved buildings, trees, hillsides into instant deadly threats and drove him like a cannon shot to open spaces.

Now, as always, the ground quivered and felt thin, fragile skin over writhing muscles of the earth thundering agony in their spasm. The town was a rickety wagon hurtling over a rocky road. Then, suddenly, the tremor was over, almost as soon as it began, the roar cut off as cleanly as if a stereo needle had been lifted from a record. The dogs stood up first, urinating immediately on their rebellious turf. Birds careened again to their perches, screaming epithets, and one by one the people straightened, dusted off, and moved away, murmuring and crossing themselves.

"Well, nothing that time," Cristóbal said, looking around. He helped Andreas to stand and watched the other men depart to check their homes, their families, their lives. His terror, he reflected, had been cold, pure, rational, unique, almost pristine. It was untainted by guilt for being present. He had no one to blame in the way that fear during battle is polluted by recriminations. Kings and beggars, he realized, would grovel equally on the fickle earth, their global plans and tiny choices ground alike to dust amid the screaming rocks.

Fear, he knew, would justify any act. Certainty of loss obliterated morals, knowledge, other people. He could see how terror worked, how it conquered all resistance, and he could also see how the knowledge that terror was coming could justify anything, anything necessary to avoid it. Terrorists would win at first, but they would create terrorists on the other side. It was inevitable. Some terrorist had bombed the barracks, and Miguel was just quiet enough, had been hurt enough . . . he dismissed the thought. Impossible.

He watched Andreas hobble anxiously toward home. There

was one who had thought terrorism could be reasoned with. Seek justice, ask for understanding, and be crushed to silence. No, it was better to avoid the issue if that was possible. But earthquakes were not easily avoided. He decided that in such a fragile place fatalism was the only rational attitude. The marvel was not that the mountain Indians were passive but that they made any effort whatever toward changing their lives, knowing the voracious ground. He sighed, and scanned the walls of his store for cracks. There was one, a long one running from the roofline to the door frame, but he wasn't sure if it had been there before. He traced it with his finger.

"Falling apart already, and just painted? Good morning, old one." He turned to see Caterina, her strong brown arm raised to shade her yellow eyes from the sun behind him. Her broad face was seamed, her body thick, her hands rough, but his scalp tingled at the sight of her. He felt something like hunger.

"The best of mornings to you, my little witch. And what do you think of all this? A bad omen, no?"

"No, I think the gods just turned over in bed maybe halfway. Perhaps a kind of insurance — now they are comfortable again and will sleep a good while." She paused, appearing to need something from him. He was instantly anxious to find and give it.

"I hope so. What are you doing? Come in and have a soda."

"Thanks. I was going to get my dreaming beans. Nobody seems to have any ideas about what we should do, and I was hoping . . ."

Cristóbal turned away, into his store.

"So what is the gossip so far?" She followed him inside.

He picked up several bottles that had danced off the shelves and lay unbroken on the packed earth. "Well, something did happen at the barracks." He told her about the radio broadcast, and she frowned. "Benedicto wants to shoot somebody, like he always does. Andreas reminded everybody we were all nice to the guerrillas the last time they were in town. And Genero" — he popped open a mineral water and handed it over — "Genero believes we will have an honest investigation and a fair trial."

"And you?"

"I believe you are very beautiful today."

"Of course." She grinned at him, conspiratorial. "And do they say anything against Miguel?"

"Yes, of course, but against everything else as well — the gods, the weather . . ." He shrugged.

"What about this murdered woman and the child?" Her persistence impressed him. He had thought her affair with Miguel was just another convenience, an amusing checkoff on the list of men in Akabal.

"Well, my love, we are all murderers, are we not?" He enclosed her hand and the soda bottle in both his beefy fists. "We give the guerrillas a chicken today, and we give the army a chicken tomorrow, and so they are strong and healthy to shoot each other the day after that. Isn't it so?"

"And if we keep it up long enough, they will all shoot each other and we will be left in peace. Is that the idea?" Her smile faded. "Do you think we can keep doing this that long? Honestly?"

He gazed into her, into the deep well that reached soft and bottomless behind her golden eyes. He moved closer. "The day will be difficult, very difficult. You must help me too."

She took her hand from his grasp and put it on his cheek. "You are wise, Don Cristóbal. We must be one on this, no?" She smiled again. " 'Bless us, old Hurakan, for we are lost and alone on the mountain and all around are demons.' Say that a few times for me." She squeezed his hand. "Thanks for the soda. I'll see you later." She grinned again and was gone.

Nine

FATHER EDMUNDO BUSCADERO watched the saints jiggle in
their alcoves, plaster feet dancing for a moment as though
they would leap to heaven. A few beer bottles fell over, top-
heavy with thick candles, and he caught two of them as they
rolled off the altar table. But Christ gazed on toward home
and the tremor's thunder ceased, leaving a thin cloud of dust
floating over the benches. The priest shook his head. Another
warning; the whole subcontinent would fall into the sea eventually. He dusted the crumbling altar step with his handkerchief, irritated at the ludicrous habit of honoring his
knees, and knelt before the sad-eyed statue. His elbows slid
forward on the plastic tablecloth and he shut his eyes hard.
Thank you, God, for our salvation this day. Now, is there some
way to do it a second time? He felt ridiculous. This was it, the
day of reckoning, and he needed strength. And answers. But
what was the question exactly? Think. What must be done.
That's a communist question. We're all communists to the
army. No, politics is irrelevant to God. Politics takes care of
itself, through proper prayers and ceremony and doctrine.
God makes the faith apply everywhere. On earth as it is. God

will provide. The church is above politics, better at it than anyone else, that's how it survived all these centuries. The church, radiant cathedral, glowing center beaming its web of light through cities, across continents, threads of itself stretching tendrils even into the mountains, even to this place, this very spot, connection to the great knowing One. He was supposed to know everything here, everyone's secrets, all their puny sins, knowing it all, but what had he known today? Nothing, nothing.

Hands clasped at his bald spot, Edmundo clenched his eyelids tighter, his mind's eye skittering birdlike from the pink clouds over the plaza to the price of wine at Cristóbal's shop. He saw the tranquil stolid block of Irene Kanak's cheeks, the sun glinting off Caterina's gold-rimmed tooth, that witch, her mouth wide in laughter, mocking him, mocking the church. She rubbed her breast when she talked to him, as though he wouldn't notice, daring him to notice . . . He jerked his mind to the soldiers, those guns flashing. The soldiers' faces blunt, impassive, the villagers' fearful, wide wrinkled lips begging him for guidance, calloused hands tugging on his jacket, tousled, dusty hair, anxious eyes, his flock of sheep. What could he do about all this? Was he supposed to deliver Miguel Angel Kanak? Did the man really rape that woman? How would he have done it? The skirts so heavy . . . ah, God forgive such a thought! He crossed himself. The poor woman. If such a thing had happened really. But of course it had happened, a thousand times, a million times; that was not the issue, guilt was not the issue, survival was the issue, and that was in the hands of God. But who was God's instrument here, after all? Surely not the army, unless as retribution for Akabal's sins, for his own sins? So great a price for such a mouse! No sins here to equal slaughter. But President Morales had promised there would be no more slaughters. Was that true? How could it be, after so many years? God's will alone . . . We are all alone here on the mountain. We are all one here . . . But who knew God's judgment? Perhaps the sins of a priest weighed so heavy, more than all their slaughter . . . if they are ignorant of God. But of course they know God, they pray over their murders. Is that really prayer? Is this a prayer? Jumbled babble . . .

He longed for a telephone, a walkie-talkie, a two-way link to God. Prayer was like a radio broadcast going the wrong way. He thought of all the SOS signals from doomed ships as the waters closed, from defeated armies as the bombs fell nearer, the wails of abandoned lovers, cries of battered children, whimpers of beaten horses and kicked dogs, probably the shrieks of agony from trees as they were cut down, from bacteria as they died in trillions in his cookpot, dying even in communion wine, all the futile prayers flying through the universe, dissipating into flecks of pain, silent whimpers in the vast eternal void. He was an empty doll of straw, the grinning magic doll Caterina shook to ward off death while he was giving the last rites, both of them with painted smiles, a vacuous lie. He spiraled in upon himself, disappearing into his confusion. Sweet bleeding heart of Mary, he thought, I cannot handle this alone.

He heard a discreet cough behind him. An odor came, of mossy earth and sunlight in green places, familiar to him but alien on this rocky ridge. He shuddered and half turned. "Father," she said. "Edmundo. Forgive me for disturbing you. We must talk."

"Caterina, please, there's no point." He crossed himself again and stood up to face her where she sat, her legs crossed, on the first board bench. She leaned on one muscled arm, her head wrapped in black cotton, her blood-red shirt glowing in the dim light. How long had she been there? "You have your ways and I have my own. We've been over this before." In a way, he thought, this stocky woman was his arch enemy, the antichrist with her fortunetelling beans and her herbs and incense. She was always summoned to the mats of the sick, the guilt-stricken or the suicidal before he got there, and he was sure they murmured her spirit charms in place of his Hail Marys. She went to bless the singing homes of young lovers or new children before he did, between his visits, and the happy couples waved him away, unnecessary. He heard of her often in his confessional, from anguished young men and guilty farmers, blurting obsessive thoughts that made him blush behind his screen. She and her two bastard children would lead today in the procession for Maximon — and he had to get ready for the procession for San Clemente. He exhaled in annoyance and relief. He had almost forgotten. That would keep him busy, too busy to worry anymore. "Anyway, I haven't got time —"

"The danger is very great. The soldiers might do anything. Miguel won't leave. Can't you send for help; don't you have a radio or something?" She rubbed her hand in slow circles on her striped skirt and Edmundo berated himself. She was afraid. She was no powerful witch but just an ordinary woman, as anxious as the rest of the villagers. Of course she had no magic powers; that was silly, it was heresy even to wonder if she did, and here he had been envious of her curing effort. He was such a sinner, again thinking only of himself.

"No, it's broken, it's been broken for months." His voice was soft. He hesitated and then sat beside her. "Caterina, we can't get any help from outside. We have to face this ourselves, somehow. But we'll be all right. Morales says —"

"Yes, I know what he says. He says all that in the capital, but here — who would care? We're just Indians." Her breath came faster, sweet as moss and heavy. "Father, you know what they do to us, the babies first and then the women, the rest of us. You know what they do. They burn everything after. They would burn the church, Father." She put a hand on his arm. He nodded and rubbed his forehead. Her grip was hard and hot through his jacket sleeve. "They want revenge this time. The barracks really was bombed. Don Cristóbal told me he heard it on the radio. They want to make an example here. We have to do something!"

Edmundo shut his eyes. What was he doing in such a place? He was a singer, for God's sake, a famous boy soprano, pride of his father the music teacher; it wasn't his fault he had grown up and disappointed everyone. He thought of the first massacre he had seen, in Tucuallpa: a mound of fresh-turned earth twenty meters square. By the time he got there it was ringed with silent peasants, eyes glazed, backs stooped with exhaustion. They told him they had buried two hundred friends and relatives, all with their throats slit. In Cuarto Pueblo, in Agua Escondido, in Chacúl, the bodies and the burning huts. In Mariscal province the bishop told him two hundred villages no longer existed and the priest had been killed; could he add that area to his circuit? Everywhere stone-faced widows, hungry babies, glassy-eyed teenagers talking to the walls, dozens of funerals every week, until the earth was full. But it had ended last year, a nightmare that was over, wasn't it, over under this new government? Yet the month before, three peasants had come to Santa Rosa from San Martín to tell of the murder of thirty-nine farm workers, members of a flour mill cooperative. An elder had removed his hat and kneaded it while he talked, eyes streaming into the leather gullies of his face.

"It was guerrillas, Father, subversives in civilian clothes. We know because they shouted, 'Down with the dictatorship!' "

"Did you see their shoes? How was their hair?"

"Boots, they wore boots, new ones. And they had short hair . . ."

"Like the soldiers? That short?"

"Yes, yes, as short as that." The old man's eyes widened. "Ah, Father, was it soldiers who did this thing?" Edmundo was silent. "But how could it be soldiers? Why would they attack a cooperative? We had a government loan! How could it be soldiers?"

Co-ops, communes, what was the difference? Edmundo couldn't try to explain. He comforted the old man. The massacres were ending; surely this would be the last. Perhaps it was the guerrillas after all. The dead would forgive, the memory would fade; soon it would never have been real; perhaps it was unreal already.

Caterina's hand burned his arm. He leaned forward and put his elbows on his knees, dislodging it. "We have to do something, Father!" Her voice shook. "Miguel is innocent. We must save him."

"So you love him then, that silent boy?" The question shocked him.

"A man, Father, not a boy. He is iron and earth. He travels in me. He is more than you think." She stared into the distance a moment, then looked sideways at him. "And if I do love him . . . ?"

"I'm sorry. It's none of my business."

"But it is your business. You must love all of us, mustn't you?" Her hand moved to touch him again. "Even me?"

He stood up. His gut heaved. "Of course, of course. A child of God. All of you." He made an automatic gesture. "But maybe they have something, proof of some kind against Miguel. What do you know really?" His voice was rough, and her eyes widened. Then, slowly, unbelievably, she smiled at him. He gaped as she closed her eyes and opened them again, a gesture so blatantly seductive he flushed. She thought he was jealous! He was suddenly furious. "They asked only for him! They're not going to kill everybody! They could have done it just now, when we were all out there together. One machine gun would have cut us all to pieces. You're wrong. There won't be any massacre."

She was looking at the candles and seemed to have forgotten him. Her voice was dreamy. "They want us to suffer even more. They want us to be hopeful first, and then they will kill us. Or maybe not, maybe they are waiting for something else . . ." She paused. "The officer said we had to do justice ourselves, that we knew what to do. He must mean he wants us all to commit murder ourselves, that's what he wants." She looked at him again, her head tilted, expectant.

"Well, that's ridiculous, that's out of some movie." Edmundo began to pace. He put both hands on his chest, shielding his heart, and looked away. He hoped Joselino would remember to bring a hammer to tack up the decorative paper fringes that had fallen loose from the rafters in a dozen places. The choir would be coming — he hoped they had practiced something that wasn't too shrill. Where was the bucket for the generator fuel? He really didn't have time to stand here talking. God, his gut hurt.

"Look, I have a lot to do this afternoon, I have to think about the homily, about the procession — I don't know what to tell you. There's nothing we can do right now." He tried to will her out of the church.

Caterina remained on the bench. In the dim light from the open door and the ventilation space between the walls and the high tiled roof, her cat's eyes were wells sucking him in. Her high cheekbones cast softening shadows on the angled planes of her face, and she smiled faintly. "Yes," she said. "You have to think. That's a good idea. I'll come back later, after the Mass, maybe later than that. Maybe tonight . . . ?" Her question hung in the air. She looked at his hands fighting with the jacket zipper. "Yes, until later then." She got up and left.

Ten

THE PRIEST TOO! She almost laughed aloud as she swept down the three board steps of the church and into the plaza. That would really be something, to seduce a priest. Odd, she had never thought of him that way before, except he was such a runty pullet, all hunched over in his Yankee clothes. She strode quickly toward Miguel's house, greeting everyone she passed in the narrow passageways, trying not to be distracted by their futures. Miguel; she must focus on Miguel. She pressed against a wall to let Joselino's daughter Juanita by, barely visible behind a wagon of early red chili peppers, and smiled into the haggard eyes. Not long to live now, that one, poor shaky thing. Edmundo would never notice her, so gaunt and bitter; clearly he liked his women solid. Most men did, thank the gods.

A few meters farther came two ancient widows who had probably arrived before sunrise after a three-hour walk from the hills near Tekan, their wired leather arms wrapped over market baskets of peeping chicks and silent, trussed-up hens. What a dismal life, trudging so far so often, and to walk into all this. They should be frantic, but it was clear they were not;

in fact, the opposite — the smaller one was so alight that
Caterina squinted, and the old crone's eyes shone like those of
a girl in love. How odd, to revel in novelty even of death. Such
untied happiness was a rare thing anywhere, and Caterina
stared after them, wondering at the cycle of grace and loss.
    She felt buoyant herself today, powerful. Somehow she
would move the priest to safeguard Miguel; perhaps, if he
had courage, he could bluff the soldiers into letting him leave,
iron messenger of God, and then he could get help, or at least
they would think of that and spare the town. She could give
him courage, all right, the courage all men felt when they had
proved their manhood, but that would take some planning.
Later.
    She turned back to her path and nearly collided with Ar-
turo, his T-shirt straining over his belly, as he emerged from
another passageway. She smiled as she did at everyone, holding
off his leer with her level gaze, pitying the sweaty forearms that
reeked to her of looming death. Such signs intruded everywhere she looked. They had appeared to her from earliest
childhood and led to innocent announcements: Aunt Nelida's
baby boy would do a red dance tonight, could she watch? Marta
won't go to Santa Rosa today because the world will turn upside
down. They laughed and she was embarrassed. But the baby
died in convulsions, spitting blood. Marta was pinned for an
hour under an overturned truck. Caterina's visions began to
frighten her family. Was she a devil's child, to see only pain?
Was she bringing it to Akabal? Speak to us when you see good
things coming, but don't call down death upon us. Still, their
aches drew her touch, glowing at her through the skin, and
where she pressed the throbbing eased, the wound healed
faster, babies stopped their wailing. She knew instantly of
pregnancy, before she knew what pregnant was.
    When she was six she had waked screaming in the morning,
wild in a dream of red sky and white earth changing places.

Scarlet rain spattered the ground, draining the sky white, drowning her parents. She ran crying from house to house to find them, but they had left early for the lime pit and were digging there by sunrise when a guerrilla patrol appeared. That month her father was the village military commissioner, one of the former soldiers named on rotation to be eyes and ears for the military police, collaborators, so the rebels said. He and his wife died in a hail of submachine-gun fire as the humid sky whitened into day above them.

After that, Caterina's uncle Jorge, the village *chiman*, declared Caterina his by her very nature. He made her a child bride of Maximon. In a white cotton robe she paraded through the rutted alleyways of Akabal beside her uncle, who held aloft the grinning wooden god in its chair, her husband ever after. She lived with Jorge from then until the earthquake of 1976, learning from him the ways of herbs and colored earths, the motions of the constellations and the names of the days, the luck of the moon and the legends of Tecun Uman and Quetzalcoatl, who rose to heaven with the morning star. Jorge taught her the legends and the ancient prayers.

> Thou creator and Maker! Look at us, hear us, leave us not, forsake us not! Thou, heart of heaven and of earth! Give us descendants forever! When there is light, give us good and wide roads, give us quiet and peace, give us good life and customs, and being. Thou, Hurakan! Chipi Caculha! Raxa Caculha! Tepew, Kucumatz, who formed us, who made us thy children! Hear us, hear us . . .

Caterina liked to say she had been born old, full of history that had not yet occurred, becoming younger as each day's events left her to reveal themselves to others. As the days drew closer to her surface, pieces of them burst out occasionally through no choice of hers, in visions or dreams. Sometimes she could coax them forth with the holy stones, fragments of the larger stone Jorge said was hurled to earth generations ago by gods angry at the Spanish invasion. If she cast the stones down again with songs to remind the gods of that act, and if the stones were mixed in their fall with certain red bean husks that evoked the people the gods defended, then the gods might make them fall in patterns that the history inside her could recognize, and it would come forth in sympathy, a pattern of words moving before her eyes, sounds coming unbidden from her lips.

This was all as it had to be, the pattern of herself and all around her, forming in one moment anywhere one dot in a vast web of life and time. The web stretched backward and forward beyond mind, endless pathways between acts and decisions made and not made: joinings and aversions, failed chases, successful kills by great beasts long dead and beetles not yet hatched. Every act of least or most of creatures wove the thread anew each moment, bringing to it force and will as they had courage for, insisting with their own particular gravity on influencing the web, creating new directions, new fibers in the weave. Therefore every pattern that existed did in fact reflect the universe, all of its growth and change, millennia of events that went into producing that arrangement at that moment — of tea leaves in a cup, nation-states on continents, cracks on a tortoise shell, entrails in a pig, beans on the ground. Any indicator would do, any dream or shadow, but she was heir to these particular ways of understanding — through the beans, the magic stones.

One night she had tried to explain the making of the world to Miguel, when he had come to her late and dusty from one of his trips, tired and hungry for her tortillas and her warm bean soup. She liked his uncomplicated needs, the smile that turned up four little wrinkles at each corner of his mouth, his perfect teeth. She liked the health that coursed under her fingers in his wiry body, and she liked the way he listened, one eye half shut in concentration.

"Everything we do has roots far in the past and vibrates

forever into the future," she told him. He put down his spoon and leaned beside her on the mat, stroking her hair. She picked up the spoon and balanced it on her finger. "Look now, tell me why the spoon is balancing here."

"Mmm, the weight is equal on both sides." He leaned to kiss her neck.

"Yes, and also because I chose to prove a point to you by balancing the spoon so that the weight is equal." She arched a little so his tongue could reach the sensitive point at the hollow of her throat. "That's the longer view. You're not wrong"— she grinned as his hand moved under her skirt — "but many decisions brought the spoon there, just as they brought you here tonight, and our ancestors to live in Akabal, and the Spanish here in the early days . . ." She pretended severity as he massaged her breast, pinching the nipple to hardness. "Everything we do alters the way everything else will link together in the future, so the future is visible now . . ."

His hand found her warm wet center and moved gently there, while he licked softly between her breasts. His other hand stroked her eyelashes. After a while she lay back, pulling the drawstring on his pants as she moved, grasping him, hard and high as an ear of ripe corn. She lifted her hips to free her skirt. He pushed the folds of cotton up around her waist and moved himself to brush gently, teasingly, back and forth across her gates. Each touch sent light electric jolts to her toes, and she gasped as he entered, filling her emptiness, and they moved together in a rhythm it had taken them many months to find. She felt each thrust as a step toward a summit over which a high wind rolled, driving scarlet clouds through the sky. Faster and faster he pushed, and they rose together, pounding, leaping finally into the wind. She soared into a panorama of sunset over water, dotted with boats and islands, spreading forever beneath them. Gradually she drifted back, the vision fading. A moment later he moved again in tiny tickles within her, making her smile and shudder, rigid once more, small earthquakes rolling outward from her groin, pulling him on. She was infinitely heavy, stuff of earth and weightless starlight, living in all time.

They lay for several minutes unmoving, locked together in the heavy lassitude that follows love. She marveled again at the world-destroying bliss of sex and sighed deeply. He raised himself on his elbows. "Which star did we just alter in its course?" His voice smiled in the dim light.

She had been surprised that he had understood, but really she shouldn't have been. He was always surprising her in little ways, like being so stubborn this morning when she had expected him to be weak with fear. That was what made him good for her, restful: she didn't find many people unpredictable. She knew most people instantly, better than they knew themselves, and they wanted her to guide them, protect them from their follies, encourage them like children, run their lives. But Miguel saw around her corners, noticing things she didn't, somehow, guarding the angles she didn't know existed. He traveled with her, not behind. Would he see now as she did that the soldiers had changed their course forever? His mother, Flora, would have seen it, would know his path. Caterina climbed the high step and knocked on Flora Kanak's door.

"A moment." The voice was sour, distracted, and Caterina braced herself. The old loon was powerful, might have been a *chiman* too if her life had gone that way, but now her energy was unfocused, scattered like buckshot from a rusty gun, and it made one smart all over just to talk to her. The door crashed open.

"Yes? Ah, you. What is it?" The tiny figure leaned out, half crouching, a scorpion startled in its lair.

"Good morning. I'm looking for Miguel to see if —"

"Not here. Nobody's here. Can't even find Irene." She half shut one eye; the other bulged toward Caterina. "You seen her? Off to get water and hasn't come back. The earth delays her, no? What happened at the church?"

"You weren't there? Ah, well —"

"Fool priest banging the bell for nothing. People have work to do. Gods shaking the place down — " She scanned her walls as if looking for cracks. "What do you want?" A gray halo escaped from Flora Kanak's tiny knot of hair, blowing back like Caterina's in the perpetual rush of time.

"Wise one, hear me a moment. There is trouble this morning and it involves your son. I —"

"Miguel isn't here, I tell you. Damn kid looking for him before. Your boy, no? With the useless arm?"

"Yes, Diego. But listen a moment. There are soldiers here, looking for Miguel. That was the bell, to warn everyone. We need to work something out, to get Miguel out of here."

Flora worked her jaw a moment and her voice was a whisper. "He left. When the bell rang. Hasn't come back. Irene's gone too. Hurakan shakes the walls. Soldiers, you say?" Her sunken cheeks stretched taut, and she raised her hand to her chin, then shaded her eyes with an arm thin as firewood. "Army knows nothing. Hurakan speaks and nobody hears . . . nothing here for them." Her voice trailed off to an anxious mutter as she turned abruptly and went back into the hut. Caterina waited, one minute, two. She pictured the old woman hunching over her beans, her stones, hidden in some secret place. Flora returned. "I can't see these soldiers. I look at the signs and they aren't there. But you say they're here? In Akabal?"

A chill raised the hairs on Caterina's arms. The old crone hadn't seen the soldiers coming either. "Yes, across the road now, on the ridge. They're waiting for us. They want Miguel." Caterina stared into the rounded eyes, their depths as dark and violent as her own, and a pit opened behind her chest. She never could see the soldiers, never found them in her dreaming beans, never knew when the rebels would arrive, saw no mark ever of the armed death that soaked the hills. Only vague troubles she saw, death in hints and shadows, pieces that said earthquake or volcano, falls or accidents, sickness or infection. The stones were healers, rectifiers, giving context and the kind of understanding that relaxed, not the kind of information on the radio. But they were infallible, eternal; it was her own distraction, her lack of concentration that made her blind.

"Well, I can't help them. He's not here. No one's here. Go tell them no one's here. No one's here." Flora shook her head and backed into the house, staring at the ground. She stopped and looked at Caterina, suddenly an old, tired woman, terribly afraid. Her voice shook. "If you see Irene, tell her to come home."

Caterina nodded and Flora disappeared. Caterina waited again. Irene, what a waste of time. She was like most of the silly women around here, boring, never said anything, never did anything but weave and cook, a lump of a life, interested only in getting married, having babies. Well, that was hard enough these days, the men dying, the children hungry; staying alive was a respectable ambition, especially now. And the cloth she made did have a little flair. That was Gregorio, of course; he designed it for her. Taking an interest in women's work, how like him not to notice it might cause gossip, seeing only his drawings everywhere instead. Hard to figure what he saw in her, such a zero, her face all teeth and gums whenever she smiled. But she did smile a lot, maybe that was it, the cheerfulness in the face of everything, permanence in all the change. Irene would cook tortillas and weave a few meters of cloth on her deathbed, on the morning of her own death, and die honest and right in every certain choice of her life, Akabal with an unlined face. Caterina sighed. She was getting impatient. The old woman wasn't going to come out again. Frowning, she turned back toward the warren of alleyways that led to the plaza.

Eleven

THE TREMOR caught Miguel and Gregorio talking by the fallow field where they had grown up playing soccer. Safe in the open, they crouched and waited. Miguel clenched his teeth. This couldn't be another big one. The country wasn't ready, the people still hadn't recovered from the last big one in 1976. Although the revolution had ballooned afterward, when masses of people realized the government had stolen most of the international aid, the country was still demoralized. Another quake would paralyze everything. No, this was just a tremor. But another big one could come any time, and what then? Gregorio was still on the other side of that great wall that separated the inert masses of the unreached from Miguel and Nahual and the Guerrilla Army of the Poor and the rest of the worldwide revolution. It wasn't right. He was going to tell Gregorio everything, today, finally, no matter what Nahual had said. Of course Nahual wanted him to wait, to be a secret weapon in Akabal a while longer, until the town was ready to greet the future. Nahual was obsessed with secrecy, and that was good, but Gregorio was different; Nahual didn't understand that. And Miguel might need help here.

Actually he needed help already, that was clear, but there was no way to contact the unit. Nahual had said to lie low after the job, just act normal, and he would be in touch. That was all fine, very good security — if he was caught, he wouldn't be able to tell them where the others were or how to reach them no matter how he was tortured. Even if they used drugs or electric shocks, even if they pulled his fingernails . . . he looked at his fingernails, dirty in the shaking earth. He was a fingernail himself, at the dirty working end of the revolution, a tiny thing that could be pulled off so the arms, the body of the revolution, could survive. He was really on his own now. Gregorio could help, would surely help, the way he always had, but how to ask him? Miguel couldn't just announce that by the way, yes, the soldiers were right, he was a fighter, yes, he had blown up the barracks.

The tremor ended and they grinned at each other, dusting off as they stood up. Little puffs of dust hovered where the earth had taken flight, and they watched the screeching birds wheel into the trees.

"Shall we talk to the earth gods?" Gregorio made a ceremonious bow to the corners of the compass, just in case, and they smiled at their own superstition.

"Not worth it. That was nothing like seventy-six," Miguel said. "If it rumbles first, it's not much."

Gregorio nodded. "We'd better make sure your mother's okay, though." They started toward Miguel's house. Flora would be upset, muttering chants, demanding blessings and apology from the raucous soil, wilder with every tremor.

If only Nahual were there to explain things to Gregorio. He could really talk, that one. He had been a student at the university in the capital before it was closed, and when he told about the oppression, Miguel could see everything as though it were happening right then. Really he had never understood anything before he met Nahual. What a waste his life would have been if that hadn't happened, if he hadn't been working on that particular plantation on that particular day in February 1980 . . . a sodden harvest, sick of eating the landowner's wormy beans and bug-filled rice, he and the other laborers angry that the overseer would not let them leave the farm to buy better food in town. Just as they had stopped arguing that rainy morning, just at dawn as they began to slog through the mud out to the fields, a big flatbed truck had pulled up to the entrance, splashing through the puddles, loaded with new laborers for the cotton. The guards looked at the driver's papers and swung open the metal gates, waving the truck inside. Instantly a dozen men jumped down from the back, wiry and tense, and pulled handguns from their dirty shirts.

"Move over! Get back! Keep quiet!" With both hands they aimed at the guards. "You! Get down! Down on your faces and you won't get hurt!"

Slowly, prodded and kicked to move faster, the beefy men got down on their knees, then to their bellies in the mud, and Miguel gaped at the sight. The rebels were nervous as they disarmed the overseers and tied them up, fairly dancing from side to side, and they waved the confiscated pistols at the cotton pickers.

"You! Listen! We're the Guerrilla Army of the Poor! We're here to organize for better wages, for decent food!" The one shouting was thinner and smaller even than Miguel; his round glasses held together over his nose with tape. "You must all help! There will be a strike here! Nobody is to come to work!"

Miguel's heart jumped. No work? What did they mean? No work meant no wages, no food. He flushed in anger. Who were these criminals?

"We are demanding higher wages! A living wage! A peasant is not a slave!" The skinny one climbed back up on the empty truck bed and waved his gun at them. When their grumbling quieted, he spoke in a lower voice, but still shouting over the rain. "My name is Nahual! I am named for the spirit of the jaguar, the revolution that lives in my heart. And you have this spirit in your hearts also, if only you will look." He glared at them. "Listen to me! You are not slaves! You have only lived like slaves, you and your fathers before you, and their fathers before them, working like animals for these rich men! Look at them! Do they look so rich now?" He waved toward the guards, belly down in the mud, hands tied, their faces contorted in fury and fear.

"These men are slaves too, slaves to the rich men who occupy this plantation! So we aren't going to hurt them. We won't hurt anyone. But the rich men oppress you all. So that time is over! We are here to tell them — you are going to work for five dólares a day, or you are not going to work at all!"

Miguel gasped. Five dólares! He and his friends murmured in horror. From one-sixty to five — it might as well be a million. They shook their heads. "Shut up!" Nahual yelled. "Five dólares a day! What's the matter? That sounds like a lot to you? Don't you think you're worth it?" He waited. "Well?"

Miguel thought. A beer, a bag of beans, a few tortillas. He worked seven days a week, that would be — he could not do the arithmetic, but he knew he had three months' wages in debt at the plantation store already, and would have very little to take back to Flora when the dry season came again. But five dólares a day! The company would never pay them that much; thousands of people waited to get these jobs as it was, and half of them Ladinos. Another worker raised his arm. "We are poor people here. We have to work. You're wasting your time."

"Go back to the city where everyone is rich!"

"Leave us alone!"

Nahual's face flushed. He raised his pistol. "You strike with us or we'll shoot you all!" He glared at them, and his expression changed. "Look. We are your brothers! We are poor too!

But listen, the poor are everywhere! We are many, many more than the rich people who have all the land. Why should they have it all and we have nothing? If we are united, we are stronger than any of the rich. We can fight together! We *are* fighting, the Guerrilla Army of the Poor. We are fighting to bring you justice, to win a better life. If we all work together we can be conquerors. You must join us. We must fight for freedom together!"

They stared at him and shifted their weight. They looked at the guards, hogtied on the ground, and back at this young firebrand, brandishing his pistol. This was dangerous talk; they'd be in trouble just for listening.

Nahual paused. He raised his arm. "We are going to burn the offices."

He jumped down from the truck and gave orders. One rebel held a gun on the guards, another on the cotton pickers. Nahual and two others dashed into the rotting shed by the gate, and Miguel saw one raise his gun butt and smash the lock on the door to the paymaster's tiny office. They staggered out into the rain with a huge cash register, an artifact from colonial times, its silvery curlicues flashing in the gray light.

Nahual hit the NO SALE key. The drawer popped open, full of money. They held it a second so that all could see, and turned it over. Hundreds of dólares fluttered to the mud, multicolored bills flapping away in the breeze, a glitter of coins showering into a pile.

"There! See! This is your money! You have earned it!" Nahual shouted. He was breathing hard. They gaped at him.

Another rebel stepped forward, a small, muscular youth about Miguel's age. He was wearing bright blue plastic sandals and had a broad Indian face. With deliberate care, ignoring his breathless companions, he lit a rag dangling from a beer bottle and sheltered the sputtering fire from the rain until it caught. He tossed the bottle into the dark cubicle.

A deafening flash exploded the window glass through the bars. Heat and flames roared out the door. They all backed away, the rebels laughing in their excitement. "Remember! No one works tomorrow! We will be back!" Nahual shouted over the roar of the burning shed. "No work! Remember! Long live the revolution!"

They dashed back to the truck and piled aboard. It gunned into reverse, mud flying from the wheels, and roared off down the road.

The peasants stood rooted in the smoke, watching the flames, staring at the bills and coins growing soggy and splattered in the rain. The guards struggled and screamed at them — "Untie us! Get over here, you sons of bitches!" — and they shifted from one foot to the other. No one moved toward the money.

"They left it all." Miguel had never seen so much cash.

"They didn't take a centavo."

"I thought they were criminals."

The guards were howling, and when they were untied they swore to kill any man who did not come to work the next day. They ordered the workers into the fields, and Miguel turned to go. Then he hesitated. What about the money? The guards would take the money and blame the rebels. Then they'd have to do something to all the workers, make their lives miserable, to keep everybody quiet. Not that the boss would believe them if they did talk. But still . . .

"What about the money?" Miguel half turned back; he was surprised to hear his own voice.

"We'll take care of the money. You get out there!" The burly overseer loomed behind Miguel, his jaw fierce, but Miguel saw excitement in his eyes. He would be a rich man in moments, in moments.

Miguel didn't move. "No," he said. His friends stopped walking and stared at him. "We stay until the boss comes. We don't want to be blamed if there's any money missing." The other workers nodded and stood with Miguel, the rain cascading from their straw hats.

So that was how it started. The guards shouted and swore and pushed and punched, but they had no guns, and finally they gave up and sent for the owner. Miguel and the others stood silent as the young man sat in the back of his car, watching his men scoop up the dripping cash. He glanced briefly at the bedraggled peasants, and then he smiled, a lazy smile, full of contempt and bored confidence, and he waved at the driver to leave.

The next day no one went to work. The strike was total at that plantation and at three others on the coast road. Miguel stayed all day at a cantina near the beach, talking with other workers around a wooden table. "They didn't touch the money," he said, again and again. "They weren't criminals. And we weren't either."

"We lose a day's pay for nothing."

"Only one day's pay, and we showed them."

"Nothing will come of it. The guards will make us miserable."

"We're already miserable. What more can they do?"

"They'll fire us all."

"They can't. It's too late."

"He's right. They have to get the cotton in this month."

"One day won't do them any harm. They'll fine us for striking."

"Maybe, but maybe not. They have to send us back out."

"It's all a waste of time. Five dólares a day!"

"Five years' pay for all of us in that cashbox."

"Twenty years! And they didn't take it . . ."

That week there were strikes at two or three plantations every day. The rains continued. Signs of mold appeared on the cotton. The following week the radio said the growers' association, because it was generous, because the harvest was good, because of love for the people, had decided to raise the pickers' hourly wage for the rest of the season, in fact to double it, to three dólares, twenty centavos a day.

The workers pounded Miguel on the back. They yelped with joy and pounded each other, and they danced on the table. Miguel sat stunned. He thought his head would burst. A bunch of useless Indians had won a doubled wage. He, ignorant Miguel Angel Kanak, had had a hand in it. He felt as though he had been walking before along a dark path, low trees and bushes meeting in walls on every side, and had emerged suddenly on an open plain that waited in sunlight everywhere he looked, waited for him to make a new path. It was dazzling, terrifying in its brightness. A few weeks later, when he saw the Indian's blue plastic sandals walk into the cantina, he went over and sat down on the same bench.

"What's your name?"

The Indian looked up and smiled. "Xocomil," he said, the relentless mountain wind. Miguel smiled back.

The rest had been easy, almost automatic. Miguel was accepted right away, and stayed on at the coast a week after the cotton was picked to be trained in a forest camp. They marched up and down the little clearing with wooden poles for guns on their shoulders, learning how to turn, how to crawl, how to shoot at shadows. In the evenings there were stories around the fire, tales of skirmishes won, spies in the army, conquests of officers' wives. Xocomil showed him how to make firebombs, how to connect wires to pins, how to mold the plastic to direct the blast. Miguel was nervous at first, but he was a natural mechanic, and Nahual had a way of putting an arm around his shoulders, talking nonstop and waving his hands; he and Xocomil made Miguel feel he was as good as anybody. Nahual himself had even gone along on Miguel's first mission, the attack on the Cotzal guardhouse late in 1980, the mission where Miguel won his battle name.

Nahual still liked to tell new recruits the story.

"There was smoke everywhere, people lying in the street, women screaming, and Miguelito was covered with dust, not fifty feet away, and he just stood there," Nahual would say, laughing. "He just stood there with his mouth hanging open, like this" — and he slumped over with a moron's face. "He was right in the middle of the soldiers, they're running out of the wreckage, running all around him, and they just pushed him out of the way! Yes! They're wild, furious, terrified, but they look at this one and they think, 'No, not this one, not those skinny shoulders, not that ragged hat, not that empty head!' " And Nahual would whoop with laughter. "And then this one goes across the street to a store there and he buys an ice cream cone!" Nahual pounded Miguel on the back. "So that's why he's Helado, see? It suits him, no? Cool and sweet. You listen to Helado."

Miguel never argued, although the truth was that he had been paralyzed at the horrific flash and din, the screams, the blood, and he had barely noticed the soldiers rushing past him. He didn't even remember buying the ice cream; in fact, when he realized he had not run to safety, he was terrified, and thought for many minutes that he had disgraced himself, an idiot Indian struck dumber than usual. But Nahual had embraced him, had congratulated him, had dragged him along in excitement to the safe house, and they had all slapped him on the back, a success, a newly forged comrade, a warrior.

Now he was the best explosives man they had. None of the others, not even Xocomil, had the same feel for the work. His fingers prickled at the thought. He teased his comrades with fuses and wires — "Here, hold this a second" — and they backed away, but they were happy to get his finished devices for their own missions. When it was his turn, he often lingered close to the blast site, as he had this morning at the army barracks, closer than anyone else would dare. He cherished

each packet as a kind of love note, a meticulous message to the
world of a heart's truth he could make heard in no other way.
When he molded the cool, quiet plastic around its wiring, he
talked to the device the way his father had to the gods in the
church, persuading them to help.

"Show the army that it cannot win. Help the people to
understand that if we are united we can never be defeated.
Tell the politicians they must listen to the people. They must
give us our land. Bloom at the moment of weakness for the
Yankee, of strength for the revolution. Help us toward peace."
The explosion always stunned him with its fury, but he had
begun to look forward to that moment of oblivion, waking
from each shock as from a deep dream. Always, after the
troops had run past him, he would marvel at the event with
other peasants nearby.

"Wasn't that incredible? Did you see the blood on the captain's face? I heard there were ten guerrillas. Yes, and five were
women. They were bare-breasted, I saw them myself." Sometimes he would saunter off, other times putter out of town on a
stolen motorbike, or have a tortilla and a soda nearby. Always,
just before he slipped away, he would repeat the line Nahual
had taught him. "Those guys were really brave. They must be
heroes to run such a risk for humble people like us."

Ah, such adventures, wonderful moments. His comrades
sometimes said ice cream was too soft for such a one, and they
called him Supercool and Refrigerator, after Yankee ball
players they heard about on *Voice of America*. But it was better
than any gringo movie, now that he had been reborn, now
that he saw how it all fit together, as Caterina said, going on
about the universe, but even she didn't understand this much.

Oh, it was too cruel not to be able to talk about it, to her, to
Gregorio, to his mother, to that fool of a mayor, to all these
people who thought they could stay out of it, that Akabal
could go on as it always had while the world changed around

them. Only people convinced of their own irrelevance could think like that, only people who hadn't been awakened, only people who were trying to stop history back at the Spanish invasion, the earth stripped bare and sown with slavery and the blinding church, the people hunkered down like rocks, thinking survival was the best they could get. How could he say anything useful to people like that? He couldn't, not if he were ordered to, really. Even Gregorio wouldn't understand, would laugh at him or tell him he was wrong, or argue with him. It would have to be Nahual, the one with the words. For himself, the bombs could speak, they talked for him, for his mother's rage, to avenge his father, to stop the repression, to spread the revolution even here. Someday it would all come here, to Akabal, equality and brotherhood and land to the tiller. But meanwhile . . . he squared his shoulders as he and Gregorio approached the Kanaks' hut, bracing himself for his mother's piercing look. He had to keep calm, keep thinking of Helado and Xocomil and Nahual, keep lying to everybody for a while yet. His heart raced.

Flora Kanak came around the side of the house just as Miguel and Gregorio reached the step. She raised her arms and wailed. "Ahh, my God, my son, my son! Will they take you from me now? Ah, dear God, save us . . ."

Miguel embraced her, feeling bones like tiny rods through the thin cotton blouse. "Mama, it's all right. There's lots of time. We'll fight them, we'll be all right, don't worry." She was so thin, her cheeks so hollow, she didn't eat right, worrying all the time, always restless, always stirring or pacing or rocking on her heels in the doorway, muttering to Hurakan or somebody, half crazy. She deprived herself for him and Irene, working all the time at that backstrap loom, driving Irene, making cloth to sell at the Santa Rosa market.

He looked at Gregorio over her head. Miguel was a failure at supporting the family; he had never been very interested in anything before he met Nahual, and the crops had always been poor even before the fighting kept everyone out of the fields. Now he was away too much; she didn't understand and he couldn't tell her anything. But someday he would set them free of all this, free of the fear and the worry, make them safe and happy, stop her moaning in the night. She looked at him with anguish, the same look she gave him the time he came back two days late from the Easter processions in Chilango, and he had let her think he had been drunk in some ditch. How that had hurt her! Someday he would be able to tell her he had been on a mission for Nahual, he was a hero, Helado the revolutionary. How she would laugh then for joy, and clap her hands! And Gregorio would admire him and marvel at how he had kept the secrets for so long. But he couldn't tell them now, not now. Nahual said women couldn't be trusted to keep secrets, that they told each other everything. Unless they were fighters too, unless they were trained, they wouldn't be able to understand. They had to be protected from the oppressors; it was for them that he worked, rebuilding the world to make it safe for his mother, and Caterina, and Irene. He put his arms around her again, putting all of it into his embrace, feeling her shudder like a bundle of sticks.

"Irene, where is Irene?" She snuffled into his shoulder. "Miguelito, you must go find your sister. Where have you been? That slut came here . . . ah, what will happen to us now?"

"Irene? What do you mean? Who came here?" Miguel held her away from himself and looked at her distorted face.

"She's gone . . . went for water . . ."

Gregorio touched Miguel's arm. "I think I know where she is. Shall I go get her?"

"Who came?" Miguel shook his mother gently. "Mama, tell me."

Flora turned exhausted eyes on Gregorio. "You worthless

fool! The girl's a treasure. You're no good for her, she doesn't want you. Go away!"

"Mama, shush, be quiet. Gregorio, go ahead, go find Irene if you can. I'll stay here." Miguel stroked Flora's hair. "Mama, it's all right, don't worry. He'll bring Irene back."

Gregorio nodded and turned away, toward the path that led down the bluff to the stream. Miguel guided his mother into the dark warmth of their hut.

Twelve

HOW HAD IT HAPPENED, all this confusion, everything upset, nothing visible, the army after Miguel, Irene with Gregorio. Worthless turd. She was right not to let his family into the house when they came singing for Irene to marry him. That whole bunch useless, all of them dangerous fanatics, old Andreas and his peasants' union or the girl Cecilia, half a boy anyway, wearing those boots, or crazy dreamers like the mother Ana and this layabout son of hers. Irene deserved somebody who'd earn a decent living. She was sixteen already and ought to get married soon, but not to him, not him, useless cornweed. Irene was too good, not very lively but hard-working and honest, that should be enough for them. But no, no, Gregorio was in the way. The other men ignored her because of Gregorio. Always hanging about, whispering with her behind the house. "Irene, get in here, what are you doing? Do you want the whole town to talk?"

"It's nothing, Mama, I'll be in in a moment." Not bothering to look guilty, and he calling to her bold as day, "I'm just going, sorry," and they kept talking as if Flora didn't exist. When she ordered her daughter to stay away from him, it didn't matter; Irene didn't answer. She didn't refuse, of course, she wouldn't dare, but she didn't do it. The kids these days were no good. But if Gregorio could find her now, that would be some relief. Stupid girl, making her worry like this. She had better make some tortillas for the day ahead. So much to do! More work now than when they were children . . . they had been such easy babies. What a smile Miguel had as an infant, a dimpled grin so dazzling, so broad, she could hardly bear to look at him for fear Hurakan would be jealous. She had lost so many that way she didn't name this one until he was a year old. If he had no name, he didn't really exist, the gods wouldn't notice him, and if he did die, at least her old shredded heart would have no name to chant. A year was not too long to postpone the dangerous moment when hope was born.

The boy needed tortillas now; look at him, talking about the soldiers. She couldn't make it out. He should lie down and rest a bit, that's right, easy, he got no sleep last night, put the blanket on him. He thought she was asleep when he came in but she had seen everything through the back of her head, felt the sweat radiating from him, that smell of secrets he always wore stronger than ever. Where had he been anyway? She would have to mend that hole where his elbow was coming out. His other shirt had holes too, and the shoulder was torn. With that slut Caterina probably. There was the cornmeal, the lime, there the water, here the board, the fire. Making the dough . . . on Miguel's first birthday she had made tortillas just so, then bundled him, smiling, in that striped blanket, gone now, carried him to the main road, two hours on her back, nothing then, she was getting old, it was still gravel in those days. A truck came by an hour later and took her into Santa Rosa for only fifteen centavos. Dusty streets, so many corners, cobblestones, looking for the register, the market women pointed to the health center at the church. The nuns wore long skirts then. They asked his name for the register and so she said it for the first time, Miguel Angel because of his smile. They smiled too; nobody could resist Miguel Angel's smile. They put him in a scale, cold on his tiny bones, he cried, and they frowned and gave her soap and cornmeal and powdered milk and lectured her like crows, too much about washing and feeding and things she knew better than they did, old women who'd never had babies, never been with a man, what did they know about children. Two more she had had, a girl, another boy, gone early, gifts to Hurakan for his jealousy, keeping him away from Miguel, coaxing Miguel to grow all the time, and finally Irene, sturdy and solid, no worry there, no need to coax the earth into her bones. She was impatient to grow and work and make a future for them, a boy to help farm and cut wood, a girl to cook and weave, to be home taking care of her mother. Flora taught them the legends.

Before the creation there were neither men nor animals, birds, fish, crabs, trees, stones, holes, ravines, grass, nor vines. The surface of the earth was hidden. There was only the sea, and it was calm, and in the sky there was nothing that could make noise. There was not a thing that existed, nothing that had being, only the sea and the still water. There was only silence and tranquillity in the darkness and the night. There existed only the Lord and Creator, Mother and Father of everything, and he lives in the water, and he is called the Heart of Heaven, because he is there and there he lives. His Word came with the lords Tepew and Kucumatz. They talked, and deliberating, consulting, and discussing in the middle of that darkness, they created all the creatures.

Now Father Edmundo had said that after the Word came light, but that was foolish because Hurakan himself was three kinds of lightning, and first made the earth and then animals. But the animals couldn't talk to give praise to the Creators, so they were punished and condemned to be food. Hurakan and Tepew and Kucumatz made the first man out of mud together, but that was a mistake because he had no mind to understand and praise them. So they called in the *chimanes* to advise them how best to make a man to do homage. The priest was blind to say the *chimanes* were evil, for even Hurakan listens to their advice. With the corn and the red beans the *chimanes* decided that a praising man could be made of wood, and the Creators whittled new men. But these men were errors too, because they had no hearts. They forgot to praise their Makers, so the animals ate them. The ones that survived became monkeys. At last the Creators got it right — they made men out of corn, men of thought and heart, men who could and would sing praise, and their singing was all that could preserve them. Silently, she sang:

> Oh, thou beauty of the day! Thou, Hurakan, thou Heart of Heaven and of Earth! Thou giver of our glory and of our sons and daughters! We pray thee to multiply our sustainers and the ones who invoke thee on the road, on the rivers, in the ravines, under the trees and vines. Give them sons and daughters! That they do not find disgrace or misfortune, do not let them be deceived, nor let them stumble and fall. Do not allow any court to judge them. Do not let them fall when they walk up and down the road; put them on the good road that nothing strike them. Do not let them have misfortune or disgrace. God, grant good customs to the ones who must sustain thee! Thou Heart of Heaven, Heart of the Earth! Thou bundle of glory and majesty! Thou who art the four corners of the Earth, let there be peace in thy presence!

She held the tortilla dough as though it were an offering, and sighed. No one knew these prayers anymore. Irene had tried but was unable to remember the words. She didn't even care. And Miguel wouldn't listen. But it was her fault, her fault, she hadn't pushed him, made him stay away from Gregorio and wily Andreas, who tried to make him read books. Lucas fixed that, her poor dead husband, told the gods in the church about it; he had sacrificed a chicken and they were letting his only son abandon him. He told San Clemente he would take the chicken back because what else would they eat if he had no help in the fields. That ended the school nonsense. But Miguel was lazy, lazy, always running in the hills with Gregorio, getting round her with that grin. Even so he might have learned if she'd been harder; now he couldn't even chant properly. That whore Caterina knew the prayers but she said them only at funerals. Too many funerals . . . that was where that *chiman* had bewitched Miguel, at Lucas's funeral, the night of the earthquake. Flora crossed herself. Poor husband, seven years dead now, Benedicto's fault. Him and his damned truck. Hot that year, so hot the old baker's wife fainted in the plaza at Christmas. Miguel and Lucas carried hundreds of buckets of water to the corn, but the stalks could not be consoled at the rain god's abandonment and spurned the river water. Irene stayed in the hut coughing all day. Lucas took Miguel for hours into the hills — he was twelve then but looked about eight, already a man — gathering wood and bringing it back in heavy bags slung from their foreheads, pennies, pennies in the square . . .

So Benedicto came, that slimy young goat, feverish, pieces of him floating off in all directions, he offered the job picking coffee on the coast and Lucas took it. She told him, warned him, the beans said evil, but Benedicto said his truck was fixed, new brakes, two hundred, three hundred dólares for two months of work, and he gave Lucas fifty in advance. She knew it was a lie; you pick fifty pounds of coffee, that's thirty centavos, so it's a hundred and fifty pounds' picking to make a single dólar. And if you break any branches, they take out for it, and for the food you eat, and the truck, and any medicine. Nobody can make a hundred dólares a month, she told him the night before, but he wouldn't listen. Lucas said the wages had gone up, he would be careful, he wouldn't drink, he wouldn't get sick. So she oiled his machete and packed a cloth with fresh tortillas and watched until the group of them walked out of sight toward Santa Rosa and the truck waiting there. That was February first. She remembered the day, because two days later the police brought in his body.

Flora slapped a tortilla on the pan and got up. The tongue was blue, terrifying in the bloody face, he smelled of shit and diesel oil, his hands were mangled, and the front of his shirt was stiff with vomit. The police had found him like that with two others on the highway an hour out of Santa Rosa; horrible; even they were gray in the face. Mother of God, may they all die, let them die in agony, fucking sons of whores, landowners, dog-sucking truck drivers. Damnation, devil on all their bastard children, may none of them live to see the morning. She damned them all, damned even the corn the night that took her husband, screaming, drove poor Miguel out of the house in terror, drove him half-blind, crying across the village all the way to the old *chiman* Jorge's house where his whore niece was, that witch Caterina, waiting for him. What was she then, fifteen? She came back here with him and Jorge and half the village, all of them wailing and yelling, surrounding poor Flora, voices helping her call down the gods. So many chants, so many times for wrongs done, dulling the knives of pain, singing curses into the night. Caterina's yellow eyes pinning Miguel through the fire smoke, saw it coming for sure . . .

Three in the morning it was, the gods heard, arrived in a thunderbolt that kept roaring, embers leaped at them out of the fire, the ground heaved. Flora thought someone pulled the mats from underneath, everyone fell over, they could not hold on to the ground. The wall bulged in waves, rippled like a curtain, then broke slowly into pieces, every particle and dusty stone drifting out over them light as pollen, floating over Jorge, pillows for his gaping mouth. The rest of them kept getting up, falling down, getting up, the door flowing away, ground a bucking horse ... then the world stopped moving, like a breath held, taut as a loom string, the gods listening to see whether it was enough. Yes, yes, enough for her, triumphant wrath of Hurakan and Kucumatz, blessings from them for her rage and grief. But not for Caterina, no, she screaming, Jorge! Jorge! and all of them but Flora digging, digging as she smiled; she knew they were too late to stop the sacrifice.

More shocks then, the mountains rattling for days after, like children crying until they could only gasp, everyone sleeping in the plaza, stars hot and blind. Only three dead here, Hurakan just, thousands dead in the towns and cities, the world sending aid, the radio said. But nothing here, nothing changed; they shoveled up the ruins and went on as before.

Yes, all of it the same now, no vengeance yet. The funeral day, for Lucas and Jorge and the other two. Joselino came back from the south and stood waiting outside her house to tell the story, how Lucas had died in the truck. The ancient truck, he said, jammed already when they got there, the driver half drunk and drinking, Ladino, didn't speak the language, Benedicto reassuring, no problem, waved them out of sight, the back boarded shut to hide the overload, full of fumes right away, nobody could breathe. Screaming, shouting, pounding on the walls but no one heard them. Lucas, shorter than Joselino, couldn't fight to the air at the top; he fell under their clawing hands. When the driver stopped to pee, he heard them, opened the truck, but Lucas and the others were dead by then, trampled where they fell.

She asked — very calmly, she thought — where the driver was now, what was his name, but Joselino backed away and then he ran from her, the fire leaping from her body. Miguel was there, crying, Irene too, thin sapling and heavy tree clinging to her skirt. She hadn't seen them in days, too big to cry

now, she told them, shut up. Ah, Miguel, you must avenge this
death, you must remember this day, this horror, grow strong
in Hurakan and Kucumatz, but he had cringed from her,
afraid, and she had seen it, he was not the one, and Irene
couldn't learn the words. So she told the beans herself still,
heard the moon speak, tried to see the soldiers coming where
they flowed in the valleys, but they slipped through her
strings, hers and Caterina's, she was blind and old and useless.
Even Irene was leaving her, half gone already with this lout
Gregorio.

At least now Gregorio would have to do the ceremonies, the
four rites. She kneaded the dough harder. Old Andreas and
Ana, toothless hag, would have to come for the formal visit to
tell her Gregorio's virtues and his faults, as if she didn't know
already. They would bring her something good to eat and
Gregorio would kneel to her, respectful once in his life. Then
they would bring the lambs on the wedding day, the soup, the
seventy-five tamales if they had enough money. She would
have to make the guaro somehow, liquor for the neighbors,
even old Honorio Luxit would come for that, and Caterina
would hang about on the edge, looking for business. The pots
and mats weren't ready, she'd have to start making them soon,
and Irene would have to learn the wedding prayers, she would
drill her until she cried:

> Mother Earth, may you feed us. We are made of maize, of
> yellow maize and white maize. Father and Mother, Heart of
> the Sky, may you give us light, may you give us heat, may you
> give us hope and punish our enemies, all those who wish to
> destroy our ancestors. Poor and humble as we are, we will
> never abandon you.

She put her hand to her mouth. Those who wish to destroy
our ancestors. My God, what time was it? The soldiers were

out there. Why hadn't Gregorio come back with Irene? Probably he had found her and they were off somewhere together. God knows what they were doing. Here she was, planning a wedding and they could all be dead by morning and no one here to help her. Miguel was asleep; how could he lie there sleeping when the army asked for him by name? They were everywhere, invisible, but that was not her fault; politics was Cristóbal's ground. He would handle the soldiers, and the priest too, if he could, poor shadow. But the spirits were thin at Akabal, winds of empty words howling in the hills, evil hissing up everywhere, closer and drowning out the Creators. Hurakan's sleep was lonely, he turned restless this morning; her small songs alone were not enough to soothe him. Soon he would wake again as he had seven years ago and wipe out the forgetful.

Miguel turned restlessly on the mat, the soft dry rustle a comfort to her, the clean swept earth beneath, the dark red embers nearby, warm and hopeful, and she knelt beside him. Lucas had been hopeful, too trusting, ignoring the warnings. Miguel was like that, forgetful. Would Hurakan forgive him? He must be forgiven.

"Miguel! Did you do it, what the soldiers said?"

He rolled over and blinked. He looked at her and seemed to fade; she stared through shadows flowing over his face. He propped up on one elbow. "No. Why do you ask me this?"

"Why are they here? You came home too late. I saw! You stink of secrets . . . tell me!"

He looked toward the door, back to the fire, a hunted creature, and she felt a sob rise in her breast. "Tell me!"

"Mama, I didn't do it, not what they say, truly. I never killed any woman or any child like that. They made the story up, it's a lie! They did it themselves." He flared like a new lamp.

"Yes . . . yes, that's true. I believe you." If only she had taught him to sing. But the shadows were still there, heavy, dark over half of him, part of him hard to see. "And the rest of it, the barracks . . . ?"

He looked away again, breathing hard. She was choking. "For you, Mama! For you! And Irene! And —"

"Aieee . . ." She covered her face with her hands so as not to see him anymore, to hold herself inside her skin, too weak a wall itself against the rotting world.

He was holding her. "Mama, Mama, don't you remember? It was you who wanted it, you told me, you told me avenge Papa's death, never forget. Well, I didn't, I've been doing that now, all the time I work for it. I've tried to tell you, I wanted to, I'm a warrior now, Mama, but it never seemed like enough, not enough for you, not for him, I meant it all to be better, so much better for you, don't you see . . ." He was shaking her and she pushed at his hands.

"What are you saying, you aren't making sense, I don't understand . . ." Her loss, her failure, her lack of faith had done this.

"Mama, I'm a warrior, they call me Helado. I do the bombs, the plastic, I'm good at it, Mama. The barracks, that was nothing, the place should have been bombed years ago. I'm a guerrilla, Mama, one of the Guerrilla Army of the Poor. You know about us, you remember when Nahual came here —"

"Nahual? A jaguar?" He was talking nonsense, nonsense.

"Yes, the leader, my leader, when he came three years ago and made a speech in the plaza, you remember, after I went to the coast . . . Mama, I brought him here, after the strikes, we got double pay, remember? It was Nahual who did that, he's my leader, don't you see?"

"No, no. I don't see anything. What are you talking about?" He grasped her shoulders and held her still to face him, pushing through the fog. She shut her eyes, hot and wet.

"Mama, listen to me. Look at me. I'm trying to tell you. I've been wanting to tell you for so long, so long. Please understand. Listen to me. It's Nahual, my leader. He runs my unit,

my unit of the Guerrilla Army of the Poor. You know what
that is. Think a minute."

She was still. But he was wrong, wrong. This was not happening. "Your leader. To what? Where is he leading you?
What is all this?" She focused hard on him, willing his shimmer to be still in the shifting light. He sat back and cleared his
throat.

"It's a revolution, Mama. We're all involved, everybody
who's poor or who understands. We're fighting for freedom,
for land and justice and our rights. We're not slaves anymore,
Mama; those days are over."

He took her hands. "Nahual is wonderful. He's a student, he
knows history and the capital, he's only one of thousands,
Mama, and we're all together, we have to be united, and we'll
never be defeated."

"United in what? You tell no one, all this a secret even from
your own mother, and you say you're all united?" She got up
and fought the shadows to see him clear. "This is all dreams,
silly talk! You're a child yet! What about me, what about your
sister? Think about Irene, how does she live with this? You
sound like something painted on a wall!"

Miguel frowned and stood beside her. Heat came from him,
an alien force, fading the shadows, pushing against her. "You
know what I mean. This is bigger than the family. The whole
country is changing, the whole world. We're getting rid of all
the crooks and the fascists who run this place. We'll put a new
government in the capital, a government of the people, of
farmers and peasants and students and workers —" His words
flowed into each other, a jabber from the radio at Cristóbal's shop.

She pushed his arms away. "That's fool's talk. Do you think
I'm an idiot? How can you talk like that? What do we care
about the government? What good ever came from the capital? This is madness . . . and you! You think they'll ever let an
Indian do anything? Your student, this leader, does he carry

his own books? Not long, not when he has an Indian around to do his dirty work. That's what we're for to them, you know it, don't you ever forget it! Oh my gods, Tepew, Kukumatz . . ." Must find the dreaming beans, ask in a different way, somehow get through the fog here . . . She fumbled in the shelves.

"Mama, listen to me." He took her shoulders again. "Think of the quetzal. I'm helping build a quetzal's nest, a place for freedom here, to bring back the quetzal even here, can you see?"

Green and gold flashed at the corners of her eyes, the bird struggling to be seen, its last strength gone, pushing at the heavy black. She turned quickly but it vanished. Darkness . . . her heart snapped. "Ah, my son, my son . . ." She fell into his arms, dark, lost. "My soul, my treasure . . . our people are all dead, our ways are gone, my mother, my father, Lucas, sisters, brothers, all gone, gone . . ."

"It's all right, Mama . . ."

"Nobody left, no one to sing . . . now you and Irene are leaving too. My heart is worn out, I'm dying. I can't — the soldiers —"

"It's all right, Mama. Nobody knows it was me. The village is on our side. Gregorio will help, the priest, we'll all fight if we have to. Don't worry about it anymore."

"Fight . . . ?"

"No, no, there won't be any fighting. Listen, sit here a while and rest. I'll go wash and we'll eat a little, and then we'll be all right. Everything will be fine, you'll see."

"But Irene . . ."

"She'll be back in a little while. I'm going out now to wash, so you heat the beans and we'll eat. Your nice tortillas are still hot, see here? We're all set. Then we'll go to the church. All right?"

"All right. All right . . ."

Thirteen

EDMUNDO MOVED from group to group in the crowded chapel, sweating lightly in his JESUS SAVES T-shirt. Smoke from scores of candles eased the ragged outlines of men and women standing, eyes closed, in the nave talking intimately to God, their palms uplifted, dark seamed hands and blackened nails heartbreaking in the soft light. He wished fleetingly, as he nodded at the old crones, smiled at their grandsons, that he could eavesdrop on the holy answers they seemed clearly to be receiving. So many people! He hardly knew Akabal had this many. Several held up baskets of corn, others a few tortillas. The drone of voices at prayer reverberated off the tile roof. The priest set Joselino to sweeping between the villagers clustered before the saints, warning him not to jostle anyone. A dozen children shoved and pulled at his shirttail, clamoring how good they had been since his October visit, and he chose three at random to fetch the stacks of long green pine boughs from the back of the jeep. "Spread them out now, all over, more in the front there. No hitting!" The sweet pine scent gentled the air, the children's giggles becoming music over the murmur of their parents pressing medallions on the crowded plaster around Saint Helena, patron of the province, protector against earthquakes.

Edmundo moved toward the altar and his late morning ritual, blessing bowed heads as he went. The beauty of simple faith always moved him more than he expected. Such refuge these people found here, which he had accidentally brought them at a time like this. It was a false sanctuary, though, the refuge of routine things, of coming to church as if no soldiers watched them, as if life would continue in its drab course if they insisted on it strongly enough. His despair and jealousy and reverence together were too much; they made his throat hurt.

He saw Arturo among the many beseeching Saint Christopher against sudden death. Ana de Córdoba had been pressing her lost causes before Saint Jude for more than an hour. The largest group murmured and gestured at Saint John the Baptist, friend to the farmer, warning him to provide good corn crops this year or else. How privileged they were to be on such close terms with God that they could threaten Him about the future in the face of death a few hours away! He shooed one of the scrawny dogs that wandered here and there, looking for handouts and licking the faces of the babies swaddled on the backs of the kneeling women, and his pain eased. He was talking to his peer. Like the dog he lived on scraps, tastes, stolen bits — just enough belief to keep going. But it was enough, after all.

The priest put his case on the side of the altar and opened it, revealing a shiny hand-held microphone. Joselino followed him through the side door of the nave into the shed and together they hauled the cranky little generator out from under Edmundo's cot. Unused since the last priestly visit, the ancient machine powered the lone light bulb over the nave, the other one over the cot, the microphone, the speakers that weren't really necessary in the tiny church. The microphone especially was a totem, a sign of the progress and modernity the church was trying to bring to places like this all over the world, places where none of it was necessary. The priest popped off the generator's dusty cover and they examined the innards.

"It won't work," Joselino said, squatting like a boy on his heels.

"Yes it will. Have faith." Edmundo found a loose wire and examined it.

"Such a lot of noise here, Father. As if a basket of corn could get Saint Christopher to save us." He scratched his stubbled chin.

"And why not? The giving is the thing; you know that. Why not a basket of corn?" He bent to strip the wire with his teeth.

"Well, Saint Christopher, he's too busy. The soldiers talk to him too. He's on both sides; he won't help us just for some lousy corn."

Edmundo grunted, splicing the wire. "How do you know? Maybe he'll help everybody — save all of us, keep the soldiers from hurting anyone, that's good for them too, isn't it?"

"Yes, but not just for some corn! We're too poor here, that's why we have no justice."

"No, now you know that's not right. Here, try it again."

Joselino hauled on the starter. "Nothing. It won't work. Listen, the whole universe runs on pull. The saints are fixers, just like in Santa Rosa. You pay enough, you get one on your side, your papers get approved, you don't get arrested, you can see the boss — it's the same as here. No different. If you pay enough to the right guy, you're all set. Otherwise —" He flicked his fingers under his chin.

Edmundo hunched over the generator, wielding the broken screwdriver, and spoke through clenched teeth. "Joselino, God is not a gangster!"

"Oh, I didn't say He was, Father, but isn't that why there are so many saints? I mean, the corn won't be enough for Saint Christopher, with him so popular and all that, but maybe it's enough for some poor old saint over in the corner. Maybe she'll do the work for you. And if she doesn't, you can take it home again and she won't be able to get back at you. Some of these saints are very lazy, you know."

Edmundo rubbed his eyes. "Joselino, if the cow dies or the crops fail, it is not because you didn't give enough corn to the right saint. It's part of God's grand plan, it's a destiny much bigger than any one single person. You know that. Remember the catechism? Anything that seems wrong really isn't, if we can only understand it. That's why —"

"That's why we need to have faith, yes, I know, Father. Poor humble creatures like us can't see very far, like ants in the grass. That's why the saints can take advantage of us. We're too poor, see, and that's why the soldiers are out there and we're in here fiddling with this thing." He gave the generator a swat.

Edmundo sighed. "Let's take it outside and try it again." They stood up and, grunting, carried the heavy machine out of the shed to the open space near the latrines. Joselino pulled the cord. On the third try the generator roared into life.

"There, you see? A little faith, a little corn —" Edmundo grinned and Joselino shook his head. They unrolled the cable from the chugging thing back through the shed and into the church, threading it between the people kneeling at the altar, and hooked it to the hand microphone.

Edmundo tapped the round metal knob and the speakers beside him blasted three explosions into the church. The babble ceased and all eyes turned to stare. "Testing, testing. *Credo in unum deum.* Testing, testing." His little joke. He turned the volume down, stepped back, and ran a hand through his wispy hair.

"Joselino! What about the choir?"

"Oh, they'll be here, Father, they're coming. They've been practicing all this month. And Genero even has a solo almost ready. You'll be pleased, it's very special, I promise."

"All right, all right." He looked at his wristwatch, plastic blue and green band, match for his jacket. Eleven-fifteen. "Well, we're late already. Might as well get started." He rummaged in the briefcase for a smudged and crumpled piece of paper, covered with the multicolored scrawls of half a dozen hands, and gave it to Joselino. "Here, get the announcements over with."

Joselino took the microphone and gazed a moment at the roiling scene before him. He held the silver cone very close, and slowly, voluptuously, cleared his throat.

The roar from the speakers shook the church. Everyone jumped. Joselino smiled broadly. "Good morning, brothers and sisters. Welcome to the house of God." A baby wailed. People surged onto the benches, shuffling, muttering, climbing over each other, pointing and calling, crowding the floor in front, the sides of the altar, the back near the door. Men and boys sat on the left, women and girls and babies on the right. A dog squealed. Several children came running in from the plaza, infants coughed and sneezed, many voices murmured in greeting and subsided into whispers. Dust and smoke misted the air.

"Today we are very lucky to have with us our most respected and honorable Father from Santa Rosa, friend and brother to all of us." He gestured to Edmundo, who stood with his back to the crowd, unpacking his case. "He'll be talking to us in a moment about all the troubles we face today. First you must listen closely." He cleared his throat again. A few girls giggled, another baby cried out.

"The powdered milk and flour will be distributed after the service right here." He waved toward the shed. "Sick babies and toothaches should go to Don Cristóbal's to wait for Father to attend them there . . ."

Miguel slipped into the church from the shed entrance, and a murmur swept the audience. People craned to see him, pointing and whispering as he pushed through four rows of women and nursing babies sitting on the floor. He nodded toward the priest's exasperated glance, genuflected, and began to light the candles on the altar table.

Edmundo mentally forgave the scrawny youth his tardiness. It could not have been easy for him to show himself, especially here where his neighbors were trying hard to deny the awful problem he had become. Edmundo unfolded the long white alb from its niche in the case and slipped the thin cotton over his head, pulling the zipper up to his chin. The high collar closed around his neck. With this ring I thee wed. Tension drained from his forehead. The muscles around his eyes relaxed, and he straightened his hunched shoulders. Ease flowed into him as it always did at this moment, but still it surprised him with its strength, and a shiver of pleasure ran down his legs. He bowed his head to welcome the shard of grace. Blessed are we who are about to receive . . . He lifted the tiny green and gold square from its hollow and let the silken stole cascade like water from both sides of his hand, impossibly long and rich symbol of hope. He kissed it, inhaling sunshine and incense. Would he have brought the red one instead, symbol of martyrs, if he had known? He put it around his neck, smoothing the square ends in front to cling to his gown.

"Father will hear confessions this afternoon, after lunch, before the procession . . ." Edmundo tied the white cotton rope around his waist, knowing every eye in the building was riveted by the dazzling white robe, ironed cloth from another planet than Akabal's. He bowed his head and turned around, noting that his right big toe was only a few threads away from emerging through the top of his running shoe. "Don Bartolomeo Torazo of Tekan sends word that he has lost three cows, all branded with his mark. He offers a reward to any who find them . . ." Miguel handed Edmundo the breviary and stood ready with the smoking censer.

The shed door banged open. Half a dozen men and women burst in, colliding with the rows of women on the floor, climbing between them, muttering apologies. Edmundo raised his eyebrows. The heavenly choir had arrived. Stumbling, bowing, genuflecting, they at last arranged themselves in two rows behind Joselino as he droned on.

"And finally the events of this morning. They are well known to all." He glanced toward Miguel, who gazed at the ground as most of the congregation turned again to stare at him. "It is a terrible thing we face today. Let us think carefully today about what is our duty, what is our responsibility to our fatherland, to the will of God. Let us take time —"

"Time for the song now, Joselino." Edmundo put his hand on his assistant's shoulder.

Joselino's narrow face flushed and he bowed his head. "Let us take time now for a song, a very special song of new things." He turned and handed the microphone to Genero, who had put on a clean shirt and slicked his hair to a gray helmet.

The old carpenter nodded and smiled. He lifted the microphone and his eyes glazed into the far distance.

> Together like brothers
> Members of a single church
> We are walking together
> To an encounter with God . . .

Caterina, looking out over the plaza from the bottom of the church steps, smiled and shook her head as the tinny speakers propelled the old man's piping through the open door. As if driven off herself, she paced ten steps from the spot where the three board steps vanished into the hard-packed earth, sighing as she moved. She wished the church were a proper home for the gods of air and water, who looked so funny in there in the robes of the immigrant saints. Then the little building would have twenty-two steps, thirteen for the layers of the heavens and nine for the layers of the nether world. She spread a striped cloth on the spot of her last step and sat down, making herself comfortable between heaven and hell.

Other villagers had established little spaces around the square, dappling the sunlight and the shade, heaping their produce for the afternoon market. Piles of cucumbers and eggs hid their faces, or waxwood kindling or bags of meal and lime for tortillas, dug from the white caves. The candle seller was counting her take from people who were already burning the long-wicked tapers on low metal platforms at the back of the church — red ones for help in love, green for business, dark blue for work, sky blue for money and health. She had probably sold many black and brown ones today, protectors against enemies, against the sins of others. Caterina closed her eyes and sang under her breath:

> The subject is single.
> Observation changes the subject.
>
> Anything is possible
> Keeping the rules.
> To know the laws
> Everything can teach.
>
> When is the test
> When is it not
>
> Women enforce for surviving
> Men break for changing.
> Allegiance is all
> Testing is all.
>
> I am weak
> I diverge from the rule without help
> I am strong
> I diverge from the rule without help
> Tell me.

She waited. Nothing. She frowned at her stones. The beans and pebbles spoke an ancient language to each other, the lives of male heaven and female earth, their children thunder and wind, water and fire, mountain and desert. Each had its own *nahual*, animal spirit, its home in a part of the body, its own personality; that vocabulary framed the questions and the answers. Had the gravity of the hulking soldier altered the stars in their courses this morning? She cast the stones again and pondered.

A pair of leather shoes appeared beside her hands. She knew them from their deep glint, like pond water under a fine haze of dust. Benedicto Tijax squatted beside her, hitching his pants to preserve the crease, and handed her an orange.

"A treasure for my treasure."

She smiled at him and took the fruit. "To the hands of the gods. You'd better get in to Mass or the Father will frown at you." She bit off the end of the orange and peeled it, pleased at its waxy nubble, its sharp aroma. Typical of him; little courtesies, small gifts.

"Your frown is the only one I notice. Listen, my heart. You must tell me if my truck in Santa Rosa will make it safely to the coast today. It doesn't look as though I'll get there to send it off."

She held out an orange section for him. He looked not at it but at her and leaned forward to lick it once, then slowly took it in his mouth. She laughed. He was a hungry lover, demanding, whispering urgency and pain, and she played him like a fish, laughing at his ecstasy on the hook. Not at all like Miguel. Miguel was like a racing horse thundering along, and it was she who exulted in hanging on, moving at a pace just short of alarming. With Benedicto she could explore his every cell, teasing him while he chafed, his gift helpless until she took it.

"No, they will wait for you there. I can see clearly they will sit in the cantina waiting, even if you do not come for days yet, and then they will charge you for the beer they drink to ease their boredom."

He grinned. "I guess I didn't need you to tell me that."

She flashed her gold-rimmed tooth at him and waited. Last night, very late, he had promised to bring her back some new shoes for Diego on this trip to Santa Rosa. The boy outgrew everything so fast these days, and Benedicto could be generous, if he didn't lose his good intentions in the bottom of a bottle. Sometimes he left for a few days and was gone a month, six weeks; he was gone a full year not long ago, and returned with only a shrug for those who asked where he had been. "Working," he had said. "In the south." She hadn't wanted to know any more.

He took another orange section, this time with his fingers. "So what have your beans told you today? Will Miguel give himself up?"

"Don't make jokes. He's innocent of all that. He just has enemies. He's not political, he's too . . ." She stopped.

"He's too stupid, isn't that right? Come on, he's nothing, he probably put his X on some petition and they're just going down the list."

"No, he wouldn't do that. But I don't understand . . ." She frowned.

"What?"

"I don't know why I didn't see this coming. I'm supposed to know these things, but I didn't. Nothing. I feel responsible." The confession made her throat tighten.

Benedicto lifted her chin with his finger. "Don't be silly. There's no logic to the army, nothing rational about it. No reason anybody should be able to tell what they'll do next."

"No, everything should be here, right here." She sifted the beans through her fingers, restless. They felt cold. "It's my fault. I've been too confident, maybe just too lucky for too long. I've become careless. I haven't been wrong too often, you know." She gave him a keen look, and he nodded, obedient. This irritated her. His readiness to say what was expected made him shimmer in her gaze, his outline losing substance like a reflection in water. "I have to make some kind of a test . . ." She glanced toward the church, at the villagers streaming in.

Her annoyance seemed to trigger something behind her eyes. She closed them and sifted the beans again. The scene trembled into focus. "The earth moves," she said. A bird called, a *cucucu*. "Indian dies." The images came in a rush. "Sharp noises. A quetzal. Four quetzals! But only one flies. Hovering, not leaving . . . A white cloth, moving in the wind." She opened her eyes. "The earth closes. That's all." She sat back, agitated, frowning.

Benedicto put a hand on her shoulder but she shrank back. "Another earthquake? Four Indians die in an earthquake?" For once he was not laughing.

"I don't know. Maybe. Four quetzals! That's the first time I've ever seen that. I don't understand it." She pressed her lips together. After a moment she sighed. "Well, what do you think? Have you heard anything?"

He shook his head. "You're the one with the visions."

"Yes, normally, but you — ears."

Instantly she felt he had leaped away from her, although he did not move. Long threads shimmered away from him toward the hills, fragments of his attention moving toward something much stronger than she. She tried to see deep into his eyes, but his pupils were tiny, closing her away.

"Yes, I have ears. I share all I know with you, Caterina. You know that." He reached for the last orange crescent and glanced around them as he savored it. The old carpenter still sang in the church, people stood at its door, unable to push in, and the plaza was full of people ignoring the service, talking, laughing, gesturing, arguing. Snatches of conversation floated past.

"But Miguel never . . ."

"The soldiers wanted him to . . ."

"You call that a chicken? So thin it . . ."

"But I thought he said . . ."

"So then if we made a . . ."

Life, raw life teemed around them in blind faith it could last forever. He inched closer on his heels and took her hand. "My heart, listen to me. We can be very good together, here, anywhere." His voice dropped to a whisper. "Come on, let's get out of here. We can leave now, together, I'm sure we can get out. Let's go."

"Go?" She looked at him in wonder. "Get out? How can we get out? What do you mean?"

He made an impatient gesture. "No, just trust me. Come on. Let's go. Please." He stood up, still clutching her hand, and she stared up at him. Then she burst out laughing.

"Ah, you old goat. You're amazing, you're never satisfied." She withdrew her hand and waved him off. "You had me for a minute there. Go on, go away. If you're nice, maybe I'll come see you tonight." She laughed again and shook her head.

He stared at her. "No, you don't understand. I'm trying — I can —" He clenched his fists. "Caterina, please!" Caterina laughed, and two old crones nearby laughed too and held up a cackling chicken for his inspection. He flushed. The whole square was grinning at him. He turned violently and plunged toward the church. A dog squealed and jumped aside, dodging his kick. The women doubled over in merriment. Caterina watched him shove his way into the church, and her laughter drained, leaving rocky unease in her chest. She picked up the stones and the beans again and looked at them. They seemed too large. She was a moment, a mote caught on the web, she and Miguel and Benedicto and the rest of them, but Akabal had its own thread somehow, and she couldn't see it. What would happen to Akabal? She cast the markers down again and closed her eyes, opening her mind, waiting for the words to come.

Bless us, old Hurakan, for we are lost and alone on the mountain and all around are demons . . . Thou Creator and Maker! Look at us, hear us, leave us not, forsake us not . . .

Gregorio, at the far end of the village, where he stood at the top of the bluff above the stream, could still hear the metallic edge on Genero's high song. "Irene!" No answer. He had asked at half a dozen houses on his way but got shrugs from the few still at home. The only place left was their listening spot on the boulders below, around a slight turn in the stream from the flat laundry rocks.

"Irene!" He loped down the ancient path. Countless times they had walked here together, laughing at whatever trick he had used to evade her mother. That old crone, what a great ravaged face she had, full of sharp angles and ravines, and he had drawn it often. He had expected Irene to laugh when he showed her what he thought were the best sketches a few months ago, but she shook her head. Too vicious; she's not as hard as that, she's just disappointed, not cruel.

"Disappointed?" he had asked as they sat on the warm stone.

"Yes. It's so hard for her, things changing so fast. She wants us to be the same as she was, the songs, the festivals, the rest of it. But Miguel can't; he's gone working all the time and doesn't care about any of it. And I can't either, I can't learn it, it's just too much. She's so disappointed in us."

"She's just hanging on to the past, as I hang on to you. I can understand that." He tried to redraw Flora's asymmetric eyes, to oust some of the fury with sadness, and found the rest of the face had to change too, the lines moving in different contours. "You're right. It looks more like her." He picked up her hand and kissed it. "My life . . . you keep me honest. My Irene . . . I need you so much. Listen, why can't we just go away from here?"

"Don't start."

"Sometimes when I think about what's happened to all of us — Cecilia, everything — I just want to fly apart, just run away. But you" — he squeezed her hand — "you've got so much good sense, you're my rock. I feel calm when we're together, like a whole person. If I couldn't talk to you . . ." He shook his head.

She had traced circles on the back of his hand that day. "Just be patient a little longer. She'll come around."

"No, she won't. She won't even talk to me."

"You should be grateful. When she gets angry the earth moves."

"Like my father."

"No, she's the opposite of him. He rages because there's no change and she rages because there's too much."

He grimaced. "They're both wrong."

"Oh, yes. Or maybe they're both right. He thinks change is good, that it's the same as progress, even. And look what happened to him — arrest, torture, the rest of it. And she's terrified of anything new. Only the old ways are safe, but they're disappearing, and she's scared."

They were quiet. "Is there anything new on Cecilia?"

"No, nothing."

His sister suffered while he sat in sunlight with a woman he loved. He had stroked the back of Irene's arm, tracing the muscle that braced her upright, and touched her dark braids, the lacy collar on her shoulder. He moved his hand down her breast, and she arched a bit. He leaned hungrily to kiss the roundness that lay heavy in his hand, and she rubbed the back of his head and embraced him. He urged her down on the stone and they pressed together, urgent, reaching. But as he moved and groped at her skirt, she eased herself sideways and out from under him. "We mustn't, my love. We've waited so long . . . I have so little to give you when we marry, I want to have that at least. Please . . ."

He had sighed and rolled over, shading his eyes from the dappled sunlight.

"I don't think Flora will ever let us. I thought we'd made some progress with the pattern business, but nothing happened."

She had laughed and nestled her head against his arm. "That's because she already thought it was a scandal I was going to the market anyway, and then you drew her into it too, so it's worse now, not better." She stroked his cheek. Irene had always been one of the fastest weavers in Akabal, sitting daily over her backstrap loom to make the striped cotton cloth that became skirts for village women all over the province. Once a month she and Miguel carried it to market in Santa Rosa, where a dozen women from a dozen other villages converged to sell identical cloth, chatting and laughing between familiar customers. It was the custom.

About a year before, she had sighed to Gregorio at their listening place of her boredom making the same patterns over and over. Not that she would want to change them. The ancient designs told history, legend, medicine to anyone who saw, stories of the quetzal and the battles and the sacrifices, but they were losing their memories in shoppers used to seeing flowered polyester and Yankee cowboy prints a few stands away. Gregorio looked at the patterns with her and she told him the stories she had learned from Flora, about the four hundred youths who marched around the skirts here, died in drunken battle there with Zipacna, creator of the mountains, and became the stars. He doodled with the chevrons and rosettes and stylized faces that interlocked in the alternating stripes of blue, black, and green, and toyed with different widths of the yellow and lavender accent stripes. He brought Irene a new pattern that used the ancient colors but spread the design over several rows, and another that arranged the chevrons into winged birds, a monkey, a stalk of corn. She was briefly shocked, then amazed at the new energy in ancient forms, and at length she was delighted, seeing the fire of the stories glow again, as though in a new language. Secretly, late at night, she wove the patterns into one new strip of cloth, and showed it one morning to her mother.

Flora was upset at first, but was at last convinced that the new cloths preserved the custom just enough to be respectable. After many chants and discussions with her dreaming beans, she allowed Irene and Miguel to take the newly patterned cloths to market. They sold out instantly. A rush of orders for more forced Flora to borrow a loom and work late herself for several months, and Irene told Gregorio with a laugh that Flora would never forgive him for the extra money they were earning.

But it had made him famous here, Akabal's cloth, for Irene had told everyone he had drawn it, and a tiny new respect came to him when he showed his other pictures to the elders, to their wives. He was not a total layabout after all, but was earning money at last, helping his family, supporting the village, contributing finally as a man must contribute to have honor and respect. His love for Irene had been strengthened by his gift to her, and it had made a place in Akabal for them both.

Her laugh rang in his ears as he plunged along the trail, his sister's fate and his fatigue forgotten. This crisis for her brother, her mother's fear — it had broken down the barriers and he would be the rock for her this time. She loved him, they would be firm with Flora, and they would marry, he would be a father — she would not refuse him tonight. "Irene! Irene! Where are you?"

He heard something and stopped. A bird? A patch of light blue caught his eye through the brush. "Here . . . I'm here. Oh, God . . ."

His heart roared and he crashed into the brambles. She was lying on the stream bank, her blue blouse torn, muddy legs naked in the water, her skirt pushed up over her body. She turned toward him and he saw the blood caked below her nose, her face bruised, one eye swollen shut.

"Oh, my God, Irene! What happened? Are you all right?" He crouched beside her.

Her face was twisted, her open eye rolled wildly. She pushed at her sodden clothes, trying to cover herself. "Soldiers, be careful, the soldiers . . ."

He looked quickly up and down the stream, but saw nothing. He hugged her close, smoothing her hair, her clothes, her arms, making soothing noises. She sobbed into his shoulder.

"I was waiting . . . for you . . . They came up the stream . . . they had . . . rifles . . . they hit me . . . pushed me down . . ." She pulled back from him and put a hand up to shield her broken face. "They . . . laughed the whole time . . . I can't . . . Don't look at me, I can't . . ."

He shuddered. "Irene, it's all right now. They're gone. I'm here, it's all right." He held her a long time, until her sobs subsided.

After many minutes, with many pauses and many tears, she stood up in his arms, leaning heavily upon him. He twisted his hands in her skirts and wrung away the water, he smoothed her hair, he kissed her swollen eye. He held her, supported her, and they moved to climb back up the bluff. Far above, they could hear people singing in the church.

> Joyful, joyful we adore thee
> God of glory, God of love . . .

PART III

Fourteen

TINY SEARCHLIGHTS probed the smoky air from holes in the church roof, igniting flowers on the women's pastel blouses, coronas on the upturned faces. The singers' keening voices surrounded the murmur of dogs and children and babies, whispers of girls braiding one another's hair, droning prayers of those in the back, their hands raised before the saints. Some nodded at the song's message to their worry:

> We will conquer, we will conquer
> All the hate with love.
> Someday 'twill be, someday 'twill be
> That Christ has conquered, we will prove.

Father Edmundo underlined the shrilling singers with his deep tenor, almost a baritone, three octaves lower than the boyish soprano that had been his father's pride. Now it had the rough edges of a fine instrument left out in the rain. Once he had offered harmony to this choir, moving without conscious effort to notes that flushed and enriched the piercing melody. But the chorus had stumbled, collapsed at once, amazed by complication. As with faith, he thought, still envious. So he stifled the lush chords in his head, tensed his ears against the knifelike harmonics, and sought to find beauty in the singers' rocky tune. He tried to savor the imprecision of it, nature's hoarseness and quaver, of flats and sharps many notes from the target, of toneless drone offered in affirmation and encouragement. He made a sincere effort to like the singing as music, resisting the urge to dismiss it as cacophony, and he found this exercise girded him again and again for the much harder task of speaking to these people.

Oh, the pain of a nodding head, sagging eyelids, gaping jaws. To care if they listened was an agony worse than hunger, for he knew their grinding lives made a quiet hour in church the only guilt-free moments of rest they might get until his next visit. The tendril of Vatican II that reached even here, the message he was ordered to deliver, made every homily a pickax excavating at four hundred years of hardpan history that buried the warriors at the bedrock of his parish. He was ordered to affirm Christ's muscle, His lively proof that even a carpenter carries weight in the universe, but here that was to ask tired lives to turn a full revolution away from four centuries of mourning His death. Four centuries of affirming the state's power to kill — the point had long since been made. The evidence was right here in front of him, waiting for rescue, waiting on the ridge.

He would speak today to those who might hear him best. He looked over his flock and sighed. Miguel stood nearby with the censer; Cristóbal chatted with his cronies in the back; the women whispered. Such a hard thing, to express an idea, and useless as scented smoke most of the time, making the eyes water, water sliding off the impervious soul. Once, months ago, he had asked the catechists here whether there was evil and injustice in the world. Of course, they had replied. Examples?

"I planted a field of onions for Don Bartolomeo Torazo in Tekan," Joselino said. "He didn't water them and they died. Now he won't pay me for the onion sets."

"You should have got the money before you planted," Arturo advised. "Now it's too late."

"No, wait," the priest said. "What did you do, Joselino?"

"I told him he was unfair. He laughed at me. He said I'd better watch out because the only enemies he has are communists."

"Could you take him to court, in Santa Rosa?"

They all snorted. "Pah, the judge is his nephew."

"We do the work and the Ladinos have the money. That's injustice," Miguel broke in.

The priest held up a finger. "Remember the story of Cain and Abel? Injustice is born when we forget we are all brothers. A brother wouldn't cheat or hurt his brother, would he? But if we forget, that allows us to be mean and jealous, even to kill, as Cain killed Abel. Here's Don Bartolomeo forgetting that Joselino is his brother —"

"Because he knows the judge is his nephew." Arturo nodded.

"— so he hurts Joselino. But what should Joselino do? The Bible —"

"He could take one of Torazo's cows —"

"But then he'd send his goons after me."

"Not if he didn't know it was you," Miguel said.

"But he'd know, or somebody would tell him."

"Right, Joselino. Stealing and lying and betraying people — everything gets worse and worse, see, when you try to take revenge yourself, just as the Bible tells us. It's right here, no? Here's God saying to Cain, 'Your brother's blood cries out to me from the soil.' And God is the one who takes revenge, not you."

"Anyone who does evil to me is no brother of mine," Miguel said.

"Well, God says he is. Even if neither one of you can see it at the time, all men are brothers. It's God's order."

Joselino frowned. "So should I ask God to send me money for a lawyer?"

Gregorio laughed and spoke for the first time. "No, Joselino, just light a black candle and he'll get sick and die."

"The point is that brotherhood exists no matter what you think. We don't have any choice about it. If you hurt another person, you hurt your brother, and God gets angry."

Miguel's smile didn't reach his eyes. "Then I think we must force people who hurt us to stop, so they won't sin anymore."

"But you're still hurting your brother. How are you different then from Don Bartolomeo?"

"I know, Father!" Joselino half stood. "We're right and Don Bartolomeo is wrong!" The others had nodded.

At such moments, Edmundo glimpsed the wild enormous flail of a half-caught idea, like a fire hose turned on too soon. That was what had got the church in so much trouble all over this morass of a continent: half-baked understanding. The cloistered bowels of the Vatican had emitted pristine theology that despots could not distinguish from anarchic calls to riot. It would have been funny, except for the result: Christian communities of illiterate farmers contributing to buy a truck were machine-gunned as hotbeds of communism. Catechists were murdered; priests and nuns died at their altars. But the church never promoted revolution. Just the opposite. The blood of sacrifice he was about to make from wine was all the bloodshed necessary to bring the world to peace, if only everyone could understand it properly. That was the key, understanding, change coming first within each heart, through the mind after torment and doubt and introspection, because only that kind of change would last. Anything that was forced would be reversed in the long run, reversed by the hand of God Himself, who forbade force by all others. Repression spawned revolution by the hand of God, and that spawned repression again by God's hand, and so it would go until everyone stopped, just stopped. Why couldn't they see that? Affirm yourselves, the ancestors who tamed the jungle mountains, clocked the stars, moved the earth, built great cities without metal tools, without the crutch of wheels or animals, be proud of this blood, of your good and valuable work on God's land, of your human being, and leave justice to God . . .

But, then, the rebels were God's tool, no? In vengeance on the oppressors? And the government was also God's hand, avenging the bombings? It followed from his own argument, and the rising wall of horror at the blood stopped all his thoughts again at that point, for the thousandth time. How could one end the cycle when God seemed to will that it continue? One sin led to another. Did every last mind have to change completely for it all to change in the slightest? If half the people changed, would that be enough? Or one over half? Surely God didn't operate by majority rule! But what was the alternative? If God is good, He is not God. If God is God, He is not good . . . Unthinkable.

Gloria, gloria, in excelsis deo . . .

Edmundo rose. "Welcome to the shelter of God. *Dominus vobiscum, pax vobiscum*, peace be with you."

"And with your spirit." The response was a soft whoosh of sound. He opened the Bible.

"Today the first reading is from the book of Daniel, chapter five, about the writing on the wall." Edmundo exulted in the knowledge that he was one with thousands, millions, of other priests reading the same text today worldwide in English, French, Urdu, Chinese, every possible click and gurgle of language, a text chosen in the dim recesses of the Vatican years ago just for today's Mass for the entire planet, magically always relevant to the issue at hand in every single place. Even, he realized, when the issue had changed that very morning, as it had here.

" 'Belshazzar the king made a great feast to a thousand of his lords . . .' " he read. " 'They drank wine and praised the gods of gold and silver, of brass and iron' " — he paused and looked up at the rapt faces — " 'wood and . . . stone.' " At least they might wonder what he was getting at. " 'In the same hour came forth fingers of a man's hand, and wrote . . . upon the plaster of the wall . . . Then came all the king's wise men; but they could not read the writing . . . Then was King Belshazzar greatly troubled.' " Always kings and lords with their exotic problems, much more delicious to think about than one's own dreary dilemmas. A high-toned collection of soap operas, really.

" 'Then was Daniel brought in before the king . . . If thou canst read the writing, and make known to me the interpretation thereof, thou shalt be clothed with scarlet, and have a chain of gold about thy neck, and shalt be the third ruler in the kingdom . . .

" 'Daniel answered, Keep thy gifts or give them to another, yet I will read the writing . . . Thou has lifted up thyself against the Lord of heaven . . . and thou hast praised the gods of silver, and gold, of brass, iron, wood, and stone . . . and thou hast not glorified the God in whose hand thy breath is. And this is the writing that was written: Mene, Mene, Tekel, Upharsin. Mene: God hath numbered the days of thy kingdom, and finished it. Tekel: thou art weighed in the balance and found wanting. Upharsin: thy kingdom is divided, and given to the Medes and the Persians.' "

Edmundo closed the Bible and looked up. "This is the word of the Lord."

"Thanks be to God." The automatic mumble was uncertain. He felt like a translator preparing his notes.

"The second reading is from the book of Luke, chapter

twenty-one." He raised his eyebrows to warn them what was to come. Well, it had been the Vatican's choice, not his. He leaned forward and pronounced each word slowly. " 'They will lay hands on you, and persecute you, delivering you to synagogues and into prisons, bringing you to trial before kings and governors for my name's sake.' " The shuffling and murmuring before him sifted into silence. " 'You will be brought to give witness, but I bid you' " — Edmundo lifted a finger — " 'resolve not to worry about your defense beforehand. For I will give you a mouth and wisdom which none of your adversaries can take exception to, or contradict.' "

Edmundo took a deep breath and moved his feet to broaden his stance. His voice boomed. " 'You shall be betrayed, even by parents and brothers, relatives and friends, and some of you will be put to death!' " The villagers stared at him. Some looked at Miguel, who gaped in disbelief. " 'All will hate you because of me! and yet — and yet' " — he shook his finger at them — " 'not a hair of your head will be harmed! By patient endurance you will save your lives!' " He slapped the book shut. "This, this is the gospel of the Lord!"

"Praise to You, Lord Jesus Christ!" The response was explosive.

Edmundo sat down in a flutter of robes and waved to the choir. The group coughed and sang:

> If thou art with me
> And strengthen my faith,
> With thou at my side
> Who shall I fear?

As the voices shrilled, Edmundo sat back in the caned chair next to the table and flipped the microphone cord behind him. He stretched out his legs and crossed his ankles, his worn running shoes showing their smooth soles below the white skirt. He knew the audience noticed his slightest gesture, rapt, but he gazed serenely over their peasant heads, ordering his thoughts. The song died and he cleared his throat. He did not get up.

"Writing on the wall always means a message from God, doesn't it? We use the idea to mean a warning of something that's going to happen. But think a minute. Daniel read the writing for the king, and it wasn't a warning at all. No, it was an announcement — it told him he was doomed, and that he'd already lost his kingdom. This wasn't a warning. No, it was a final judgment. The writing on the wall is a judgment, not a warning." He paused to let this sink in.

"God had sent lots of warnings to Belshazzar before. The Bible tells us the king had ignored many signs — his father's history, his counselors. So by this time, God was fed up. He didn't give Belshazzar another warning. When the king saw the writing on the wall he finally got scared, but by then it was too late. It was too late! He couldn't do anything about it then, because judgment time had come. He lost his kingdom, he lost everything."

Edmundo stood up and walked thoughtfully back and forth across the small open space around him. "Now we receive messages from God all the time, don't we? Our mothers tell us what God wants us to do. The Bible tells us over and over again. But we ignore the messages. We aren't scared yet. We know it is wrong to say bad things about our neighbors, don't we? But we gossip anyway. We spread rumors. We know it's wrong to cheat even a little, but we think we can get away with it. And we do! No lightning strikes us. No voice comes down from the sky —" Edmundo scowled and made his voice a roll of thunder. " 'You have done wrong!' " He saw a smile or two. "So we go on. We know it is wrong to hit a child, or to make someone work a long time with no pay. But we do it anyway and nothing happens to us. So we get bolder. We worship false gods, gods of money, or gods of wood" — he raised his eyebrows — "we know we're not supposed to respond to insults with violence, because the Lord says turn the other cheek, that revenge belongs to Him. He tells us do not lie, do not steal, do not desire our neighbors' wives or husbands — but we do all these things anyway, all the time, because we don't listen, and because nothing happens to us right then." He stopped and faced his congregation.

"What are some of the things we do that we know we should not do? Anyone, give me an answer." Edmundo waited. Arturo stood up.

"We don't help our neighbors when we should." He looked around the church, his chin jutting.

Edmundo nodded. "Yes. Another example?"

Joselino stood up. His voice was loud. "Some people spread false stories about their kinfolk." He sat down abruptly.

"That's right. More?" The priest waited. "Is it the will of the Father that there are hungry children? That the little ones only seven or eight have to work to feed their families?"

"No, Father."

"It's wrong."

"Is it right to make threats against people? To shake a fist like this in someone's face, to make them do what you want when they don't want to?"

"No, Father!" More voices joined in.

"It's wrong! So God doesn't do that either! He doesn't shake His fist. He doesn't threaten us. He has given us the Bible. We know what we're supposed to do. God just watches us to see whether we do it."

Edmundo sat down again. He surveyed the seamed and anxious faces before him, the brows furrowed in the effort to understand.

"Now here's the important thing. If we don't do what we're supposed to, if we keep on lying and spreading rumors and cheating, if we ignore what we've been told, then it's too late! It's too late! The judgment comes. Then comes the judgment! No warnings, no threats, just a judgment. And then comes the message we can't ignore. Then — and only then, after it's too late — comes the writing on the wall." Edmundo stood up. Even the babies were quiet.

"Today we face a very serious test here in Akabal. We've been threatened. The army has come and shaken its fist in our faces!" A hundred mouths inhaled in a soft rush of air. Edmundo looked at Miguel, standing straight against a side wall, and nodded, indicating him with one hand. He opened the Bible. "Just as the Bible says, innocent people are in grave danger. 'They will lay hands on you, and persecute you . . . You will be brought to give witness. You shall be betrayed, even by parents and brothers, relatives and friends, and some of you will be put to death.' "

"No! No!"

"We'll fight!" Several men stood up. "Miguel is innocent!"

"There must be justice!" Arturo shouted. "Justice!"

"We'll die, we'll die!" A woman began to wail. A dog barked.

"The answer is here! Here in the book of Luke!" Edmundo shouted over them all. He waved the Bible. The noise subsided. "Here, right here, it says, 'I bid you, resolve not to worry about your defense beforehand.' That is, the Bible says that if you have obeyed God's will and lived with justice, there is nothing to worry about." The priest paused, his finger on the passage, and looked up. His eyes shone.

"God says here, 'For I will give you a mouth and wisdom which none of your adversaries can take exception to, or contradict.' That means God Himself will defend us, right here in Akabal! We are strong in faith! You are children of God! So we will be able to convince the soldiers when the time comes. They will understand that what they have threatened is wrong! It is wrong and evil in the sight of God, evil in the eyes of the world! They will know, because God will make them hear our words! They will know that God Himself, the God of Luke and Belshazzar, God and His holy justice forbid any violence against Akabal! God will give us the words to convince them!"

The audience gaped. Miguel stared at the priest. Edmundo waited for the nods, the amens, but none came. The faces were supposed to be relieved and joyful, but instead they looked incredulous. Didn't they understand? "See here! God says right here, 'By patient endurance you will save your lives. Not a hair of your head will be harmed.' Did you hear that? 'Not a hair of your head will be harmed.' This is a promise from God Himself! This is the word of the Lord!" He clapped the Bible shut and stood triumphant, smiling before them.

"Thanks be to the Lord." A few voices mumbled the automatic response. Genero raised his arms. "Praise God!"

Miguel sagged against the wall, the censer hissing, color gone from his face. Cristóbal stood up and raised his arms for quiet.

"But Father, please, with your permission." He waited for silence. "As you said, we are all still sinners. We have not always done what we should. We've ignored many messages before this, about how we should live. Some of those things you said" — he shook his head — "we are not always good, Father. Some of us would even look guilty to the soldiers. Maybe not Miguel, maybe not most of us, but some of us, we haven't always been as firm as we should be, and the soldiers — some of them aren't good Christians either, some of them might not listen when you tell them they shouldn't hurt anybody. Isn't there something — "

"No! It's not too late for anybody! Confess your sins! Come to God! The Lord on high will defend all of us!" Edmundo raised his hands over them, a guardian angel. "God's love is complete, it is unconditional. He forgives more than any of us; He forgives seven thousand times seventy-seven; He loves His children. God will defend everybody! 'Not a hair of your head will be harmed!' Oh, yes, there is much to do, many changes must be made, we are all sinners, but yes, there is time." Edmundo's smile radiated belief to the corners of the sagging building. "Listen now, let us pray together . . . I believe in God the Father, maker of heaven and earth . . ."

Slowly, some bowed their heads and joined in, murmuring the ancient words a beat behind, as though hearing them for the first time. Miguel stood rubbing his brow, shaking his head, and Cristóbal sat frowning on the bench, kneading his hat in his hands.

Fifteen

LIEUTENANT GOMEZ could hear the singers as a faint tinny wail a kilometer down the dirt track. Not a great place for a camp, but the rocks were big enough to offer some shade at least. Two men had caught a goat for lunch, its owner's contribution to national security, and others tended a fire. The rest sprawled under scrubby trees.

Gomez lay against a rock, his throbbing knee propped on his rifle. His head ached. There was rum in his pack, good stuff; it might help. Then again it might not. Later. It wasn't even noon yet. He'd need some for tonight too. He damned himself at the thought of the long night ahead. He should have set a sunset deadline. Now he'd have to keep patrols up all night to make sure nobody got away. Melinda was right, it was time to get out of field work. He was slipping. He should spend the time he had left at home, with his kids. Little Antonio and María Elena, a real handful, a girl just like her mother. Two was enough, but Melinda wanted more and probably would have them, too; he thought of her dark hair cascading on the pillow, her warm brown flesh, her cave of forgetting calling him, secure for the deepest part of himself, salty refuge for everything he was. He sighed down to his aching knee and wished mightily he were home with her, tongue and hands tangled in her long brown hair.

The singing wafted over the hills. He could not make out the words. He fingered the Saint Christopher's medal and cross on their cord around his neck. A long time since this old choirboy had been in a church, three years, not since Julio's funeral. Hadn't been much point after that, after he had cursed the church and everybody in it. He ground his teeth. Justice and mercy, the Father had said, God's will, and he had screamed bullshit, this beautiful boy, a mere boy, studying to be a priest, how was it justice that he should be blown to bits on a sunny Sunday afternoon? It could have been anybody else walking past the Cotzal guardhouse just at that moment, anybody else bouncing a soccer ball, anybody but his inno-cent brother, getting his legs blown off, strings of red flesh and bone trailing off to a gushing nothing below both knees. Then the stinking bandages, a wormy infection for three weeks before he died, delirious. It could have been five sec-onds earlier or later and Julio would be a priest today, twenty-one. How was that justice and mercy?

Prospero Jesús Gomez had bought Julio that soccer ball for his eighteenth birthday, presenting it suddenly, no ceremony, a proper army man. Julio whooped, grabbed it, dropped it to the ground, and kicked it with those doomed feet out the door of their house in one fluid motion. The two of them raced after it, laughing and pushing as they maneuvered for posi-tion, kicking the black-and-white treasure back and forth down the street. Smaller boys gave chase, shouting and dart-ing in to intercept. Julio scooped up the ball and stopped, panting, as they reached their father's store.

"Ah, I can never be a poor priest now, with no property whatever." He laughed, holding the ball high over the clamor-ing children. "This is much too wonderful to give up."

"So be the priest of the Regulars. All the teams have their own, don't they? You'd bless the goalies or something." The brothers laughed, thinking of free tickets, chats with the mayor, cocktails with the generals, nights out with the team. How simple their dreams had been then! Julio faced off the two nearest boys and hurled the ball down between them, and the youngsters were off, kicking and shouting up the street.

"I think I'd rather be the priest for that team there," he said, his eyes soft.

That was Julio, all right, always giving away his books, even his clothes, to those ragged kids who hung around the house. When their mother scolded him he only shrugged and smiled, and she would soften, as everyone did. The boy was a saint.

Another memory surfaced, the day ten years before that when his father first opened the store as his very own. How proud they all were, fussing and rearranging the meager stock of boxes and bottles to take up as much room as possible. His mother wore a new dress, the color of the jacaranda blossom in her hair; his father wore that permanent half smile, always about to say yes may I help you for the rest of his life. Prospero and Julio had stumped around, delighted in their new shoes, two sizes too big. He had not realized until that moment that it was possible to have more than one set of clothes.

His older sister, Margarita, bullying bane of his childhood, had put on a bright blue dress, dazzling, and turned before his eyes from a sister into a person, a woman. What a day that had been! So many people, so much drinking, everybody singing and happy, giving him sips from their bottles until he was dizzy.

And Luis, small and wiry, one of the soldiers from the barracks, one of the new customers that day, with his quick grin that fastened on Margarita in her blue dress. Prospero's lip curled at the memory. Luis the jokester, tousling the boys' hair, making his sister laugh and blush. He visited Margarita every day after that, until one afternoon when Prospero came upon them in the cornfield, rolling together with little grunts and cries. He backed away before they saw him. Then he would find them talking earnestly, his sister shaking her head, often in tears, Luis insisting. They would fall silent when Prospero came near, looking at him with wary eyes.

Luis vanished a few months later, and Margarita stopped talking. She walked around with heavy feet, her hair tangled, doing her chores as though asleep. Soon it was obvious she was pregnant. Her father slapped her twice across the face.

"Where is he, slut? Whore of a daughter, why did you let him do this to us?

Her chin came up. "He's gone with the rebels in the hills. You'll see him again soon enough, when the revolution comes!" Her father had knocked her down.

It had taken Prospero much too long, but he had avenged Luis's insult to his family. He won a secret commendation for it, from General Barcos in 1979. He had been tracking a rebel unit in the hills like the animals they were, and they had walked into his trap. Lining them up, he had recognized Luis among them, the unit leader.

In his memory he sighted down his pistol at the point where Luis's eyebrows nearly met. "Such a pleasure to see you again after all these years. You don't remember me? Little Prospero from Cotzal? Surely you remember Margarita? Where is the smile that charmed my sister?" The pig's eyes rounded in horror. He waited. "You cannot smile? You don't remember? Then this is for her."

He pulled the trigger. He watched the face disappear into a black hole as the back of Luis's head exploded onto the tree trunk behind, painting it a shiny, dripping red.

Afterward he had made it a practice to order the soldiers in his patrol to question subversives they caught individually, apart from the others, and then to shoot them personally, as he had done. It hardened them to this kind of life, and they always learned a great deal from the last two or three to die. Gomez's breath came a little faster as he leaned on his rock. That time, with Luis, most times, he hadn't needed anyone to tell him what to do. But today . . .

All this fucking around made him crazy. Meddling Yankees were the problem, talking half the time about killing communists and the other half about human rights. Sure, let's kill them all, but don't hurt anybody. If the fucking generals couldn't figure it out, how could anybody expect him to? Joyabal had it right: just shoot them and be done with it, then say whatever you want to later. But even Joyabal was waffling these days; hadn't had the guts in that speech he made to tell them they were all dead. Or maybe he was ass-kissing some more, thinking Gomez would want the privilege. That was stupid. Or maybe he wasn't stupid; maybe he was being smart, being careful not set himself up for when the second guessing started later. No, he wasn't that complicated; this was all in Gomez's own head. Joyabal was just like the rest of them, standing back and waiting for orders, not wanting the responsibility.

Well, Gomez could handle the responsibility, but he had orders too and he was a soldier. But what kind of stupid order was "Get the bastard"? Was this under the new rules, and he should show the flag and make speeches, or the old ones, and he should even the score? And did that mean he should kill two of these animals and break the legs off ten of them? What he should do was something so grand it would stop anybody here from planting any more bombs ever again, no matter what. He grunted at himself. Stupid notion. Nobody would ever hear of this place no matter what he did, or what he didn't do, and another dead peasant or two or twenty wouldn't stop the revolt. Ah, that Lorenzo was slick all right. Even in his underwear with that damn fool dog, he had given orders as though he were saying something real, and Gomez had believed it. The explosion must have mushed up his brain.

What was obvious was that Lorenzo would take the credit if the high command in the capital liked whatever Gomez did, and Gomez would take the blame if it didn't. But there was no way he could know what the generals wanted; they didn't know themselves, jockeying back and forth in that castle with the pastel walls and the painted woodwork. The speeches didn't help any. Some of them, most of them, were just propaganda to soothe the Yankees into more military aid, but the formal directives were harder to figure. One day Joyabal had come to him with a thick headquarters bulletin in either hand and stood there with his eyes closed, weighing them. "General Figueroa is slightly heavier than General Alarcón," he said, and Gomez had had to laugh in spite of himself. Another time they had put contradictory orders on the wall and thrown knives at them to decide which ones to ignore. Too many cliques, coup plots, rumors bursting left and right. As well the bleating goat over there might judge which soldier was safe to butt.

Gomez heaved to his feet. He looked around for Joyabal but saw only a laughing clump of soldiers, and he lurched toward them. All four snapped to attention. "At ease, at ease. What's so funny?"

"Sir, Private Chucút here was telling us about the Akabal girls, sir." He grinned. "He said he had one up at the stream just now and she was delicious." They all tittered. Gomez looked at Chucút, who gave an uncertain smile.

"Hunger makes even a goat taste good," Gomez said. The four laughed.

The lieutenant walked on and spotted Emidio Tijax hunched like a boulder, staring at his feet. He looked haggard, as though he had just been sick.

"So, what's the matter? Don't get up." Gomez sat down heavily beside him in the dirt. "Don't you like it here? I thought this was your territory."

"Nosir. All fine, sir." He didn't look up. Gomez offered him a cigarette and lighted it for him. No reaction. The stone-faced bastard was not going to let his guard down. The lieutenant was briefly irritated, but reminded himself that high walls shield empty lots as easily as bank vaults. The kid was probably thinking about people he knew here. That could be useful.

"Listen, Tijax. Tell me what you know about this place. Did the army recruit here?"

Tijax shrugged. "Very ordinary village." Gomez had to lean forward to hear him. "Just farmers. No subversives. Army recruited in Santa Rosa but not here. When they come, the people give them food."

If they haven't given it all away to the subversives the day before, Gomez thought. "You, you seem like a nice kid. Why'd you join the army?"

Tijax narrowed his eyes in the cigarette smoke and shrugged again. "I'm a farmer, no money, no family. I go to Santa Rosa, to the cinema, the army comes there, poof! All of us are in the army."

Gomez grinned, and Tijax smiled, exposing brown teeth with gaps on either side. "When was that?"

"Since nine months."

Lucky for the army the rebels hadn't gotten him first. He probably wouldn't have cared, probably didn't know the difference. Forced recruitment by both sides would keep the war going as long as new babies were born, as long as guns kept coming in for them to play with.

"The subversives must have come here a lot?"

"A few times. They make speeches. But people don't believe them, nobody pays attention."

"Like this morning." Tijax shrugged a third time. Gomez could picture some bony teenager with a bandolier and a red scarf, haranguing the same stolid faces from the same spot where he had stood. He tried to imagine the villagers' deep-set eyes lit with enthusiasm at promises of land, riches, electricity, roads . . . but he couldn't. Everybody made the same promises; he had promised all that and more himself, many times, and it was all lies, everybody knew it was lies. What could anybody promise those peasants that they might believe? If he told them to work hard, save their money and be sure to vote, that capitalism would make them rich and happy, they'd laugh in his face. They lived here slaving to work off debts six, seven generations old, for people who treated cattle better than they treated Indians. Even he could see that. He was a soldier, on the fringes of it all, born to take orders and keep the peace, but his bosses ran the world, and they weren't about to turn it over, that was sure.

There was simply nothing to say to these people. If communist troublemakers told them they had nothing to lose but their chains, they'd be suspicious, and they should be. But he could see the appeal of something like that. A lot of people would fall for it in a place like this. That's what this was all about, just plain greed, people wanting more than God gave them. It was simple, really, but the Indians were too dumb to see that, too stupid to see it was just another pack of lies. They really had to be taken care of, watched over to make sure the troublemakers didn't take advantage. That wasn't so bad, being protected. They could have it pretty soft, actually, if they were a little patient, waited until there was some extra money so that they could have schools and so on. Even now, they could go to church, grow what they wanted, work at whatever they liked. They couldn't do that under communism, but they didn't know that, of course. When they were educated properly they'd understand, and when they developed some manners, then they could do a little more for themselves. In the meantime they'd have to be guarded from the subversives, like sheep from the mountain lions, until they figured it out, and that was the army's job. At least he was on the right side.

He shifted his weight, stretching his right leg slowly so that it wouldn't crackle too much. Where did that leave him? This Tijax, for example — he was a kind of sheep himself, under

Gomez's protection in a lot of ways. He was a soldier and he was young, and he was an Indian besides. He was probably pretty confused right now, wondering what he was going to have to do to his own village. Gomez opened his mouth to ask Emidio about Benedicto Tijax, Gomez's ear in Akabal, but he changed his mind. No need-to-know here. He pretended instead that he hadn't been listening. "You say you have family here?"

"No, no family. Parents dead. No money for wife. A brother, but he left for the plantations a year ago." Tijax stubbed the cigarette out on a rock. "Nothing since then. I think he died there."

"Well, you know we have a job to do here; we have to make an example of this place, about what happens to subversives." Tijax's face reminded Gomez of the old Mayan masks in the capital museum — empty eyes, sunken cheeks; all he needed were ear loops. "We're acting with firmness here, to defend the nation, so if you have any worries about that —"

"Lieutenant, sir!" Martín Joyabal appeared and saluted smartly. Tijax scrambled to his feet and stood at attention.

Gomez looked up in irritation, shading his eyes from the sun. "Yes, Sergeant?"

"Sir, would you like to choose the patrol relief now, sir?"

Gomez sighed and got up. Four two-man units guarded hills and roads around the town, and another pair watched from the ridge. The afternoon would be critical, hard for anyone to stay awake. "No, Sergeant, you pick them. But why don't you take the ridge yourself? That's the key spot. And Tijax here can keep you company, maybe tell you something about this place. All right?" That would fix them both. "Get something to eat first."

He saluted and dismissed them, noting their mutual distaste with satisfaction. He walked back to the rock where his pack beckoned. It had to be after noon by now.

Sixteen

FLORA KANAK DE CANIL, flower of the corn, daughter of Hurakan the absent, what good were motherkind words for this bleeding girl, stupid willful child, raped and ruined? Better to give consolation, reproval, whispers of vengeance, and warnings of love, some soup later. She stroked Irene's mud-caked hair, brought warm water, rinsed her hair, wrapped the blanket close. More was gone than just the tilted nose, the maidenhead, if she had had that to begin with. Irene's mind was a wisp in the room, eye blind like hers, soul drifting like mist, unseeing, spit running down her cheek.

"Mama, I'm cold . . . It's a new design though, I'm sure you'll like it . . . I'm sorry, I can't . . . don't do that . . . where's my basket? Why did you do that? I'm cold . . ." She sat up.

"Quiet, quiet, girl! Lie down there, that's it, that's right, you're all right now . . ." She wiped Irene's face, smelled the sweet sticky male smell on the wet clothes, undressed her as they hadn't bothered. She felt the back of her mouth open up, her stomach heave. She stifled it; no time now, time later to pour it out, all of it. She piled the rags in a corner, forced her lips to open over her few teeth in a terrible smile. At least

Irene was visible, clear to her, not like Miguel, poor Miguel, a killer, terrorist, lost to her too . . .

"Is she all right? Tell me. Oh, God, I'm so sorry . . ." Gregorio's voice was harsh, out of place here.

Irrelevant men, they knew nothing of women's pain. Another one, another killer . . . He sat there on the mat with his head in his hands, useless, in her way as she moved, always in the way. "Stop bothering me, no earthly use. Sorry for what. Punishment is mine, not for you, arrogance, like Miguel, that too, soldiers, get the whole family, forgetful, nobody has any sense . . ." She rummaged in the shelves for the broken pot and stepped around Gregorio to get water from the jug.

"The family? What do you mean?" Always mumbling; nothing was clear in Gregorio's head. "The soldiers? Get the family?"

"All of us, too late. Lucas in the truck, Miguel in the army, Irene now, nobody left . . ." If she had been able to make them sing, if she had never cursed the corn, Hurakan would see her now, save her and Irene and Miguel, keep the soldiers away. Stupid boy here, staring at her, ought to get out . . . she knelt before the fire and poked it viciously.

"The family? You think the soldiers — they picked Irene deliberately? They knew she's Miguel's sister? What are you talking about?"

She waved him away. "He's gone, they'll take him too, kill all the rebels, anybody connected." She turned on him suddenly, waved a finger in his face. "You should have stopped him, Gregorio, you could have talked him out of it, but oh no, you don't pay attention, nobody listens, can't see him right, even I can't see him . . ."

Gregorio scrambled over and grabbed her by the shoulders. "What are you saying, old woman? You're crazy, you know that? What do you mean? I could have talked him out of what?" He shook her hard.

Flora glared at him. "Stupid baby! You idiot! He's killing soldiers, setting bombs, he thinks he's Kucumatz, won't even tell his own mother — " She pushed at Gregorio's hands. "And you blinder even than me, Irene ruined and what for? Here we are all of us dead already, fly spit waiting to dry up. Hurakan, why do you stand for it, why do you wait?"

Gregorio found it hard to breathe. He shook the bony shoulders until the woman's teeth clacked. "What do you mean, he's killing soldiers? What do you mean?"

"Bombs, soldiers, death to them too, my son a killer, full of words, how can you wait? Hurakan! Hear me! Aagh, you fool! And you did nothing to save him, nothing! You stupid, useless — " She struggled against him. He opened his hands and she raised her fists, beating his chest once, twice, and staggered back sobbing. "Oh, gods in heaven!" She raised her hands to the dark rafters. "Open the earth! Let us all be swallowed! Let blood death rain down on me, on my son, all of us, the soldiers, on the sins of Akabal!" She sank, wailing, to the hard floor.

Gregorio reeled away from her and slumped against the wall. The wattle was cool on his back, then hot. He knew it, he had always known it, there was never any doubt; Miguel had been with the guerrillas for years. It had been obvious, but he never let himself see it, he had refused to know. He saw dreams and visions and made-up Miguels, he saw them clearly and called them what he wanted them to be. That open smile, those thin shoulders — of course. The days he disappeared, the long silences, the steady looks, the darkness in his eyes; it was all there plain as granite, the oddball stories and the strange trips. Gregorio was breathing as hard as if he were running, and he was, he was running away, he had always been running away. There had never been a need for questions between them because he knew Miguel. Didn't he? He saw the long twilights when they sat smoking in a doorway

while the sun set, all the times Miguel had stopped in midsen-
tence and he had babbled on — there had been clues in every
moment, but he never looked at them. His Miguel was simple,
gentle, passive, open — a mirage, a painted image, clutter he
had generated to obscure his own view of a lying, violent
killer.

Ah, and what would Miguel do now? What was he capable
of now, now that his sister had been raped, his family violated
directly? His father's death had been a murder, but distant,
institutional, the guilty party hard to single out. Yet Miguel
was a rebel and Gregorio was not, although his own father, his
own sister —

He looked at Flora sobbing on the floor. Poor old crone,
Miguel had fooled her too, or rather she had fooled herself.
He bent down to her and tentatively, touching a snake, he
embraced her. It was like holding a bundle of cornstalks. He
helped her sit up and sat next to her, leaning against the wall.
She sagged against his shoulder. Irene moaned on her mat,
but neither of them moved. The sunlight poured in the door.

> Praise God from whom all blessings flow!
> Praise Him all creatures here below . . .

The Doxology floated over Akabal, and Gregorio pictured
Father Edmundo lifting the Host and the chalice, his friends
and neighbors shaking hands in brotherhood and lining up to
dine on God. They were a thousand years ago, a thousand
kilometers away. He stared dully at the shadow of the door
frame across the floor, watching the dark edge move slowly,
imperturbably, across the tiny motes of the packed and dusty
earth.

An hour passed, perhaps more. A familiar *click-click-click*
came at the open door. A chicken approached, pecking in
eternal optimism at the barren ground, and Gregorio looked

outside. Flies droned in the alley's hot sunlight, circling a scrawny pariah dog as it nosed a thin piglet snoring in the shade. Envy rose in Gregorio's throat. The animals were obscure in their constant presence, ignorant that they would starve and sicken and die young because their fundamental conditions were intolerable. Ah, he had been like that once; they all had, generations of them mindlessly living and dying without questions. But that was over now, gone like Eden and for the same reasons. He had a thousand questions for Miguel, a thousand more for himself, but he shrank from asking them, not sure he would survive the answers.

Irene's chest rose and fell. She slept at last, freed a while from the wounded world. She was very beautiful, with her smashed nose, her matted hair; and his longing for her was so strong he nearly wept. But under the tears was a cold place, a hard future requiring them to turn from each other in order to watch their backs. Her destruction was his as she was, and now he would have to think always of protection for them both, a new dark line under his desire. It pulled him a little out of his mourning, back to the day. He spoke as if from another body. "I'd better go get Miguel, to tell him." Flora nodded and wiped her eyes. Slowly, helping each other, they got up. He went to the door.

He could not move. The little distance from the Kanaks' house to the church loomed before Gregorio like a journey to the moon, the path a muddy sewer strewn with boulders. He thought of entering the chapel, breathing the sweaty darkness and the pungent smoke, and it made him dizzy. He tried to picture Miguel there, swinging the censer near the priest, but he could not make out the face. It was a blur, the features washed with blood. He leaned against the door frame and blinked in the white sunlight of the shining day.

Seeing Miguel would be to see — what? He willed Miguel's shapeless image to hold still. The smile, that open smile that

crinkled at the corners, eyes that now seemed bottomless, a pit
that drew him in and down, down to a darkness he recognized
from his nightmares. At the bottom of the well behind Miguel's
eyes lay the unthinkable, the other side of wild, screaming fear,
the thing worse even than terror — the capacity in oneself to
inflict such terror, even to enjoy it. The bloodbath that animals practiced on prey, on weaker beings, the capacity for
bloody acts beyond description — it was the other face of fear.
One could choose at the bottom of the pit: the madness that
was terror or the other madness that was terrorism. Miguel
had chosen one way, Andreas the other. Cecilia? Irene? He
shrank from the vision. Quetzals swooped and flashed in his
mind, beating themselves to death against all cages, looping
into free extinction. How he envied the birds! Without choice
each found a vacant corner of the universe to occupy undis-
turbed, a niche to fill that let them live and fly and sing and
die without interference. Mindless life, that was freedom; his
father had been right to choose that in his torture, to confess
and live. What had mind got Gregorio but platitudes and lies
and pain? His father, his sister, Irene, Miguel — how much
better to have a mind stuffed with vacant space than to want
and rage and suffer.

Gregorio half fell, half stumbled out of the house at last. He
lurched along the path, supporting himself on either wall,
and came into the plaza as his neighbors began pouring out of
the church. In a moment he was engulfed in a murmuring
torrent of white lace, gentle colors, black braids twined with
ribbon, red-and-black skirts and blankets. He was pounded
on the back, his lifeless hand pumped a dozen times. His ears
roared, he heard only a babble, saw only yellowed teeth glinting here and there with gold, saw mouths moving in meaning-
less noise, and he heard himself as from a great distance
making useless noises in response.

"Have you seen . . . fine, thanks . . . and you too . . . no,

Miguel, I'm looking for — yes, thank you . . . but where is . . .
yes, and your family . . ." How could everything be so normal?
Why was no one else weeping, no one else devastated by the
blue, blue sky? He stared upward, dazzled by the sun, and saw
there the drive of life, life at all costs, life that roared in the
flash between the finger's twitch on the trigger and oblivion,
life that surged even here, even now, washing over them all.
He saw himself as an arrogant, pompous blatherer of irrelevance in this teeming rush of life, a common moment trying to
merit drama, pathetic, ridiculous. Brown arms plopped straw
hats atop scores of heads, circled pastel shoulders, shook outstretched hands, dragged squalling children down the steps.
A dozen angry-looking men brushed past him, shaking their
heads.

"Idiot priest . . ."

"Maximon's day too. It'll be better . . ."

"Where's the *chiman* now . . ."

Gregorio looked inside the chapel, where men crowded
before San Clemente, women huddled near the shed, others
lined up to make confession. The priest was removing his
white gown amid a hubbub of children. Miguel was nowhere,
and Gregorio turned back into the plaza.

Miguel had followed Don Cristóbal as he strode from the
church, certain from the mayor's reaction to the priest's unbe-
lievable homily that he had an ally there. The priest wasn't
going to do anything, just talk to that fat lieutenant as though
he were a normal human being, as though God would talk to
such slime. Edmundo would just stand there and let the soldiers take him, but the mayor didn't want to give him up, and
the rush of hope and gratitude in Miguel's chest surprised
him. He hadn't thought he was that scared. But the mayor
could do just about anything. He would be mayor forever,
even after the revolution came, and why not? He always

helped the people, even though he was rich and his prices were too high. Miguel pushed through the crowd around Don Cristóbal as he moved through the market, but then he hesitated. What exactly did he want the mayor to do? He couldn't just walk up and say here I am, save me. He needed a plan, some idea to offer that the mayor could make work. What would Nahual say? Miguel felt helpless, alone on an island far from land.

"What incredible nonsense!" Arturo nearly deafened Miguel as he pushed past to Cristóbal. "What was he saying? Does he think we're all idiots?"

"Calm yourself." The mayor didn't turn around, threading his way among the rich aromas that rose from piles of peppers and bags of seeds. The squeals of a dozen piglets on tethers nearly drowned him out. "He's just a man, like anybody else. He wasn't spouting papal orders."

"Yes he was, Don Cristóbal!" Genero hurried to keep up with them. "He says God will make the soldiers listen —"

"God gives the words to appeal to any rational man, Genero. But is the lieutenant a rational man?" The mayor reached the door of his shop and turned as they gathered around him. "He's probably got his own ideas. Plus his orders. He's a soldier, for God's sake. You know two officials never agree about anything." They all turned to look at Miguel, their problem. In their eyes Miguel saw compassion but also appraisal, as if he were a sheep they might offer at the market.

Joselino put an arm around Miguel. "Let's tell them Miguel got away. We can say we saw him heading down the back path to the stream and they must have missed him. We can hide him somewhere while they search." He gave Miguel a grin. "We can bury him somewhere, with a straw to breathe through."

Arturo snorted. "You think they'd believe that, you're crazy.

And what if they did? Then they'd shoot us all for protecting him." He spread his hands. "Can't you just see it? Miguel would be the only one left alive, and the only one buried!" They all laughed briefly. Cristóbal unlocked the shop door but did not enter.

"But why do they want Miguel anyway, of all people?" Genero was nearly wailing. "Miguel, what did you do?" The others looked at Miguel.

Miguel told himself to stay calm. The ancient simpleton knew nothing. "I? I did nothing, nothing. What do you think, old man? That I go around killing women and babies?" He smiled gently. Nahual would be proud of him.

They looked at him for a long moment. Then Arturo waved dismissal at Genero. "It's true. If they come after Miguel, nobody here is safe." Arturo nodded at Miguel's grateful glance and lowered his voice. "Our luck has run out. But we can still get the better of them. We can fight back."

"Fight back! What with, Arturo?" Cristóbal laughed. "Shit shovels versus machine guns at fifty paces?"

"We can fight, I tell you! We can trick them! We have guns, not many but enough. We —"

Genero put up his hands to shield himself. "Don't be crazy! Just because you have nothing to lose —"

"We can get them as they come up the hill —"

"Yes!" Miguel's heart raced. "They won't be expecting anything. We can do it! We've been humiliated long enough —"

"We'll die fighting if we have to!"

Cristóbal raised his hands. "Just a minute —"

"We'll kill as many as they do." Arturo was fierce, glowing. "Better to stop this now. If we do what they ask this time they'll just keep coming back, again and again. We'll be the sheep of the province; they'll just kill us all off one by one. If we fight, we'll be heroes!"

"If you fight, you'll be dead." Benedicto had come up behind Miguel, and they all turned. "You weren't listening, Arturo." They looked at him, frowning. "The lieutenant said we had to show our loyalty. That's all. Nothing else. We do what they want, they leave us alone."

"He never said they'd leave us alone," Joselino pointed out. "They might kill us all even if we do what they want."

"No, they won't. They know what's going on here. They want to teach us a lesson. They don't want to kill everybody. What good is a country full of dead patriots?"

"It's peaceful. That's all they really want anyway, for everybody to shut up and sit down." Cristóbal shook his head.

"Right." Benedicto lifted his shoulders. "So Miguel gives himself up and that's it, he goes to jail for a while and gets out. What's so bad about that if the whole village is at stake?"

"That's bullshit and you know it." Arturo glared at him. "You fucking excuse for a shithole. You want Miguel to volunteer to be shot, just to get him out of your way. That's right, isn't it? You dog piss. Suppose we decide you're the terrorist, not him? They got the wrong name and it's you they should shoot?" He cocked his head sideways. "You know, that's an idea. Maybe it's even true." He leered at Benedicto. "Where were you last night anyway? Where were you that whole year, come to think of it?"

Benedicto half closed his eyes. "Be careful, you fat pig. Can you tell us yourself where you were last night? I've been thinking, you know — Miguel probably wasn't alone when —"

Arturo lunged. He knocked Miguel to one side, his meaty hands reaching for Benedicto's throat. But Cristóbal and Joselino shoved themselves in front of Benedicto and grappled with the bigger man.

"All right, all right! That's enough!" The mayor grunted. "Stop it!" Joselino had Arturo in a hammerlock. "Stop! Arturo! Don't you see, this is just what they want out there, to divide us, get us fighting with each other!" Arturo stopped struggling. Joselino relaxed his grip. "This is all we need. If we fight each other how can we fight them?"

Arturo scowled and finally nodded. The others stepped back, and he dusted himself off. He dismissed Benedicto with a wave. "If there's any fighting, keep this insect away from me." He looked at Cristóbal. "So what should we do if we can't fight?"

Joselino held up a finger. "We need allies. Maybe we can get word out somehow. The priest — they have to let him leave, don't they?"

Cristóbal shook his head. "No, he's stuck here with us, and besides, who would he bring back? The bishop?"

Miguel stared at Arturo. So he wasn't the only one who hated Benedicto. Maybe there was something . . .

"How about our natural allies, the boys in the hills?" Benedicto asked. His sneer made Miguel's teeth clench. "Our protectors, our saviors? Where are they now? Maybe they don't know we need them to come back now and keep their promises. Let's cry to the mountains. Come on!" He cupped his hands and shouted. "Help! Help! Save us! Help!" He burst out laughing. "Come on in and fight it out with the Special Forces! Here's the prize!" He waved at Miguel and out at the bustling plaza. The noise was increasing as the churchgoers found friends, squatted down to talk and bargain, pinched the pigs and chickens.

The familiar sight of his friends and neighbors made Miguel's chest hurt. This was what he fought for, these simple people who lived and laughed and died unknowing how they could be free. It was parasites like Benedicto who kept them slaves, pandering to the landowners, seducing everyone with penny wages and dirty labor, leeches the revolution was picking one by one off the body of the people. It would be simple justice to let the army take Benedicto, to do the job the revolution would have to do later.

"Benedicto," Miguel began. Slowly, this was dangerous. "Where *were* you last night?" The others turned to look at him. "Maybe Arturo has a point. Weren't you supposed to be at the church, with Father Edmundo?"

Silence. Benedicto's eyes narrowed. "Me? You're asking me where I was?" He gave a short laugh. "Who do you think you are, you little punk? Why don't you tell us where *you* were?"

"Answer the question."

"This is incredible. You hear this? He's a coward, he's trying to save his own skin. He really is a terrorist and he's looking for a scapegoat. He's the one the army wants and they've probably got a good reason. You're the one who needs an alibi, not me!"

"You can ask Caterina where I was. What about you?"

"Caterina!" Benedicto's eyes went wide and he laughed explosively. "Caterina? You're saying you were with Caterina?"

Miguel nodded. Something was wrong.

"Hah! I was with Caterina, not you! That's amazing!" Benedicto gestured wildly. "He says he was with Caterina! Let's get her here, ask her about it! She'll tell you. She was with me, not him! All night!" He leered at Miguel. "And we had a fine time together, too!"

The others gave them both startled looks. Miguel raised his fists. "You fucking liar." He leaped at Benedicto.

The older man stepped back, his hands up. The millisecond was enough for Cristóbal and Joselino to jump in front of him, and then he punched at Miguel, who clawed back at him around the two big men in the middle.

"God dammit, stop this! Both of you!" Cristóbal shouted, pushing. "Jesus!"

The struggle was uneven, and all four lost their balance, toppling over together like a collapsing building. Cristóbal fell half on Benedicto, who gasped and went limp, his wind gone. Miguel flailed away on top of Joselino, who put out a burly arm and flung him around hard on his back. The peacekeepers kneeled over the combatants, panting.

"Good Christ! Enough of this!" Cristóbal got up. He kicked at Benedicto's leg. "Get up! Get up!" Benedicto moaned and rolled onto his side, breathing in short gasps. "You too, Miguel! That's enough!"

Miguel sat up, arms around his knees, breathing hard. "That asshole. Sonofabitch!"

Benedicto at last sat up. Cristóbal hauled him to his feet. "Get away from here, why don't you? Goddamn troublemaker, go on — " He shoved him toward the market, where every face looked back at them, astonished.

Across the square, Gregorio had also spotted the scuffle, and he zigzagged through the crowd toward his friend, pushing and calling. He came up short behind a wall of men who had been watching the fight, and as he pushed to get through he saw Benedicto, who was dusting off his trousers and his shirt, half bent over, his hands shaking.

"You're all crazy, all of you." Benedicto breathed more deeply. "You just wait, you just ask Caterina who she was with last night. She'll tell you." He spat once at their feet and shouldered past Gregorio into the crowd, unseeing.

Joselino stood in front of Miguel, blocking him. Cristóbal put a hand on Miguel's shoulder. "Now calm yourself, just calm down."

"Oh, leave me alone. I'm all right." Miguel wiped his forehead. "Lying bastard. I'll shoot him myself, to hell with the army."

"Come on, let's go in and have a drink. Come on."

The crowd eased and Gregorio burst through. "Miguel!" He ran up, panting.

Miguel looked at the contorted face and went cold.

"Miguel! It's Irene! She's — you've got to —" His hands flailed as if to pull words from his own mouth. "The soldiers, they caught her —" He reached for Miguel with one hand, touching his chest, and with the other gestured vaguely behind him. "At your house."

Miguel stared at him. Then he pushed past Gregorio and began to run. They had killed his father, they had ruined his mother, now they had killed his sister, his innocent sister. They were closing in on him, the walls were falling, he was being crushed slowly like Jorge the *chiman*, dying in an earthquake he had no way to stop. He shoved through the crowd, stumbling on animals, ignoring the cries of protest, a truck through reeds of grass.

Seventeen

MARTÍN JOYABAL and Emidio Tijax lay propped on their elbows in the shade of boulders just below the ridgeline of the hill opposite Akabal. The plaza surged and shimmered through their field glasses.

"That tall one got the worst of it both times," the sergeant said, his voice husky with the pleasure of watching other people fight. They watched the lone figure work his way through the crowd toward the broad path that led across the cemetery and down the hill. "Everybody's mad at him. Maybe he's the one we want."

Emidio focused on the tall man's face. "Mother of God . . ."

"What? You know him?"

Emidio swallowed. "My brother." He had not been able to see clearly before, but the walk, the slump of the shoulders, that brushfire hair — no question now.

"Your brother? I didn't know you had family here."

Emidio clenched his teeth and cursed himself for letting surprise loosen his tongue. Pig-brain sergeant was delighted. No right, he had no right to know, to interfere in family business. He forced his jaw to relax but kept his face expression-less. "I didn't either."

Questions flooded his mind, collided and shattered into silence. After a few moments, Benedicto alive was a fact to him; a minute before, the truth was that Benedicto had vanished for a year in some far-off place. He had simply risen from the death of coastal dysentery or fever or a drunken brawl where Emidio had imagined him when he did not return from the coast.

Joyabal waited a full minute before he was certain Emidio would say no more. "So? What do you mean?" He blew his nose with his fingers and wiped them on his pants.

Emidio looked slowly at this restless Ladino creature. "He disappeared a year ago. I didn't know he returned."

"Well, where was he? What was he doing? Why was he fighting with those other guys? Who were they, did you recognize any of them?"

Emidio heard his own questions in the mouth of a puppy yapping at nothing. He shrugged, determined not to answer. "Just a fight. Who knows?" He turned away to look again through his binoculars. Benedicto was moving through the crowd toward the road, stopping, then slowly working his way through the brush below the edge of the ridge. Behind Cristóbal's shop, which backed on the gully, he opened his pants and relieved himself against a tree. Reaching beneath the shop's cement block foundation, he pulled out a bottle, took a quick drink, and tucked the bottle inside his shirt, under his arm. Then he ran his hand through his hair, climbed back up the ridge into the square, and disappeared into the market kaleidoscope.

Joyabal poked Emidio in the side. "Hee, hee. Your brother's going to have himself a little party, hey? How about that?"

Emidio watched the market. Cristóbal, Arturo, Joselino — he recognized them easily by their bulk, and the smaller man in the fight was probably Miguel, judging by his stance, but Emidio wasn't sure. He felt secretive, cornered by Joyabal's proddings.

"So now what? You think they're gonna do anything?" The sergeant scanned the crowd and sighed. "Doesn't look like it." He put down the field glasses and rolled over on his back. "Damn, it's hot! Dumb shit Gomez oughta be here himself." He put an arm over his eyes. "What about that priest? You know him?"

"Yes. Ladino."

"Not from here?"

"Santa Rosa. He comes every month, two months."

"He talk politics much? Human rights, freedom, oppression, that sort of stuff?"

Emidio looked away. "No. Always Jesus." He decided to be amiable, to avoid talking about Benedicto. "He was very hard at first. Four years ago, he didn't baptize babies if the parents weren't married. Always angry at us. He hates Maximon. But he brings flour and medicine. I think he is a good man."

"I knew a priest once who was a communist." Joyabal grinned, glancing sideways at Emidio. "He was a real rabble-rouser, an honest-to-God communist; he even told me he was." Emidio said nothing. "It was up in Benen, when I was driving my truck, before I joined the army, in the jungle — ever been up there?" Emidio shook his head. Benen was as far as the stars. "Really different country, wet and rain like you wouldn't believe. They still have quetzals up there, even. I heard one once. But this guy, I met him when I was taking out a load of logs for this company I worked for, a really good operation. They paid better than I'd ever seen before . . ."

Tijax took a deep breath. Another Joyabal story that would round the bases of his humble origins, his poor family, his amazing luck and success in every effort, and finally score the point that he held secret power and you'd better be friendly. Ladinos were all alike, transparent.

". . . and here was this broken-down jeep in the road, mud to your balls and dug in deep, with a guy pushing in back. When he turned around he had on the collar, see, so I knew he was a priest, and I was kind of disappointed, you know, because you can't charge a priest anything, it has to be a gift for God, blessings on us all. So I offered to pull him out of the mud for free with the chain on the truck but he said no, he'd only get stuck again, and he was just trying to push it off the road if he could get a ride with me down to the highway. So that's what we did. He climbed in and we talked about an hour. It took us that long to get down the mountain in those days. Now you've got that Yankee highway right up in there, you know, but not then. Anyway, I asked him what was he doing in such a godforsaken place and he said he was working in solidarity with the people, people like me." Joyabal snorted in derision. "People like me! I'm getting rich driving this big fancy truck and seeing the country, having a great time, and he's in solidarity with me. Well, right away I knew he was a communist. Nobody else talks like that. So I let him talk. He told me he was working with a bunch of nuns up there on some nursing school they'd started in the hills, midwives and such for the Indian women, but he didn't like the idea. He said the school was a front, just a way to make the women feel better, but there wouldn't be any real change for them, and it would just slow things down.

"I asked him slow what down, and he got real serious." Joyabal puffed his chest and made his voice pompous. " 'A change in the structure of society, fundamental change.' So, well, what could I say? He went on about how he was working with land rights on the side and that a lot of people would be moving up there pretty soon, and that would change things for sure. That made me kind of mad, so I asked him right out, 'Won't people say you're a bunch of communists?' And he said, 'So what if they do?' And he gave me a funny smile. He wasn't offended, so I knew he was telling me he was one. Isn't that something? So I played along, I asked him what about the church, didn't the bishops give him any trouble."

Joyabal rolled over and squinted at Emidio. He raised an index finger. "And I still remember what he said. He said, 'The church is an obstacle to God's will on this. There's a big difference between the bishops in the cathedral and the true religion of Jesus Christ.' Can you believe that?"

Emidio grunted.

"Well, that was it, I had his number then. He went on about how the time was coming when all the priests might have to leave the church, when it would die so the true religion of Christ would survive, or something like that. He talked about Poland, of all places. The church died there but Christianity was stronger than ever, he said. Poland, Russia, they're all communists over there if you ask me. Obviously this guy was a real nut. Anyway, he kept talking and when we got to the highway he gave me his name and address and said to keep in touch." The sergeant's smile was triumphant. "I did that, sure enough. I joined the army a few months later, right around the time all those squatters moved in up there. I told my commander about this guy and poof, that was the end of him."

Tijax kept looking through the field glasses.

"Pretty good, eh?" Joyabal prodded.

Tijax grunted again.

"The army cleaned out the squatters too. I felt damn good about the whole thing. That's the only way to deal with communists, you know. You can't reason with them; it's all tricks and lies on their side. You've got to get them one by one or whenever they turn up, *bam bam bam*, and then the other ones get the message and lie low. Otherwise they just wait for you to relax a little and they're right in there, pitching the poison. It's a real disease, a cancer like they say. These are not nice people. You can't just sit back and hope they'll go away."

Emidio put the binoculars down and looked at his sergeant.

Slowly, enunciating each syllable, he said, "This priest in Akabal is not like that. He talks only about Jesus."

Joyabal looked surprised. "Well, I'm glad to hear it." He seemed annoyed.

Tijax turned back to watch the market. Neither spoke.

Martín Joyabal was sweating heavily, and he scratched his crotch. "This is stupid. Nothing's going to happen. I'm going to take a nap. If anybody does anything, go ahead and shoot 'em."

Tijax murmured assent. Joyabal settled into the rocky slope, his hat over his face, and sighed. In seconds he was snoring softly.

A wave of fatigue washed over Tijax. His eyes felt full of grit against the binoculars and his face was as sticky as the khaki shirt on his back. His shoulders ached. He couldn't see his old house from this angle, but he could summon up its dark cool room, the low fire, and the peaceful smell of tortillas cooking. He wondered whether Benedicto was living there now, whether he'd had to evict some squatter who moved in when Emidio didn't come back from the movies. When had Benedicto returned? Why? Where had he been? A rush of longing and concern for his brother surged in Emidio's chest, surprising him. He hadn't worried about Benedicto in years, not since he had grown out of his childlike admiration for his big brother's cleverness and seen the nervous bully underneath. But now both of them were back in Akabal, he up here on the ridge, waiting for the lieutenant's crazy deadline, and Benedicto down there, fighting with half the town. What was it Joyabal had said, that Gomez called the whole village a bunch of traitors? What did he mean by that? Maybe Miguel had gone bad, but was it really possible the subversives had taken over everything here since he left? The gods knew they had tried often enough. But so had the army. Benedicto sneered at one side the way he sneered at the other, after they were out of earshot. He tried to imagine Benedicto joining a cause, any cause, and smiled to himself. If there was money in it, or a woman, or some business deal, his brother was capable of doing anything: knifing babies, raping women, bombing the barracks, whatever, wearing a third or even a fourth face. But believing in it — that he would never do. The fucking sergeant had said maybe he's the one we want, but that was ridiculous. He didn't know anything.

He remembered the day Benedicto was arrested, two years ago, after a bombing made the army set up roadblocks all over the province. Emidio had been along for the ride to the coast when the soldiers stopped Benedicto's truck. A corporal listened stone-faced to Benedicto's nervous jokes, but Benedicto just couldn't shut up. When the jokes turned to bluster, the soldiers got annoyed and dragged him and three others off the truck. They let Emidio go on with the truck, although he barely knew how to drive it, and they stood by laughing as he clashed the gears, wobbling away. Benedicto came home two days later, but the others never came home at all. His brother waved a hand in dismissal when Emidio asked what had happened.

"Aah, I told them a story that my sister was sick and gave them ten dólares. Fucking assholes'll believe anything for enough money." But he had tousled Emidio's hair and brought him a glorious present, a new shirt, bright red, with a Yankee cowboy cut and mother-of-pearl buttons. When Emidio put it on, it was tight across the chest, which surprised Benedicto — Emidio was six years younger, always the kid brother, but he was growing up faster than Benedicto thought.

Emidio's chest felt tight at the memory. He had been wearing that shirt the night the army caught him at the movies, and it lay in his footlocker back at the barracks, although he could only wear it completely open now, with the sleeves rolled up to disguise how short they were. He sighed. Across the gully he could focus on a dozen or so people at a time through his field glasses, and many wore a similar bright red. Some were sitting vacantly beside their piles of wood or peppers or chickens, but small huddles of men argued here and there, waving a hand, now jabbing a finger. Were they all subversives arguing strategy? Maybe by this time tomorrow they would all be dead. Maybe they would be lying in a bloody pile right there, where they stood now.

He had seen such piles before. Four times in the past nine months he had been part of mop-up operations when the Special Forces cleaned out rebel campsites. He had been scared at first, but he was a good shot and managed to fire fast enough to stay alive. Terrorists deserved to die, and he had kicked the bodies in satisfaction and helped throw the pieces on the oozing pile. He even had souvenirs back at the barracks: a Chinese rifle and a Russian knife. He scanned the plaza and saw people he knew, poor Juanita with her peppers, so thin now, and the foolish old carpenter Genero. No Russian weapons there. His brother was around somewhere. Subversives? A shiver ran from Emidio's chest to his toes and back up to his scalp. A trickle of sweat itched his neck. He saw the dogs lapping at scarlet puddles, the first vultures circling overhead. The silence was always eerie, after the earthshaking gunfire. In a hut a baby would wail and someone would be sent to shoot the baby too — in kindness, the lieutenant always said. Emidio's vision blurred. He saw his brother's seamed and stubbly face as though through cross hairs, the feathery hair backlit in the sun, the eyes bleary and unfocused. Maybe he's the one we want. Emidio's index finger twitched on the binoculars. Subversive. Bombed the barracks. The pile of bodies lay before him, Cristóbal, Arturo, Miguel, Edmundo, Genero, Juanita. They lay agape, their eyes wide, astonished, empty. Collaborators. Traitors. Communists. His hand shook. He pulled the trigger again and again and again.

Eighteen

GREGORIO wandered in the market, nodding at his neighbors, his vision streaked as a rain-washed drawing. He stepped carefully among the pigs and chickens in cautious greeting, hoping only to avoid disturbance. He was a sack emptied recently of its contents, retaining his shape out of habit, and as he had nothing much to do anymore, nor ever would again, he smiled and moved about, appreciating things, fitting himself in the spaces of this real world. The sky was a dark thick blue he had no paint to catch, thinning into cobalt as it touched the mountains. The piled white lime was dazzling and he stared at it a while, comforted by the gray and ivory shadows in its chunks and drifts. Even in such purity there were grades and variations, enriching for the whole, not wrong, not shameful. He wandered over to the babble of Juanita's little radio, its tinny salsas dancing in and out among commercials and soccer scores. She squinted up at him and said something, but he couldn't make it out, and smiled at her. He moved on, pillowed by the surging chatter and breezes of the plaza, freed of all decisions, moving with the other shadows. After a while he felt a strong grip across his shoulders.

"Hey, why the sick look?" Benedicto punched him on the elbow. "Come on over here. You don't look so good. Wanna have a drink?"

Gregorio felt mild surprise that he merited attention. Benedicto pulled and pushed and led him out of the comfortable hubbub, toward the desolate corner of the plaza by the church. Gregorio did not resist. He was probably wrong about Benedicto too, this cheerful character, the way he had been wrong about everything else. It didn't matter. They went around to the side wall of the shed, and Benedicto spread a white handkerchief in the narrow shade. He sat down, adjusting his creased pants with care, and looked at Gregorio. "Well? Come on."

Gregorio sat. He slumped against the cool wall and left his legs limp in the sun. They looked out over the hill that sloped to the stream below, the rocks down a way to the left, the dry hills beyond white in the shimmering heat. Layered puffs of cloud rolled away through the dark secret blue overhead, every tendril solid as marble, every shadow gray as death, hundreds of soldiers on silent parade. The two men were alone on the planet, specks of dust in a sky-blue desert.

"Here. Do you good." Benedicto unscrewed the bottle cap and took a long swallow. He gasped. "Damn!" The bottle was caked with dirt, half full of colorless liquid, sparkling innocence under the crusted glass. Gregorio raised it and drank, fire filling his nose and pouring down inside. His eyes watered and he took several deep breaths.

"Drink and eat and be happy because we die tomorrow. Like the gringos say," Benedicto confided. He took another swallow.

"Fuck the gringos." Gregorio reached for the bottle and drank again. Liquid heat flowed down his arms, into his knees.

"Right, fuck 'em all." Benedicto took the bottle back. "Listen to that buncha fuckin idiots back there. Buying, selling, yammering on about the damn chickens. You'd think they were gonna get a chance to cook 'em." They shook their heads. The buzz of the market rose and fell like insects calling in the night.

"Tomorrow we die." Gregorio made no effort to care.

"Yeah. Buncha fuckin communists."

Gregorio nodded, but then he stopped. "Communists? Who's a —"

"The soldiers, the whole army. Fuckin communist bastards."

Gregorio tried to focus on him. "The soldiers?"

"Yeah, communists, fascists, what the hell, same thing."

"Right." Gregorio had another swallow. "All the same when we're dead."

"The same right now, the day before we're all dead."

Sadness flooded Gregorio. Poor Irene, poor Miguel, poor Cecilia. Ruin and death and damnation under a sunny sky. A sob rose in his throat, but he took another swallow and forced it down. "Some of us are dead already."

Benedicto looked at him. He shut one eye and held up a finger. "You mean your buddy. Listen, Miguel's a fuckin idiot. You're a lot smarter'n he is." He drank. "What about him, anyway? Is he gonna go quietly tomorrow, save the rest of us, or what?" He looked again at Gregorio. "You talk to him? Where is he, anyway?"

Gregorio shrugged and closed his eyes. "His house. Told him . . . the soldiers. They got Irene." He waved toward the stream. "She was down there, this morning . . ." His hand felt like lead and he dropped it. "Four of them." His chest heaved and tears gushed from his eyes.

Benedicto shook his head. "Ah, Jesus." He leaned forward and clumsily patted Gregorio's leg. "Jesus." He drank again. "Listen, that wasn't part of the — it was an accident. They were just — ah, Christ." He waved a hand and drank. "So what's he gonna do?"

"Nothing. What can he do? Nothing we can ever do."

"Yeah." They sat in silence, passing the bottle back and forth. Benedicto drained it and tossed it into the gully. "Y'gotta be a moving target, that's what. Problem with us is we sit still too much."

"Dumb Indians."

"Army's Indians too. So's the commies. All of us taking orders all the time. Rich guys give the orders, Indians take 'em."

"No rich guys in the mountains."

"Sure there are. Who you think started the subversion anyway? Rich kids in the army, wrong side of some coup, long time ago."

"Miguel's not rich."

"He's a dumb shit. Soldiers all dumb shits, both sides. Emidio, he's a dumb shit too, joined up while I was gone."

"We're all dumb shits."

"Not me. Not gonna be some chicken, sitting around squawking, just waiting for it. Rich guys sitting up there, nothing to do. Top of the pile so they want to rearrange it, want everybody to hold still so they can move us around the way they want." He poked Gregorio in the arm. "Lefties too. Talk about classless society — that's bullshit. Even cows have ranks, and people are gonna be different? Sure. The runt chickens will be the top peckers. That's just moving the pieces different places."

Gregorio remembered a drawing of Napoleon moving toy soldiers around on a table map. Now the generals had bigger maps, markers for thousands, millions, of men. The clouds had lost their sharp edges above, but they marched on, rolling relentlessly to the horizon, under orders.

". . . chickens, buncha chickens getting ideas, moving themselves around, that's your revolution whichever side. Guys on top, nobody wants that, no matter who they are." Benedicto swayed and slumped against the wall, his eyes shut. "Everybody wants armies, keep out the troublemakers, make everybody hold still. So you kill a few chickens here and there" — he waved at the hills and started to laugh "— and nobody notices."

"Chickens don't notice either." They both laughed. Benedicto turned his laugh into a rooster's crow, and Gregorio cluck-cluck-clucked in agreement. They laughed some more. "Grawk! Miguel!" Benedicto raised an imaginary gun and fired. "Blam! Grawk! Gluck-gluck! Cristóbal!" He fired again. "Ka-rawk!"

Gregorio flapped his hands. "Gruk-gruk-gruk!"

Benedicto put his pistol finger at Gregorio's ear. "Blam!"

"Rawwwwkkk . . ." Gregorio's head slumped sideways. Benedicto collapsed onto his shoulder, laughing. They chuckled into silence, leaning together, propping each other up. The sun was hot. Benedicto's breathing became regular. Soon he was snoring. Gregorio's head swam, his vision full of dancing chickens. Some wore peaked roofs as hats, some soldiers' helmets, and a few had black bandanas. He couldn't hear any music.

"Well, look at this." A cool shadow fell across Gregorio's legs, and as he opened his eyes, Caterina's dark skirt brushed his arm. "Are you all right?"

"Yeah, I guess. I don't know." His stomach seemed to be sloshing back and forth.

She squatted beside him and took his hand. "What happened?"

"I dunno. Nothing."

"I saw Miguel go running off. What was that about?"

"No, too late. 'S all over. Blind dumb shits." Gregorio's head was loose on his neck. "I'm drunk."

"Yeah, you sure are. Here." She slipped her arm around him and sat beside him, pulling his head down on her shoulder. The rough cotton scratched his cheek; the smell of her made him dizzy. She patted his head. "You're so good, so sweet . . ." Benedicto rumbled softly on his other side. Caterina sighed. "So here we are, just waiting for the end. Everything's gone now, isn't it? The way everything used to be . . ."

"Buncha dumb chickens."

"Yes, chickens, can't even lay anymore." She stroked his hair. "Your drawings no good, my holy stones don't talk to me. So what do we do, hmm?"

"Gotta keep moving. Stay outta the way."

"Ah, it's too late already. No more time."

"Outta time. Poor Miguel. G-rawk!" He put his finger to his temple and fired. "Pshiaow! Hah. Poor Miguel, po-oor Miguel, Mii-guel, mi guerr —" He lapsed into tuneless Spanish song. "Mi guerrilla, guerrillero, Miguel." Gregorio shook his head. "I knew it all the time, all the time . . ."

She stroked his forehead, frowning. "What all the time? You knew what?"

He sang softly to himself. "*Los maté, si señor . . . y si vuelvan a nacer, yo los vuelvo a matar . . .* I killed them, yes, and if they're born again, I'll kill them again . . ."

Caterina sat up and took Gregorio's head in her hands. Her yellow eyes were hot on his face, and Gregorio looked away. "What are you talking about? Look at me!" She shook him.

"You know, you know all about it." He reached up and took her wrists, pulling her hands down his cheeks. He held them there. "Miguel, our buddy. Been fooling all of us. Me too. All of us. Blew up the place —" He stopped at her confusion and released her hands, exhausted.

"He never . . . I didn't . . . Why didn't he tell me?"

"He did. Told all of us. All the time. Didn't listen."

Benedicto stirred in his sleep and coughed. Gregorio shut one eye and put a clumsy finger to his lips, then shook it from side to side.

Caterina stood up in a swirl of skirts. She reached across Gregorio and poked Benedicto. "Hey! Benito! Wake up!"

He grunted and sat up. "Caterina?" He squinted up at her and reached for her hand. His feet scrabbled under him. "Been waiting for you. Let's get out of here." His feet wouldn't cooperate, and he fell back on Gregorio. " 'Scuse," he muttered. Gregorio waved forgiveness.

Caterina hauled him upright. "Sure, sweetie, let's go. Let's go right now and make sure everything's still okay, all right?" She put one hand on the bulge in his trousers.

"Yeah, right." He swayed toward her. "We can get out, let's go. Let's get out." She put his arm over her shoulders and they staggered two steps. He stopped and held up a finger. "Wait. Have to wait until dark. Not now."

"Right, we'll wait. Let's go home." They moved away. She looked back at Gregorio. Her eyes were wide, yellower than Gregorio had ever seen them. "I've got to make sure. If I can get him — if he can do it I'm okay."

"Yeah, right." Gregorio's head bobbed several more times than seemed necessary. Caterina and Benedicto disappeared around the corner of the shed, into the noise of the square.

Gregorio let his head sag back against the wall. He stared at the hills. Caterina, Cecilia, Irene. He wanted to go tell Miguel the rest of it, the whole sordid mess. But he would rest a while first.

When he opened his eyes, the shadows were longer. His mouth tasted like rotten bananas and his groin ached. He got onto all fours and with great care, one foot, the other foot, managed to stand up. He lurched toward the latrine but couldn't wait; he peed a river against its door. Then he turned back toward the plaza.

Nineteen

BLESS ME, FATHER, for I have sinned . . .
". . . lusted after my neighbor's wife . . ."
". . . touched myself, but only when I couldn't sleep . . ."
". . . taken the name of God in vain . . ."
Go ye and sin no more.

". . . gave them food and water."
"Did they threaten you?"
"Yes, but later they paid me a little. I was still afraid."
"What else did you do for them?"
"I delivered a message. And I lied about where they were."
"Nothing else?"
"I was happy to see them. Father, is that wrong?"

". . . and so I shot them. God forgive me, Father."
"But you had orders to shoot them?"
"Well, yes. The sergeant yelled, 'Fire!' and everybody started shooting. It was very dark."
"How do you know it was you who killed them and not somebody else?"
"I had them in my rifle sight. I'm a good shot, Father."

"Then what happened?"

"Then we made sure they were all dead. We . . . we took their guns and things."

"You kept these things?"

"Yes. No. I mean I gave them away, later. To my son. This was years ago, Father."

"Why did you wait so long to confess?"

"Well, you said . . . today . . . if we were honest . . ."

"I have impure thoughts, Father."

"I understand. What do you — no, have you repented, have you stopped these thoughts, woman?"

"Father, they obsess me. My need is very great. Even now, I —"

"Be stronger than these thoughts. God will forgive you. Now go and —"

"Even now, listening to you, I am wet and heavy, Father. Please, you are a man, as a man you can help me. I —"

"Caterina, I — this is impossible. You can't — you must control yourself!"

"Father, I can't, I think of nothing else, your —"

"Stop this at once! You shouldn't even be in here, you're not a —"

"Where else, what else? You're the only one left, I need you to —"

"Quiet! No! You must leave, this is a desecration."

"But Father, you might see, you might like —"

"You must leave at once."

"Father? Father? Just one more word . . . Father, are you there? Edmundo? Listen, I know you're still there. I'll come back later, all right? Edmundo? You'll be glad to see me . . . I'll come back later."

"She begged me not to, but I went ahead. I was scared, but the other guys, they were laughing, they said I was a pansy . . ."

"This is very serious. When did this happen?"

"Two weeks ago. It was late, Father, she shouldn't have been out. We were coming back from Santa Rosa —"

"Drunk, were you?"

"Just a little, not very much. But she started screaming, Father, and so I — I had to hit her . . . "

"You hit her. And then what?"

"Well, she wouldn't stop, so I guess I — I hit her again. Forgive me, Father."

"First you must make up for this thing. What have you done to make amends to this girl? I can't hear you. Now, crying won't help. You must go back to Tekan, to this girl and her family, before you can receive absolution, do you understand?"

"Yes, Father, but —"

"You must send word to them asking forgiveness. You must offer to help the girl, you must ask her what you have to do. Then when you have done it, you can come back here. Is that clear?"

"But Father, she's not there anymore. She's — the family left, Father. They all moved away somewhere. To the mountains."

"With the rebels, you mean?"

"No. Well, I don't think so. They're just in the mountains."

"I have sinned greatly, Father."

"The Lord is merciful. Tell me about it."

"I've been selfish and lazy and stupid, and other people suffer because of me."

"Miguel, no one is blaming you for —"

"No, Father, not that. It's the soldiers; they're here and they got Irene, and it's because I —"

"Irene? What happened to Irene?"

"They raped her, Father. Down at the stream, this morning. I thought she was dead when I got to the house, but then she moved and she told me. She's just barely alive, Father, and she's not right in the head now —"

"Dear God, bless her and preserve her. But that's just shock, Miguel, that'll pass. I'll go to her later. Don't blame yourself, my son —"

"Yes, it is my fault. I was stupid to do it the way I did. If I'd been smarter I'd have done a better job, used more — I wouldn't have stayed so long, they wouldn't have followed me here, none of this would have happened. I was stupid and arrogant."

"Stayed so long? What do you mean? Stayed where?"

"At the barracks. I was — Father, I was just waiting to make sure, about the mission. I didn't expect — I didn't think they'd see me, and I never thought they'd be able to track me here. Forgive me, Father."

"Track you here? From the barracks? You bombed the army barracks?"

"Yes, Father. I confess it, and you must keep it secret, you know that, but it wasn't what you think, and I never did the rest of what they say. I never raped or killed any woman or child, that was a fucking lie, the soldiers are trying to —"

"You bombed the barracks. And you want forgiveness for what?"

"My pride, Father. I thought I'd get them all, I would get away from there, I never thought they'd manage to follow me here."

"Miguel, think for a moment. Listen. You bombed that barracks, you killed people. Isn't that more of a —"

"No! That's not a sin, that's justice, for what they've done to us! You said yourself, the sins of the fathers will be —"

"Miguel, pretend a minute that you have a brother, maybe Gregorio. Suppose Gregorio was a soldier and he was in the barracks. Now, would you —"

· "Gregorio would never be a soldier. Never!"

"But suppose he was. Listen, Miguel! Everybody has relatives in the army. You know that. Don't you see? It's as if you bombed Gregorio in there, or your mother —"

"No! That's backward! I'm doing it for them, to save them! It's justice, for all we've gone through, here, everywhere! Don't you understand —"

"Miguel, vengeance is the Lord's. We've gone through this before. You're just putting yourself on the same level as them, as the army, if you do this kind of thing."

"No, it's not the same. They're just little pieces of the corruption, the entire rotten system, and the revolution has to —"

"Don't talk slogans to me. You're not the revolution, you're Miguel Angel Kanak, one person, and God sees and judges you that way. Miguel? Are you listening to me?"

"I believe that any god who says we should do nothing in a stinking mess like this one is no god at all. That's what I believe. I'm leaving."

"Miguel, listen to me. Miguel, wait! Where are you — Miguel!"

Dear God, there were better ways to have handled that. Of course the situation should have been obvious. Why hadn't he seen it before? He was as blind as Miguel himself; he thought the whole episode was a misunderstanding, an exaggeration, an accident. But there aren't any accidents. Absurdities, yes, constantly. Like these confessions, godless revolutionaries making confessions, to whom? For what, what did he expect? And the others, what did they expect? A people of no gods or too many gods, mocking the church, warping the very idea of forgiveness of sins. More of them all the time, mechanically disgorging their blasphemous murders, rapes, cheats, torture, no thought of ending any of it. The confessions lay in the church like bloody vomit, the sinner purged, pure, exhausted, waiting for the priest to wipe it up, make everything clean, to bring the putrefaction into himself, hold it quarantined. He taketh away the sins of the world. And what doth he do with them? Where does the rot settle at the last?

Stupid priest. He should never have gone in the damn church, full of moaning old women and spineless idiots. The whole place is still part of the problem, understands nothing. Lets you think you can make up for your mistakes, start clean when you've done something wrong, but it's a lie, they only want you to shut up and spread your legs, just lie back and take it, don't make trouble, be a good little boy, let God take care of it in a million years or so when He's good and ready. Fuck that. Those days are over. This is history we're talking about here, a revolution. If the priests don't get the message, to hell with them. The hell with all of them and anybody else who can't figure it out.

Joselino's knees wobbled, but he would be extra careful and would maintain his dignity in the procession, he was sure. Carrying the heaviest corner of San Clemente's pallet was not too much for a man of his strength, for a man of his weight in Akabal. If only the streets were wider. Some of the turns were difficult. In the glass coffin the protector of Akabal reclined, glowing, magnificent in blue velvet, the faded folds luminous today, surely a good sign. When he felt the saint speaking, Joselino rang the little bell, sweet and clear as his sacred voice must have been. Down one alley, up another. Joselino made sure all the women and children in each doorway made the sign of the cross before he nodded at the boy in front to move on. Little Daniel Malik, grandson of Honorio Luxit the baker, exuding grave responsibility in every centimeter. This was his first time to lead the procession carrying the church's proudest treasure, the little square flag of filigree brass and silver. He looked so young, the back of his neck so soft and smooth above his grimy T-shirt, not like all the leathery men carrying the pallet, smiling, nodding, shuffling behind at this stately pace, cords of their necks bulging with effort under those tightly buttoned collars. Some of the sweat was fear, of course. Such a day! Everyone here weak in sin and temptation. Only with proper honors and respect from everyone in the village would San Clemente have the courage to call upon God Himself to save Akabal.

Maximon was floating, not really touching the blocky chair that the two capering boys below him carried along by one leg each. Caterina shielded her eyes from the critical sun and encouraged Diego to run on ahead a bit, to turn and dance and enjoy himself, running up to collect cigarettes and little bottles offered by the villagers watching the procession, running back to put them in the baskets she and the other women carried. The two children were so different, the boy so cautious, the girl strutting along beside her like a queen already, proud of her gap-toothed grin, the baby incisors on a string around her little neck. She would be a handful in a couple of years; the men were eyeing her already. She stroked the girl's hair, her back, her arms. Look, Maximon, how perfect she is, a treasure. Strong back, strong hands, sturdy legs — see how she strides along! — and beautiful hair. She has good hips; she will have many healthy children to honor you, Maximon, if you let her grow up and then find her a good husband. We will burn many candles to you then, Maximon. Hear me in your groin where men listen deepest and you will know that I am honest, I do what I do only for her and for Diego. Let me be strong tonight, Maximon; open to me once again the truths of your moon.

Twenty

MIGUEL KICKED the clod of earth hard with the side of his foot, as though sending a soccer ball to the end of the world. "And Irene thinks it's all her fault. That's the impossible part."

"I've been thinking it's all my fault, and you say it's your fault." Gregorio's tongue still felt thick and he rubbed his forehead. The fallow field radiated late afternoon sun and heat that made his ears ache.

"It's the fucking pig soldiers, the fascist government, that's who it is. Don't you see, we're all slaves, we've got to get rid of them, then we can be free, we can have enough land —"

"Yes, and Cadillacs will appear in the plaza and we'll all sprout patent leather shoes and wings and fly away." He spread his arms and did a clumsy arabesque. "These guys have pumped you full of so many words, they're blocking your eyes, Miguel. You can't see what you're talking about; you can't see what's really out there. You sound like my sister."

"Cecilia's right and you know it. She's been right all along."

Gregorio took a deep breath. "Miguel, Cecilia's dead."

They stopped walking and looked at each other. "I guess I thought so, but I didn't —"

"I've been wanting to tell you since I found out, last week, but you weren't around. Nobody else knows, not even my folks. I haven't had the nerve yet. I think it'll kill my mother."

"What happened?"

They sat down cross-legged in the dirt at right angles, as though waiting for a third person. Gregorio had the sensation of preparing to lift a great stone out of his chest. He took a deep breath and shut his eyes.

"About four months ago, you were away, Captain Lorenzo came to the house." He heard Miguel's sharp breath of surprise; the infamous head of the provincial garrison appeared only on distant daises, never near ordinary mortals. "Yes, we were astonished too. He came right up the hill in a jeep, all alone, no guards or driver or anything, and about half the people in town followed him to our house. You can imagine what that was like. Well, he was very polite, took off his hat and asked my mother if he could come in. She said of course, and he sat right down on the mat like a villager. Of course his eyes ran in the smoke and he tried to dust his boots off a couple of times, but mostly he seemed relaxed. I stood off to one side, behind him, watching him in case he went for his gun. But I don't know what I would've done if he had.

"Anyway, he told my parents he brought them greetings from Cecilia, that she was alive and well and being questioned at a secret place. He said he couldn't tell them where, but he admired her strength. My mother got so excited she practically kissed his hand. He said we should all be proud of Cecilia, that she was very beautiful and very strong, and by the way, did my mother happen to have a little something to eat around the house? He had come a long way.

"So my mother ran out and got some eggs and borrowed some beer and a little cheese — she couldn't give tortillas to this man who had so much power. She made him a meal, right then, and he sat there and ate it, stuffing his face while we all just sat and watched him. He took his time, too, and didn't say anything, just nodded that it was good. After he finished he wiped his face and told us we were really very lucky he was stationed here. 'You know, Cecilia is being very tough, very tough,' he said. 'But I am trying to make sure she isn't harmed. You know that isn't easy with things the way they are.' He was very serious. 'It would be easier if she would cooperate a little, you know,' he said. I felt so bad for my father. He just looked at the floor the entire time and never said a word.

"Mother said, 'If we could only see her, we could talk to her,' but the captain said that was impossible. He said he would use what little influence he had, and then he said, 'Of course, it would help if I had something I could use to persuade the others, you know, some little token, a few dólares perhaps.' "

"Ah, of course," Miguel whispered.

"Yes, of course. So they gave it to him, thirty dólares, all they had in the house, months of work. He said, 'Well, it isn't much but maybe it will do some good.' And he got up and left."

"The fucking bastard. So what—"

"He came back two weeks later. He said things were looking good, he might even be able to get Cecilia released. My mother clasped her hands together, she cried, my father cried, even I got a little hopeful. 'Let's drink to that!' Lorenzo said. So my father brought out a bottle and the captain drank almost all of it. Then he wanted something to eat again, and my mother fed him again. This time he told stories while he ate, things about Cecilia, what she had said, things about Akabal she must have told him. He said how wonderful it must be to have the baking cooperative and was it going well, things like that, and could he see some of my drawings. I said I didn't have any around at the moment and he gave me a look. Then he said it was too bad, but Cecilia still wasn't being very helpful. He said he was having a hard time protecting her and he would need some more money for bribes to the others. He said he needed a lot this time, really a lot, and he shook his head. Finally mother asked him how much, and he said it would take at least five hundred dólares."

"Five hundred dólares!"

"Yes. They told him they could never raise that much, that nobody in Akabal had that much. Then they got to figuring, this much for the sheep, that much for the chickens, borrow from the co-op, and beg from everybody and maybe they could raise two hundred. He said, 'Well, maybe that would do.' He said he would see and he went away.

"After that we had an incredible fight. They wanted money from me and I told them it was useless, that Lorenzo was just robbing them. 'You couldn't leave it alone, could you?' I screamed at my father. 'You had to get it all going again, you had to get back involved, didn't you, even after what they did to you the first time? You had to use her to spread your poison, your talk of revolution and the unions and the Agrarian Institute! You see what it got you, what it's got Cecilia? This is all a lie! She's probably dead already!'

"He hit me across the face. That old man, I didn't think he was so strong, but he nearly knocked me down. And he screamed at me, 'You, you're a useless parasite, sniveling around here, doodling and complaining, daydreaming when your people are starving! You won't lift a finger to save your own sister!' He swung his crutch at me, but I caught it and threw him down, my own father. He yelled up at me, 'You're a frog, hiding in the cracks. You think you're safe, but there aren't any safe places anymore. Either you fight or you die. You think you can be lukewarm — I'll spit you out of my mouth.' And he spat at me as hard as he could."

Miguel gripped his friend's arm. After a moment Gregorio continued.

"I just got out of there. I don't even remember where I went. We didn't talk to each other for a week." He drew a long breath and made circles in the dust with his forefinger. "At the end of the week my mother went to Santa Rosa with the money. I gave them everything I had, of course — hardly anything, but they sold everything in the house. It was all in ones and fives and change, stuffed all over in her clothes, and she had to wait outside the barracks half the afternoon as always, and when she got in, Lorenzo was furious. Why had she come there, she should have waited for him to come back, she might have ruined everything. She was petrified, barefoot and dirty and all alone in this big shiny place, so she just pulled all the money out; she counted it all out for him there on his desk.

"And you know, he calmed down watching her. He sat back and started smiling. She said there was a little dog in the room and he picked it up, a funny-looking little dog wearing a lampshade on its neck."

"A lampshade?"

"Yes, around its neck. He patted this dog and talked to it as my mother was counting out the money, and he told her the poor dog had a skin disease, mange probably, and had been scratching too much, so he put the lampshade on it to keep it from hurting itself." Gregorio made a face. "Such a kind man."

Miguel shook his head. "Then what?"

"Then nothing happened for about three weeks. My mother was crazy with worry. Finally Lorenzo appeared and this time he looked really grim. He didn't even get out of his jeep, just sat out there in it with the motor running. He didn't want any food, he was very serious. He said he hadn't been able to get Cecilia released and the others were about to give up on her. We knew what that meant, he said. Mother was just about hysterical. Then he said Cecilia was sick too, that her fingernails had gotten infected, she was bleeding a lot, and that made it hard on them, they wanted her out of there too really." Gregorio stopped and swallowed. "He said things were so desperate he might be able to arrange an escape. That was something we hadn't even considered before, and it took us a minute to believe he'd really said it. The problem, he said, was that the two hundred just wasn't enough for that kind of arrangement, that he would have to bribe a lot of people.

"So my father said, 'Give us a week and we'll raise more.' And he nodded and drove off. And Miguel, I swear this is true, those two old people managed to raise another two hundred fifty dólares. They went begging from door to door and they borrowed a hundred from Don Cristóbal and another hundred from the priest. Yes, even from him, they told him the sheep had all died and they needed a loan to buy more. And they took the money to Lorenzo again." Gregorio drew a long unsteady breath. "He said that would help and to wait for word. But nothing happened, no messages, nothing. It was awful at home, my mother crying all the time, then laughing about how wonderful it would be to have Cecilia back, and then crying again, and my father watching the road all day long. I couldn't stand it. So two days ago I went to Santa Rosa to — to find out . . ."

"What did you think you could do?"

"I don't know, but I had to do something. So when I got there I was really angry, I was ready to wait in line all day and all night, I had food with me and everything, but they let me in right away, he didn't keep me waiting at all. And when I came in he was there with the dog, the one with the lampshade, and he put the dog down and got up and came and put his arm around me, and he said, 'I'm so sorry, it hurts me very much to say this, but I have to tell you your sister has died.' He said, 'It was very disappointing to me. She was really a subversive, you know. There was nothing I could do.'

"I should have killed him on the spot. But I went numb

instead. I guess I had really been hoping inside that something would happen, that this time we'd be all right . . . Well, I didn't do anything. I asked when we could have the body, and he acted real surprised. 'The body? She's been buried for many days already. She was very sick before, you know, and — well, we couldn't wait for you. But listen,' he said, 'She was very special, very special, and you remember those boots of hers? She loved those boots. So I took care to bury her with those boots on.' I guess I stared at him, I couldn't believe it. So he explained, 'Don't you see? That way, later on, after all this business settles down, you'll be able to be sure it's her body. Nobody else has boots like that.' "

Miguel sat with his hand over his eyes. Gregorio rubbed his hands as though he could clean them of the captain's touch. "And then — you'll like this — he said because of security he couldn't tell me where she was buried yet, but if I wanted to make sure the site wasn't disturbed I could bring him a few dólares every month and he'd take care of it. I just stood there and stared at him with my mouth open, like an idiot. Finally he rang a bell and a soldier came in and pulled me out of the office."

They sat in silence. Miguel prodded the ground with a stick.

He took a deep breath. "Now you must join us, don't you see? The bomb was to do justice for you, for Cecilia." Gregorio stared at him, and Miguel rushed on. "If that didn't get him we'll take care of him together. We'll find him and we'll stuff that dog down his throat, lampshade and all. Even that will be too good for him."

"Yes, I want to kill him, you're right. But then —"

"Then what? Then you're free, you have revenge, you're a man! Gregorio, look at me. Every time I make a bomb I think of that truck driver who killed my father. I think of the coffee growers who rob us, and the soldiers, and the rest of them, all of them, paying them back a little finally for what they've done, just a taste of what they've made us suffer. It's just the tiniest part of the beginning of paying them back —"

"Yes, that's just it, that's what scares me. Don't you ever feel — swallowed up by it? That it's so big, there's so much blood already and so much yet to come? It's too overwhelming, I feel I'd be sucked into it and never come out, I'd just disappear. You don't talk about just Irene, or just Cecilia — it's not just making up for my father, or for yours, or anything like that. It's forever you're talking about, all our ancestors, all of history. It's too much. Just thinking about it makes me feel panicky, like I'm dying. I'm not strong enough for that, Miguel. I don't have enough to offer."

"You! Nothing to offer?! I used to think that too, but you! You've always been the smart one, your drawings, your fancy talk. You'd be wonderful, you could do anything. You could do the posters, the picture books we give to the ones who can't read, the letters — it's the pictures that make people understand. You could do that; you wouldn't have to make bombs."

Gregorio saw Miguel as if he were calling across a great canyon, urging him to take an impossible leap as though everyone knew naturally how to soar as Miguel had. What was it that enabled other people to be sure about things, about anything, when all he was sure of was doubt? Certainty was a glorious fire lit by miracles for a happy few, and he felt limp beside the energy of Miguel's conviction. Tears rose in his throat. He shook his head. "Listen, there's another problem. Benedicto — does he know about you?"

"I don't know." Miguel frowned. "I don't think so. We had that fight; Cristóbal and the others were there. He would have said something then, I think. Why?"

"We were drinking. It's pretty clear he'll make sure tomorrow that you — that the soldiers —"

"Yes, he was saying that all day. Let him try. The bastard,

he's the one that ought to get it, the worthless shit, not me. He'll have to go anyway in the revolution; you know that. People like him are useless, just parasites on the people." He stopped and looked carefully at Gregorio. Was it too soon or too late? He put his hand on his friend's shoulder. "Listen, Gregorio, I thought about this a while ago — we can convince the army it's Benedicto they want, not me."

"What do you mean?"

"Let them take care of him for us. They're looking for someone to blame for the bombing, they don't know who it is, they just got my name by accident. You can figure out what to say, we can tell them he's the one who . . . What's the matter?"

"No, it won't work. I couldn't — I don't know what you're talking about."

"Like hell you don't." Miguel's voice was hard. "Listen, my friend, this is war here. You think it's some game they're playing? You think those soldiers are sitting out there for the fun of it?"

"No, of course not, but I — the times have changed, Miguel. They aren't going to blow the whole town away anymore. They're bluffing about that. They have orders, like they said. If you go in, there'll be a trial, that's what they've promised, and we'd all go in to make sure, with Don Cristóbal —"

"Cristóbal!" Miguel jumped up. "That fat snake will survive if he has to sell us all! You can't be serious!" He crouched with his face inches from Gregorio's. "Listen. Those soldiers are here for a purpose, and that purpose is to kill me. Do you understand that? To kill me!" He stood up again, waving his arms. "These people are animals, fascist, imperialist pig animals. Think a minute what they did to your father, to your sister, to Irene. Just now, right now, to Irene! Is that the way times have changed? Don't you get it? That's what I'm trying to tell you. I don't have any choice. If you don't help me — they've got my name, Gregorio. I'm all alone in this.

If we don't convince them it's Benedicto they want, I'm a dead man."

They stared at each other, breathing hard. Birds wheeled overhead, the earth rolled hot beneath them. At last Gregorio looked away. "Yes. You're right, I agree. I'll do it. Whatever you say. Just tell me what you want." He lowered his throbbing head onto his arms.

Miguel stood above him. After a minute he opened his mouth and closed it. He turned away and turned back again. Then he spoke.

"No." Miguel crouched again. "You're right. I can't ask you to do this. No man can tell another what to do. You're not me; you have to do things your own way. You don't have to do anything." He put an arm around Gregorio's shoulders. "But listen. Don't say anything about it, okay? You just stay out of it. I'll go talk to Don Cristóbal. We'll figure it out, and then if we need you I'll let you know. All right?"

Gregorio nodded. He didn't look up. Miguel patted him on the shoulder, soothing a fretful child. "You just go on home now and keep your mouth shut, okay?" Gregorio nodded again. He heard the earth's soft crunch as Miguel walked away.

He sat up and watched the shadows a long time, noticing the way they circled and filled the field's dips and hollows as they lengthened. How beautiful. Even shadows had a place. But where did shadows go when the sun went down? Did they mourn their destiny in the mornings, knowing that evening doomed them? Where were they on cloudy days? Did he have as much substance as a shadow?

Twenty-one

EDMUNDO patted his rumbling gut and took another sip of wine. He tilted his chair back against Cristóbal's plastered wall and held the glass to the firelight.

"A fine dinner. Many thanks."

Cristóbal waved his own glass and blinked several times. The elders' meeting on Miguel's fate would start in a few hours, at midnight, and he would never be coherent without a nap. He yawned enormously.

"When you enter a new world, you suspend disbelief," Edmundo said, oblivious. "Have you ever seen the movie *The Wizard of Oz?*" Cristóbal shook his head, irritated. "It was in Santa Rosa a couple of years ago. Well, a good, beautiful witch floats down in a bubble. And nobody runs in panic or anything because they're not in Kansas anymore. Anything is possible, you see, when you go to a new place. And you tend to assume the new things are innocent; that's my point."

Cristóbal's jaw had gone slack. Edmundo leaned over and poked him with a forefinger. "Like babies. They assume everything is friendly. You go somewhere new and you assume there's an underlying order, that things are basically all right even if they look really strange, and all you have to do is figure it out. That's why we read books, we go to the movies, we listen to stories — to visit new places. And anything can happen — bubbles of witches, beauties with green skin, people going to heaven on clouds of butterflies. And we accept it all, we hardly notice them as artistic symbols." Cristóbal grunted. "And in life we do the same thing. We go to a new place, we have ritual greetings, expressions of friendship that everyone understands, or at least nonaggression — the hand up, a smile . . . We go in hoping for acceptance or toleration, and we're ready to believe anything can be normal there. It's a fundamental thing, it's a readiness to cooperate. I believe that may save us all in the end." He tilted his glass to his lips and noticed Cristóbal's suspicious look. He waggled a finger.

"No, truly. All the world's religions talk about this — everybody's first assumption is the same, a hope for good relations. When you see a stranger, you don't shoot right away. You assume he's friendly until you see otherwise. That means there's never any reason for fear. If everybody's hoping for cooperation, then we should all be able to live together peacefully, like children."

"Brotherhood of man."

Edmundo ignored Cristóbal's sarcastic tone. "Exactly. Be as a little child. The innocent expectations of children."

"And the child winds up skewered like a pig. Look around, Father." Cristóbal's voice was weary — not cynical, just realistic, he told himself. "The world's an armed camp, the visitors are looking to rob or kill or worse. People cooperate as long as they think they'd lose if they didn't. Your witch in a bubble — she's full of poison gas. I think we travel with a smile ready, but we must also keep a gun handy." The mayor aimed and cocked his finger.

Edmundo smiled. "You know, the Mayans had no idea of private property. Everything belonged to everybody, so there was no such thing as robbery. And before the Fall there was obviously no ownership of anything. So in a way you're right, really. It's a sign of our original sin that we're divided into people who have things and people who don't, and that we have governments to stop the stealing, to rule over our wickedness. And of course the more we sin, the heavier the governments become later — sins of the fathers and all."

"Well, our ancestors must have sinned very greatly, for all their lack of property, to give us such a heavy government now." They smiled. The mayor refilled the glasses. Outside they could hear singing as their neighbors wandered home from the last market sales.

"But Cristóbal, you must admit we begin in trust. Babies have to be taught to avoid the fire, the cliff. Even so, the children don't believe us half the time, they insist on hurting themselves. What is that but innocence, optimism, a will to goodness?"

"But falling off a rock doesn't give a kid a will to be bad. Pain by itself doesn't make a killer." Cristóbal's tongue was slow with sleep and he yawned again. "Danger is one thing, you can teach a child about that. It's not the same as evil."

"Although evil is dangerous."

"Yes, but for evil you need something else —"

"Betrayal. Betrayal of that first trust. Eat the apple. Push the kid off the rock, that's evil. And you know, it's inevitable in life, isn't it? We even expect it, we prepare for it, don't we? I mean, children playing — they're always pushing each other, playing tricks and laughing when the victim cries, really mean tricks sometimes. Do they learn that from their parents? No, we scold them for it. But even animals — kittens and puppies are forever pouncing, stalking and pouncing, practicing to kill some unsuspecting creature." He paused. "Now the scientists would tell you this is genetic, that it goes back to when we were all monkeys or lizards or even microbes, or farther back

than that, to when we were subatomic bits. Pushing and pulling forever, like electrons and protons, going forever back
and forth, bonding and breaking up. No choice about it,
doing it forever. Yes, forever, ever since the angels' fall from
heaven . . ." He fell silent and stared into the fire. "Opposites
attract, Cristóbal. Evil is monstrously seductive, monstrous.
We rush toward that which will destroy us." He reached for
the bottle.

After a moment he continued. "We do it to ourselves, really.
You know betrayal is coming, but by definition you don't know
for sure, you don't ever expect it, so you set yourself up to be
vulnerable, but you hope maybe this time . . ."

Cristóbal's chin had sagged to his chest, but Edmundo
hardly noticed.

"That's the thing, you see. If nobody betrayed anyone else,
we would all live in peace, like children, like brothers, all
vulnerable but safe too." He drank. "But it doesn't happen.
We warn the children about the fire and the cliff and they can
see it for themselves. But we warn them about evil and there's
nothing to see, to touch. What is the face of evil? The pictures
of Satan, with horns and a tail, flames and smoke? He leers at
us, he's red and evil, watch out for the devil, we say! Ah,
Cristóbal, if only people actually leered more often! If only we
knew evil when it appeared, if there were a sign, a mark of
Cain really, a number on the forehead, six-six-six, something
to make it easier. Then we would not be fooled."

He stopped. "But then nobody would ever have to do any
thinking, would they? Really, that's all we do in life, isn't it?
We choose this or that, better or worse, watching for danger.
And we can only learn by our own experience, or our par-
ent's." He waved the wineglass. "Think of all the millions who
have died in the learning! Don't drink this, don't eat that . . ."
He shook his head. "Danger everywhere, even in the good.
Maybe in the good especially, like parents who love their

children but let them down. A moment of inattention, exhaustion, temptation . . . Betrayal is inevitable, Cristóbal."

Cristóbal snored gently.

"And why, my friend? Why do we strive forever to avoid the inevitable, a cosmic game of " — he held the glass aloft — "of dodgeball? We can't win, the destroyer always comes. We drink in some new disease, we fall into the same hole that claimed our grandfather, we shoot someone who would later have saved us from the earthquake. Or we don't believe what we learn, we don't trust our own perceptions. Truly, God must be entertained, watching us forget or choose wrongly! Perhaps He — or perhaps it is a she? Why not a she? I don't see why God cannot be a she — perhaps She casts lots after all, which raindrop will reach the ground first, which of us will evade the most destroyers. How far can this one get? How much evil in how many wonderful disguises can that one discover and avoid? What entertainment!" The priest raised his glass as in a toast. After a moment he raised his other hand and held the glass aloft with both.

"So God created evil out of boredom. Ah, yes. Boredom." He lowered the chalice. "You know of the big bang, Cristóbal? Before it there was unity, perfection, total order, everything in its proper place and orbit, nothing different from anything else — without form and void." He gave a bitter little laugh. "Perfect, perfectly dull. Then, then . . . just one quiver of deviation, by one primordial particle, one speck of change — one Word, and bang — collision, explosion, total change, chaos! Nothing was related anymore to anything, all was independent, solitary bits, each one another perfection, alone and absolute. But it was the same thing — silent, boring! Only the potential of the other remained, the memory of it — and with no links anywhere, all links were suddenly possible. Think of it — what wild joy then! What infinite possibility — yes, infinite! How much more exciting than closed predictable perfection!"

He thought for a moment. "And gradually, here and there, a collision sticks, becomes a link, a rejoining, another word — bits collect other bits, fall apart again, surviving here and there longer and longer, making up rules and strategies . . . eventually stars, light, planets, you and me, every subatomic particle in us driving us to keep at it, this task of linking up, even in the teeth of inevitable destruction."

He sighed and sat back. "So here we are, Cristóbal, condemned by God to get together with others, forge alliances to clear a little space around us of danger. That is how we form society, my friend — we are all vulnerable, all about the same in threat and promise and need, so we cooperate, to give ourselves strength and breathing space, time to reproduce, raise the children, teach them how to survive as much as we know. But we know so little, there is so little understanding and so little will, and even less generosity. Obviously we have to have rules and leaders and organization and division of labor . . . and we fight over it all, don't we? Every union gives off heat, every border is drawn in blood." He sat forward with a thump of the chair legs, and Cristóbal woke with a start.

"This is our hell right here, my friend." The priest's eyes burned and Cristóbal blinked at him. "In this place the clearing is very small, the evil is so pervasive — early death is a mercy. Blessed are the stillborn who go directly to God!" He drank a toast and Cristóbal frowned, then got up, stretched his arms out to either side, shook himself, and poked the fire.

Edmundo hardly noticed his friend's irritation. "The children — what do they have here? Initiative is stifled, flattened, a rose trying to grow on a highway. How can anyone learn to know life when all choice is in the hands of others? A man can be disemboweled for a sarcastic remark — to speak isn't courage but idiocy, so how can he learn courage? To live in this place is to lose understanding of cowardice or courage, of success or failure, of hope and heartbreak, because there are no choices under the guns." He drained his glass. "Despair has no music, no art — they require hope or anger. Yet, and yet . . . again and again the children teach us, Cristóbal. They laugh in welcome of everything, expecting all to be good — the baby smiles and reaches up to touch the bayonet as it plunges toward his belly . . ." He stared blindly into the fire.

Cristóbal shook his head. "That's too bleak, Father. You're just tired. Akabal isn't that bad. We've survived a long time now, hidden away here. It was a paradise for me once, poor as it is, a home when I needed one, and we'll find a way out of this. There's always hope. Even in the worst places new things come always. The radio, the politicians, the doctors, the teachers — even you, talking your new Jesus. Even in this province new roads are being built. What you say is defensive; you make it sound as if people just live in fear all the time, building walls against threats." Cristóbal rubbed his eyes. "People are more ambitious than that. We go out every day looking for opportunity, something to use, something to do, some way to get rich. Today the market was full, even today. People don't just sit around hoping not to die." He gave the priest a sidelong look. "And what about Christ? Isn't Christ always with us?"

Edmundo took a deep breath. "Of course. Of course. He can save us all. If we have faith and do as the Bible tells us. But we don't. And people don't want change, Cristóbal. They fight it. Even good changes. And that's why God moves so slowly. People have to accept change willingly or it won't last. If you force it on them, they'll wait until you leave for a chance to have their own way again. A change must first affect the heart before it can affect the society. This is why revolutions are doomed to failure. Violent change is just the rule of the strongest again. No, if you let people alone and do not betray them, they are innately good, as God says."

"With all respect, Father, that's bullshit. Armies have changed history permanently since time began. If you let people alone, they try to take advantage of each other. The strongest do win and later they write the history that makes them look good."

"Well, you prove my point, Don Cristóbal. Evil people will have only evil governments. How can we have a tolerant government over people who solve every argument with a gun?"

"Perhaps a good government can seize power and force the people to be good to each other at least for a while, so they learn how. Benevolent dictatorship of philosophers like ourselves."

Edmundo grimaced and spread his hands. "You know that won't work. These connections have to be made by free will. If one person links to another, both become open to new worlds, each learns from the other new tricks to stay alive —"

"New torture techniques, new types of machine guns. Come on, Father. How long have the Indians turned the other cheek here, and what has it got them? Here we are, deciding tonight whether to betray an innocent man, a man at least who says he is innocent, or to die ourselves. This is hardly a new problem, and it's no easier now than it was the first time, probably back in the Stone Age."

"But innocence is not the issue. Don't you see? It's a test for us precisely because Miguel is not innocent! He is guilty, as guilty as sin itself! We are all guilty, of course. But that's irrelevant. For us the problem is the army, not Miguel, because the army usurps God's right to punish. He alone can judge Miguel, not the army, and we simply must not join the army in this terrible thing."

Cristóbal's eyes widened. Miguel guilty, of what the army said? He felt a wash of fear. Had he heard right? Was that what Edmundo had said, or was he hearing his own thoughts? "But perhaps the soldiers are right about him, Father? Do we know for certain what he did?"

"It's not relevant, what he did or didn't do." Edmundo

waved a hand. "He's just a symptom, a very small part of all this. What he did was unforgivable, unforgivable — but God will judge, only God."

Cristóbal's blood pounded in his ears. Miguel had done something unforgivable. He squinted at the troubled priest, willing him to speak clearly, knowing he would not. The mayor's voice was pleading. "But Father, by your own argument, if Miguel is guilty of something unforgivable, then the soldiers are God's instrument in his punishment, no? Or whatever he did, maybe that was God's punishment on the soldiers for something else —"

"No, no, no. That's —" Edmundo's face contorted. "That's too complicated. Miguel is guilty as we all are guilty, no more, no less. The army cannot judge him, we cannot judge him. No, the issue is how people are to learn to do God's will without giving up on anybody, even somebody as misguided as Miguel."

Cristóbal sat still a moment and regarded Edmundo, swaying slightly in his seat. The priest was telling him Miguel had been misguided in something he did, something unforgivable. But everybody was equally guilty. No. Miguel had done the bombing, Cristóbal knew it suddenly, knew with a cold certainty that meant he had known it a long time. The priest knew it too, but differently somehow; somebody had told him. Miguel himself, in the confession? Useless to ask that. Not even necessary. The mayor understood at last, Miguel's quiet simple face, that smile. He had been driven into that fatal commitment long ago, and Cristóbal had long ago decided not to notice, willing the strong young man to be an ally in staying on the fence. Cristóbal felt weak, betrayed by his own foolishness. He had thought of himself as leading the way through a dangerous forest, but in fact he was alone, still weaving this way and that, pushing on, while the rest had halted here or there, stopped at last by exhaustion and fear and loss. Only he had not yet said enough, this far and no further.

Well, on with it then. Miguel had chosen; he had not. He would not, not yet. He didn't have time. He drew a deep breath and braced himself. He slapped his knees. "Well, Father, I'm sorry, but I have to give up on this argument. I'm just too sleepy." He stood, fired by new energy. He would save them yet, he would continue somehow. There was much to do before morning.

"Yes, of course." Edmundo stood and teetered, then moved unsteadily to the door. "Sorry." He opened it. "I'll see you later, then, at the meeting."

"Yes. Good night."

"G'night. Oh, ah, thanks for dinner." The priest was slightly dizzy, but he felt lighter, almost cheerful for a moment. He aimed himself toward the church across the dark plaza and concentrated on steering between the piles of litter and banana peels and chicken bones, the debris of the day. A gust of chilly air blew him through the church door. It startled the candle stubs guttering before the saints and made the shadows dance wildly, like his thoughts. Perhaps the soldiers are God's instrument.

He sat down heavily on a bench and stared at his crucified God. The image's shadow rolled and leaped inside the dusty glass cage, a spirit clamoring for release. Miguel's too? The pathetic boy, deluded, playing at revolution, understanding nothing. His death would not save Akabal, that was sure. Would anything? Would even God? He leaned over to pray. The priest had learned nothing since morning, had been no good to anyone, had led no one to God, had brought no soul closer to any other. He saw himself walking down a narrow, howling tunnel, long robe whipping his ankles, dispensing the Host right and left, *pax vobiscum*, dropping each pulsing bit into a black void, becoming wispy and more insubstantial

with each dispensation, finally evaporating without conse-
quence into the seething murk. A hillside appeared, and he
was lying on it face down, breathing warm earth, a hand
stroking his hair. He had died and she mourned him, his
beautiful hair, his thin and wispy hair. He sank deeper into
the grass, its damp warmth prickling soft against his groin.

"Father. Edmundo. Wake up." He started violently. Caterina
sat beside him, her long hair loosed and blowing, her patterned blouse glowing in the candlelight. She stood and took
his hand, pulling him up as she backed toward the front of the
church.

He staggered forward. "What are you — no, I don't . . . let
go . . ."

"Come on. It's all right. Come with me, here, in here." She
led him like a sick old man past the table ablaze with candles,
then sideways toward the shed door. Edmundo looked up at
the crucified god, the lights dazzling on the spotty glass, but
the eyes were dark, gazing over his head toward heaven,
peaceful, oblivious. He half fell after Caterina into the shed.

The red stripes in her blouse glowed crimson, wine, black
and bloody in the flickering light, and he stared at it as she
took his limp hand and thrust it underneath, onto her breast.
"Here, here is truth. Here is communion. Here, and here . . ."
She closed her eyes and he stared at her. She tugged her
blouse over her head. For a blinding moment he saw only her
long throat and his own right hand, hot as if welded to the
fullness of her breast.

She grasped his hand and bent to kiss it, rubbed it against
her cheek, and reached for his other hand, pulling both
of them to her breasts. His breath came in gasps, and he
tried to back away. The brown nipples were hard against his
fingers, stabbing them, nestling between them. His knees
buckled. Caterina fumbled with his belt buckle and snapped

open his jeans. She pulled down the zipper and reached inside.

Edmundo cried out as she grasped him, liberated his straining sex from its long confinement, sending an electric jolt up his chest and down his legs. He was fully ready and she sank to her knees before him. She ran her tongue down one side of his penis, then down the other, as he groaned above her, his hands now on top of her head as though in blessing. She licked the tip and tasted the salty wet, and opened her mouth to receive him just as he came. He moaned again and again, sending jets of himself into her throat.

He looked down at her, eyes wide. She let him go and sat back, and he sank to his knees to face her. He reached tentatively to touch her bare shoulders, to stroke her arms. "So beautiful. So beautiful." She radiated heat, her muscles firm as furniture, and her yellow eyes burned like a cat's. But when she looked away she seemed demure, contented. Only in her eyes did he see something else, something dark, something, he thought, rather like a leer. He moaned. "My God, my God, what have I done?"

She smiled at him. "So I am right. I do understand you, this much at least. And you are human too. Is it so very difficult?" She reached to touch his chest, but he shifted away from her. He sat beside the wall of the narrow shed and leaned his head against it, his eyes closed. She touched his leg, but he withdrew it as though he had been stung.

"No. Please, no. Please, just go away. You don't understand anything." She didn't move and his voice rose. "For God's sake, Caterina! Just get out of here!" He opened his eyes and looked at her. The contentment in her face gave way to confusion. She groped for her blouse and put it on, then hesitated.

"You know, Caterina," he said, looking at the wall, "you've taught me something important." His tone was conversational, as though he were addressing a class. "I'm exactly what

I always said I was, but I never really believed it before." He sighed. "I realize that now. I am so deep a sinner, so hopeless . . ." He shook his head. "I have said that since I was in seminary, but until now I never understood it." He turned and looked at her, a hard gaze like a blow to the belly, and took another deep breath. He shuddered. "May you be damned in hell."

She recoiled. "No, it's for your own good. I'm only showing you —"

"You are damned, and everyone here with you. All of you. God's judgment."

She gasped. His stare was an iron wall. She got up and ran from the church.

Twenty-two

CRISTÓBAL left his house seconds after Edmundo, crossing the rutted paths between buildings to the shack of Andreas de Córdoba, fifty feet away. He knocked softly and called in a low voice. Inside he heard scuffling, a few curses, and Andreas appeared, blinking. The two men whispered together.

"Well!" Andreas said, drawing back. "I never thought he had it in him."

"This makes it all that much harder. We have to go talk to him now, before the meeting."

"Doesn't change a thing, as far as I can see. I never thought any of us were innocent in the first place. And a man's entitled to a trial."

"Right. Tell that to the soldiers."

"I expect to."

"Andreas, be reasonable — "

"I am reasonable. That's always been my problem."

"Is Gregorio here?"

"Yes, he's sleeping it off. Came home drunk. Shall I get him?"

"No, leave him alone until the meeting. Do you think he knows?"

Andreas shrugged. "Let me get my jacket."

In minutes the two were passing the soccer field that the moon had turned to dimpled silver, heading to the Kanaks' dark house. Thin fingers of smoke rose from every roof toward the chandeliers of stars, so close the smoke appeared to hold them up. Andreas's crutch made tiny white puffs of dust with every step.

"You know what might have saved us, Andreas? Tourists. If we'd only had tourists in Akabal, things might have been different."

Andreas stifled a laugh. "Tourists! What tourist in his right mind would come here?"

"That's my point. If we'd had tourists — well, take Miguel for instance. When he was little he had such a smile" — Cristóbal shook his head — "he had the kind of face that lights up, you know. A little dirty, a little pinched, but still angelic, the kind of face that a smile turns into the face of one's own son. Tourists melt when they see such a face; they give candy or a tip, they let the boy guard the rented car, they use him as a guide. And the kid learns a few words of English, or German or French, he makes a little money, he sees a different kind of life is possible, he starts wanting sunglasses and wristwatches. He becomes ambitious. If we'd had tourists —"

"We'd have thieves and hustlers and prostitutes, venereal disease, trash, noise — and ambition, yes, but what kind? And it wouldn't stop at sunglasses. No, people would start wanting television and credit cards . . ."

"As if we don't already."

"But not as much."

"We'd have a little wider world, a little hope to offer young people. But now they leave for the cities . . ." Cristóbal sighed. They came to the Kanaks' house, rounded the corner to the door, and nearly tripped over Flora where she crouched in the shadow.

"Aagh! My God, you scared me!" the mayor cried. "Are you all right?"

Flora rocked back and forth, heels to toes, heels to toes. She did not look at them. "He's not here." Andreas opened his mouth, but she was faster. "Caterina."

"And pardon, old one, how is Irene?"

Flora turned her head slowly, her good eye glittering like a cat's. "Alive. Leave me alone."

The two men backed away. "If Miguel comes back, tell him we just want to talk to him. At the elders' meeting, at midnight. All right?" Cristóbal waited. Flora began to murmur and he leaned forward to hear.

". . . thou, Hurakan. Chipi Caculha! Raxa Caculha . . ." The mayor straightened and looked at Andreas as Flora's voice grew louder. "Tepew, Kucumatz, who formed us, who made us thy children! He's doomed, you know." She was nearly shouting.

"Now don't get excited —"

"Doomed, dead already. Like all of us. Tepew! Kucumatz! Hear us!" Her voice fell again to a mutter.

The men retraced their steps toward the church and the plaza. They looked in at the big arched doorway, dazzled by the flickering candles, and saw only a few chickens huddled under the empty benches. They went on across the square to Caterina's leaning shack, just above the cemetery, but no one answered their knock.

"Well, this woman could be anywhere, but where else would Miguel go?" The urgency in Cristóbal's voice woke Miguel with a start where he lay trying to sleep on Caterina's sweet-smelling mat. His skin prickled. They were hunting for him; they were going to turn him over. He sat up and listened.

"He wouldn't run without telling somebody, his mother at least," Andreas said. "He'll turn up in time for the meeting."

"Let's go tell the others and come back later. Caterina always knows everything."

Miguel listened to their footsteps move away. His heart was pounding. So they were going to drag him before the elders. Those old farts, what did they know of revolution? He thought of the men who would be there. Diego Saraf was at least seventy; nobody had ever been so old. The baker Honorio Luxit had paid for so many celebrations and processions he would be complacent the rest of his life. The sniveling Joselino, of all disgusting people; even the whining simpleton Genero. How could such a group begin to understand him, Helado, shaper of the future, maker of devices of wire and love? Cristóbal, perhaps a little, and Andreas, yes, he had a hero's past, he would be sympathetic. But he was only one voice, and they had to reach a consensus. Would they turn him over? Should he go to the meeting and argue with them? He told himself to relax and think. With shaking hands, furious, he lit a cigarette and inhaled deeply.

It was too late to escape. Caterina had been right this morning; he should have tried then, but he had been excited by the situation. Cocky, too proud. They had all thought he was innocent, he had tricked everybody; he wanted to see what would happen next, as though he were watching a movie about innocent Miguel. Stupid! Well, he could hide, the mayor had hinted at that, and they could tell the soldiers he wasn't there. Caterina would hide him, and if they searched the village maybe she could cast a spell and the soldiers wouldn't see him. But everybody knew he was there. Benedicto would insist on a search. Maybe he knew Caterina's hiding places, or he could make her tell . . . he had been with her last night, right here. Miguel scrambled to his feet, irritated. Everyone was abandoning him. He would have to fight, maybe alone. No, Gregorio would help, he would try again with Gregorio, and maybe there would be a couple of others. Together they could hold the soldiers off, maybe escape in the confusion. But they might be hit, and the soldiers would surely burn the town after that. Everyone dead . . . He shook his head to erase the vision and stubbed out his cigarette.

He'd been screwing up the whole day. He should have used more plastic, he should never have stayed so long at the barracks; he was just too damn cocky. And then when he knew they'd seen him he should have made a real effort to cover his tracks. If he'd been more careful, they'd never have come here, Irene would be okay . . . he wouldn't have lost his head and wound up in that damn church. What a dumb move that was, to run to the church as though he were still twelve years old. It was just as Nahual said: You've got to remember your battle name; that'll remind you what's important, where your friends are. Helado, helado; stay cool and smooth. All right. What were the options now?

Well, he would get Cristóbal to agree to turn Benedicto over to the soldiers instead of him. Would that work? Benedicto would deny it, shout at him, and mock him as he had today. Miguel's arms tensed at the thought. Stupid of him to lie about being with Caterina! Almost got caught there. The scurvy bastard had a slick tongue, he'd be too fast; Miguel would wind up tricked somehow and would confess in public. His head began to ache and he rubbed his forehead. Would Cristóbal go along with it? How did he and Andreas find out about him? From Gregorio? It wasn't possible. Surely not from his mother or Irene or the priest. What did they mean, Caterina always knows everything? He hadn't told her, hadn't been able even to get close to her today.

Where was Caterina, anyway? He felt a surge of desire and impatience and moved to poke the fire. He had come to

Caterina's an hour before, after a tense and silent dinner at home, watching Irene toss with fever in her blankets, enduring his mother's endless muttering. He had walked aimlessly a long time, trying to decide what to say to Cristóbal, what to ask Gregorio to do, and had looked up to find himself at Caterina's house, just the way he had found himself in the same place, when the hut belonged to the old *chiman*, in another emergency seven years ago. Waiting for her, he had fallen asleep on the other side of the warm fire where her two children slept in piles of blankets.

Diego moaned in his sleep. His dirty bare feet were exposed, round and smooth as sausages, and Miguel went to him to adjust the covers. Only the girl's braids were visible. He sat back down on Caterina's mat. When would he have a son of his own? With Cecilia dead now, that was no longer a question of time, no longer something that would happen without further effort. Now he would have to find a wife, go through the whole courtship business — a couple of years at least. He thought of the young women he knew. Not one was remotely interesting. Caterina would make fun of all of them. Would sex with such women be the way it was with her? The thought of her solid body, her soft heavy breasts, the way her face would light up when she came in and saw him here — his chest warmed and he smiled to himself. He sighed and looked at the children's tousled heads, the blankets moving slowly as they breathed. They were good kids, funny and smart; he was half father to them already. He wondered idly who their fathers were. But he didn't care really. He couldn't do much for them. Or for Caterina either. In fact, thinking about a wife was ridiculous. He couldn't support even his mother and Irene with the fields so dry and all the time he spent with the revolution. And now . . . his situation came to mind again, and he frowned, rubbing his palms together. It's as if you bombed Gregorio in there, or your mother . . . He cursed the priest. Putting yourself on the same level as the army . . . what bullshit. Nahual would know what he should have said to the priest; he would know what to do now. Maybe somehow Nahual would find out what happened and the group would come, there would be a fight . . .

The door burst open and Caterina swept in, flushed and disheveled. She seemed to give off sparks that dimmed the fire, and Miguel caught his breath at her rough beauty. Seeing him, she gasped and her eyes narrowed.

"Hey, easy, easy," he said, getting up. He put out a hand to soothe her.

She touched her lips and composed herself, smoothing her skirts. "Welcome to your home," she said. They smiled at each other.

He gathered her in his arms. "What's the matter? Did you see a spirit so late at night?"

"Worse than that. The soul of a man." She spoke into his shoulder.

"And did it survive the meeting, or was he already dead?"

"Doomed, like all of us."

He stood away from her. "What do you mean by that? Who was it?" *Caterina knows everything.*

She rubbed her forehead. "I see blood tomorrow. The stones say death is sure but the number is unclear." In the plaza, with Benedicto, that brief moment of seeing had jarred her, but it had been incomplete, like everything else these days. She knelt on the mat and reached for the water jug, took a drink, and looked at Miguel. "But it is Indians who die, not Ladinos — I heard a *cucucu* call."

Miguel sat beside her and took off his sandals, then began to unbutton his shirt. "The army is full of Indians." She reached over to rub circles on his chest, and he took her hand to kiss it. "We haven't got much time. Cristóbal and Andreas were here looking for — were here a moment ago, and they'll be back soon."

"Let them wait." Her voice was low. He took the hem of her

heavy blouse and pulled it over her head. As her breasts swung free, a shudder went through him. Would he ever again see that incredible sight, touch those hard ebony nipples, hold this warm soft flesh? He moved his hands carefully over her body, memorizing each curve and hollow. He watched her as from a far distance, imprinting as she lay back each sigh and twist of her head, every arch and moan, each breath of her dark green scent. So he noticed her glance toward the children, her distraction, the tension in her arms. He rose twisting within her, now gently, now fiercely and she stroked his arms and held his hips, encouraging him, smiling, moving with him, but still distant. He groaned in frustration, every cell yearning to push closer to her, to merge with her and disappear into a new unity. Hungrily he kissed her neck, her shoulders, nestling his face under her ear. But she turned her head and he saw worry in her eyes. He let her go then and drove hard, harder toward his own release, and burst free into shuddering exhaustion.

She lay quiet beneath him as his breathing eased. For many minutes they held each other in silence. Then she told him of a dream. "I was underground, looking up through the earth from a kind of crouch. I was anxious, maybe hiding from something, but it was warm and safe there, and I could see the bottom of people's feet as they walked around above me. It was like being under water. I could see the undersides of houses and roots of the corn, but not the tops. And then you were there too, but above me, lying on your back. That was all I could see of you, your back. I reached for you, but you were rising up, out of the ground, and then you disappeared. I felt a terrible sense of loss."

He raised himself on his elbows. "You would miss me, then, if I die tomorrow?"

She didn't answer. Then, "In some ways you've left me already. I think that's what it means. I don't know you anymore."

"You know me better than anybody." He stroked her face.

"No. I should have, but I didn't see . . . any of this. Nothing told me who you were." She arched a bit, uncomfortable, and he withdrew, rolling to his back beside her.

"What do you mean? I'm the same — "

"I've lost my powers, Miguel. Or they don't trust me anymore. I can't see when I need to. I didn't see the army coming, I didn't know what had happened with you, I didn't understand the priest. I wonder now how long I haven't seen things clearly." She raised herself on one elbow and looked at him, her eyes as yellow as the fire. "Tell me about the life of a revolutionary."

He drew a long breath and closed his eyes. "What do you want to know?"

"How does it feel, to kill someone?"

He looked at her across inches that were miles between them. "That's what you want to understand? Out of all the things it means, being what I am, you want to know that?" He looked away, at the sticks and straw of the roof, the smoke hazing the room. Justice, retribution, dignity and freedom, his father's life and his mother's rage, the passions of strength and change and joy, all of it lay heavy as a granite slab between them, impassable, indescribable. "You get used to it." His voice was rough.

"You're good at it?"

"Yes."

"Why didn't you tell me?"

He sat up violently. "Mother of God, Caterina! It's for you that I do it! Don't you see? It's all for you, and Irene and my mother and Gregorio and the rest of you who can't do it yourselves! And anyway I did tell you."

"How? When?"

"A hundred times, when I went away, when I came back. I just never said it out loud. I was sure you knew." He leaned to touch her hair. "Can't you understand, my heart? If we'd spoken of it, you'd have been in danger, every time the soldiers came. You'd have been worried by it. You'd be casting your stones to see if my bombs would work, if I'd be caught, but I'd still have to follow my orders . . . It would have been impossible." He turned away. "Besides, you're happy living in the past, keeping the old ways as though they still mean something. You're already the town witch; you can get away with anything here, sleeping with anybody — ah, I'm sorry," he said at the flicker of her eyes. "I didn't mean that. I just meant — you're strong, you can take care of yourself with things the way they are, so I wanted to keep all the ugliness away from you as long as possible."

"You thought I was a rebel, didn't you? That I was like you in my own way. But I thought you were a simple farmer, anchored here forever. I guess we were both wrong." She studied the blanket. "But you're right too, about the revolution. Everybody here feels rebellion every day, hoping for change even as we fear it. We can't move for the fear, of what the soldiers might do, fear of failure, of suffering, and we're paralyzed by hope too, hoping someone else will do it for us. And you" — she shrugged and smiled ruefully — "a common farmer, a nobody, just like everybody else. But the gods picked you for some reason, to be the one to go ahead. You were the one who acted for us, maybe not the way we would have, but we didn't act at all, or maybe we acted by not doing anything. The thing is, we acted through you, in a way, and now we're all involved in your consequences."

"Yes, but I didn't mean that to happen."

"You didn't have any choice. We're all bound up in it together. I don't need any holy stones to tell me that."

Something that felt like hope stirred in Miguel's chest. "What are you saying? You mean there's a way to stand against the army?"

"I don't know yet. The elders will have to decide. Is that what you want, to fight?"

"Yes, to fight! Yes! It's the sitting and waiting that's impossible. If we're all united, we can cut them down, as they come up the hill . . ." He stopped and looked at the sleeping children. "But I can't . . ."

"You can't what?"

"I want to fight for myself, but it's a terrible risk. If it doesn't work . . . I can't ask the children to do it, or you, or Irene —"

"Or Gregorio? Or Cristóbal? Yes . . ." She was thoughtful a moment. "You're right, you can't ask anyone to fight your battle. No one can tell another what to do. But it isn't just your battle, is it? And I can't send you out there to die alone for no reason either. Don't you see? Whatever we do, we have to do it together, all of us. The whole town. Just as you said before."

Miguel put his head on his knees. He saw the two children, his mother, his sister, Caterina, Andreas, the town lined up beside him as the soldiers aimed and fired. Tears stung the corners of his eyes. "I still don't know what I should do."

She rubbed his shoulders a long time.

PART IV

Twenty-three

GENERO HESITATED at the door of the empty church. Wrapped in a brown striped blanket against the midnight chill, he crossed himself and waited a few moments, but no one appeared. Raising his chin, he entered and strode to the front row, where he crossed himself again and sat down on the bench, twisting his straw hat in his hands. Christ writhed above him in the candlelight. Miguel was a good boy; nothing bad would happen to him. Surely there would be a sign telling them what to do.

Joselino came in, genuflecting at the door, and spat into a corner. He sat down in the row behind Genero, adjusting the pistol in his belt. He was certain that trouble would shatter the quiet night before long, and he was ready.

Behind the church the generator sputtered and roared into life, startling both men. A few moments later Arturo, muttering to himself, stomped down the aisle, dusting his hands. "Let's have a little light in here," he demanded of the plaster saints. He flung open the door to the shed and reached inside for the light switch.

"Father! Time to get up!"

A yellow glare imposed order on the twisting shadows. Edmundo lay sprawled, fully clothed, on his cot, a pillow over his face. He moaned and flung the pillow to the floor, shielding his eyes with one arm. "All right. I'm coming. What time is it?"

"Midnight, Father. Time for the meeting."

"Right. I'll be right there."

Outside the church the sudden light sent Miguel leaping back into the shadow of the open door. It was too early for him to go in; he couldn't sit still that long, he was too agitated. Unseen, he stared at each entering face.

Cristóbal and Andreas came in together, yawning, and sat with the others. Fatigue had aged them, and Miguel thought he saw anger in their knotted brows. But surely they were angry at the soldiers, at the hour, or at life in general as much as at him.

Two more men entered, Honorio Luxit, the baker, erect and proud, and Diego Saraf, hobbling and stooped, both with lower lips pursed in what Miguel decided was stubbornness. He admired that. The stolid endurance of men like these had preserved Akabal through generations of unspeakable crimes. Their eyes were dull from centuries of weeping, but now they would catch fire, here, nationwide, all over the world, and the revolution would triumph here and everywhere because of these men of corn, no matter what happened to him. Miguel felt light-headed. He thought again of escaping, making a run for it through the cornfields, the sheltering corn that had received him near the barracks. He could feel the harsh leaves stinging his face, whipping his arms. He heard the shouts behind him, the first shots zinging over his head. Then the thud into his back, lifting him forward off his feet, an instant of flying, his arms out, and then the blackness. Blessed silence. His hands trembled and he paced back and forth beside the door. If he were shot in the cornfields it would be all over, the army would be satisfied, the town would be spared. They would carry his body back, Cristóbal and Arturo, and the women would cry and wail, and the priest would pray. He would be laid in a coffin . . . Gregorio would weep and draw his portrait. He would be a martyr, perhaps become famous; maybe Nahual would name a fighting unit after him . . .

Miguel cursed himself and wrenched his mind back to reality. The army would never be satisfied with just stopping him. The fat lieutenant would kill everyone in Akabal if he tried to run, would call them all traitors and collaborators, whether he escaped or not. His back ached suddenly. A fog seemed to swirl over him. He blinked as he stepped aside, out of the mist, and walked into the light billowing from the church door. Dazzled, he took a deep breath and pushed his way into it, into the church. No one noticed him and he sat down at the end of the last bench.

The elders and the man they would try sat together in silence for several minutes. Gregorio's mother, Ana de Córdoba, slipped in and stood in shadow at the back wall. Gregorio followed, his eyes on the back of Miguel's head. Two women entered, Flora whispering encouragement as she supported Irene, who limped and wore a scarf draped to hide her beaten face. Skirts rustling, they moved to the other side of the door against the back wall, where they crouched, hands to mouths, silent.

Caterina came next and stood near Ana, and Benedicto slipped in behind her. In twos and threes, more people entered the church, and then more, until nearly half the town stood behind the benches where the eight men sat. At last Edmundo emerged from the shed, pale and staring at his feet. He did not look up. He sat on the front corner bench and said nothing.

Several more minutes passed. At last Cristóbal stood and

turned to face his town, three-score pairs of eyes dark with worry, anger, fear, and hope.

He had a moment of vertigo, a sense that all the faces of his forgotten life, his lost family, and his youthful dreams were here in this crumbling church. He drew in his belly and stood as tall as he could in order to be worthy. "Good evening," he said. A murmur rolled across the room. "We are here tonight to discuss our answer, Akabal's response to the soldiers. You all know the demand. The good Father here has spoken wisely. God will defend us all." He indicated Edmundo, who did not look up. "But God helps those who help themselves." Many heads nodded. "We must make sure we agree on what we are going to do, with God's help, so that all of us, even the children, will understand what comes next. Is that all right?" There was a general murmur of assent. He cleared his throat.

"You all know that the lieutenant says we have a terrorist here. He says we are collaborating with the subversives." Cristóbal gave a thin smile all around. "The lieutenant fears that in our hearts we are all collaborators, perhaps we are all infected with this microbe. He wants to eradicate the source of this infection." He spoke slowly, pausing between each phrase.

"The army says it wants us to do justice to Miguel Angel Kanak here. He bombed the army barracks yesterday morning." The mayor said it flatly, calm in his own understanding, and waited out the general rustle as his words sank home. "And the lieutenant says that if we do not do the army's justice for him, we may all die." He stopped, and all heads turned toward Miguel, who sat looking at his hands. "We may all die anyway. If we give them Miguel, they may still do their worst here. The army's view of justice is hard to understand. The danger is very grave."

The mayor looked down, waiting for silence. "Maybe there are other things we can do. We have to talk about it. The decision is in the hands of the elders, as is the custom. But any of you will have a chance to speak." He waited a moment. "Miguel, do you want to say anything?"

Miguel got slowly to his feet. "Yes, thank you." He looked around and flushed. Most of the faces were blank, expressionless, and he gave a nervous smile. "Pardon me, my friends, my neighbors. I'm not used to this." He toed the dusty floor, his arms tightly folded. Those behind him leaned forward, straining to hear.

"I want to say first that I'm just a humble farmer, a peon. I'm not a terrorist. I'm like you all, a poor man trying to make a living in difficult times." He knit his brow and looked at the floor. "You know my family, my poor father, how he was killed by a landowner's truck driver. You know my mother, my sister, you know we are ordinary people." He stopped and swallowed. "A few years ago, I met a man who helped me understand things. I saw how the landowners exploit us, how we suffer because the government is corrupt. I understood that we are poor because we are kept that way by the rich people, and how they take our land and would keep us poor forever if we let them. I saw that we have nothing now. But what could I do, a poor peasant who can't even read and write?" Miguel looked up and around him. "I have no land, nothing. Who would listen to me?"

He made a broad gesture. "I asked a lot of people what I should do. Most of them said there was nothing. One or two said I should go to the mountains, take my family, and join the revolution. But my mother is old; how would they eat? So I couldn't go. Some other people said I should complain to the officials, but I saw what happened to Don Andreas and his — to people who did that. I would get no work, they would call me a communist and maybe arrest me. So I couldn't do that either. Then the government had an election and everybody promised us things would be different. You all heard them. But the soldiers came on election day and told us how to vote — you know that story. So for a long time I didn't do anything."

Miguel cleared his throat and paused. The audience shifted and coughed into silence. "Then this man I met told me I could help with the revolution and still stay here in Akabal most of the time. He said I would have to keep it all a secret from everybody. So that's what I did." Miguel put his hands in his back pockets and stood straighter. "It wasn't so hard. I didn't carry a gun or anything. I ran messages at first, when I went to Santa Rosa or to the coast. I had some training and then I — I got involved in other things. But I want you to know I never killed any women or children the way the army said. That was a lie, an evil lie, I swear it."

He shifted his weight and looked at Gregorio. "I never told anybody I had joined the revolution. Not even my best friend. I didn't want to put anybody else in danger." His eyes sought his mother, his sister, Caterina. "I never even told my own mother." He looked at the floor. "Now it seems I have put everybody here in danger. I am very, very sorry for this." A sympathetic murmur swept the room. "I didn't mean to get anybody else in trouble."

He looked up, and his voice rose. "But I want to tell you something. If I had to do it over again, I would still put a bomb in that army barracks." Flora gave a muffled cry and covered her face. Miguel turned and looked at her. "These soldiers are peasants too, Indians like us, some of them, but that doesn't matter to them. They kick us and shoot us like dogs, worse than dogs." He waved one hand. "They've been brutal to us for four hundred years, and now they're starting to see what it feels like to suffer a little themselves." He took his hands out of his pockets and raised them in fists, as he had seen Nahual do. "This is the beginning of justice, don't you see? People are acting as I did all over the country. Everywhere peasants like us are demanding freedom. The revolution is growing, the revolution is going to win! If we are all united, we cannot be defeated!"

In the silence a dog barked outside. Miguel lowered his arms. The only sound was the muffled chugging of the generator. Miguel's voice was steady. "Now this army dog says he wants justice for the bombing of the barracks. I tell you that justice was in the planting of that bomb, just the beginning of justice, and we owe them thousands of bombs more! The revolution at last is bringing true justice to the entire country!" His heart was pounding, and he paused until he could speak again in a low voice. "In the morning, when the army comes back, we have to stand united here. If we stand together and resist them, they won't dare to do anything. The soldiers are bluffing. They're afraid of us, afraid of the people, afraid of the revolution. If we are ready to resist, they will see that. They know the entire country would rise up against them if they tried to do anything to us."

He fell silent and looked at his feet. "So I say it again. I'm very sorry for getting you into this problem. I didn't mean to do that. But I know nothing will happen if we stand united against them." He stopped. "That's all I have to say." He sat down. There was a commotion of feet, voices, shifting bodies.

"That's just garbage!" Benedicto stood away from the wall. "It's total garbage!" He called over the noise. "He's a traitor to his country. He's sold out to the communists, and everything he said was a twisted lie!"

"Quiet! Quiet!" Cristóbal spread his arms for order. Miguel sat frowning at the floor, grasping one quivering hand with the other.

"Where are all these revolutionaries?" Benedicto shouted. A space cleared around him. "Where are all these people united when a whole village is in trouble? I don't see them charging to our rescue. They're all in hiding, that's where they are, just like our young warrior here." He waved at Miguel. He raised his hands, and his voice became pleading. "Don't you see now? Miguel was tricked by this communist he met. It was all lies, a big lie about land and rights and the people united. The terrorists are criminals who want to take what isn't theirs, and they dress it up with all these wonderful-sounding lies. They don't have any land to give us. They're going to protect us — see how well they've protected us today! How many times have we heard these promises — roads, schools, freedom? And what do we get but guns and bombs! No, the reality is that Miguel is a criminal and that there are soldiers outside who want him, and their guns are aimed at all of us."

Benedicto drew a long breath and dropped his voice. "Face reality, my friends. We are poor and humble people — Miguel got that right — but at least we're still alive. That's because we haven't gone with the revolution, and at the same time we haven't become an army camp. But the truth is that the communists are losing the war, not winning it. The new government is better, they're actually doing some things now, and maybe things will get better for us. But the terrorists don't want that. Oh, no! That would mean things can get better without a revolution, and they can't have that! No! So they have to keep blowing things up to keep the army mad, to keep them shooting, so that things get worse for us, not better! They actually want more massacres, more repression, not less! They don't want it to end, because then there'd be no reason for a revolution. And the more repression, the faster the revolution comes! That's what they say, believe me! Oh, yes, the terrorists are losing, and they need help, they're desperate, they'll say anything to get more people involved. They want to drag us all down with them."

Benedicto wheeled and pointed to the ridge beyond the open door. "You all saw the soldiers. They'd love to blow us all away, just to make an example of us. They are not bluffing about that. You know they have done it before. And this —

this revolutionary," he sneered, waving toward Miguel, "he killed a bunch of soldiers, he killed women and children and God knows who else, and now he's trying to talk you into standing out there and fighting the entire national army, just to save his own hide!" He paused and glared around him. "I say we take him out and shoot him ourselves."

Gasps hissed through the church. Benedicto stood with his hands on his hips and shook his head. "I don't think we have any choice. We know him, we know now that he's a terrorist. If we do it ourselves, the army has no excuse to attack the rest of us. And anyway could we be safe here with him around, now we know what he's done? Could we —"

"Shut up! Shut up!" Flora Kanak de Canil rushed at Benedicto, her hands clawing at his face. "Liar! You're the murderer! You're the one who —"

Pandemonium. Cristóbal's shouts were drowned out as people grabbed at Flora, pulling her away from Benedicto. Irene screamed. Miguel leaped up and lunged through the crowd, pushing to grab his mother. He hugged her, pinning her flailing arms, held her fast as her struggles ceased, her cries became incoherent and subsided into sobs. He murmured into her ear as she wept against him. Gradually the noise died away. Benedicto stood scowling with his back against the wall, his arms folded.

After a few moments, Joselino stood up, wringing his hat in his hands. "I'd like to ask a question. Just a question. I'm not saying this is what we should do, understand me." He looked up through his eyebrows and waved one arm. "Is it possible we could escape somehow, all of us? Right now?" Cristóbal raised his chin. "I mean, the soldiers are probably asleep mostly. We know the area; maybe we could go down through the cornfields a few at a time and get away. They wouldn't know we were gone until morning. We could even maybe dig some traps in the houses, or set nets or put out the wire snares. That would delay them even more when they got here. We can go into the mountains tonight and go to Tekan or Santa Rosa in the morning. They don't know who we are. We could come back later when this is all over."

No one spoke. "Lots of other places have done it. If we leave them some money they might not even burn the houses." He stood in silence a moment and sat down. The only sounds were the generator and the flapping of moths hurling themselves against the light bulb.

Cristóbal took a deep breath. "Joselino has asked a good question. Perhaps this is a possibility. We would have to leave all the animals and almost everything we have. Somehow we would have to keep all the children very quiet." He stopped. "The soldiers would probably burn the village in the morning, even if we left money for them. Certainly they would kill the animals, or take them. If they didn't catch us and kill us too."

"Some of us would have to stay here whether we wanted to or not," Andreas said, hoisting himself on his crutch. Honorio Luxit nodded. "Those left behind would surely die." His voice rose. "But I say the rest of you ought to stay too. Not to save Miguel. He's just a kid, playing at revolution; he doesn't understand yet what he's gotten into. But we should all stay to save ourselves." He looked around and shifted his balance. "Who among us is not just like Miguel? Haven't we all felt a little thrill, a little happiness, when we hear that some landowner is dead? Didn't we all shake our fists behind the soldiers' backs after they came to arrest someone? Didn't we all give a chicken or a tomato or a drink to the boys when they came in from the hills, and not always out of fear?" He raised a fist. "Look at me. I tried to change things without using a gun. You see what happened to me. You know that; you're afraid to do anything yourselves so you let the boys do it for you. Let them run the risks. Miguel did it, he got caught here. But how is he different from the rest of us? Where do we draw a line?"

Andreas paused and hoisted himself around to face the rear of the room. "Benedicto!" Tijax jumped. "Why don't you say we should take Andreas out and shoot him instead of Miguel? Hah? What does it matter who we shoot? We're all the same here."

"Not me, old man," Benedicto replied.

Andreas waved dismissal. "I say we take a stand here. Now. We have half a dozen guns, a few pistols. When the soldiers come up the road in the morning, we'll be hiding, and we'll shoot them, one by one." His hearers inhaled as one, a long hiss. "Everybody will have a target, everybody with a gun will be hiding and ready, and we'll kill all of them. Then we can think about disappearing, at our own speed."

"What if we miss, even one soldier?" Benedicto called. "They have machine guns. Even one of them can blow us all away. And even if we don't miss, the army will hunt us down to the last baby, they'll arrest everybody for miles around and torture them —"

"I'm not talking about being martyrs!" Andreas shouted. "I'm saying we should stand up for ourselves for once!" He waved at Miguel, still holding Flora tight. "This boy here acted for all of us, and I say we act for him now, while we have the chance." He turned and sat down.

The room buzzed. A couple of men went to Benedicto and clapped him on the shoulders. Ana de Córdoba stood with her eyes closed and streaming, shaking her head. Arturo stood and raised his fist toward Cristóbal.

"I agree with Andreas! The time has come to take a stand. We have nothing to lose, really." Arturo turned to the rear of the room. "Think about it. We can't trust the army. How many times have they lied to us about what they were going to do, the roads they would build, the water pipes they would bring? How many times have they laughed at us when we tried to file a claim against the Torazos or some big shot in Santa Rosa?

Every time they betrayed us. If we shoot Miguel, the soldiers will laugh at us: 'Stupid Indians, they kill their own people, they're too stupid to live.' And they'll come in here and shoot us all anyway. Think about it. We don't have any reason to believe this lieutenant. All he says is that if we don't do his justice for him, we'll all be shot. That's a threat; it's not a promise that he'll leave us alone if we do what he wants."

Arturo stopped. He was sweating despite the chill breeze from the open door. "You know they have killed thousands of people like us, thousands, innocent people. Why would they let us go after we admit we've let a terrorist live here all this time?" He shook his head. "No, we can't get out of this one. We can't escape; they're watching the paths and there's a moon like a searchlight until four o'clock. If we tried to run they'd love it, they'd say it proves we're all subversives. They're going to shoot us all anyway, so I say let's shoot them first. That way we at least have a chance to live."

Heads nodded around the church. Arturo sat down amid a general murmur of approval. Andreas shook his hand.

Genero stood, rubbing his hands on his thighs. He clasped them then and stood very straight. "With all respect, my friend, you are too suspicious." Arturo snorted a laugh, but Genero raised his chin. "You laugh when I say this, but the new president has promised us justice." He ignored Arturo's shaking head. "The bloodbath has stopped, at least six months, you know that's true. Now I'll agree, you're right, the lieutenant spoke to us very harshly. But maybe that's just his custom. Our esteemed mayor has spoken with him. Is that his custom, Don Cristóbal?"

The mayor nodded. "Yes, it's true he is belligerent, but once he showed signs of being sympathetic. These things are always uncertain."

"I think the lieutenant respects our mayor as we do." Genero bowed slightly. "Akabal is a patriotic village. Everybody knows that. We've never had any trouble before. The soldiers didn't come in shooting, no, they came and talked, they explained what they wanted. So it seems to me, with all respect to you, Don Andreas, and you, Don Arturo, that we should obey the army's orders here." He held up a hand against the rising murmur. "I don't mean we have to shoot anybody. They didn't ask us to shoot anybody. We can arrest Miguel and take him to the soldiers, and tell them we will watch and wait to make sure he gets a fair trial in the —"

"A fair trial!" Arturo hooted. Others smiled and shook their heads.

Genero looked pained. "How can we ever live in peace if we don't believe anything they say? Think of the children! The poor little children! They can't shoot anybody; they only learn horrible things from the fighting. What are we teaching them if we say everything is a lie? We have to give the soldiers a chance. We can't jump to conclusions all the time. We should let them prove themselves honest."

Cristóbal raised an arm to quiet the murmuring crowd. Gregorio stepped away from the wall. "Don Genero, please. I agree with you that we can't jump to conclusions." The room turned to look at him. Gregorio stood with his hands in his pockets, looking at the floor. "I am the proof of that, as you all know. I made so many wrong assumptions . . ." He shook his head and was silent, as though he had forgotten his hearers. Then he looked up. "I fear your assumption would be wrong too, Genero. Think of my father, of what they did to him after he was arrested. My sister Cecilia — " He swallowed and looked up. "She has not been treated well in prison." He stood straighter. "Under this government which has made so many promises, my sister has been tortured and raped and . . . probably even murdered," he said in a rush, without looking at Ana.

Behind him, his mother wept.

"If we turn Miguel over to the soldiers, we are saying to them, 'Here is your subversive terrorist, your revolutionary. We don't want anything to do with him, he's a communist bomb thrower.' And what will they do then? You think they'll shake his hand and give him a drink? You think they'll name a lawyer to defend him?" Gregorio shook his head. "No. It'll be horrible, what they'll do to him. He'd be better off dead." Miguel stared at the floor, an arm still around his mother. Gregorio turned and moved through the crowd to Miguel's side. He put a hand on his friend's shoulder.

"This is a man of honor," he said, his voice cracking. "All his life he worked hard to feed his mother, his sister. He has done his part in the societies, always he paid for the ceremonies when it was his turn. He saw how we suffer from injustice and he tried to fight it, maybe not in the way he should have, maybe not the way we would have done it, but he was trying to help all of us. He didn't even ask for any help or any credit. He tried to keep it a secret." Miguel gave him a grateful glance. "Now when he is in trouble he hasn't pretended anything. He hasn't tried to get out of it. He is an honorable man." He squeezed Miguel's shoulder, his mouth working.

"This is a poor village. With all the fighting, too many good people have died already. We don't want to lose another one." He took a deep breath. "We can't risk the children either. We can't try to escape. We can't try to shoot it out; that's crazy. We'd all be killed and it makes no sense. Akabal needs Miguel. But Akabal doesn't need everybody. It doesn't need . . . me. I volunteer to die in Miguel's place."

"No!" Miguel staggered. The room erupted. The young men stared at each other, then embraced. Above the confused hubbub, Ana de Córdoba's voice keened a long wail of protest and despair.

Twenty-four

"YESSIR, just about the whole town is in there, sir, over."

"Can you see what they're doing? Over."

"Nosir, the ones we can see are standing in the door. It's been going on a couple hours now, sir. Over."

"All right. I'll be there in a few minutes. Keep on it. Over and out."

"Yessir, over and out."

Gomez yawned and stretched and checked his watch, plain in the moonlight. Two o'clock. He sat up and rubbed his knee, looking around at the dark mounds of his troops sleeping in the slanting silver light. The guard hurried over. "All normal, sir," the boy said, saluting.

"Good, good." Gomez touched his forehead. "Wake — ah, Ilmo and Moran. They'll relieve the watch on the ridge and I'll go with them. Everybody up by five and come down, got that?"

"Yessir." The private saluted again and moved off.

"Private! One more thing."

"Sir?" the boy said, turning back.

"Get Sergeant Joyabal too."

"Yessir."

Two shifts of men had watched Akabal from the ridge since the sergeant and the tracker Tijax had been relieved. Gomez had questioned those two closely about the fistfights, and all his warning bells went off when Joyabal revealed, with malicious glee, that the two Tijaxes were brothers. It was another headache in this stupidly complicated case. He could no longer trust the tracker if it came to a shootout, and yet letting the ear live would make the soldier suspicious. He almost wished Joyabal had kept his mouth shut.

In five minutes the four men were walking toward Akabal, Gomez in the lead. His moon shadow lay black before him and he stumbled repeatedly in the rocky path. He cursed his knee, his age, the task awaiting him. Joyabal, openly irritated at being forced to return to the ridge so early, brought up the rear. Gomez was determined to be cheerful. "We've got three more hours at least before sunup. You all okay?"

"Sure, no problem, sir," Moran said. He was cocky, talkative, sent out from the capital with a star by his name, a comer like Joyabal, Gomez thought with annoyance. "With permission, sir, what happens then?"

"Depends. We'll see." Gomez muttered.

"What?"

"I said it depends! We'll see what happens. But we're back at the barracks tonight for sure, no matter what."

"Great." The privates relaxed into easy lopes. Gomez clomped along, each step turning a fine knot of pain on and off like a light bulb deep in his knee. It was easy for these kids, just follow orders, no responsibility; trained to be killers and damn good at it. They were secure in the right, doing God's work against evil, wearing their crosses. They had no conception of the riptide of conflicting policy around them, undercurrents that could drown everybody. Maybe they'd all be court-martialed together someday, like the Argentine generals, or maybe the soldiers would be ordered to arrest their own officers. These two would handcuff him and lead him off to prison, and Joyabal would testify against him. Not while he had his pistol. He listened to the rhythmic clank of the soldiers' gear and chided himself. He was being foolish. He would apply this week for a desk job back in the capital. At least then he'd be able to keep track of what he was supposed to think.

They came to the ridge opposite the village and turned to climb it. Crawling to the edge, they lay on their stomachs and peered over.

The view was very different from what it had been the previous morning. The church floated, luminous on the hilltop, light billowing from the ventilation space under its eaves, glowing down the outer walls and spilling over into the square. The building seemed to hover, translucent, in midair, suspended in a basin of light edged by the dark houses ringing the plaza. Figures crowded the doorway, intent on the proceedings within. Beyond the village the moon etched the looming mountains in silver and shadow, hinting of vast worlds sleeping far away.

"So what are we waiting for now, Lieutenant?" Joyabal whispered, licking his lips as he lowered his binoculars. "If I may ask. We've got them all in one place again."

"You think they're all terrorists, then?"

"If they're not, they're doing a good imitation."

"How?"

"Well, they sure didn't seem worried this afternoon. It's like they know something we don't. Maybe they've got reinforcements coming; I don't know. It seems to me we should take care of them while we can."

Gomez considered. It wouldn't hurt to take precautions. He snapped on his radio and gave the password. "All troops up and get here as soon as possible, but no noise. No formation,

just spread out along the ridge." He waited for an acknowl-
edgment and closed the antenna.

After a moment, Gomez rolled over on his back and
stretched. The stars were close enough to touch. "Advise me,
Sergeant," he said. He felt Joyabal go tense beside him.

"Sir?"

"Suppose we attack now. One or two will probably get away
in the dark; they usually do." His voice was casual, almost
dreamy. "That means the communists will start yelling eventually, making propaganda to the Yankees, and there'll be
denunciations and investigations and so on, and some more
bombings and memorials and all that. A royal pain."

The sergeant stifled a sneeze. "Yeah, so?"

"Well, it won't hurt us, of course. But does it ever stop? I
mean, nobody will ever hear our side of it. Just more bombings, more chases like this, a lot of shooting. It's a waste, a real
waste, and I'm sick of it, Sergeant, I have to tell you. I'd like to
stop it once and for all. Any ideas?"

"Ideas, sir?"

"If you would do me the favor." He couldn't help the ice in
his tone.

"Ah, well. Ah, perhaps we can make sure no one gets away.
That would —"

"That's not likely. What about Morales?"

"Morales, sir?"

"Haven't you been listening to President Morales? Justice,
fair trials, human rights. No more killing. The Yankees are
breathing down his neck and we need more weapons. New
guns, new uniforms — your boots are at stake here, Sergeant."

"My boots, sir? With respect, sir, I'm not sure what you
mean. President Morales — that's all fine in theory but when
you've got a real situation like this one, with a terrorist setting
off bombs and killing innocent people, you can't tip your hat
and say please, sir, honor us by coming to jail. The Yankees

have a different class of criminals from ours; they don't know
what we're up against here. And you've got a whole town full of
them here, sir, collaborators; it's obvious they've been hiding
this guy." His voice rose. "I mean, the Yankees have no idea
what this is all about. They have no idea. They used to have
it right: the only good communist was a dead communist.
But now they won't follow through. They don't know what
they want anymore. I say the hell with them and let's get on
with it."

"Yes, but about stopping it all?"

"It'll stop when they're all dead, don't you think, sir?"

"I suppose so. But it's been thirty years, Sergeant. Thirty
years already."

"Yessir. I don't think it'll be much longer, sir."

"I guess not." He lay silent.

"Sir?"

"Hmm?"

"So are we going in, sir?"

"At dawn, Sergeant. I gave them until sunrise. Just a couple
more hours."

"If you say so, sir."

Cristóbal gave up trying to keep order in the church.
Clumps of villagers formed and reformed, heads shaking,
arms waving, fists pounding on open palms, fingers jabbing
chests. Here the seven other elders huddled on the two front
benches, whispering, a double ring of townspeople offering
advice around them, trying to hear. There a group clustered
around Benedicto, nodding, arms folded, glancing now and
then at the side bench where Miguel sat with Gregorio, near
the priest. The two young men stared at the floor, not talking. The priest had not moved from his slump and gazed
continually at Christ, his eyes glassy. Most of the women and
some of the men sat nodding along the walls, cradling the

heads of sleeping children. The candles had long since gut-
tered out, leaving the bare bulb to etch lines deeper in the
tired faces.

Outside the church, Caterina sat with Flora on the plaza
spot between heaven and hell. They cast huge and shapeless
shadows across the square as they rocked back and forth,
chanting:

> Hurakan! Tohil! Hacawitz! Receive us! Your House of
> Darkness, House of Shivering! House of Jaguars, House of
> Bats, House of Knives! Houses of Hell receive us! We shall
> burn! Abawab of Xibalba! Gods of Hell! Ahawab Tucur!
> Tamazul! Zaquicaz! Camasotz! *Wac c'o! Wac c'o!* The Ahaw
> of the Deer has come! Hurakan! Tohil! Hacawitz! Receive
> us, receive us . . .

"We've gone over that already." Arturo's booming voice was
weary, but it carried above the noise in the church.

"I know, but I am old and forgetful. Let me hear it again."
Diego Saraf's slow baritone quieted the others like an invo-
cation.

Arturo sighed and rubbed his eyes. He was hoarse. "My
point is that Gregorio's plan won't work." His tone was flat.
"The ears here will tell the army that Miguel is still alive and
that he is the subversive, not Gregorio. They will come back
for him. And they'll probably kill all of us for trying to trick
them."

"They may do that anyway right now, for collaborating,"
Joselino said.

"At least now we know they're out there."

"The village is all but dead already in any case," said Honorio Luxit. "The cooperative made no money this year. The
crops wither. The young people leave, the old die . . ." He
shrugged.

"Doesn't anyone have any hope of an honest trial?" Genero asked. One by one the others shook their heads.

"He wouldn't even make it back to Santa Rosa," Andreas said.

"It is a terrible sin to kill a man like that," Genero said.

Diego Saraf nodded, and looked at Genero. He was silent a moment. "This is an important point you raise, Don Genero. Who will bear the sin if Miguel is killed? Let us ask the priest."

Cristóbal leaned back and asked the nearest child to fetch Father Edmundo. She darted through the adults to the priest and stood in front of him. He appeared not to see her. Hesitating, she tapped his knee, and he jumped. He stared at her a moment, as if he did not understand her message. She pointed. Then he stood and worked his way across the front of the church to stand near the mayor.

"Father," Diego Saraf began, "if a man is slain today, who has sinned: the army lieutenant who gives the order, or the man who pulls the trigger?"

Edmundo blinked. "Both. Both have sinned mortally, beyond redemption, beyond hope. Both. Both." He spoke rapidly, mechanically.

"And if there is a battle, who bears the sin for the deaths that follow?"

"If thine adversary smite thee on one cheek, turn unto him the other. A soft answer turneth away wrath . . . all who offer battle are sinners. All are sinners."

Diego Saraf's eyes narrowed. "If we try to escape and the army shoots, who then sins?"

"The man who shoots and the man who provokes it, both have sinned . . . By patient endurance you will save your lives. Not a hair of your head will be harmed." He stared dully into the middle distance.

"Thank you, Father." Diego's voice was kind. The elders watched as Edmundo turned and went back to his corner.

Cristóbal shook his head. "May God have pity on his soul."
He sat back and looked at Diego, who nodded.

"We must decide. It will be light soon. There is gray in the
sky already. But I think we have decided." He looked around
the circle. Behind him excited voices whispered the words:
"They've decided! They've decided!" More people clustered
around.

Cristóbal stood up. "There is no difference in the sin," he
said to everyone present. "It is clear we are all guilty. We have
helped Miguel in this deed, one way or another. We cannot
escape. We cannot kill one of our own in the prime of his life.
We will help him now." The others nodded.

All the elders stood up. They turned toward the corner
where the two young men sat. "We have decided," Cristóbal
called. Gregorio and Miguel looked at each other, then at the
mayor, and slowly stood to face him. "Miguel —"

"No!" Miguel raised a hand. "Stop. Don't say anything. I'll
decide myself." He swallowed. "I want it this way. I — I —" He
swallowed again. "I will die so that Akabal may live."

His knees buckled. Gregorio grabbed his arm as the room
once again erupted in noise. Some faces lit with relief, others
collapsed in pain. Irene cried out and sank to the floor.

"No, it won't work! It won't work!" Andreas's voice rang over
the tumult. "They'll kill us all anyway! They don't care! We
have to fight, we have to get them first! Or we'll all die
anyway!"

"Yes! Miguel, don't be stupid."

"This way you have a chance . . . "

Miguel, half sagging on Gregorio's arm, shook his head. He
detached himself and raised his hands, opening his mouth to
speak. But the noise was too great. The villagers hushed each
other. Miguel's throat worked.

"No, uncle. It's true, I wanted you to say that. I thought
that was what I wanted, and I'm grateful to you, more than I

can ever say. But it is wrong." He stopped and rubbed his hands on his shabby pants. He blew a long breath. "I have thought as I sat here tonight how wonderful it is that you debate this thing. I feel ashamed because I kept my life a secret from you all these years, believing you would betray me and kill me right away if you knew. I never thought you would worry about it so much. I didn't trust you, my own people." He looked at the floor and swallowed hard again. "Now I see we are truly a family, more than I ever thought." He gestured toward Gregorio. "I got Akabal into this by keeping everything a secret. I was afraid. Now it is my duty to get Akabal out of it." He stood up straighter and raised his eyes to the women and children asleep along the walls. "Look at them. They are innocent. Why should they die? It's true, we don't know what the soldiers will do after — afterward. But this way there's a chance." He nodded toward the families. "I'm not being noble. This is just reality." He took another deep breath. "I'm not afraid anymore. My life has been good, but I'm not worth any more death. Don Diego? Don Honorio? Don Cristóbal? Isn't it so?"

They met his gaze. After a moment, Diego Saraf nodded, and Honorio Luxit bowed his head. Cristóbal looked away.

Miguel looked at the other elders and named them, one by one. Slowly, one by one, they agreed. Arturo's eyes were wet, but he nodded. Miguel raised his eyes to the roof and breathed a great sigh. Then he turned and put a hand on Gregorio's shoulder. "All right, then. That's it. Now I ask one favor. Gregorio, you must paint a quetzal on my coffin."

Gregorio's mouth fell open. He shook his head violently. "No. No, I can't. You can't do this. I should — let me be the one . . . you can't —"

"Gregorio, listen. It's the only way out. I'm sure of it now." He held Gregorio's shoulders. "You have to do this. Please."

"I can't, I won't. I have no paint —"

"Yes, you do." Miguel's voice was soft. "Now listen. My friend, my brother, listen to me." He shook Gregorio gently. "You must take care of my mother and Caterina, and you must make many children with Irene. To carry on the fight. Promise me."

Gregorio's head dropped and he shook it again. "I can't, I don't know what —" He choked.

"Yes, you can. You know what to do. You were always stronger than I was. You were always there, even when I thought I was alone. Now you have to live for both of us." Gregorio's face streamed with tears. The two embraced.

Slowly Miguel let him go. He turned to the elders. The room was silent. Outside, far off, a rooster crowed. "I guess that's all. My mother will be all right?" They nodded. "Well, good. That's it, then." He took a deep breath. "I'm ready now. I'm in your hands."

Twenty-five

LIEUTENANT GOMEZ lay propped on his elbows on the ridge overlooking Akabal, just able to make out the cemetery through his field glasses. The crypts once again were smudges on the opposite hillside, the low crosses silver in the gathering light, knee-deep in marigolds. The yellow glow had faded within the church, leaving it dark and forlorn against the fringe of treeline in the distance. The lieutenant's shoulders ached, his cheekbones were sore from the metal eyepieces, and a damp chill had seeped from the ground into his belly, his aching knee. He was tired; he would give them ten more minutes. As he looked at his watch, a huddle of men came out of the church, pushing into the crowd at the door, carrying something long and low. In a dark slow knot, the crowd moving as one, they worked their way across the plaza toward the cemetery. A few moments later three more shadows emerged from the church. One wore a long white robe that appeared to float empty, ghostlike, as the three moved slowly across the plaza. That was clearly the priest. The bulky figure with the rifle had to be the mayor. The third appeared to be a young man, thin, wearing a white shirt and a high-crowned straw hat.

"That must be our man," Gomez said. "They're going to turn him over after all." Haltingly, as slow as the rising sun, the three men approached the crowd and its edge surged forward to absorb them. Arms reached to embrace the man in the hat. He stopped and reached back. One after the other he hugged them, men and women, cradling faces, kissing, embracing, ruffling the hair of the children. An older woman shrieked and hurled herself at him, throwing her arms around his neck. He held her a moment, then freed himself, kissed her, and moved on. Another woman wailed, and he held her too. Gomez was impressed by how well the cries carried across the ravine. The light grew and the man embraced all who came to him, moving as though through water toward the cemetery at the top of the road.

The sun's rim appeared over the mountain ridge. Gomez squinted, then got to his feet and raised his arm. "All right, prepare to move." Swiftly, like flowers opening, his troops stood up, one after another, all along the ridge. Gomez looked back at the square and then looked again, startled. The crowd had parted at the cemetery to reveal the dark pit of an open grave. The young man in the hat stood on one side of it and the priest stood at the head, his hand raised. On the other side were the mayor, clearly recognizable now in the pink light, and three other men, all with rifles. "Hold!" Gomez called to his men. He lowered his arm. He was confused. What were they doing?

The priest's voice across the ravine was a low drone. The crowd made the sign of the cross and murmured something, and the young man followed suit. He removed his hat and tossed it to a young boy with a withered arm, who caught it. Then he raised his chin. After a moment he nodded, and thrust his right fist high in the air. The four men raised their rifles.

Puffs of smoke were visible an instant before the shots

reverberated through the hills. The man's body jolted sharply backward and sagged to the ground, the fist still aloft. Gomez exhaled a long breath. Two men darted forward and seized the man's arms, holding him upright. Blood poured down his chest, and a woman began to wail. From behind the priest four men emerged carrying the long, low object, a coffin. They brought it to the edge of the grave. To Gomez it looked strange in the half-light, streaked or defaced in some way, but it was obscured by the marigolds and by milling arms and legs. The two men holding the body half carried, half dragged it to the coffin and laid it gently down. They stood back, and as they moved away, a flash of bright orange leaped from the coffin side, and a wash of green. It looked like — yes, it was a quetzal, painted head up, bright breast forward, emerald tail glowing in the dawn. It was poised on the side of the coffin as though ready for flight across the field of corn.

Gomez muttered a curse and clenched his teeth. They were going to make a martyr out of this murdering punk. He scanned the crowd for anyone with a camera, but saw only the usual ratty Indians, holding their straw hats, clutching their babies, heads bowed. Two wailing women pushed forward, dragging their companions, and sank to the ground, clutching the sides of the coffin. The priest made the sign of the cross above them, and other women pulled them slowly away. Gomez shifted from one foot to the other, watching through his field glasses. Hurry up, for Christ's sake, he thought.

A young man, bigger and more muscular than the others, stepped through the crowd with the coffin lid. He stood it upright on the ground, holding it so the top faced the ridge. Another quetzal. Gomez cursed and lowered his binoculars, checking how much detail his men could discern without field glasses. The colors vibrated in the sunrise, the bird clearly identifiable.

Then he gasped. The villagers tipped the open coffin up

on end next to the lid, facing the ridge, so that all the soldiers clearly saw the bloody body sagging within, the quetzal soaring beside it. Gomez noticed his hands were shaking. After a moment, the tall young man moved forward with the lid and nailed it on, the coffin still upright. The hammer blows were like duller rifle shots across the gully, each one thudding a millisecond after Gomez saw the blow land.

The men stood back then and turned to stare up at Gomez, at the ridgetop, at the line of soldiers poised along the edge. There was no sound. The women too now stood erect, looking across the ravine. One by one the villagers turned to look, until the entire crowd stood silently behind the coffin and the quetzals, staring into Gomez's metal eyes.

The moment seemed eternal. Gomez was transfixed by the bird aimed at the whitening sky, the electric shimmer of orange and green in that sea of brown. The mud-colored buildings, the field, the ragged people vibrated on the edges of his vision as the bird writhed on its coffin, restless to soar up and out of this barren, lifeless place. He stared at it until his eyes burned, and he shook his head. At last a man stepped in front of the coffin and lifted its lower end. Two others passed ropes under it from the sides, and together they lowered the box into the grave. The birds seemed to struggle one last moment before they disappeared.

All life and color seemed to vanish from the earth. The men dropped their ropes and picked up shovels. The first clods of earth landed with soft thuds, then fell in apparent silence.

"Sir? With your permission —"

"Hah? What?" Gomez swiveled hard on Sergeant Joyabal.

"We await your order to move, sir." The sergeant's eyes were wide and scared, and his face was gray.

"Not yet. Just wait a minute." Gomez turned back to watch the hill, dull and shapeless once again, more devoid of hope than it had ever been. The two men were still shoveling. The priest stood well back from the grave, praying, his white robe flapping in the morning breeze. Nothing moved but the two diligent workers, their shovels glinting pink in the sunlight.

A couple at the edge of the crowd suddenly turned away and walked back into the plaza. A heavyset man followed them, his head down. A white-haired man hobbled away on a crutch, leaning on an old woman. One by one the crowd dispersed, some back to the square to stand talking in small groups, a few into the church, most into the narrow passageways between buildings. A few children trotted toward the stream, carrying buckets. Soon all had left but the priest, who had not moved, and a stocky woman in a red blouse, standing alone. Two other women huddled together near the grave, and the tall young man stood with Don Cristóbal, watching the two shoveling men.

At that moment the ground began to tremble. Another earthquake. The rumble was upon them. Pebbles jumped off the ridgetop and all the soldiers crouched, their eyes staring. Gomez turned to look at Akabal below, half expecting to see the earth open and swallow it up. In the square the priest raised his arms, the women opened their mouths, and the others crouched in the dusty plaza. Birds wheeled in the air.

It was over in a moment. Another shiver, a twitch of the restless land, nothing more. Gomez stood up. His knee didn't hurt at all. "Well, that's it," he muttered. The quetzals were buried. He looked down the line of his men — Joyabal, Tijax, all of them. They stared at him, waiting. For a long moment, he stared back. Then he shouldered his rifle.

"All right, fall in. Let's go home."